GODDESS

BOOK THREE OF THE PERCHERON SAGA

FIONA McINTOSH

An Imprint of HarperCollins*Publishers*

This book was originally published in 2007 by Voyager, an imprint of HarperCollins Australia.

EOS
An Imprint of HarperCollins*Publishers*
10 East 53rd Street
New York, New York 10022-5299

Copyright © 2007 by Fiona McIntosh
Map by Matt Whitney
Cover art by Greg Bridges
ISBN 978-0-06-089913-4
www.eosbooks.com

First Eos paperback printing: July 2009
First Eos trade paperback printing: June 2008

HarperCollins® and Eos® are registered trademarks of HarperCollins Publishers.

Printed in the U.S.A.

10 9 8 7 6 5 4 3 2 1

For Steve Hubbard . . . slainte!

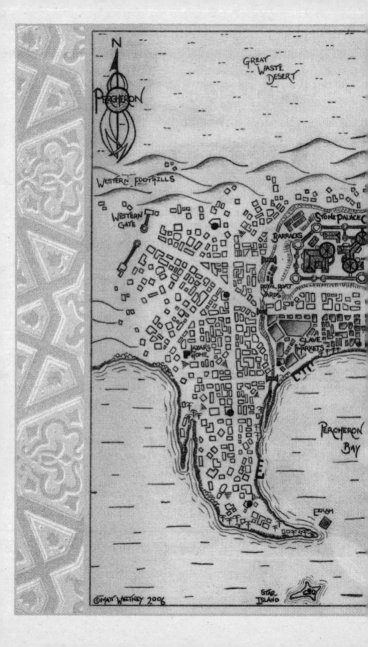

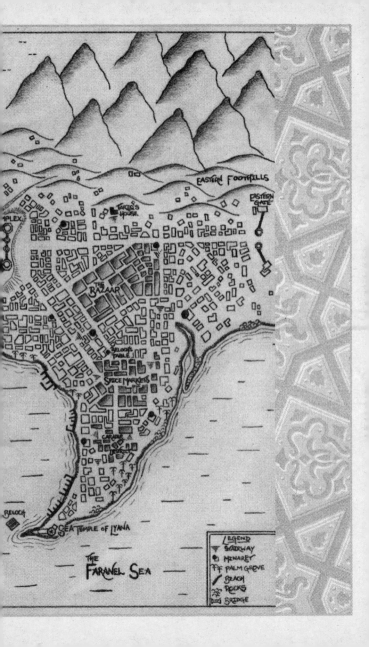

Acknowledgments

Ah, the final volume . . . It is always such a relief and a pleasure to bring closure to a sprawling tale. It is especially satisfying for this writer, who never has a plan—never knows what's coming next—and works instead only to the vaguest story line. I am always genuinely surprised that the end does miraculously arrive and all the threads of the story do somehow weave themselves back into the main tapestry . . . as if . . . well, by magic!

My thanks to the usual support crew on this series—Pip Klimentou, Sonya Caddy, Gary Havelberg, Judy Downs. Thank you to Matt Whitney for his great work with the maps, and to Trent Hayes for his much-valued work on my website and bulletin board that keeps me in touch with more than 700 readers around the world.

Thank you to the booksellers of America and to the librarians who have encouraged readers to take a look inside this exotic, make-believe land of Percheron and its struggles. My gratitude to the team at HarperCollins, especially Kate Nintzel for her dedication to this story, to my work, and for her friendship as we have edited two trilogies together.

Finally, my focus comes full circle to rest on the three people who put up with all the magic and mayhem associated with crafting these big books of otherworldly adventures and who constantly remind me that I do live on planet Earth. Thanks to my beloved Ian, Will, and Jack for being my real world. Fx

GODDESS

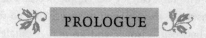

PROLOGUE

The man took her elbow gently and guided her. It was a polite gesture, but there was no choice; Ana would go wherever he chose to lead her because she was his prisoner, in his fortress, amidst his private army. And this time there were no Elim to rescue her, nor any of Boaz's elite mute guard . . . and she was a long, long way from Spur Lazar's protection.

Ana was alone for the first time in her life since she had been found as a newborn in the desert after a Samazen storm.

She had been here by her reckoning perhaps three moons. She couldn't be sure, for her existence had been solitary. She was kept in a locked chamber that was positioned high within some sort of fortress. The monotony of hot, stifling days and freezing nights was interrupted only by the twice-daily delivery of simple but surprisingly nourishing meals and fresh water and the removal of her waste pail. Treatment had been mostly silent, broken solely by her barrage of questions at the various robed men who took care of her simple needs. The men were rotated constantly, she assumed to ensure that no relationship developed between prisoner and keeper. A single brief but courteous inquiry as to her health was a daily ritual and Ana had been tempted several times to claim she was ill in the hope of a change of scenery or to engage any one of her captors in conversation beyond the cursory question. But experience had taught her that lying rarely led to the desired outcome, and so she erred on the side of caution, leaving alone as best she could the minions and waiting instead for the man who had taken her captive, their leader, to make his move.

He finally had done so, on this day, fetching her himself, leading her silently through a maze of chambers and corridors and many sets of stairs until they were out into the searing heat of the afternoon. She was blinded by the intense light and dizzied by the sudden inhalation of fresh air and high temperature. Her gloomy chamber with its tiniest of windows, affording her the barest of drafts, had its advantage in being cool by comparison.

Blinking beneath the ferocity of the sun's brightness, Ana was struck by the irony of her situation. Isn't this what she had craved? Wasn't the tantalizing lure of freedom a drug for her . . . something she had risked her life for in the past? And yet here she was, free from all palace constraints for the first time in more than a year of her young life, and she was trembling with fear as the mysterious Arafanz led her out onto the rooftop of his fortress.

She felt the dry caress of the breathless desert heat kiss her grubbied skin whilst reminding her that it did not love her, did not love anyone. The desert's treacherous welcome was one of death if you were naive or careless, as the royal party had surely been when Arafanz and his men had stormed their camp. She realized now that she had always been their target—Arafanz and his Razaqin had intended to abduct her; the killing and the humiliation of the royal party, and especially Spur Lazar, had been nothing more than sport. She remembered how many of Arafanz's own men had died; from her recollection of that night, he had not so much as blinked in sympathy. Clearly this man was ruthless, so there would be no escape, not into this seemingly endless panorama of parched emptiness.

It was as if he could read her thoughts. "Look out here, Ana," he said in flawless Percherese, his free arm sweeping in a wide arc to encompass the wilderness stretching out before them. "Beautiful, isn't it?"

"It is. The desert frightens many, but not me."

"That is because you belong to it."

Despite her anxiety she liked the sound of that sentiment. "I was born in the desert, the day of a Samazen, I'm told."

"Yes, I'm aware of your story. It wasn't just any day, though, Ana. It was midsummer's day. An auspicious day."

"Because of the superstitions surrounding it, you mean?"

"They are not idle. It is the boundary of sunlight and shadow, when the night is no longer than day. That is the day when powerful magics are rampant, can leak through one world into another."

She nodded, distant memories surfacing. "Where the sea meets the land it is most potent, I believe."

"The edge of worlds," Arafanz said, his voice heavy with portent. Then his tone lightened and he swept a hand in a wide arc. "Isn't this what you have hungered after for so long?"

"I have craved freedom, this is true," she said with care, tearing her gaze from the sweltering landscape to focus on the narrow, softly lined face of her captor. It was hard to tell his age behind that closely shorn beard, but a glance at his unblemished hands told her he was likely of an age with Lazar, perhaps slightly older. A bead of perspiration slipped down her back and she couldn't be sure whether it was only the heat that provoked it. Fear was coursing through her.

His gaze, dark and rarely still, briefly danced upon her before moving to another point over her shoulder, returning to her in an instant. "I give you this," he said. "I have freed you from the entrapment of the corrupt royals and their debauched ways."

"But I am not free, sir," she said. "I am as much your prisoner as I was of the palace."

"No one here will force you to lie down with a man."

"But you do oppose my will."

"I ask only your obedience."

"Then are you so different from Zar Boaz, sir? He asks nothing more from me."

Beneath the beard a smile ghosted across his surprisingly generous mouth and she was struck instantly by how that small gesture changed his intense expression from severe to almost welcoming . . . almost. "Perhaps not, except that I win absolute loyalty from those who surround me, unlike your precious Zar."

"He is not mine, although we are married. He belongs to his people and they are all loyal."

"To the death?"

"Who can say until they face it?"

Now the creases in his face deepened as genuine amusement touched his restless gaze. "Well done, Ana. That was truly the right answer. Come. I wish to show you something." He walked

her to the very edge of the rooftop and Ana looked down, not
to the sand as she expected, but to another rocky roof below
them. Twenty or so men were assembled in neat, silent rows.
They wore the dark robes she remembered and, as before, she
could not see their faces. "These are some of my loyal subjects," Arafanz said.

Ana remained quiet but felt a fresh tingle of fear climb up
her spine.

"I wish to demonstrate what true loyalty is," Arafanz continued. "Choose one of these men, Ana."

"Why?" Her voice shook.

He shrugged. "I want to explain something."

"Can you not simply tell me?"

He gave a short laugh. "I was told you were clever with
words."

Ana swallowed, hoping to steady her voice. "Forgive me,
sir, I wish only to understand."

His eyes glittered now, their gaze finally resting upon her at
length, turning into an intense, unsettling stare. "I want you to
understand in a way only something visual can explain. Choose
one of these men, Ana."

She shook her head slowly. "I cannot."

"Give me a reason."

Ana knew there was no rational explanation, for hers was
an irrational fear. She gave an excuse instead. "I do not know
them. I cannot even see them."

"Would it make it easier if you did or if you could look them
in the eye?" Arafanz didn't wait for her answer, immediately
barking a harsh order in an ancient language that Ana recognized and that chilled her despite the heat.

She watched the men instantly move at his command, waiting in awkward silence during the minute or so that it took before they emerged onto the same rooftop that she and Arafanz shared, arranging themselves once again in straight rows.

"I will have them take off their headdresses."

"No. Do not."

"But you said—"

"What do you want of me?"

"I want you to choose a man," he said smoothly, his tone untroubled by her lack of cooperation. "Walk toward one, pick one. He will thank you for it, I assure you."

Ana felt hope flare inside. She looked away from Arafanz to the gathered men, anonymous behind their head-to-toe robes. She moved hesitantly.

"Take your time, walk amongst them. One will call to you for one reason or another," he urged. "The choice is yours alone."

Did she hear cunning in his voice? It mattered not; she was on a path now from which she couldn't step aside. If she refused, she was sure there would be recriminations—Salmeo had taught her this, if nothing else—and it was clear she was not in a position to deny Arafanz anything.

She passed down two of the rows of men before a flash of brightness caught her notice, sunlight glinting off a curved blade at his hip as one of the men lifted his chin, shifted position at her approach. In that small movement he had drawn her attention, unwittingly committed himself to her.

Ana stood before him, stared up into dark eyes that did not see her, would not look at her, and with a heart filled with dread, she raised her hand and laid it against his hard chest, hoping somehow to reach his heart through her touch. "I choose you," she said, feeling faint with fright.

"Return to my side, Ana," Arafanz said, and she did as she was asked. He switched to the ancient language. "Are you prepared?" he said to the chosen one, his voice taking a more sonorous timbre.

"I am, Master," the man answered.

"Show yourself, then!"

The man emerged from the rows and peeled away the linens that covered his face and body. He undressed to billowy dark pants and soft boots. His hair was tied loosely back, accentuating a face whose youth was not very well disguised behind a sparse mustache. He displayed proudly his lean, hard body, burnished from the sun.

He undid the scimitar from his side and handed it to Arafanz with a reverential bow. "What is your command?"

"Do you see that blade, wedged between those rocks in the distance?"

The man squinted slightly to pick out the weapon and Ana swallowed hard, her legs shaking as she, too, followed his line of sight to where Arafanz had pointed. She could see the blade winking at them ominously.

"I do," the man said.

"Good. I wish you to impale yourself upon it."

"It is done, Master," the man said, turning briefly toward Ana and bowing. "Thank you," he said, before striding away across the rooftop from where the men had first come.

"What?" Ana screamed, using the ancient tongue. "He's to kill himself?"

Arafanz did not look at her. "I am impressed that you understand. We shall discuss that later. Now watch, Ana."

"No! This is madness." She ran to her captor, beat at his chest. "Stop this! You cannot do this."

Arafanz was unmoved. She could feel how strong and wiry he was beneath her fists. He turned to her. "As he said, it is done. And as I promised you, he knows only gratitude to you. Look."

Ana wheeled around, desperately wishing she could shield her eyes but knowing that respect was the least she could give this man she had chosen to give his life. She watched, nausea threatening to overwhelm her, as she saw the man running blindly at the blade, howling a war cry not dissimilar to a chant of prayer. His devotion to Arafanz became complete as he thrust himself as hard as he could at the vicious blade, its tip expertly parting flesh, bone, sinew, and organs in its cruel passage through his body, finally breaking through the skin of his once strong, flawlessly sculpted back.

The man's body halted against the boulders but it didn't rest, trembling and twitching for an agonizing few moments until his brain accepted that his heart had stopped beating. The initial burst of blood slowed to a trickle, its stain already bright against the golden sand as the young man slumped forward.

Ana choked back a sob. "What was his name?"

"What does it matter?" Arafanz replied. "He is happy. He has gone to Glory."

"Glory?" The despair was still evident on her pale, unveiled face, despite her contemptuous tone. "Glory, did you say? I think not, *Master*." Ana loaded his title with every ounce of derision she could pull together. "I think he has gone nowhere but to hell, on your orders. There he is, heaped against the unforgiving rock. You make a mockery of his young, beautiful life, whoever he was." She was breathing hard and knew she must sound as if she were babbling.

Calmly he turned to her. "He didn't think so."

"How would you—"

"Choose another!"

Ana stared at him, mouth agape. She could feel a ringing in her ears and the blood pounding through her head. She glanced over at the corpse. The man's helplessness—and courage in the face of it—reminded her of Lazar after his whipping and she felt rage rise within her, quashing her fear and steadying her nerves. She turned back to Arafanz. "No. I refuse you."

"Then you shall die."

Her courage intensified as she laughed at his threat. "Do it!" Ana had been prepared to die for many moons. The thought of it did not scare her. But even as she baited him, she knew in her heart that Arafanz had not brought her to this place, wreaked so much havoc, revealed himself to the royals and to Lazar, simply to kill her. He could have done that back at the camp—he could have killed them all.

"I had heard you have spine."

"From whom?"

"Someone I trust. Someone who walks the corridors of the Stone Palace but goes unnoticed."

Ana's mind raced. Who could that be? Mentally dismissing it, she declared, "Then if this person advises you truly, you will know that Spur Lazar—"

"I know all about Spur Lazar, Ana. And you should know that his life was never in danger. Shall I tell you why? Because he was always going to make the decision he did. I knew that; that's how well I know him."

Her thoughts now fled to weeks previous when she had lain in the warmed sand of the dunes with Lazar, when they had made love and bound themselves to each other in a way no other vow or act of marriage could. She bristled at her captor's presumptuousness. "You have all the answers, and all the power over me. But I will not bend to your will. Kill me now as you threatened."

Unfazed by her scorn, he fell back into the other tongue, the ancient one he had used earlier. "It's true, my threat was empty, but there is still a point to be made. You!" he said, pointing at a man. "Throw yourself from the roof onto the rocks below. You," he said to another as the first man nodded and began preparing himself, "swallow your blade." To that man's companion he pointed. "Kill the man to your right with your scimitar and then kill yourself. You—"

"Stop!" Ana screamed.

He did not so much as look her way as he continued barking orders; within moments she was witness to seven men's deaths, either by suicide or by a companion's hand. And each man, before his passing, bowed reverently to Arafanz and thanked him for the opportunity to offer sacrifice.

By the time the last condemned man took his final, rasping breath, Ana had withdrawn into a squatting position, her eyes closed tightly, her hands pressed to her ears to shut out the groans of death, tears trickling down her cheeks as she made an involuntary soothing sound to herself in a vain attempt to block out the hideous noise of swords being drawn, of Arafanz's voice hurling sadistic new torments at his men. But she could not blot the tangy, harsh smell of spilled blood from her nostrils.

In her torment her mind fled from this place—as it had once before when she had felt under siege. *Pez!* she screamed in her head. But he did not answer and, remembering the dwarf's still body at the campsite, she wondered if he was dead. She tried once more calling his name but received only silence, causing her to weep harder.

How long Arafanz left her to her own comforts she did not know, but finally she registered a soft whisper and then strong arms first cradled and then lifted her. She opened her eyes to realize she was in the embrace of one of his men. As the man lifted her, the linen covering his face slipped aside momentarily and she recognized him.

"How—" she began, confused.

"He will see to your needs," Arafanz said, gently stroking the hair from her damp cheeks. "We shall talk again soon. But this is your home now—at least for a while, until that babe you carry in your womb is born."

Unseen amidst the chaos of carnage, perched on a high point of the fortress, Iridor shared the horror and the revealing conversation. To hear Ana screaming for him and to feel so helpless was almost more than he could bear, but to reveal himself now would be unwise. The only help he could provide was to remain unseen and take news of her back to Percheron. His only comfort lay in knowing that Lazar had survived the attack in the desert. Now it was left to be seen whether the Spur had gotten himself safely back to the city. Without him, surely they were lost.

Iridor had failed. He had failed everyone loyal to Lyana.

Silently, but heavy of heart, he lifted into the sky. It would be a long and perilous flight back but he had to find Lazar. As he turned east toward Percheron he began to pray, begging Lyana that the Spur had survived the desert itself.

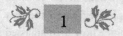

1

Herezah slapped away the ministrations of her slave. "Stop fussing! It's hot enough without your feverish activity."

The attendant was saved further criticism by the arrival of an Elim, who bowed. "Valide."

"What?" Herezah's brow creased with annoyance. "Can you not see I have taken to my bed?"

Annoyingly calm, the man simply blinked. "Grand Master Salmeo wishes to see you, Valide. May I show him in?"

"Oh, do what you will. It's like the bazaar here today anyway. I can see that I shall have no peace."

The Elim withdrew and moments later the doorway was filled amply by the chief eunuch, giving his best gap-toothed smile. "Valide," he began, bowing more extravagantly than his size could comfortably permit. He'd brought her delicate ferlise blooms, fragile bells in the palest of mauves and pinks found only in the alpine regions of the very far north.

She couldn't imagine how he'd amassed so many. And they were beautiful but she wasn't going to let the fat eunuch know how exquisite she considered them. Instead the Valide sniffed. "I thought you'd forgotten me."

"How can you say that, Majesty?" Salmeo said in a tone of feigned injury. He handed the flowers to Elza, who arrived on cue, bobbed a curtsy, and hurried off to find a vase. "I have visited no fewer than a dozen occasions and have been turned away on most."

"I am in pain. Does no one realize that? And this heat! It cannot be summer already."

"The weather is curious for sure. And we do appreciate your pain, Majesty, but the physics need to understand the extent of it. They are not keen to reduce your discomfort with their herbs and medicines until they are sure of what is happening within."

"Because they are cruel!" she hurled at him.

"Because you are too precious to risk, Highness," he soothed. "Their methods are sometimes challenging, I grant you, but you must persist and let them take care of you in the way they know best."

She heard the soft lisp and gave him a scornful glance. "I returned with a broken ankle, Salmeo. It can't be that hard for the physics to work out."

"Nevertheless, Majesty," he said, a finger raised to suggest caution. He smiled again, his chins quivering. "You seem"—he paused, frowning, searching for the right word—"restless."

She knew it to be true; her ankle was not so troublesome anymore—although it did still hurt—but she wasn't going to allow Salmeo any sense of smugness at knowing her so well. "Restless? Do I?"

"Is there anything I can do for you, Valide?"

"You can turn down the sun's heat, you can mend my ankle, you can tell me about my son—who I haven't seen in days—or you can stop second-guessing my moods. I don't mind which you pick."

Salmeo's bright demeanor dimmed slightly but he ignored her sarcasm, smoothing out the folds of his pale silks as he replied. "Ah, the Zar is very busy with war preparations, Majesty. I am told he eats little, his temper is short, and his periods of wanting to be alone are long and frequent."

"What is the new estimation on timing?"

"The doomsayers would have us believe that war has begun, but the word on the streets is that the Galinsean fleet is not yet close to our waters, Majesty. The fishermen are keeping the palace well briefed . . . but it can't be long before enemy ships return."

"When was the last time you saw Boaz?"

Salmeo shrugged. "Not in more than a week. He is preoccupied, has not called upon anyone at the harem, of course."

"That shouldn't surprise you, eunuch."

"Well, your news that Ana is likely pregnant is playing heavily on his mind, I suspect, from what the Elim tell me, although the looming war must be taking a hard toll also. He is, of course, assuming she is still alive."

Herezah nodded, tapping an elegantly buffed nail against her teeth in thought. "She has the lives of a cat, that girl. And he probably misses that wretched dwarf as much as anything else. Still no word of the freak's whereabouts?" The huge man shook his head. "And the Grand Vizier? Is he fully recovered now?"

"He was not injured, as you know, Valide," Salmeo replied pointedly, before softening his tone. "He is working closely with the Zar, as I understand it. Has recently been away, I gather."

"Well, I wish to speak with him," she said, pouring herself a glass of chilled minted tea and yawning, feigning distraction as she waved a hand carelessly. "Set it up, would you." She phrased her next question carefully, keeping her voice disinterested and remote. "And what news of Lazar?"

"None at all, Majesty."

"But surely the palace needs his input now more than ever?"

"From what my sources tell me, the Spur refuses to emerge from his house."

"What, still?"

"He is sickening, I hear, although I cannot substantiate this."

"Well, you certainly are the bringer of glad tidings, Salmeo. Not a single positive item have you given me."

"I have learned not to insult Your Majesty with idle gossip. I have lived long enough beside you to know that the running of the realm is your only true interest."

She eyed him with a look that combined contempt for and amusement at his slippery manner. "Help me up, Salmeo, I'm going out."

"Out? Valide, you are in no fit state."

"Oh, tosh! I'm bored. I can be in pain outside the palace just as easily as I hurt inside its walls and I cannot sit around and do nothing."

"But what do you plan to do?"

"I'm going shopping," she lied. "Now leave me and go make preparations for the Elim to take me where I wish. And send in Elza. She has no mistress for the time being—she can help me ready myself."

———

The owl alighted on the balcony, exhausted. Would he ever remember the way back from where he'd flown? He prayed he would—as he was the only one who knew where Ana was—and with that last thought in his bird form, Iridor shifted shape and became Pez, jester to the Zar of Percheron.

The doors had been carelessly flung open to welcome the breeze off the Faranel into the house but he could see stray leaves from the nearby tall Lashada trees had blown in and evidence inside that the late-blooming reeka had blossomed deeper into the season than normal, its petals strewn over the tiles. Going by the detritus inside the house, these doors had obviously been open for a while. He tiptoed around the debris, surprised he could walk as steadily as he was doing after the long journey, and moved across the familiar chamber.

"Ho!" he called. He anticipated only silence, but heard a muffled sound from the bedroom. "Lazar?" he tried.

The voice was clear now and Pez smiled despite the tone. "Go away, whoever you are," growled the occupant.

Pez stepped into the room, its shutters closing off the light, and peered into the murky darkness. "Lazar?"

The figure on the bed didn't move, although the voice managed some semblance of a roar. "Begone, I said!"

"It's Pez," he replied.

Lazar remained silent for a long moment, then croaked, "Prove it."

Pez limped to the bedside; he really was fatigued. He took the Spur's cool, dry hand and placed it against his own rough cheek. "It is I, old friend, and I have found her. She's alive—she's all right."

A low groan met his tidings and Pez couldn't be sure

whether Lazar wept at the reassurance or was in pain.

"Forgive me," Lazar said, composing himself. "Welcome back—I'm glad you're safe. I'm feeling low—I think losing Jumo is only just making its impact; I miss him. And I thought Ana as good as dead. So many lives lost that night," he said, as mournful as the atmosphere in his sleeping chamber that was neither day nor night. Light seeped through the shutters but not enough to illuminate, and so Lazar was living in a curious void. "And this wretched illness makes my mind as weak as my limbs," he admitted.

"Is it the same thing that afflicted you after the whipping?"

The Spur nodded.

"It will pass, then. Ellyana did warn that it would shadow your life."

"It will pass but not soon enough. I shall need some more drezden—I've finished the stocks that I took from Zafira's hut. Tell me about Ana, so I can go after the murdering bastard who abducted her."

Pez hoisted himself onto the bed and took Lazar's hand again. He wondered briefly how many other men the Spur might permit to be so intimate with him. He'd never seen Jumo touch Lazar; the Spur was not exactly easy to be affectionate with. But Pez felt his energy returning just to have Lazar's presence in his life again. He was still convinced Lazar was the "difference" that Ellyana had warned about for this battle between Lyana and Maliz. Clearing his throat, he pushed away his private thoughts and focused on the present moment. "Well, she is safe, that's the main thing. It took me a long time to so much as glimpse her. I suspect they've had her locked away. The strange thing is that I couldn't reach her via a mindlink, but when I finally sighted her a few days ago, she did not look mistreated in any way. And then I dared not trust the link; I couldn't be sure who might be listening. The truth is, from what I could see, they were treating her with deference."

Lazar frowned. If the news made his heart leap, it wasn't noticeable to Pez. "How many?"

"Hard to tell. I watched him organize the slaughter of seven of his men."

"What?"

"His way of showing Ana what true loyalty means. He was criticizing Boaz—I'm not sure how the two points match up, but I think Arafanz was demonstrating his power over his people as a means of displaying to Ana that the Zar of Percheron did not have similar loyalty."

"So we still know nothing about Arafanz?" Lazar asked in frustration.

Pez shook his head. "An enigma. I've never heard about him in all of my years around the palace and he reveals little, other than his contempt for the Percherese, although he speaks the language like a local. I suspect he is older than he appears but that is purely a private feeling—I could be wrong. I got the impression that he has abducted Ana for reasons of faith more than anything else."

"A mystic?"

"Possibly. He has amassed his own renegade band of fighters and he is not at all frightened to lose them. You saw how he allowed his men to be decimated at the camp for no good reason. And again, in front of Ana just days ago, I watched him command the slaughter of more men simply to make a point. He is mad."

"He is ruthless, I know that much." Lazar tried to sit up and only half managed it, falling back onto his pillow. "What does he want with Ana?"

"Apart from the obvious attraction of a nubile young woman?"

Pez ignored Lazar's sneer. "I fib. I don't think he has any carnal interest in Ana whatsoever—not by the way he behaved toward her. She is pregnant, by the way."

Lazar's closed eyes shot open. He gripped Pez's hand so tightly it hurt the dwarf. "So it's confirmed. She carries Boaz's heir. You're sure?"

"I'm sure that she's with child, yes. Her belly is swollen and Arafanz mentioned her pregnancy openly."

"If he lays a hand on a single hair of hers or the baby's, I shall tear him limb from limb, I will raze his fortress to the dust of the desert, I shall—"

"Well, you can't do anything lying in bed. You need to—" Pez stopped talking suddenly, cocking his head to one side. "Hush, I hear something. Let me check." He waddled over to the window, opening the shutters slightly to sneak a look. He returned to Lazar's side, his large mouth in a lopsided grin. "You're not going to believe who has just arrived. I must hide. We shall speak later."

"Wait! Pez!"

"Say nothing of my return," Pez warned, and disappeared before Lazar's disbelieving eyes, adding silently: *Remember, I can't hold this trick for long.*

Moments later, Lazar heard a small commotion at his front door. More muffled sounds were audible before the doors of his sleeping chamber burst open and Herezah swept into the room.

"Leave us!" she commanded her accompanying Elim, and

they dutifully closed the doors behind them. Lazar knew they would be standing on the other side, that the house would be fully secured by the elite harem guard. "It stinks in here, Lazar," Herezah said, regarding him from a distance and wrinkling her nose. "You stink." She bowed. "Forgive me. Good morning, Prince Lucien."

He hid his shock as best he could, along with his nudity. He dug deep, covered his vulnerability with sarcasm. "Hello, Valide. Bored at the harem?"

"Yes . . . can you tell?"

"The desert can do that to you."

"What do you mean?"

He let his head fall to one side, holding her gaze steadily, not permitting it to roam, mindful that he was naked save the scant covering of the corner of a sheet. "Are you restless?" he asked, withholding the scathing tone he usually took with Herezah and hearing his own restiveness in the question.

Herezah gestured at a small wooden seat. "May I?"

"Of course," he said, tugging the sheet farther across his body. "Forgive my poor manners, Majesty." He felt so weak he couldn't be sure he could make it through whatever conversation the Valide had in mind. And he no longer had the strength to fight her. "How is your foot?"

She waved away his apology, limped to perch on the stool's edge, and sighed. "Lazar—I prefer to call you that, by the way—to tell you the truth I don't know what's happening to me. My ankle is healing fast but I can't say the same for my mind. I seem to be sharing Zaradine Ana's plight in chafing at the bonds of the palace. I would hardly describe myself as one of its easiest members—I too craved freedom—but the kind that power brings. Ana could never appreciate that, I don't think." She gave a sad laugh. "And still, in spite of her complete disregard for the ways of the harem, she has achieved the high position of Zaradine faster than most."

Lazar remained silent, unsure of where this was leading. For it seemed to him that the Valide had set out to say one thing, but had in fact said something entirely different. He could sense her confusion and unhappiness. In spite of their past differences, he found her new vulnerability refreshing.

Herezah looked up from her lap to regard him. "Something must be wrong with me if I am being this candid with you, of all people. Can you believe it, Lazar? Us two talking like old friends?" Lazar did not answer. She sighed. "Yes, I am restless. And I think you're right. The freedom that the desert allowed me to glimpse has done this to me. I still desire my position as Valide, don't get me wrong, but suddenly everything at the palace feels utterly tedious and my moods are out of kilter."

"War is coming, Valide. You may live to desire the monotony of harem life more than anything else."

"Maybe I will, but right now discussing whether one girl has learned her steps of the Shezza dance accurately enough seems altogether pointless. There are such bigger things at stake and it galls me that I am kept from them."

"Have you seen Boaz?"

"No. My son is avoiding me. Not deliberately, I don't think. He's preoccupied with the Galinsean threat, and rightly so. How could I, a mere woman, help him?"

"A woman has two arms, two legs, a brain . . . just as a man does. Save brute strength, she is his equal, Valide."

"Zarab save me, Lazar, do you really believe that?"

He nodded from his pillow, his stare earnest. "I always have."

"And yet there is no more chauvinist man in Percheron, I don't believe! You keep the company of men, you certainly show no interest in women in general to my knowledge."

"I am not prejudiced, Valide. You know only the interest—as you call it—that I do not show in you. Unless you're spying on me, then you know nothing about time I have spent with women, or your spies are hopeless." He watched her bristle, unsure of whether it was the barb about having poor spies or the fact that he might be engaged in amorous pursuits with other women that irritated her. He continued, but in a more soothing manner. "I do believe men make better fighters. They can be more ruthless—save present company of course." She smiled ruefully at his cutting praise. "Women undoubtedly make better caregivers. I generalize, of course, but I think we all have roles we can shine in, though I still say we are equal. We balance each other; we need each other." ·

"You don't seem to need the balance of a woman, Lazar."

"Oh, but I do. You just told me how much I stink and my house stinks. A woman, better than any, can fix that."

She reacted girlishly to his sarcasm rather than angrily, smiling as she hurled her silk purse toward him, loving the feeling of freedom it gave her to act so thoroughly out of the character everyone expected from her, especially him. "Oh, how dare you!"

His mouth twitched in genuine amusement that Herezah was capable of taking the jest and laughing at it. He tried to move his head but was far too slow. The soft silken sack landed across his face, lightly; there was nothing in it save a square of voile.

"Oh, Lazar, forgive me," Herezah said, standing quickly to remove the purse.

He laughed beneath the silk despite his mood. "That's about

as uncontrolled as you've ever behaved, Herezah. You should reveal yourself more often in this way."

She bent into a crouch by the bed, took the purse that he handed her. "I could say the same for you. I do like it when you call me by my name."

"I shouldn't," he said.

Herezah unhooked her veil. "I like it even more when you are not snarling at me."

Fresh, spicy perfume wafted over him and she was close enough for Lazar to smell the fragrant herbs on her breath that so many of the Percherese chewed. "I snarl at everyone."

She shrugged. "Well, I suppose it's reassuring that you know you do, but I do believe you save your worst for me."

"It's because you disappoint me." He saw the shock flare in her eyes as if she had been slapped. "You have so much to offer Percheron. That's why Joreb chose you in the first place. You raised a son we are all proud of, groomed him perfectly for his royal role. You are arguably the strongest, most talented, and most beautiful Zar's mother Percheron has ever seen."

Her gaze intensified as the air seemed to thicken around them. "I've never seen any indication of this admiration you speak of. I have craved your approval for so long—why are you only giving it now?"

Lazar felt unnerved by her honesty but there was nothing to lose. He might never again have the opportunity to be equally candid. "Because you focused on the petty squabbles within the harem instead of looking outward to what was crucial—Percheron's welfare. Our personal history with each other is long, Valide, but you have wanted something from me that I would have been more insane than Pez to give you. But that aside, if only you'd put that bright, sharp mind of yours to Zar

Boaz's needs instead of using your cunning to bring down a mere odalisque or to hurt the Zar's loyal soldier servant, the realm would not be facing war."

She stood, her expression incredulous, her hand flat against her chest as though she were suddenly breathless. "You blame me for the Galinsean threat?"

"Partly. You and your cruel, effeminate sidekick. If you had not pushed Ana so hard, frightened her so much, she would likely not have tried to escape the harem that first time. And if you had not campaigned for her punishment quite so enthusiastically, I might not have had to offer myself in her place. And if I hadn't done so, Salmeo might not have felt sufficiently maligned to manipulate the use of the Viper's Nest or the drezden poisoning . . . and Horz, a very good man, need not have died, and Jumo would not have rushed off to find my family."

"You have no proof of the chief eunuch's involvement."

Lazar shook his head sadly. "And still we both know it to be true. It's an old gripe. We can't change what's gone but its effects linger—because here I am useless to Percheron for the second time because of the sickness that the drezden provokes."

"I don't understand this malady of yours—what is drezden? I believed you were avoiding the palace because you were so angry about what occurred in the desert."

"Nothing so simple. The drezden that was used on the whip has weakened me for the rest of my life and lives alongside me. Whenever I am physically tested, I suspect it reemerges to claim my body again. The long trek, on foot, back from the desert tested me." He shrugged.

Now Herezah really did appear shocked. She sat on the side of the rumpled bed, laid a manicured hand against his arm. "You mean you will never be rid of this sickness?"

He shook his head. "It follows me, hangs around and within me. It waits until I'm weakened and then strikes."

Herezàh turned away. "I had no idea."

"What is done, is done. As I say, we cannot change it. But you can change . . . you can help your son shape a future."

Lazar had been slowly pulling himself up, the emotion behind his words charging him, giving him a false energy. He groaned now and fell back on his bed. "I'm afraid I remain useless."

"No. This cannot continue," Herezah suddenly said briskly. "We're going to get you well, Lazar, and you are going to help Boaz. You are wallowing here. You said I can change; well, here's the first of my changes." She strode, despite her limp, to the windows and pulled back all the shutters, ignoring Lazar's squeals as he fled beneath the sheets, covering his eyes from the agony of light.

Get rid of her! Pez suddenly burst into his mind. *The magic dwindles!*

"Valide, please, I—"

"Don't argue, Lazar." She had continued throwing open shutters around the room. Now she marched to the doors and flung those back. She issued crisp orders at the Elim before turning to the shape beneath the sheets. "I shall see you back at the palace, Spur. Ready yourself. I am going to nurse you back to full health." She left him with that terrifying notion, slamming the doors shut behind her.

Pez winked back into existence on the other side of the bed. "That was close."

"What did she mean?" Lazar croaked, emerging hesitantly and blinking.

"I think it means she finally has you at her mercy," and Pez chuckled in spite of himself. "I cannot stay here. This place is crawling with Elim."

"What are you going to do?"

"I'll go to the Sea Temple. I'll let myself be found shortly. I think she meant what she said, by the way."

"Is it my imagination or did she sound different?"

"Different, I agree, but don't trust it. Herezah is too old to change her ways entirely."

"Pez, I'm too weak to fight this."

"Then don't. Let her get you well. Once you're strong again, we'll think about what's next."

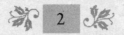

2

Boaz glumly leaned against the balcony of his private salon. His personal servant, Bin, interrupted his thoughts, his expression a mask of worry at his Zar's sorrowful mood.

"It's hot out here, Majesty. I've brought you some chilled apple tea. The Grand Vizier is here to speak with you as well. May I show him in?"

"Yes, why don't you," Boaz answered, his tone detached. At his servant's urging he took the goblet of tea and sipped, feeling the fruity but slightly bitter liquid cool his mouth and throat as he swallowed greedily, realizing he hadn't eaten or drunk anything since the previous afternoon. Food held little interest for him these days. He saw Tariq enter and bow, and rallied himself from his gloom. "You look better," he said in greeting his senior counselor, wiping his lips with his fingers.

"The sea air helped after our time in the desert. But you look older, Majesty. The mustache suits you."

"This has only taken the four weeks of your absence. I shall wear a beard by year's end. What news?"

"No news is good news, Highness. Our ships have scoured the approaches into the main bay, and there is no sign of the Galinsean fleet."

Boaz was unimpressed. "That does not mean they are not coming, Tariq." The counselor simply nodded and Boaz spun on his heel in a show of frustration. "Oh, what are we thinking? This is not the traditional work of the Grand Vizier—you shouldn't be at sea! We need Lazar and he's too sick to move! I need my Zaradine and she's been stolen from me by some madman in the desert. Even my jester has abandoned me."

"Well, my Zar, your understandable dismay regarding your new wife and the loss of the dwarf aside, while you are right that we could certainly use Lazar's soldiering prowess, in all honesty, what good is one man against a fleet of ships? I do think we should consider planning your retreat and escape route."

'I don't wish to leave Percheron."

"Majesty, you have no choice. We must secure your safety and that of your women at all costs."

"I will not flee the realm, leaving the Percherese to Galinsean justice. You know what that would mean."

"But what purpose would your death serve?"

"At least I'll die bravely, alongside my people, facing my enemy, not cowering in some cave on the edge of the desert in the vain hope that my crown might resurrect itself through the bravery and deeds of others."

The Grand Vizier bowed again. "Bravo, Majesty. I applaud your courage. But what is Percheron without its royal? The Zar must be protected at all costs."

"On your return from the aborted trip to Galinsea, you and

my mother believed Zaradine Ana to be with child. There is my heir. Find Ana, find my son."

"But we cannot be sure, Highness. The Zaradine was sickening as if with child. We are assuming, that is all."

"I want my wife! I want to see her expectant belly! I want the dwarf returned to me!" Boaz didn't care how petulant he sounded. As it was, he was only just controlling his anger.

The Grand Vizier studied the Zar. "Forgive me, Highness. I don't wish to upset you. I can see how the loss of those close to you is hurting you but—"

"But nothing, Grand Vizier! Do not presume to understand me at all times. You cannot know what I am feeling. What I want is for my orders to be adhered to. A party of soldiers must be sent to find Zaradine Ana. It has been three moons and your counsel to wait and see if she be returned or if any demands be made might have been wise at the outset but no contact has eventuated."

"Zar Boaz. At the risk of your wrath, may I ask if you are prepared to discover that Zaradine Ana is dead? And that your jester is almost surely dead? My last memory of the dwarf is of seeing him struggle up a sand dune carrying two huge swords. They were for the Spur, of course, for the man came down the sand dune like a berserker not moments after. I never saw Pez again. Even if he survived the attack, he couldn't have survived the desert. If Lazar hadn't had the single camel, we would never have made it out of the Great Waste with our lives. And as for the Zaradine, it's true I'm only surmising, but she was a lone woman in a company of men. That doesn't bode well for her."

"They are both alive, I'm sure of it."

"How can you know that, my Zar?" the Grand Vizier asked calmly, irritating Boaz.

"I would feel it to my very core if either were dead. I feel connected to both of them."

Boaz saw the flare of interest that registered in the intense gaze of his Grand Vizier. "You can feel them?" Tariq repeated.

"Not in the obvious way," Boaz replied. He sauntered away to stare out to sea. "Perhaps I just want to believe I am emotionally and spiritually linked to them. I suppose you find that amusing, do you, Tariq?"

"No, Majesty, not at all. I can assure you that I do not sneer at such things."

Their conversation was interrupted by Bin, who whispered privately to the Zar. "Your mother wishes to speak with you. She awaits my message, Highness."

Boaz nodded. "And she says it is important?"

"She used the word *crucial*, your Majesty."

Boaz addressed the Grand Vizier again. "Tariq, you'll have to excuse me. My mother has asked for an urgent and apparently crucial audience. I gather she's rather worked up about something."

"Oh? Can I help?"

"I don't think so. She has asked if I could meet her in her private salon in the harem. I haven't spoken to her in many days, so I am loath to ignore her further. She would not use the word *crucial* lightly. We shall speak later . . . er, perhaps over supper, Tariq."

"As you wish, Highness." The Grand Vizier bowed but Boaz didn't miss his disappointment.

Herezah had only recently returned to the harem from her visit and had expected Boaz to take at least the rest of the day to find time to see her. She was as surprised as Elza was shocked to hear that the Zar was entering the harem.

Salmeo, of course, preceded any royal entry, flouncing into Herezah's suite in a noisy rustle of silk taffeta. "The Zar is coming," he announced unnecessarily. "Did you request an audience?"

"Yes. I trust you don't expect me to ask your permission before I make arrangements to see my own son."

Salmeo was not permitted to answer, for the Zar had arrived. The eunuch sighed silently as he began lowering his bulk in deference to the royal.

"Mother, forgive my absence," Boaz said, crossing the chamber in three short strides and helping the Valide straighten. He kissed her cheek. "You look radiant, as always."

She touched his face lightly, her fingers near his new mustache. "So handsome," she said, smiling, but she knew him too well not to see below the facade to his sorrow. "Thank you for coming so quickly. Can I offer you some refreshment?"

"No. Let us speak privately," he said, looking at the two servants still waiting to be given permission to stand. Herezah sensed that her son relished the opportunity to make the Grand Master Eunuch, breathing heavily in his uncomfortable position, struggle on a little longer. He finally gave the command that would surely bring relief. "Rise, Salmeo," he said and, once the huge man had labored to his feet, added: "What are the physics saying about the Valide's foot?"

Salmeo caught his breath. "Her progress is excellent, Highness. She will be walking without the stick by the next moon, they tell me."

"Good. She is to have anything at all that she needs. Now I wish to speak with my mother alone."

"Leave us, Elza," Herezah bid. She glanced at the towering

eunuch. "I shall speak with you later, Grand Master Eunuch."
She kept her tone neither deferential nor overbearing. She did
not need Salmeo as an enemy.

Salmeo shot her a glance that was hard to read, though she
suspected he had hoped she might ask him to stay. Silently, he
followed Elza from the chamber. When the doors had closed,
Boaz turned to his mother.

"I think you used the word *crucial* to summon me, Mother.
How can I help?"

"It's how I can help you, son," she said, again deliberately
not coloring her tone.

He looked up sharply from the ottoman on which he was
making himself comfortable. "Go on?"

"It's Lazar. I've been to see him."

Herezah could hardly fail to notice how one of Boaz's eyebrows arched slightly in tandem with a twitch at the corner of
his lips. So, he was amused. "And?"

"Well, he needs to be looked after properly. He explained
his illness to me. It's connected to what made him disappear
from us the first time. We can't lose him again, son. He is too
important to you now."

"I've had my people look in on him but he chases them away.
What are you proposing?"

"I shall nurse him."

"You?" He stood, regarding his mother with obvious incredulity. "Is this some scheme to put Lazar, when he is too weak
to resist you, under your control?"

She shook her head, held his gaze, said nothing. She assumed that Boaz anticipated that she would take umbrage at
his accusation and he was clearly surprised when she took his
words so calmly.

"Why, then?"

"He has been deathly sick, Boaz. I could smell the illness from him and around him. He is not getting any care from what I can see and is clearly willing himself to death."

"Surely he—"

"No, Boaz," she interrupted. He looked momentarily surprised but she didn't apologize. "I may be reading this wrongly but I doubt it. This is about honor. Lazar gave you his word that he would protect your wife and your mother. But I suspect he believes he has let you down. He had a devil of a choice, as I've explained, and I would have put my very title—my life, in fact—on his choosing Ana over me. But he didn't." She shook her head in disbelief, repeating softly, "He didn't." Sitting down down directly opposite her son, she looked at him openly and honestly, revealing to him that she was not trying to make mischief. "To this day I remain shocked that he came after me—killed a dozen men single-handedly to get to me—and saved me from their cruelty."

"Why should you be shocked? You are the Zar's mother. He had pledged to serve you with his life."

"He had surely pledged the same for your wife, Boaz. And we all know that Spur Lazar has . . . well, let's just say he possesses a soft spot for Ana."

She watched him bristle, sensing her son's jealousy.

"He chose you out of duty," he said carefully.

"And that's my point." She continued as if insensitive to his feelings. "This is about duty and honor. The choice was evil. He had to make the more daring choice and that madman knew it; I now realize he fully expected Lazar to save the Zar's mother. Any one of us could see he meant Ana no harm—if he had, she would have been killed before our eyes. No, in those few seconds, Lazar worked out that my situation was more precarious than Ana's and that they would kill me if he didn't risk his life to save mine. But, even given that choice, I firmly believe that he feels he has let you down."

"Don't be ridiculous. He brought you and Tariq back to safety. You said yourself he carried you a great part of the way."

She smiled at the memory. "When it was too painful for me to sit on the camel, he carried me. He was so gentle, so kind. I . . . I don't know—"

"He chose duty because that's what makes up Lazar. Surely you know that?"

She looked back at him, puzzled. "I was so sure he'd choose Ana."

"He did the right thing. You really believe that Ana was in no immediate danger?"

"I honestly believe she wasn't. Have you been avoiding Lazar?" Herezah asked, her tone curious but comforting.

"I have found it hard to face him, yes."

"He should have died a dozen times that night. He fought like a man possessed; I've never seen anything like it. We were all so helpless. Even though he's Galinsean, he made me proud to be Percherese and to know that the heir to the enemy crown fought for us."

"You almost make me wish I'd been there."

"Well, all I'm saying is he did you proud. Don't blame him, son. Do everything in your power to hang on to him. We are losing him because he can't forgive himself for losing the Zaradine. Tell him you don't blame him."

"Mother, what's gotten into you?"

"How do you mean?"

Boaz stood. "You don't even sound like the Valide I knew from before."

"Before what?"

"Before the desert," he said, shaking his head as if unsure of what he meant himself. "Anyway, when did you visit him?"

"Today. I have just returned."

"And?"

"I want to care for him, nurse him back quickly to good health. If Ana is carrying Percheron's heir, as we suspect she is, then we have to find her, especially with war coming. Only Lazar can take us back there. He is useless to you lying in a bed and wishing himself to death. Do you still blame him?"

Boaz held his mother's gaze silently for few long moments. Finally he sighed. "No."

"Then see him."

"I look at him and I know I will experience only the pain of loss. Ana is gone. There are moments in my bitterness when I think he did this deliberately."

"What?"

"Well, you've hinted often enough at his desires for her."

Herezah knew that a tender touch was needed now, along with the truth that Lazar had behaved only with honor throughout the journey. "Boaz, my Lion. I was there. Nothing happened. For all my bitterness and all my secretive wishes that I could catch your wife in some moment of infidelity with your Spur, they were very distant, very sensible of their positions and duty. Ana was withdrawn and quiet for the entire journey—she was sickening constantly. Lazar was respectful to all of us and dutiful, but absent for virtually all of it. You know how he is—not there in spirit even when his body is!" She tried to catch Boaz's gaze again but he avoided her eyes.

She continued: "Lazar hardly looked at her and I feel ashamed for worrying you so unnecessarily."

Her attempt at apology only seemed to accentuate Boaz's distress. He shook his head as he spoke. "He has never behaved toward Ana with anything other than grace and courtesy. It is wrong to suspect him of anything dishonorable."

"Perhaps I was blinded by my own frailty toward our Spur."

Now Boaz did look at her, hard and quizzically. "This must be the first time you've ever been so truthful with me."

"No, it is not. But it is possibly the first time I have been so candid about Lazar in front of you."

Boaz looked away, refusing to acknowledge Herezah's confession. "So they never behaved secretively?"

"Never. In fact, Tariq spent the most time with your wife. The dwarf, of course, was always flitting around her, serving her food and fussing about her in his strange, demented manner, and the man Jumo was always very diligent and courteous toward Ana, but Lazar was consistently remote. The only moment I could cite when the Spur let his guard down might have beeen when his servant, that same Jumo person, perished. It cut deep into Lazar and we sent Ana to speak with him—yes, to comfort him. They are both such fringe dwellers, aren't they? Tariq agreed that if anyone could get through the ice fortress of Lazar's countenance as he grieved, Ana might."

"You left them alone?"

"No, son. I was with Ana the whole time. But I allowed Ana to lead the conversation. And she did so with elegance and grace. She did not let us or you down. Why do you pursue this?"

He gave an ironic laugh. "Coming from you, that is amusing. No reason at all, Mother. I'm jealous that you all had time with Ana when I didn't. And now she's gone."

"We will find your Ana. But you must help me get Lazar well. No one else knows where she was taken to."

"But surely he doesn't either?"

"I think Lazar may have some idea."

"What makes you say that?" Boaz shot back.

"This fellow—Arafanz, he calls himself—he knew all of us and he certainly knew Lazar. There are clues in that show of knowledge. Lazar's too sick to focus on it but he's the only one amongst us who knows the desert, who knows in which direction Ana was taken. If you want Ana back, you need your Spur."

She watched Boaz raise his head to capture a soft swirl of breeze that blew in through her apartments. It seemed unnaturally warm and still for so early in the season, so this gust was a welcome respite.

"You want to bring him into the palace?"

Her pulse quickened. "Yes. Near to the harem so I can attend him each day. Elim can be present at all times but I want to supervise the care. He needs this drezden poison—it alone can restore him."

"From snakes?"

"They have to be found and milked and he must ingest copious amounts in a tea, apparently. The pure venom will restore him only for a short while. The tea heals, makes him well."

"You have my authority to organize it."

Perhaps he expected a squeal of delight, a sense of triumph maybe? Instead Herezah very deliberately showed no overreaction; she simply quietly stood and hugged him. "Thank you, darling. I give you my word, we shall find your wife and we shall bring home your heir."

3

Ana stepped into the chamber with trepidation, afraid of what ghoulish event she might have to witness next. To her relief, all that confronted her was a sparsely furnished room consisting of a shallow clay basin with pails of water nearby and a wizened man who was waiting to offer her some drying linens.

The man bowed slowly, reverently. "You are to bathe," he said in the ancient language she had heard spoken earlier that day, "and then Arafanz will see you."

She looked around, fearful. "Where is he?"

"Not here. He awaits you but he asks that you feel free to take your time."

"Where does this water come from?" she asked, perplexed, as she gratefully reached for the towels.

"A fresh spring feeds the fortress. We do not squander it but Arafanz has commanded that you have access to it. Three pails

39

are warmed, the other tepid." The man shrugged. "It is all for you."

"But why? Just an hour ago he was—"

"I am a servant only. Save your questions for him alone. Bathe, please. Do you need any assistance?"

"Er . . . no," she stammered. "I can manage."

"Then I shall leave you now. I will not be far away should you need anything."

Ana watched him leave, her mind racing. She had believed these past few months that her captor's intention was to ransom her, but today's display of power had nothing to do with money or desire for it. Why his people were being so polite to her, why he himself was so courteous to her, whilst he was so ruthless to others, baffled her.

She undressed and stepped into the clay basin, reaching for the first pail of heated water and the mug, which she used to tip the water over herself. Ruefully, she recognized that despite all her bitter words about the decadence of the harem, she had taken its bathing rituals for granted. As the clean water broke over her head and splashed down her body, Ana felt herself gradually relaxing. She spied a pot of paste, presumed it was soap, and was secretly delighted to discover that it wasn't made purely from goat or camel fat as she'd expected, but was lightly fragranced with cinnamon and rose water. It was mixed with sand and dried petals and they acted to slough her dried skin. She couldn't help but feel pampered again as she applied the low-lathering paste, smoothing the gritty substance across her swollen belly, enjoying the tautness as its precious cargo began to make room for itself. Until now Ana had deliberately pushed all thoughts of her child firmly to the back of her mind. She had refused to acknowledge him—it was a boy, she was sure of it—

because she had been certain her death was imminent and didn't want to feel guilty for the child. But now she found she could not ignore him any longer. It was a shock, realizing that at nearing sixteen, she was to be a mother. Her lack of knowledge and her inexperience scared her but it seemed her body knew what to do and so she would leave the tiny mite to his own devices and try hard not to think too hard upon his fragility. She smiled in spite of herself. One night her belly had been tender but flat, and the next day it seemed to have popped. Her jailers had obviously kept Arafanz well briefed.

This child would be Percheron's heir, she suddenly realized, and she stumbled in the basin at the thought that the Stone Palace would claim her son. Perhaps she was better off here as the desert's prisoner than the harem's? She sighed and put the futile thought from her mind, turning her attention to cleansing her hair. Before she knew it, all three buckets of warmed water had been utilized. It felt wicked to use the last pail but she did, in defiance of Arafanz's deeds this day.

Twenty less thirsts to slake, she thought as she used their water. Her anger at the men's senseless deaths returned and she sucked in her breath as the cool of the water bit, awakening her. She stepped out of the basin and began toweling herself, rubbing hard to revive muscles that had felt too little exercise. When she was finished she called to the man outside, who emerged holding two candles on a tray of braided grasses, along with some combs and a brush. Ana hadn't registered how dark it had become and she shivered now at the realization that dusk had obviously fallen in the desert. It would become cold very rapidly now.

"Sit, please," her aide said, gesturing toward a small wooden bench. "I will brush your hair."

Ana wanted to decline but kept silent and did as she was asked. The man began working behind her; his touch was careful, his fingers coming into contact only with her hair, not even grazing the skin of her shoulders. He began to hum softly as he worked.

"What is that tune?" she asked, equally quietly, enjoying the rhythm of his combing.

"It is about frankincense and myrrh. It is a song my mother used to sing."

"I don't know the language. What does it mean?"

"It's about a woman singing to her husband that she would rather have the smoke of the crystallized sap than the glint of gold from the ground."

"Ah. It's nice. And what is your name?"

"We don't use names here, although I was once known as Soraz."

She could tell she'd made him feel uncomfortable and so Ana fell silent again. After a while the man put his combs back on the tray. "Your hair is still damp but it's shiny now," he said. "I will leave you to dress it as you wish. I'm also leaving you with a small pot of sandalwood oil should you care to use it on yourself as perfume. Someone will fetch you soon. He will bring fresh robes."

"Thank you for your kindness," Ana said, turning to stare at him.

Soraz said nothing in response, simply bowed his head to her and departed.

Ana tipped some of the thick dark oil into her hands and rubbed it onto her neck, chest, and pulse points as she'd been taught in the harem. Its deliciously spicy perfume filled the air and she was reminded of the time that Elza had been given permission by Salmeo to use the expensive sandalwood fragrance on Ana before a visit to Boaz. "This is the perfume of the gods alone," the servant had whispered as she had smoothed it onto Ana's skin. Ana shivered slightly at the memory. Pez believed she was a god. A wave of sorrow rippled through her on behalf of the dwarf, for despite his dedication to this notion, she knew she was no such thing.

Another robed figure, with only his eyes showing, appeared within a couple of minutes bearing simple linen robes. He turned his back whilst she pulled the soft swath of fabric about her.

"I am ready," she said, unsure of what was expected.

He bowed. "Follow me," was all he said, and then, in the silence she had begun to expect from these faceless, nameless men, she accompanied him on a journey through the fortress. She ran her fingers along the rough-hewn walls, watching the soft light of the oil lamp that her guide carried bounce ahead of them. Once or twice she thought she saw symbols cut into the walls or engraved above doorways, but they were moving swiftly and illumination was brief, the symbols swallowed by darkness in the instant they passed.

Finally, they arrived at a low doorway. Her navigator nodded, and silently pointed toward the dark doorway. She had no choice. There was nowhere else to go but inside. Ana took a deep breath and pulled at the handle of the smooth timber door. She stepped in and was taken by surprise with what she saw.

Lazar was sweating, twisting in bed from the pain that even a weightless silken sheet seem to provoke. It hurt to lie down but it hurt more to sit or stand; there was no position that might bring him peace. But he had been here before, recognized the familiar sense of nausea and dislocation as fever swept through his body and claimed him. Oh yes, he remembered this suffering all too well from his time on Star Island. It had been different then—he had not been able to so much as hold a thought; all he had been able to do then was drift abandoned on its waves. But this time he felt more anchored in reality. He could think; he was aware of himself and his surrounds—that much was a blessing—but the pain felt sharper for that greater level of consciousness.

He rode the pain until he thought he could take it no more, until he was sure he was screaming at the top of his lungs. In reality he was not screaming, although his eyes were shut tight and his mouth was pulled back in agony.

Open your eyes, someone commanded.

The sound of the voice stunned him into consciousness. He blinked, slowly, expecting light, but saw only darkness, tasted the tang of salt, and heard the slosh of waves.

Fully!

Lazar obeyed. He could do no less. And felt instantly terrified. He thought he dropped to his knees, clung to the cool of the stone.

I don't understand, he gasped.

You will not fall. Raise yourself up. Look at me.

I am dreaming.

You are not. You are here. Say my name.

You are Beloch, Lazar whispered.

Louder!

Lazar gathered his courage, lifted himself straight, and stared into the stone-carved eyes of the giant. *You are Beloch,* he stated clearly.

Good. And my brother?

Is Ezram.

And you?

I am Lazar.

State your real name, the giant growled. *Don't hide behind that alias.*

He complied, murmuring, *I am Prince Lucien of Galinsea.*

Indeed you are, the giant said more gently now. *Welcome, Prince Lucien.*

How is this happening? I am dreaming.

You are dying again. You were saved once and will be again if you take the help you are offered. You must accept the aid, despite the person who offers it. You must get well and you must find Ana.

I know.

She is with child.

Lazar thought he might have nodded.

A new voice joined them. It was Ezram. *You must bring the heir back to Percheron. It is important to restore the balance.*

Lazar looked up, puzzled. *Balance?*

My brother means "for the chaos that is coming," Beloch explained.

You will need all of us, Ezram confirmed.

I don't understand.

You will when the time arrives.

But I want to understand now. What does Ezram mean?

Beloch sighed in a low rumble. *You must free us, Lucien. All of us—not just us twins, but Crendel, Darso, Shakar.*

But how?

Fret not, at the right time we come at your call.

At my call? Lazar repeated, totally confused. *What is this time you speak of?*

The coming of Lyana. It is what we have waited for.

But the old stories tell us she has come and gone before and none of the stone statues of Percheron did anything.

This time it is different, Ezram said.

So I am told, Lazar replied, a bleakness in his tone. *What is my part in this?*

You do not know? Beloch asked, surprised.

I have never known.

Then it is not for us to say. One of your duties is to release us, Lucien. That is your part for us.

Release you! How do I do such a thing? You are set in stone!

We are alive! We have always been alive! We are imprisoned through magic. You must thwart the magic.

How?

Only you know. You must find the solution fast. War is upon us.

Lazar hung his head. *I don't—*

It is within you. Beloch cut across Lazar's despair. *You must go back now. Someone attends you.*

Hurry, Ezram urged.

Through their voices and through his own breathing, above the pounding of his heart and the whoosh of blood coursing through his ears, fringing his fever and cutting through his confusion, Lazar heard a whisper, a voice he recognized, calling to him. Yet he turned back to the darkness, to the stone statues.

Answer me this! he cried at the brothers.

There is no—

Answer me! Is Ana the Goddess?

No, they replied together. *But the Goddess rises.*

And Lazar was flung backward, his eyelids springing open to regard Herezah leaning down, looking into his face. He read fear in her eyes.

———

Arafanz stood before a small fireplace that did little to ease the chill of the room. He was dressed in loose-fitting trousers and shirt, looking more like a soldier, less like a cleric. He looked suddenly younger. In his hand was a clay goblet, from which he sipped as she entered.

"Welcome, Ana," he said, voice soft, melodic. "I trust you are refreshed."

"I am, thank you," she stammered, unsure how this cozy scene matched the prison she understood this place to be.

"Come, sit, warm yourself. I should have sent a blanket to wrap around your shoulders. Forgive me."

"There is no need to fuss. You did not trouble yourself for the past three moons of my incarceration. It can hardly matter now."

He held her gaze intently and Ana was pleased she did not wither beneath it.

"Would you like me to explain?"

She nodded. "I would like to understand what this whole business of my capture is about. If you have no intention to kill or even ransom me, what use am I to you?"

"Come join me. I will tell you what I can."

She dabbed his lips with a soaked sponge. "Be calm. It's me, Herezah. You are feverish and hallucinating."

"But Beloch and Ezram are—"

"Still in the bay, yes, where they're meant to be. Lazar, pay attention if you can. The Elim are here to bring you with me. They are going to carry you in a special karak. Can you hear me? Lazar?"

He shook his head from side to side, his face a mask of confusion.

Herezah turned to the two senior Elim with her. "Just take him. Ignore him if he resists. This is on the Zar's orders."

Salmeo stood nearby. "Rather intriguing to see him look so wasted. At the flogging he at least appeared strong, but now he's just a shadow of the Spur we all knew."

"Not once I've finished with him, Grand Master Eunuch," Herezah said, her tone crisp. "Let's get him back to the rooms we've prepared."

Under the amused gaze of the chief eunuch, six Elim lifted Lazar's struggling body, which was too weak to be anything more than a nuisance to their efforts to carry him.

"The Zar wants this house aired properly and cleaned," Herezah said, not even looking at Salmeo as she swept by him. "See to it, eunuch."

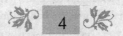

4

Ana sat, feeling nervous as she watched Arafanz reach for the carafe of whatever he was drinking. Despite his seeming relaxation this evening, she realized that Arafanz was not a man who was ever tranquil in thought. His gaze was restless and his hands were rarely still. He didn't sit, preferred to stand.

"We have no ability to chill our food or wine, but this is Dorash, a sweet and mellow blend from the north," he explained as he poured. "It can be served cool rather than cold." He blinked. "Ah, Dorash is a grape from the region where one of your companions came from—the one who perished in the desert."

"Jumo? You knew about it?"

"We watched."

"But you did not help," she admonished, a gust of pain rippling through her, reminding her of Lazar's despair.

"It was not our place to interfere and we had no intention of disrupting the special surprise we had planned for later."

"What else did you see?" Ana asked, suddenly fearing that his men had also shared her night of love in the Lazar's arms.

"How do you mean? Your party was followed from the moment you left the city of Percheron."

Ana was so shocked by this news that she could say nothing in response. She chose to hope that her betrayal of Boaz was not common knowledge amongst the Razaqin. She did not have the courage to find out for sure.

"Taste your wine, Ana, please," Arafanz urged, and she did, if for no other reason than to cover her anxiety. "Is it to your liking?"

"Does it really matter?" she snapped, trying to regain her equilibrium.

He shrugged. "I suppose not. I am not sure I can make you happy here but we shall try and do our best to treat you with courtesy."

"Really? So the murder of so many before my eyes is your idea of making a guest comfortable?"

Arafanz impaled her with a cool stare. "I explained to you I was making a point about what true loyalty really is—and how ugly it can be."

"Well, it was meaningless! All I saw was men squander their lifeblood. Loyalty had no part in this. To me it was about convincing young, impressionable men that giving up their lives so cheaply had some reason."

"But that's it. There was reason. Proving loyalty to their cause."

"Proving loyalty to stupidity more like," Ana countered angrily.

"You have spirit. I'll grant you that," he murmured, and came as close to a full smile as Ana thought she might ever see from him.

"I care not that I impress you. Why am I here?"

"I want to cleanse Percheron of its sin."

She stared, uncomprehending, at her captor. "What do you mean?"

"We are going to kill everyone in the palace, including its servants and all of the priests at the temples. We shall spare the innocents—the Percherese people who know no better—and we shall help Percheron to make a fresh start."

"A fresh start? As what?"

"A new regime."

"And you Zar, I suppose?" she said, her tone all scorn.

"No, in this regard you have me all wrong. I have no aspirations of that nature."

"Then what do you want, Arafanz?"

"Your child on the throne, Ana, and the faith of the Goddess restored. That is what I want."

Ana's horror couldn't have been more complete. She stared at him openmouthed, her goblet of wine forgotten, tilted in her lap with some of its contents spilling out onto her fresh linen robe.

Arafanz continued, "You are here for your protection and that of the child's. We nearly lost you in the palace—we shall not risk you again."

"We?"

"Ellyana and—"

"Ellyana!" Ana stood. The goblet dropped and splashed what little wine was left across the floor as the clay shattered. "What has *she* to do with this?" she demanded, eyes glittering with anger.

"Everything."

"So you are a follower of Lyana?"

"All of us here are."

Ana felt her bile rising. "And those men killed themselves for her?"

"Certainly not for me, or you," came his reply. "I am purely their leader and her disciple. I will restore her to Percheron. This time it is different."

"And me? What is your interest in me, then? Simply my child?"

He nodded, looking away. "An heir to the throne. A follower, faithful to Lyana. We know you are. We know your child will be. We know the Goddess wants you safe, your child crowned."

"But who is Lyana?" she asked, feeling the question catch on her breath.

He shook his head. "No one knows, this time not even Iridor."

"Iridor has risen?" Ana asked carefully. She must not betray anything she knew.

"I don't know. I am told it is all playing out very differently this time. I know only what I am permitted. Perhaps it is the same for you?" Ana said nothing and Arafanz continued. "But I want to assure you that I am not your enemy, even though it may seem that way." He bent to pick up the clay pieces of her goblet. "Can I pour you another?"

She shook her head. Her anger had fled, had been replaced with confusion and no little despair.

"Then at least share some supper with me. I am your protector."

Ana didn't want to mention that she already had one of

those. One she loved with all her heart. "You have a funny way of showing it. Why did you leave me to rot in that room?"

"I have been away. That room kept you safe. Away from prying eyes and also away from temptation."

She gave a mirthless burst of a laugh. "Temptation? In my condition?"

"I didn't mean you. You are the only woman in this fortress. I believe that men, no matter how firm their resolve, can be undone by a woman."

"So, for all your claims of loyalty, your men would under-mine you in a blink if I offered my affections?" she baited.

He regarded her sadly. "Some might, others would. Men think they have power but it is not always so. It's women, I fear, who hold the ultimate power. Power over our bodies, power over our seed and what becomes of it, power over our hearts and souls. Another reason why Lyana is right to be our god. This morning's demonstration was important to impress upon you that we are serious in our intention and that these men are loyal to their cause. I think I ordered it as much for their sake as yours. They needed to be reminded that our cause and our lives beyond the fleshly ones of this existence are more important."

Ana shook her head, disbelief in her expression. "You've stolen me from my people. The deaths haven't impressed any-thing upon me save your cruelty. Don't you think I realize how serious you are?"

"No. Until this morning you had no reason to fear me, or my men, as much as you fear us now. Now you know that noth-ing earthly can stop us. We are committed to Lyana's cause. She will prevail this time. Not only Maliz but the followers of Zarab will die."

"Lazar will stop you," she warned, unable to help herself.

Arafanz nodded. "He will try. And how sad it is that he and we are working toward the same cause."

"Lazar works only for Zar Boaz and the good of Percheron. He does not share your crusade."

"Not knowingly perhaps, but he shares the same ideals; he admires Lyana. If he were with us right now, he might well see the sense in what I am proposing."

"Never! He would never be disloyal to the royals, and he will protect Boaz to the death. For all your spying, you don't seem to know the Spur all that well if you think he would ever condone senseless murder of any Percherese—or anyone, for that matter."

"Then, alas, he will die too. But let us stop this talk of death, Ana. You are what . . . ? Perhaps nearing three moons with child? I am informed you became pregnant the first time you lay with your Zar." Ana felt herself blush at both his knowledge and his candor. "We have up to another six moons together before anything can happen. You are my guest and your welfare is my concern."

"I want nothing from you," she said as coldly as she could.

"We shall see," Arafanz said, summoning one of his hooded men. "Now, let me organize some food. You carry the most important life in all of Percheron in your belly, and if you won't eat for yourself, I insist you eat for him."

"How can you be so sure my child is male."

"Ellyana told me."

Maliz, the demon who hid beneath the facade of Grand Vizier Tariq, couldn't really have cared less about the petty mortal war that was certainly coming, but recently he had decided that his next body would be that of Boaz. And so preserving the life of the present Zar and perhaps even his delectable harem, was of some concern.

The Zar's invitation to sup together had eventuated and now Boaz leaned back against silken cushions. They had begun eating very late, although Maliz noticed the Zar hardly touched his food.

Boaz reached for a fig, nibbled on it. "Have you heard that the Valide is bringing the Spur into the palace? She's determined to ensure his return to good health."

"Yes, my Zar, I'd been informed," the Grand Vizier replied, his own supper appetite still not sated even after a plate of rice blended with chicken and vegetables, a pyramid of lamb cubes on skewers crusted with herbs and cooked over an open flame, and the jug of the fermented mare's milk he habitually took with his evening repast. He ladled some thick meaty soup into a bowl. "You are not eating much, Highness."

"Forgive me. I am not hungry tonight."

Maliz thought that Boaz had likely not been hungry since he first heard of what had unfolded in the desert. "You must keep yourself nourished, Majesty. You health is now more important than ever and you look extremely thin." He had no intention of inhabiting a frail Zar's body if it could be helped.

Boaz nodded, distracted. He put the uneaten fig aside and took a draft of watered wine instead. "I'm going to send a party into the desert to find Zaradine Ana."

"I assumed you would, Highness. In fact, I'm more surprised at your patience."

"I've had to be patient, for I can't find her without Lazar and he has not been well enough to have anything close to a discussion with. But I'm hoping my mother's efforts will return his vitality."

"So you're sending him back into the desert?"

"I plan to."

"What about the Galinsean invasion? Do you not think the Spur is best left in the city once he's well?"

"If my wife is carrying Percheron's heir, I think that child is more important to our future than any of us realize."

"I don't agree, my Zar," Maliz cautioned, his interest in the soup forgotten. He could not risk Boaz being so uncaring of his people's lives—all Zarab worshippers—or especially of his own. "Ana, lovely though she is, is but one of your women. You have several dozen, of which at least thirty must be ready for bedding. Get more of these girls with child—start tonight, Majesty—sire ten new sons upon them, and if need be, secure them somewhere outside of Percheron. The royal line must be preserved, I agree, but you are in a position to do so now without compromising the realm's security. We need Lazar here, my Zar." He held Boaz's gaze steadily.

Boaz regarded his Grand Vizier with a cool stare. "Perhaps I haven't made myself clear, Tariq. It is only the heir in Ana's belly in which I'm interested."

This intrigued Maliz. He knew Boaz was fascinated by his new Zaradine but he hadn't realized that the young Zar was so smitten that he had ruled out any other relationship and even other heirs by another wife. Despite his exasperation with the young ruler, he responded calmly. "But, my Zar, you had her executed no fewer than four moons ago. If not for Spur Lazar's theatrics, she would certainly have succumbed."

"That was then, when she was neither my Zaradine nor the carrier of my heir. She was merely an odalisque—and may I remind you that it was not I who called for her death. The harem, as you know, has its own rules and internal politics. In these matters of punishment I have little say. My only role in that whole sorry affair was to make the pronouncement of her death—and I can assure you that did not please me. In fact, it sickened me."

"You hid your despair admirably, Majesty." Maliz didn't succeed in hiding the sarcasm in his tone.

Either Boaz didn't hear it or he chose to ignore the bite of his Vizier's reply. "I would have shamed my father had I done anything other than veil my true feelings. I had no choice politically but to follow the ways and laws of our land."

"So it is different now—" the Grand Vizier began, but Boaz cut him off.

"Of course it is! I have secured her future by making her my wife. Now she is mine and the child of hers belongs to me. I will declare him my heir immediately if necessary."

The Grand Vizier frowned, unsure of why there was so much vehemence driving the Zar's words. His eyes narrowed slightly as he regarded the young ruler and his curious choice of words. What was at play here that he didn't understand? Something was not right, he was sure of it—there was an undercurrent that he couldn't pinpoint. He moved on carefully. "Of course, Highness. That is your prerogative," he soothed. "I can see now why you are giving this your priority. How can I assist you?"

Boaz drained his goblet before answering. "I want you to help the Valide in any of her needs regarding Lazar."

"You have my word."

"I assume none of our networks have revealed anything about this Arafanz or the Razaqin he speaks of?"

"None yet, but I am meeting with someone shortly who may know something."

"Who?"

Maliz put a soft expression of sympathy onto the Grand Vizier's face. "Ah, Majesty, you know I can't reveal the sources of information. We have discussed this previously—that I don't wish to compromise the Crown in any way. You are always furnished with whatever information I can discover."

Boaz nodded, showing he understood. "Then the moment Lazar is fit, he will be sent to find her. I'm giving him another four moons at most. I cannot wait any longer. The child will be due and I don't want it born in the desert."

"They why risk waiting? Send other men."

The Zar shook his head firmly. "I trust no one else to survive the desert or survive whatever fight might be involved to wrest her back from that madman's clutches."

"You will send Lazar alone?"

"He is as good as a dozen men—you should know that from what he did to save your life, Tariq. And it seems obvious now that the more people involved in any desert party, the more vulnerable it is. Lazar was right. He warned me at the beginning of the journey to Galinsea that he wanted no more than Ana, Jumo, himself, and perhaps one other."

"No one could know that Arafanz would strike, Majesty, not even Lazar."

"He could not know it. But he understood better than any of us the dangers. Look at what happened to Jumo. That could have been you, Tariq."

Maliz let the lightly couched insult pass. "And should Lazar perish in this attempt to find the Zaradine?"

Boaz surprised the older man by shrugging. "Then he dies. We all die, Tariq," the Zar said, with condescension. "Even Lazar would put Ana and especially the child first, I'm sure."

Maliz hesitated, caught by something in Boaz's voice, but before he could respond, the Zar burst out, "Zarab strike me! What does Arafanz want? He takes my wife, my heir; he makes no claims upon us for their ransom. What is he aiming to achieve?"

"Perhaps he wants her, Highness," Maliz offered. "He seemed to know when and how to strike effectively; he knew precisely who we were—in fact all about the individuals in the royal party. This was no opportunistic attack that hoped to yield a few jewels, my Zar. I believe Ana was always his intended prize."

"But why, Tariq? She is one woman, not worth risking so many men for."

"Is she not, Majesty? You staked your whole realm against her name in sending her to Romea. You entrusted her with the lives of all of your people by choosing her as your emissary. The future of Percheron rested with this young woman."

Boaz looked down, nodding. "And nothing has changed. She holds Percheron's future in her womb. If I die, that child is all we have."

"You are not going to die, my Zar. I shall see to it," Maliz assured with far more determination driving his sentiment than the ruler could appreciate.

Boaz found a rueful smile. "Thank you, Tariq, but I fear even your faith cannot spare me a Galinsean sword."

Maliz nodded. He could not win this argument, based more on passion rather than good sense. "We must redouble our efforts to protect you, my Zar," Maliz replied.

"Salazin, your most elite of the Mutes, perished. And I think we have lost our finest of the royal guard in the desert," Boaz said.

"Many lives were lost, yes, and I regret that Salazin was one of them, Highness, but still we must intensify the guard of the Elim about you."

"As you see fit, Tariq," Boaz replied, waving his hand as if it meant little to him.

The demon hesitated, confused by Boaz's reaction. "What else troubles you, Highness? It cannot be all about Zaradine Ana. Let us presume she is safe."

"And Pez?"

"Ah, Highness. Forgive my candor but I would hazard the dwarf is likely dead. What use was a babbling imbecile to us"— he held up his hand as Boaz looked up angrily—"other than as the harmless amusement that brought such pleasure to your father and yourself alike?" Maliz tried hard to make it sound like the compliment he had contrived but still it came out a sugared insult.

Boaz batted the fig off his plate in a rare show of peevishness. "Oh, he was so much more, Grand Vizier, but none of you knew it!"

Maliz felt all of his internal alarms begin to sound. He carefully kept his voice even, his body language unchanged from the languorous position he had adopted, his fingers loose around the goblet of wine he had been twirling. "I don't understand, my Zar. What do you mean?" He frowned casually and nearly hurled the goblet across the room with unfettered rage when Bin suddenly interrupted them.

"Zar Boaz, please forgive me, Majesty," the servant said, appearing in the chamber, bowing and shuffling and unable to be still.

"Really, Bin," the Grand Vizier snapped, "hasn't his Highness any time to himself to eat?" Maliz slammed down the goblet before he answered the urge to hurl it at the secretary.

Boaz gave his Grand Vizier a quizzical look at the tone of and aggression in the admonishment. "It's all right, Tariq. I told you, I'm not hungry anyway. I'll hear this news outside in the salon. You'll have to excuse me—we were finished anyway, I'm sure."

Maliz felt his gut twist with fury but he pasted an avuncular smile on his face. "Of course, my Zar."

He watched the tall young Zar move away from the supper table and the huge salon doors close behind him.

"What is it, Bin? Please don't tell me Galinsean warships have been sighted?" Boaz held his breath and couldn't believe it when the servant smiled.

"No, my Zar, I bring only good tidings. Pez has been found."

The Zar leaped to his feet. "Pez? Alive?"

The servant nodded, grinning widely now at His Majesty's pleasure. "And rambling as usual, my Zar, making no sense but thrilling everyone that he's back. He is unharmed. Very disoriented, very thin, but he is whole."

"Where is he?"

"He demanded to see the elephants, Majesty, and then he insisted he be taken to the the florack bushes in your father's private garden. He wanted to pick some of their petals we gather. He plans to throw them at the stars . . . or so he told me. I thought it best to let him have his way, Highness."

"Is he there now, in the gardens?"

"He is, Highness. I'm sorry we didn't rush him straight

here, my Zar, but I didn't want to risk upsetting him. I know how you've missed him and I imagine he's terribly confused. It seemed wiser to keep him calm for you."

"You did well, Bin. I shall go to him immediately. This will be a private time for us. No one is to be permitted. No one! See to it."

"At once, Highness."

5

Pez saw Boaz burst through the courtyard doors, and watched his friend cross the distance in four strides to lift him hugging him tight, laughing and weeping at the same time.

"I thought I'd lost you," Boaz gushed.

"What a welcome. I should obviously get lost in the desert more often, Highness."

Boaz laughed, wiping at his eyes. "If you tell anyone I wept, I'll have you impaled."

It was the dwarf's turn to smile, his features going through that curious change that made him lose all the ugliness for which he was famed. "I'll write a song about it and sing it loudly everywhere."

"Not that anyone would understand your gibberish," Boaz followed up.

"No, but I'd make sure you did, Highness."

"Oh Zarab! Pez, I've missed you," Boaz said, squeezing Pez

again before setting him down. "You are well, not hurt?" he asked, spinning the dwarf around to be sure.

"I am unharmed, as you see."

"You look so thin."

Pez couldn't explain that it was from the long flight.

"I could say the same for you, Highness," he admonished.

"I have been fretting! Tell me everything."

Pez began to craft his tale. "I had to exist frugally. I lived off some meager supplies I found at our camp. Fortunately we had fresh water. There was a camel, too," he lied. "I was able to drink her milk and she kept me warm at night, and each day I struggled to get up on her, but she was a gentle beast. She saved my life."

"Where is this camel? I shall have a statue carved in her honor."

Pez thought quickly. "I set her free, Majesty. As I approached the western foothills, I came across a small herd and I allowed her to join them. I was so thankful to realize I was all but home."

"So you were lost in the confusion of the attack?"

"Totally. I was knocked out and remained unconscious for a while," Pez lied. "They must have thought me dead. I regained my wits only to discover the dead around me. All those I cared about were gone. What of Ana, my Zar?"

"No news. I cannot allow myself to think she is dead."

"She is not, Highness." And now Pez began to tread as carefully as he had ever done before.

"You know! What do you know?"

"Not much. As I explained I was knocked out but I came to my consciousness and heard voices. I feigned that I was dead but I heard that man Arafanz give Lazar a horrible choice. I couldn't see very well, but knew he had chosen to save the life of the Valide. Ana was safe, the Valide was not. Lazar had to make the most appalling decision, but he chose to help the royal in most need. Please tell me, Zar, that Lazar survived?"

Boaz nodded. "Lazar is alive and saved my mother and the Vizier too, although our Spur is sickening again. Salazin, who protected them, also disappeared, according to the Grand Vizier, and likely perished from his wounds."

Pez felt the wound of Razeen's death cut deeply. Razeen had been handpicked by himself and Zafira to pose as the Grand Vizier's private spy, under the name Salazin. They had played a dangerous game with this young man's life and Pez had never lost his fear for the youngster. Now to discover that the youth had in fact lost his life was crushing and Pez was reminded of Zafira's warning that they were squandering the lives of innocents. "I heard Lazar leave but not before he promised Ana that he would return with the anger of the Crown burning brightly in his heart to reclaim the Zaradine and the heir to Percheron."

"He said that?" Boaz asked, his eyes shining.

Pez nodded, warming to his guile. "I heard him, my Zar. His wrath on your behalf could not be mistaken. He told Ana that her husband would not rest until she was found. He warned Arafanz that Zar Boaz might be young but that you made a formidable enemy and your rage at his theft would know no bounds."

Boaz smiled faintly, confusion creasing across his forehead. "Lazar threatened the thief in this manner?"

"He did, my Zar," Pez assured, inwardly begging Lyana to forgive his necessary deception. "And then he rode away on the camel. But I heard Arafanz say to Ana that she would not be harmed in any way. She is alive, Majesty."

"Did he say why he was taking her?"

"No."

"And do you know where he was taking her?"

"I do not, although I watched them and they headed in a firm westerly direction. The Khalid may know exactly where they were destined."

"Khalid?"

"The men of the desert who accompanied us."

Boaz frowned. "I didn't know there was anyone in your party save those who left the city."

Pez shrugged. "Tribal men moved with us—not many. It was bargained with Lazar. I gather he wasn't happy about it but they supplied our camels, became our friends."

"So they did not perish in the attack?"

"They fled, I presume."

"Not truly friends, then," Boaz said, bitterness in his tone.

"Everyone, save the few you know about, was slaughtered, Highness. The desert men would not have been spared. They did the right thing in fleeing, for we were no match against the attackers. Only Lazar and Salazin felt any measure of success. How is Lazar?"

"I gather the same sickness that had him in its grip after the flogging has reclaimed him." Boaz grinned. "You'll never guess . . . my mother has decided to care for Lazar."

"The Valide?" Pez deliberately exclaimed with just the right balance of disbelief.

"She is determined that she alone will see to his care. He was brought here only today, I gather. I plan to see him tomorrow."

"And her reasons are simply for the good of Percheron and strictly platonic?"

Boaz gave him a wry sideways glance. "Nothing my mother thinks or does is ever simple, Pez. But Lazar is not helping himself and he won't ask for the help he needs. I sense he may even succumb to his sickness, and happily, because of the darkness that he has plunged himself into . . . but we need him. He has a duty to all of us—to Percheron. The only way to make him better is to force it by royal decree and I suspect nothing would terrify him faster into good health than knowing my mother has him at her mercy."

Pez smiled. There were times when he was sure none of them gave the young Zar enough credit for his mature insight. "Does she know how to look after him?"

"Apparently he needs some special bitter tea."

"What he needs immediately is the pure drezden poison, milked direct from a snake."

"How do you know?"

"As I understand it, that's how Zafira kept him alive last time. The tea is important to bring him back to full health but the pure poison is essential for him to survive. Has he been through the wasting fever yet?"

"I don't know." Boaz frowned.

Pez knew Lazar had not. "That is when he's at his most vulnerable, apparently, when we genuinely nearly lost him last time, although of course then there was the complication of the vicious flogging. I imagine it was hard not to consider him on the brink of death for the entire trial."

"How long will he go through this?"

"He took a year to recover last time. Now perhaps three or four moons."

Boaz nodded. "That's all I can give him. So what should the Valide do?"

"You'll have to tell her what I've told you but beware not to betray me—lie if you must." Pez knew he didn't have to remind Boaz of their secret but he had never felt himself in a more precarious position than now. "Give her this." He handed the Zar a scruffy-looking scroll of parchment.

"What is it?"

"A recipe for the tea that Lazar will need. I found it at the Sea Temple," Pez lied. "Zafira must have written it out. Tell anyone who asks that you found it on me when I was discovered at the temple."

The Zar read it. "We shall have to get the fresh poison. I'll order snakes to be milked immediately."

Pez nodded. "How is the Grand Vizier, by the way?"

"Unharmed—the only one who came out of the desert unscathed, to tell the truth. He's just returned from a brief tour with our ships." Boaz shrugged at his friend's look of surprise. "I needed someone senior I trusted to do some reconnaissance."

Pez masked his feelings about Maliz's being in such a position of trust. "No Galinsean ships yet?"

Boaz shook his head. "I don't know what to think."

"They're coming, my Zar, don't think otherwise. But I imagine the dignatories took the precaution of first sailing back to King Falza to advise him personally of developments. No doubt they gave Lazar long enough to reach Romea, or at least for your emissary to enter the capital. I imagine they'll be deciding around now, if not already, that no diplomatic party is arriving."

"And the ships will be returned," Boaz finished for him.

Pez nodded. "You have perhaps five moons at most before they are in our harbor."

Boaz gave an unintelligible growl. "And we shall be ready for them."

Lazar grimaced. "Valide, please—"

"Call me, Herezah," she urged, dabbing a soft flannel over his brow. "Does that help?"

He reached to stay her hand, noticed the flash of delight in her eyes above her veil at his touch. "You should not be nursing me," he croaked.

"Why ever not? My son has little need for me as counsel—he takes all the advice he requires from the Grand Vizier these days. And as I told you, after my time in the desert the harem is tedious. Furthermore, with the threat of war, it now seems altogether pointless. I might as well make myself useful by helping you to recover."

"The worst is yet to come," he warned, his voice cracking. "I have yet to confront the wasting fever."

"So be it. I shall see you through those times, Lazar. You saved my life—I feel obliged to reciprocate. I shall be your slave for a while." Her eyes glittered with the innuendo of her words.

Behind the Valide, Lazar saw a woman enter.

Elza bobbed a curtsy. "Excuse me, Valide, I have been sent to warn you that His Highness, the Zar, is approaching."

"Ah," Herezah said evenly. "Please, bring the Zar in."

Moments later Boaz arrived.

"My Lion, be welcome," Herezah said, standing to greet her son and removing her veil in a practiced motion before dropping to a low, elegant curtsy.

The Zar took her hand and raised her. "Mother," he said, planting a kiss on her cheek.

Lazar struggled unsuccessfully to raise himself from the pillow. This was the first time since he'd returned from the desert and handed over his precious charges that the Spur had seen his Zar. At that moment of return he had croaked an anguished apology that all had gone so wrong. Boaz had been stoic but cool toward Lazar. Now at least he wore a smile.

"Please don't, Lazar," Boaz admonished at his Spur's struggle. "Let us ignore protocol for the time being. It is good to see you, brother," he said, reaching for the Spur's raised hand and grasping it, making a fist of it in the way Lazar had taught him when he was a young lad.

The Spur found a twitch of a smile as the fond memory flitted across his thoughts of a young prince striving to become a man, his father rarely present and a royal soldier his next best option. "Majesty," he croaked, "Forgive—"

"Don't, I beg you. You have our collective gratitude for returning the Valide and Grand Vizier to Percheron alive. I can see what it cost you to save my mother. I can only imagine the more hidden effects."

Inwardly something snagged at Lazar. Boaz's words seemed genuine enough and yet to him they seemed to carry an uncomfortable undercurrent. "What news, Majesty?" he asked. His mind was beginning to swim. He must ask Herezah not to wear such a heady fragrance if she was going to look after him. Look after him? How ridiculous. The Valide, of all people!

"I do bring news. Good news," Boaz said, his bearing changing to that of a young boy with a secret.

"Boaz, tell us," his mother urged.

"Pez is returned!" the Zar exclaimed triumphantly.

"Gods be praised!" Lazar said, relieved that he no longer had to keep his knowledge of Pez secret.

The Valide kept her own counsel, although her eyes showed she was more bemused by her son's childish pleasure than delighted by the news itself.

"I told the Grand Vizier this is the first reason I've had to smile in a while," Boaz admitted.

"I'm pleased for you, son," the Valide finally deigned to say. "Keep him away from here, though. Lazar is not well enough for the dwarf's antics."

"I don't believe Pez will be up to any antics, Mother," Boaz said. "The desert took its toll on all of you. He's lucky to be alive and essentially doing little more than drooling at present," he lied, turning to wink at Lazar.

"How?" Lazar croaked. It was the most he could say amidst his dizziness and nausea, but knew Pez would be expecting the Zar to craft his lie fully.

Boaz gave a confusing version for his mother's benefit, just enough to suggest that he had managed to make some sense of what the dwarf had been through although most of it had been gibberish. "The fact is, he did survive, and that's all that matters to me," he said to his mother, whose eyes were filled with query.

"Tens of men died," she exclaimed, shaking her head. "How did that pathetic, befuddled dwarf survive?"

"None of us will ever know."

"How did he have the sense to know in which direction Percheron lay?" She turned to Lazar, who had already closed his eyes. This conversation was lies within lies: he was lying to Boaz about Pez, Boaz was lying to his mother about the dwarf, and Pez, he was sure had lied to Boaz as well.

"He muttered something about the Khalid," Boaz said.

Lazar, keeping his eyes closed to steady himself on what felt like a floating bed, took up the reins. "They are desert men. They would have known him from our party and perhaps guided him back. That would explain how he found his way."

"Yes, I think that's likely what occurred." Boaz turned back to his mother and changed the subject. "So, do you know what to do with Lazar? Apparently he's meant to be given a dose of pure drezden."

"I've already taken it," Lazar said. "That was the last of the stocks I had and what has kept me alive thus far. I will need more of the pure poison for the future but now I have to start drinking the tea. The delusions and restlessness will begin any moment."

"Mother, here—luck is on our side," Boaz said, reaching into his pocket and pulling out the scruffy-looking parchment. "They found this on Pez. I think he must have stolen it from the belongings of the priestess Zafira. It tells you how to make this tea of drezden."

"Ah, how convenient. Again the dwarf triumphs," Herezah said coolly. Nevertheless she took the parchment, glanced at it briefly. "I can ask Salmeo to organize this."

"No," Boaz said. "I command you not to involve Salmeo in anything remotely connected with our Spur's welfare. If you are going to take on his nursing, Mother, I insist he is tended to only by the people I appoint."

"Why, Boaz?"

"You know why. Either it's done my way or not at all."

"All right, son. As you command."

"And Pez is to have private access to him at all times."

"You know that's ridiculous," Herezah replied, a petulant note creeping into her otherwise respectful tone.

Boaz took a breath that was clearly meant to signify soft irritation at the old argument. "Pez made a difference when I was grieving, Mother. It's hard to explain why or how. But he is someone who transcends the ordinary conversation; sometimes just his presence can have a positive effect on those who like him. I can't expect you or Salmeo or even Tariq to understand this, but Lazar does. This is another of my commands. Pez has access everywhere in the palace. Lazar's sick room is no exception."

The Valide did not take her grievance further, although it was obvious from her dark expression that she was furious. "He must learn to be quiet whilst the Spur rests."

Boaz nodded. "I shall get you all that you need—"

Lazar heard no more, could feel himself already slipping toward a familiar abyss. He didn't want to be in the palace but he also didn't want to die—not yet, not with the unfinished business with Arafanz of the Razaqin. And so with a soft sigh of regret he gave in to the ride down the slippery slope of half consciousness, into the feverish state he remembered all too well. He knew it would be several moons at least before he spoke to these people again with any clarity.

6

Ever since the night that Arafanz had told her of his connection to Ellyana, Ana had felt a lessening of the strict rules that governed her care. She had been moved to a different chamber in the fortress, one that was closer to the suite of rooms that Arafanz inhabited. Previously she had ignored her jailers but knew they were constantly rotated; now she noticed a single guard took care of her immediate needs. As his face had become familiar to her, she tried to be friendly.

"Thank you," she said as the man, no more than eighteen summers, replenished her water jug and the tiny basin that served for cleaning herself.

He nodded but didn't smile.

"I wonder if I might be permitted to take a walk today?" she asked in the ancient tongue that Arafanz used with his men. She didn't expect an answer, just the usual dark-eyed stare. It was simply something to say.

"I shall ask for you," he surprised her by murmuring before turning to leave.

"Oh, wait, please," she begged, leaping up from the cot on which she had been sitting. "Please don't go. I'm grateful for this chance to talk with someone."

"We are allowed to speak freely with you now that our leader is returned, Miss Ana," the man replied shyly.

"Thank you," she said. "I know names are not used here, but am I permitted to know yours?"

"I was known once as Ashar. I have no name here—he names only a few."

"Do you speak only Sharaic?"

"We all learn it. It's the language of the fortress. It is what we speak, yes."

He had not answered the question. Perhaps Arafanz had taught his men to be evasive as well, she thought. "But that would take years, Ashar."

"I have been here many years, Miss Ana," he said, and she understood that was all he would say about it.

She nodded in thanks, not wishing to damage this fragile bond by being overly inquisitive. "I look forward to hearing about my walk."

She didn't expect to hear that day but he returned swiftly with the news that Arafanz would be accompanying her.

"Oh no, I didn't mean—"

"He wishes to take you somewhere, Miss Ana," Ashar said gently, cutting across her protestation. "You are to wear full robes of the desert," he added, handing her fresh garments before departing.

She was fetched not long afterward. Ashar led her through various corridors and down stairs, emerging at ground level for the first time. Again she blinked beneath the vicious sun, even though it was barely near the heat of the day.

Arafanz strode over to greet her, looking entirely comfortable and untroubled by the heat. "We should be doing this in the cool of the dawn or early evening, but I do have to check something and it was the perfect excuse to give you the fresh air you crave. I'm sorry I have not offered until now. We will not walk, but ride. Is that to your suiting?"

She nodded. "Thank you."

"I see you've covered your face fully. That is acceptable for the desert but please don't do it on my account."

"I do it for my own comfort," Ana assured him.

She saw the ghost of what could have been a smile move briefly over his mouth, crinkle the corner of his eyes slightly. It was gone before she could fully register it, frustrating her. The man was so controlled with his emotion it was almost an insult.

Arafanz gave orders to the two men who waited with them as Ashar assisted Ana onto her camel. "She is called Farim," the Razaqin whispered. "She is a gentle, beautiful beast, as her name suggests."

Ana badly needed an ally at the fortress if she was ever going to escape Arafanz's clutches. So she took her chance and smiled at Ashar as she ever so gently reached to touch his hand, ensuring that he felt her gratitude. "I shall be gentle with her, thank you, Ashar," she murmured for his ears only.

Arafanz led the way, Farim dutifully lumbering after his camel. Months of despair and loneliness began to leach away from Ana as they moved off from the fortress and entered the desert proper. The sun's heat tried its best to burn through her linens but the fabric took the brunt of the rays bravely and saved her skin. She had wrapped the tail of her headdress about her face as Lazar had taught her. It didn't feel like a veil, even though it had the same effect; it felt as though dressing this way gave her a connection to Lazar. This is how he had looked just before the heat of each day in the desert. Suddenly she felt at one with the desert—as if she were coming home. Despite the hostility of the sun's heat and the parched sands, that notion calmed her. Was it because the desert had kept her safe when she had been abandoned as a newborn? Or was it because the desert was where she had finally lain in Lazar's arms? She could pretend that the man ahead was Lazar, leading her deeper into the sands. A daydream of just the two of them. Another welcoming sand dune, the luxury of the second chance to know each other's touch, lips, love.

Once again, as if he could steal into her thoughts, Arafanz dropped back to ride at her side, cutting into her reverie. "How are you, Ana? Delving into happier memories?"

She could not help but like his voice. He had an economy with words, too, not dissimilar to the Spur, and like the man she loved Arafanz had the ability to be caustic in one breath, gentle in another. "I'm well, thank you," she answered, matching his brevity.

"The child?"

"My baby grows, perhaps flourishes, in spite of the imprisonment of his mother."

"Do you feel many changes? Motherhood has always intrigued me."

She twitched a smile, even though she didn't want to, at the naïveté in his question. "It intrigues me also. I have no experience with it. I feel like I'm still a child myself."

"Old enough to conceive," he said softly, not looking at her.

"Some men would consider a girl of nine summers old enough. That her body has ripened early does not make her sufficiently mature for the trauma of pregnancy or the trials of parenthood." She tried to keep her tone even but the words still came out taut.

"But you are, Ana. You talk like an ancient. I feel sure your maternal instincts are strong."

"Do you remember your mother?" she asked, deliberately trying to catch him off guard.

He smiled gently, not in the least perturbed. "I do. I have been gone a long time from her but I can remember her clearly. She was a quiet, long-suffering, endlessly patient woman—I had eight brothers, you see—and I loved her deeply. I still do; it matters not that she is long dead. She will be the last person I think of as I draw my final breath." His voice thickened as he spoke.

Ana felt his candor deserved a response. "I have no memory of my mother. I was orphaned, left in the desert and found by a goatherd, the only man I have known as father, whom I love dearly."

"I remember the day you were born."

She swung in her saddle to face him, filled with surprise. "You knew me then?"

"I knew *of* you," he corrected. "I was told of the newborn protected by the Samazen."

Protected? She had never thought of it that way. Ana had always thought the famed desert wind had killed her family, and although she had been spared, she had never viewed it in a kindly light.

Arafanz broke into her thoughts. "And your stepmother? Do you love her?"

"I despise her. But the feeling was mutual. No doubt that is why she sold me into the harem."

"Was she jealous of you, Ana? As jealous as the Valide is of you?"

Ana looked sharply sideways at him. "How do you know about the Valide?" Then she answered her own question. "Ah yes, Razeen, the traitor. It was certainly a surprise to realize he is one of your men. He was known as Salazin in the palace. How did you meet him?"

"I have known him since he was born."

"I heard that he came from the Widows' Enclave. Found by the Grand Vizier, who was impressed by his fighting prowess and especially the fact that he was mute."

"He is not mute."

Ana looked at him aghast. "Not mute?" she repeated, imagining all those occasions this past year that Salazin had escorted her to the Zar's rooms or fetched her from somewhere to meet with Boaz. The young man had never uttered a sound. "But he worked as one of the elite Mute Guard that protected the Zar."

Arafanz nodded. "I know. He tricked everyone. That was the point."

Ana refused to believe this. "But why?"

"I needed someone in the palace."

"To spy on the Zar?"

"That was an additional advantage. No, Ana. Razeen's most important job was to spy on you."

She stared at him, bewildered. "But if you have known about me since my birth, been so interested in my welfare, why did you permit me to be sold into the palace in the first place?"

Arafanz shrugged. "Another of Ellyana's secrets."

Ana couldn't even begin to think that comment through. There was too much pain attached. She shook her head to clear it of Ellyana's machinations. "So Salazin betrayed us all," she said sadly.

"Not at all. He protected you all, in fact. It was Razeen who fought courageously against his brothers when the attack on your camp came; he was the one who kept a formidable ring of protection around you, the Valide, and the Grand Vizier until Spur Lazar arrived. And it was Razeen who once again killed his own in order to keep the Valide and Vizier alive long enough for the Spur to deal with their pursuers."

Ana was stunned by the ruse. She took a few moments to find her voice. "And did Razeen continue to ensure their safety?"

"I know you're eager to find out about the welfare of your companions, Ana."

"Only about the health of the Spur," she corrected.

Beneath his beard, she saw Arafanz smile. "I know. Razeen made sure they were all alive and then sadly succumbed to his wounds," he said sardonically.

"He was injured?"

"He suffered many cuts but he inflicted a wound upon him-self—in his belly—that would have looked fatal at the time. They had to leave him behind and I made sure he was picked up as soon as they had departed."

Ana shook her head at Arafanz's complexity and cunning. "How interesting that you would go back to save the life of a fallen warrior and yet you cast so many to their unnecessary death. Is Razeen special?"

"No more special than any of the other men who commit their lives to Lyana's cause."

The heat was intensifying around them and Ana recalled how Lazar during their journey had often suggested that silence conserved energy. But despite today's sapping temperature, she was not about to let this topic drop. It galled her that Arafanz had controlled them all with such ease. And worse, she had always liked Salazin; so his betrayal cut even deeper. "You left the dying in the desert after the attack. I heard a few of your men groaning. Did you go back for them or was their 'Glory' calling?" she asked, her tone scornful.

Arafanz did not rise to her bait. In his calm, steady voice he answered, "No, they had already pledged their lives. Razeen's work is not yet done on this plane. He was saved for another day, for he still has an important duty to perform."

"And what is that?"

"I do not know. I know only that his life is precious and he is still in the service of Lyana."

"Why was he chosen? Why is he so different from any of the other men who have pledged their lives?"

"I had no say. He was selected and groomed from birth."

"By Ellyana?"

He nodded and she sensed for the first time a tiny indication of discomfort in her captor's manner.

"So you took Razeen from his mother's arms and committed him to this crusade of yours. Did she have any say in this?"

"His mother is dead," he replied, his tone flat. Ana was secretly surprised that he was being so honest. She was also beginning to suspect that this man shared another quality with her lover; like Lazar, he preferred to deal only with truth. Lazar had lived with a lie for so long it had made him distant, cold, perhaps even constantly hating himself. The candidness Arafanz was showing now, she believed, was far closer to the real man than the tricks and subterfuge that the leader of the Razaqin had used to beguile them in the desert.

"And his father?"

"He's alive," he said, sitting up straighter on his camel and scanning the rock face they had been following. "We are close."

"And Razeen's father is happy about his son's vocation?"

"He is."

"And when Razeen dies, as he surely will?"

"Then he has glorified himself for Lyana."

"And you will feel glorified, too?"

Arafanz hesitated. "No. I will mourn him, if I'm alive."

"Mourn him?" she scorned, breathing hard with anger. "And what of the other young men whose deaths you've ordered on a whim?"

He turned, his eyes also blazing with the anger she had wanted to provoke. It thrilled Ana to see that she had finally pushed him into revealing a true emotion.

"Mourn Razeen?" she persisted. "Why?"

"Because he's my son," he said. His voice cracked ever so slightly, and Ana glimpsed the sorrow in his gaze before he turned away.

All the fury went out of her in a gust. "I'm sorry," she murmured.

"Don't be. He's not. He's the most committed of Lyana's followers." He sighed. "I knew even before Razeen entered the palace that the Zar's mother feared you."

"She had nothing to fear from me."

Arafanz gave a soft grunt. "She had everything to fear. You

were the single-most-important threat since the early days of her rise through the harem."

"How old are you?"

Again she sensed his amusement; he had found his way back to his protective shell. "Old enough," he said.

"Not married?"

"To Lyana, perhaps."

Ana was intrigued. He was so like Lazar in his self-containment. "Never a need for a woman?" she pressed.

"I didn't say that. I've already told you that Razeen is my son."

"Do you—"

"I permitted you to ride with me, Zaradine Ana, not interrogate me. Did you question Spur Lazar in this manner?"

"You remind me of him."

"In what way?"

"Your aloofness, your single-mindedness, your arrogance, your terrible vulnerability."

He turned now. "And how about our attraction? Do I fire your heart in the same way that Lazar has?"

It was her turn to feel invaded. She refused to cave in under his intense scrutiny. "No."

"Why?"

"Because he's not a murderer."

They locked stares for several long moments, long enough for the heat to win fresh beads of sweat from her skin. She traced the silent descent between her breasts until Arafanz spoke again. "We are here," he said, his voice devoid of all emotion.

"Where?"

"I shall show you." He plucked a sack from his camel and pulled it across his body. "We'll need some light."

He helped her climb from the gentle Farim and led her toward what looked like more of the rocks their camels had been keeping close to. But when they were just inches from the rock face she noticed a gap, cunningly hidden by folds in the rock.

"How clever," she breathed, unable to stop her admiration from spilling over. "How do you find it?"

He grinned and the amusement again touched his eyes. "I have taught these camels from calves how to find this place. Neither has ever been used for any other journey. The secret of this important location lies with Farim and her companion."

Ana was struck by the notion that Arafanz had invested such faith in a pair of dumb animals. "And what if something happened to either of the camels?"

"Then the secret is lost," he said calmly, easing himself into the gap and reaching for her. "Let me lead you. It can be precarious."

She took his hand, felt the strength it possessed as it closed around her own, and let him gently guide her into the cool dungeon-like cave beneath the vast rock face.

Once inside, Ana looked up from the ground where her gaze had been carefully picking out safe spots to plant her feet and found herself confronted by a magnificent, huge rock pool. Water dripped deliciously with a sound that echoed off the cave walls. She sucked in her breath at the beautiful cool atmosphere that soothed her.

"This is our spring. Beautiful, isn't it? I needed to check on it," Arafanz murmured. Ana could barely speak for pleasure. He knew it, too, she could tell from the deep amusement in his eyes. "But it gets so much better. Let me show you." Again he took her hand, this time leading her down a tunnel. It was so dark that her only connection to reality was Arafanz's warm, reassuring grip. He halted and she heard flint strike and sparks explode a couple of times as her surroundings were illuminated for only an instant before being plunged into darkness again. Finally, a flame and then a candle was lit. She looked slightly above them to a roundish opening.

"We're going in there?"

"Trust me." Once again he reached out his hand.

Ana took it. In a blink Arafanz had encircled her waist, his mouth close to her ear as he quietly spoke. "I'm going to lift you. Just crawl in. At the other end of the very short tunnel is an opening. Don't panic at the end. It is dark but I shall be right behind you and will bring the light. Just crawl out of the tunnel and you will be on a wide ledge. I promise you will come to no harm, but the light will have to be extinguished momentarily."

She turned. They were close enough to kiss. His eyes glittered darkly in the subdued light. Ana nodded and lifted her robe, glad that they had given her trousers today, and then felt herself being swung easily into the air by Arafanz's strong arms. She got purchase on the opening within moments and began crawling down its dark depths. As he'd promised, she found herself on a ledge. Arafanz was beside her seconds later.

"Are you all right?"

She was bemused by his concern. For someone who had gone to such lengths to terrify her, he was incredibly cautious about her physical well-being. "Yes, it was all as you said."

Their voices were the only sounds in what felt to her to be a cavernous space. It was so black where they sat, Ana began to lose the sense of where she was in the space. His body, its warmth, his voice, were her only anchors.

"I've brought you to my most private place. No one else has

ever visited here with me, not even my son. No one else even knows of it."

"Other than your two camels," she said, giggling.

She didn't know if he smiled but she heard a wistful tone when he spoke. "I think of it as mine."

"Then why am I here?"

"I'm not sure," and she heard the ruefulness in his voice now. "Because you are special," he whispered, so close to her ear that his breath stirred her hair.

Ana heard the strike of the flints again and a first candle was lit, then a second. Arafanz stood and moved gracefully around the space he obviously knew well, lighting lamps that had clearly been left from previous visits. And as the illumination increased, so did Ana's awe. By the time Arafanz returned to where she sat, the cave was bathed in dewy light and a tear of joy slipped down her cheek.

He smiled fully and she saw genuine pleasure in his face, wondered how long it had been since he'd looked so happy. "I did warn you it got better," he said, and reverently kissed her hand as he helped her down from the ledge.

Ana was surprised by his tenderness but didn't overreact by flinching, snatching away her hand. Instead she nodded graciously, unsure of how else to behave. "What is this place?"

"I think of it as my place of worship. It's where I feel closest to my Goddess."

And Ana understood. The roof of the vast cave arched magnificently as though it were the ceiling of a grand temple. Hanging from the rocky roof and growing from the rocky cave floor were spellbinding columns that sparkled with more incandescence than any of the jewels people had swooned over in the harem.

"These are the Crystal Pillars of Lyana. I like to think of them as sentries to her finest natural temple. I come here to pray."

"Are my eyes deceiving me or are they changing color?" she asked.

"No deception. Come, touch them. Feel their beauty, listen to them."

"Listen to them?"

"They will speak to you."

She walked over to one glimmering column and touched it. It felt warm to her touch. She leaned close to its rocky, glistening crystals and put her ear close.

"Do you hear?"

"A sighing sound?"

He clapped. "Yes!" She had not previously seen Arafanz so animated. She laughed, their enmity forgotten for the time being. "They are whispering to us, Ana."

"What do they say?"

"They speak only to the individual listener, Ellyana tells me."

"She has been here? I thought you said no one else knows of it."

"I have not brought her here. I have no idea if she has seen it, but I described the pillars to her and that was her response many years ago. Do they speak to you?"

"I hear no words."

"Perhaps you must be alone. This is how Lyana speaks to me. The pillars told me about you. That's how I knew when you were born."

She stepped back from the column, unnerved by his words. "Lyana told you this?"

He nodded.

"Arafanz, I am not Lyana."

He smiled sadly. "I know. But you are important to her. I do not yet know why. But she will reveal all to us as she chooses."

"I have been given no instructions."

"But still you remain the central figure in her fight."

"She has never communicated with me."

He nodded. "She will. You must trust her."

"What if you're all wrong? What if I am simply a goatherd's daughter who has created a lot of problems within the harem and drawn undue attention to herself?"

"We are not wrong. Too many people are involved with your life for it to be inconsequential to the fight. Do you know who Iridor is?"

"He's the owl," she said, deliberately evasive.

"And his mortal incarnation?"

"I have no idea," she lied.

"I thought he might be Lazar. But the Spur used no magics to save you, or himself. If he were Iridor, he would surely have employed his magic to help his friend Jumo, certainly to fight me for you. No, Lazar is simply a man in love with you. It is understandable." He held her gaze.

Ana cleared her throat. "I am Zaradine to Boaz."

"That does not mean he owns your heart."

"No," she said carefully. "But I am fond of Boaz. He is a good ruler. He will be a great one for Percheron."

"A new regime will not permit him to sit the throne. He comes from a long line of followers of Zarab."

"That is not his fault. As a ruler, he is just and loyal to his people."

"I'm not interested in his ability to rule his people. I'm interested only in the Zar's pastoral care of his people. If he worships Lyana, so, too, will they. If he outlaws Zarab worship, they will ultimately fall in with his desires. Zarab was forced upon the Percherese centuries ago. Now he will be driven from their lives and Lyana will prevail. Boaz is not the man to help in this regime change."

"And my son is? A baby?"

Arafanz nodded. "With the right guidance, yes. He will come to the throne when he's old enough, with no preconceptions of the life that preceded him. He will not know his father. He will be taught Lyana's ways. He will know his mother follows her way, shares the Goddess's name."

"Not know his father? How can you deny a son his father when you yourself keep such careful watch over your boy?"

"I have put my son into much danger and his life has always been forfeit. Boaz is not worthy of his child."

"I cannot believe that Lyana would allow such a thing. She would surely want my son to know his father."

Arafanz shrugged, ending the conversation. "I have another treat for you. Please, wait here."

"Where are you going? I don't want to be alone."

"Not far, and I need only a few moments," he said, agilely scaling a series of ledges until he reached a long wide platform. He pointed. "This is not rock, here," he called down.

She nodded. "I can just make it out . . . a circle of timber?"

"I had it made to exact specifications. There is only one particular hour of the day when I can do this and it changes with the season. Now is the hour."

Ana looked up at him puzzled. "For what?"

"Watch," he said, and with a flourish, he tugged at the rope that led from the disk. The wooden trapdoor fell away and instantly the central part of the chamber was flooded with a glorious light. The rays bathed the columns and fractured into rainbow colors whilst the columns themselves seemed to sing, their crystals sighing as the warmth hit their cool surface. Their voices became a chorus and their colors began to shimmer and change rapidly.

Ana felt tears wet her cheeks again. This surely was Lyana's temple. She realized that Arafanz was at her side once more.

"Come, stand amongst her throng," he said gently, and led her to a special raised plinth that was encircled by the largest of the pillars. "You must go to the parapet alone," he said, nodding to the naturally carved steps that would lead her to the platform. With the choir of pillars singing to her, the magnificent colors shimmering around her, Ana walked up the stairs and stepped onto the rock platform encircled by the sentinels.

And she heard them.

"Welcome, Mother," they sang.

7

Five moons later . . .

Lazar stared out toward the hills and the desert that he knew lay beyond. "Ironic," he commented to Pez. "Seventeen moons ago I was looking longingly toward the Stone Palace, desperate to be here. Now I gaze out from it with equal longing to be gone."

"You are over the worst, are you not?"

The Spur nodded wearily. "Well enough. I must make ready to leave."

"Boaz can't wait to see you on your way."

"This time I go with no one in tow. Just us." He swung around to face the dwarf. "I wish you had made that trip once more so we can be sure."

"But I'm not sure I could survive it, my friend. It was a perilous journey last time. If I took the chance and succumbed to the heat, to loss of direction, to any one of the many hawks that want me for a meal, we would lose our only chance of finding Ana. No, we do it once and we bring her home. We know she is being cared for, I'm sure of it, so this wait has been wise. In fact, I've had this niggling feeling that all of this somehow has to do with the rising of the Goddess."

"I thought we'd cleared that up," Lazar replied wearily. "Ana is no such thing."

"I shall believe what I wish. You are welcome to your own theory. The Goddess is rising, Lazar, I feel it even if I don't understand it."

"What about Maliz?" Lazar murmured.

"I've been clever at staying out of his way. The Grand Vizier is busy with Boaz and from what I can glean seems more concerned with setting up an escape route for the Zar, Valide, and harem."

"What's his plan? He should consult me."

"As far as I know, it's the eastern foothills. I overheard the Grand Vizier telling Boaz that he knows them well." Lazar smirked. "Yes, my thoughts exactly. Tariq wouldn't know what any foothills look like. But Boaz's mind is too filled with responsibility and private mourning over Ana to take note that his Grand Vizier is suddenly so knowledgeable."

"Boaz has visited me often these past moons and from what I can tell he has no intention of leaving the city."

"The Grand Vizier is relentless in pushing for him to abandon the palace and its seraglio. That said, he isn't planning for the Zar to be anywhere near the harem women in their escape. Only the Valide would be permitted to accompany Boaz. As for Salmeo, I don't think Tariq cares what happens to him."

"What's his motivation, do you think?"

Pez shrugged. "He claims he is preserving the palace hierarchy, or so he assures the Zar."

"It's a lie, of course."

"The curious part is, Lazar, I do think he cares about Boaz—well, *care*, that's an odd word, I know. But there's certainly an element of desiring the Zar's survival."

"That's madness, though. What happens to Percheron is irrelevant to Maliz. His interest lies only in the destruction of Lyana, whenever she turns up. He's simply biding his time. All of this mortal angst with war is purely sport for him, wouldn't you agree?"

"Yes. I can't explain his concern . . . not yet."

"And speaking of explanations . . . Have you thought of an idea to explain your absence when we go?"

"No, but now that I know that we are on the brink of departure, I shall dream up something. Boaz is preoccupied with war anyway. He is not going to miss me. He will miss you, though."

"The Zar wants his Zaradine and heir back. I have given Ghassal instructions. He is a good soldier—the best; he knows what to do, how to set up the Protectorate for maximum security. Have we heard anything?"

"Nothing. You would be one of the first to learn anyway. Boaz defers to you as Spur despite your illness."

Lazar sighed. "He treated me very coolly when we first returned, but he's warmed. I don't doubt his mother's determination to see me fit has helped in that regard."

"It's about Ana, Lazar. It's always been about Ana."

"She is his wife. I cannot stand in the way of that."

"Not in the palace, perhaps," Pez commented, giving a soft shrug of apology. "Don't pretend you didn't know I was part of the guile. She told me she just needed some time with you that night. I was her cohort."

The Spur blushed in a rare show of emotion. Pez pretended not to notice. "We needed to talk. There was so much left unsaid between us, not—" Lazar stammered.

"You don't have to—"

"Not just around the time of her marriage," Lazar continued as though Pez had not spoken, "but long before that. There were things I needed to say to Ana that were overdue from the first wretched evening I brought her into Percheron." He banged his fist on the balcony rail with frustration.

"You don't need to justify that time with Ana to me, Lazar," Pez said softly.

"I do. You were her accomplice and took a risk for us. I never thought I'd have the chance to say any of the things I did to her on that sand dune. She contrived the meeting—I would never have dared—but I am ever grateful for the opportunity . . . to talk." He cleared his throat and sent a prayer to anyone listening that Pez would never know what had actually occurred.

"It's odd, you know, that night . . . before our lives were changed."

"What's odd?"

"I was sickening for something. I don't know what it was about. One moment I was fine, the next I was vomiting into the sand as Ana came away from you on the dune."

"You were there?" Lazar heard his voice break slightly on the last word.

"I was awake. Just looking out for her. I had to in case anyone discovered she was not in her tent." Lazar nodded. "But I was not the only one awake, I've just realized."

Lazar's eyes flared with shock. "What do you mean?"

Pez looked stunned. "Forgive me. I've just recalled that the Grand Vizier stepped out of his tent as she came back to the camp."

"What?"

"It wasn't important. I think he was probably emerging to relieve himself, stretch, I don't know, and her presence perhaps startled him. They spoke briefly and Ana was smiling, the Vizier scratching. A coincidence, and in the scheme of what unfolded that night, inconsequential."

"What happened?"

"Well, he said he was disturbed. He mentioned this to Ana, and to her credit, she didn't miss a beat, told him she'd tripped over one of his tent ropes or something."

"And he accepted it?"

"What else could he do? She told him she'd just stepped away from the camp to relieve herself. It was a well-crafted and well-executed lie. She didn't sound abashed, just apologetic for disturbing him."

"Well, good. She didn't arouse any further mystery, then?"

"No, but that's my point, I'm embarrassed to say and only now recall. She never did."

"I don't get you."

"Well, it didn't strike me at the time, but now that I'm thinking about it, I know that Ana arrived soundlessly. She made no noise. My hearing is exceptional, and I knew she was back in camp because I could sense her, not because I could see her or hear her."

"Am I being a dullard in not understanding what you're saying?"

"I'm saying that no noise disturbed the Grand Vizier and still he was woken from his deep sleep. I know he was sound asleep because I checked on him." Lazar stared at the dwarf with incomprehension. Pez continued thinking aloud. "I don't know what dragged him from his slumber but something did. Lyana!"

"What now?" Lazar asked, alarmed that Pez had paled suddenly.

"Perhaps his disturbance was more than coincidence, for just moments earlier I had vomited for no good reason and Ana had just stepped silently back into the camp."

"Ah, I get it. You're on your Lyana pedestal again. That was one of the things we spoke of that night, Pez. Ana admits that she is not who you think she is. She feels saddened for you that you pursue this dream. And why would Lyana announce anything to Maliz anyway?"

"Lyana, Iridor, Maliz. We are all helplessly connected. We do not necessarily choose to communicate but our lives our irrevocably bound. Something disturbed Maliz and Iridor when Ana was present—albeit silent." Pez suddenly fell on all fours and began barking.

Lazar deliberately turned away, striking a bored pose as he leaned over the balcony. He heard the click of a heel and the smell of perfume reached him before she did.

"We'll talk on this later," Lazar whispered to Pez. The dwarf reared up on his legs and began beating his chest as the Valide swept onto the verandah.

"Good morning, Lazar. You have lots of color in your face today."

"I feel the brightest I've felt in a while. It must be your fine care, Valide."

She demured with a soft shrug and a smile behind her veil. "Oh, begone with you, dwarf! Your noise is enough to set anyone's health back." She called behind her to an Elim who had followed her into Lazar's chamber. "Please take Pez away. I wish a private conversation with the Spur."

The man nodded and urged Pez to follow. The dwarf meekly took the man's hand, ambling at his side as the monkeys did with their handlers in the Zar's zoo. He left quietly but not before loudly wiping his nose on the corner of the Valide's silken shift.

She shrieked, scowled at the Spur's helpless amusement. "Why does he entertain you and Boaz with such vulgarity?"

"It's not him, it's you, Valide. You give him so much fun to work with. In his addled mind he still seems to sense that he can provoke a loud reaction from you every time. You must learn to ignore him as we all do, then he'll likely leave you alone."

"Why you tolerate him around you is beyond me. Has he been barking like that for long? It must set your nerves on edge."

"No. I hardly notice him. A lot of the time he sits quietly and picks his nose."

She made an involuntary sound of disgust before she noticeably softened. "Are you cold? Let me fetch you a blanket."

Lazar sat down. It was obvious this would be no fleeting visit and he dared not be rude after all her care. "Herezah, you don't need to wait on me like this," Lazar called over his shoulder, although he was grateful for the warmth when the soft rug was placed around him.

Herezah had come to Lazar's quarters this morning with a mission in mind. She had deliberately distracted the Elim with Pez and then left a message for that same Elim to run some errands for her. She was counting on him being kept busy for a while—

long enough for her needs. She was also gambling with the notion that the more senior Elim would not realize that the single day and single night guard they maintained around the Spur were compromised. The guards were token, simply a show of respect toward the harem. The Elim trusted the Spur implicitly but it was a matter of principle, a man living relatively near to where the women were housed warranted the show of a guard. Herezah had earned the Elim's respect these few moons, always seeing to it that the Elim were informed when she was visiting the Spur's quarters, diligently ensuring that she was never without her escort. She neither removed her veil in the Spur's company—even when he was too far gone in his fevers and hallucinations to be aware of anyone around him—nor touched him below his neck. Instead she supervised the Elim in this regard. Trust had been earned and she intended to take full advantage of her weeks of patience.

She leaned against the railings, her back to the Faranel and her sheer, rather revealing costume for today ensuring that the full glory of her still-firm, voluptuous body was showcased for her guest. "But I enjoy looking after you," she admonished in a lazy voice. "I'd be lying if I said I'd been happier in my life than these past five moons in caring for you."

"Please don't say that aloud to anyone else. Don't even say it to me again, I beg you."

"But why, Lazar? Why not to you?" She made her move, crouching near his side now, careful not to crowd him but close enough to place her hand over his. "Surely you cannot deny that I have always been honest with you about my feelings."

He shook his head. "It is unwise—"

"Why? You are well now—or much fitter than a few moons back, when I swear to Zarab I thought we'd lost you. But—"

Lazar surprised her by covering her hand with his own and she helplessly shivered at his touch. "And I haven't thanked you for that. You saved my life but—"

"You saved mine in the desert."

"That was my duty. Helping me back to good health has surely been unpleasant and you didn't have to do it."

"No, but I'm glad I have. And yes, you do have to thank me, but do so properly. I don't want your carefully chosen words, Lazar. I want you. Don't look at me like that! I've never hidden my desire, and although we've often felt like enemies, for my part it was a result of frustration over how you ignore me." She put her hand to his lips. "No, wait, let me finish. Every man has a sexual drive," she urged, "every woman, too," she added ruefully. "I am not bound by who I might take as a lover anymore—and you have no one in your life. I know I'm desirable to any man. If you didn't have such a strong opinion about me, you would feel the same yearning. Why pay for a whore who has been with a dozen men before you that day alone when you can have me, untouched for so long, and at no charge? Why not satisfy us both? I will accept your thanks only once if that is all that's offered. I promise, there will be no repercussions."

"Herezah," he began, but again she stopped him.

"I want nothing from you, Lazar, except your body riding mine. I'm not naive enough to think you might suddenly fall in love with me. This is about lust and relief, nothing more. I have never been with any man but the Zar and he was not out of choice—can you imagine what that's like? I know you pay women, Lazar—not that you'd need to but I imagine it's cleaner that way, no messy relationships attached; you choose with whom and when and where. An odalisque, a Zaradine, has no such choice. We are no better than whores but with none of their freedom. I will not lie to you; although I liked and respected Joreb, he disgusted me physically. What I did for him sexually I did out of duty. He gave me Boaz and I cannot regret that, but I am in my fourth decade, Lazar, and I might as well shrivel up and die soon if I don't get some satisfaction for this magnificent body and its desires." Her words had come out in such a torrent, and with such feeling, that she was breathing hard by the end of her monologue.

She knew Lazar could see the perfect shape of her breasts, her dark nipples chafing at the gauze of her near-translucent linen chemise. If not for its loose cut, her body would have been naked to him. But she'd taken the added precaution of unfastening the front so Lazar could clearly view the rounded flesh, the inviting cleavage, the pulse at her throat. She was sure that at this close proximity to such an invitation any man would be victim to his own body's betrayal, including the man of ice himself. And she was right. Herezah watched with untold delight the unmistakable swell beneath Lazar's loose garments. She thrilled to the knowledge that she had finally won a response from him—and best of all, Lazar was well enough to be seduced and she was close enough to take advantage of him.

This was the greatest risk she had taken since becoming Valide. The killing of the heirs, the persecution of Ana, the cunning and deception of so many years in the harem; all of it amounted to naught in comparison to this moment when Herezah, Valide Zara of Percheron, bared herself to the one person who could break the heart she had protected for nearly two decades. She moved her hand and placed it on that swell of his body, felt the answering throb beneath her fingertips, and could have wept.

Instead she pressed her luck still further. "Even the Elim have left us alone. We are free to make our own choice. No one owns us, Lazar . . . and what's more, no one cares." Her voice was husky, sensual, and when he couldn't react negatively to her touch, she took a further chance. "Thank me, Lazar, in the only way I'll accept."

Herezah bent her head and placed her lips against his. She began tentatively, exploring his mouth gently. She tasted his reluctance; his lips were politely soft but unresponsive. But she was not to be deterred. She risked everything, gently squeezing the hand that was still nestled quietly in his lap. And won the response she'd dreamed of—Herezah felt the instant response in her palm and it was suddenly mirrored by the hungry yearning from his mouth. She knew any woman could probably achieve a similar reaction—couldn't convince herself otherwise—but nevertheless she felt breathless at the knowledge that Lazar was finally beneath her. Determined not to shatter this fragile moment, she began working her fingers, working her tongue.

Lazar groaned and Herezah celebrated inwardly.

At last he was hers.

Although they had been preparing for this moment, Boaz's expression was still one of undisguised shock.

"Anchored off the Isles of Plenty?" he repeated.

Ghassal, the Spur's deputy, bowed. "Yes, Majesty. We count more than thirty war galleys, more still arriving. One flies the royal pennon of Galinsea."

"Falza is here?" Boaz asked, his eyes wide with disbelief.

"We do not know, Majesty. It could be one of the sons, but either way, Galinsean royalty is near to our waters. The Grand

Vizier has given orders that I am personally to fetch you."

"We're to make arrangements to meet with the royal, is that the plan?"

"I am to take you on the barge."

"Barge?" Boaz frowned.

"We go by river upstream, he says. A team of Elim will accompany you and—"

"Ghassal!"

"Majesty," the man said, suddenly kneeling, arrested by the tone in his ruler's voice.

"Don't you ever dare to presume that I do as the Grand Vizier bids. I am your Zar. You will follow my orders, or your Spur's, not Tariq's."

"Highness, I—"

"You are a good man, Ghassal, and come highly recommended by the Spur, whose judgment I trust above any other man I know. Now live up to his expectations and mine."

The soldier adopted a chastened expression. "Forgive me, my Zar. How can I serve you, Highness?"

"We must avoid confrontation as best we can—extend a hand of friendship, but not flee. That's an open invitation for the Galinseans to sack the city. I don't plan to fight them but fight them I will if we are cornered. In the meantime we will use every diplomatic weapon we can. Now, I shall be here to face King Falza whenever he is ready to enter our bay. He is permitted to bring only the royal galleon into the harbor."

"For now they are not coming closer but simply biding their time, Highness, it seems."

"They have intentionally made their presence known. They likely await our first move."

"What should we do?"

"Nothing yet. I must speak with Lazar. Await my orders and tell the Grand Vizier I wish to see him. He is to await my pleasure."

The soldier bowed deeply as the Zar swept past him, calling for Bin. "Tell the Grand Master Eunuch I shall be visiting the Spur, who I assume is in the company of the Valide."

Lazar was gripped in Herezah's fist. She pulled back from his mouth, her fingers rhythmically working, not allowing his helpless need for relief to wane. "Why waste this?" she said, impressed.

"Herezah, don't, I beg you." His expression was one of pain and he was breathing shallowly, vainly trying to control his own lust.

"I do enjoy it when you beg anything of me," she murmured, her hand moving faster. "I want you inside me, Lazar."

"I . . . I." He looked lost, almost panicked.

Neither had heard the swish of the silks but both smelled sandalwood overlaid by the fragrance of violets.

"Valide, I—" Salmeo's words were cut off and a ghastly silence ensued as Herezah jumped back as if burned. "Oh," Salmeo tittered, taking in the scene at once. "Oh my, forgive my interruption, Majesty. And, Spur, my sincere apologies. I really hadn't expected you to be quite this . . . um, recovered," he lisped.

"Salmeo, how dare you just walk into the Spur's chamber," Herezah spat. "This is a private room and you will announce yourself in future." She noticed that Lazar had not moved. His eyes were closed, his erection wilting, and this only served to intensify the fury she felt at being denied what had been rightfully hers.

Her chest heaved with the angry words. "What the Spur and I choose to do—"

Lazar's voice cut across her. "We do not need this complication," he said to her alone, and Herezah knew he was being kind, knew what he was truly saying was that he didn't need her. She could see the relief in his eyes now that they were open. He was grateful for the interruption.

"Salmeo, you will suffer for this," she warned, unable to rein back her despair. Nothing, save the death of Boaz, could have upset her more than what had just occurred.

The Grand Master Eunuch bowed, and adopted a virtuous expression. "I think you'll both ultimately thank me for this intrusion—even though it seems so painful to you at this moment. I came to tell you that Zar Boaz is but moments away. He wishes to speak with the Spur and anticipated that you, Valide, would be with him. It would have been, um . . ." He paused deliberately, searching for the right word as the shock of what could have happened had the Zar discovered them registered with Herezah. "Let's just say it might have been indelicate to have been found by the Zar in the same position I found you both. I suggest you reveil yourself, Valide, or risk the harem's wrath, not to mention that of your Zar. I shall overlook it this time, put it down to your both still being traumatized from your experiences in the desert." He grinned angelically, his tongue flicking between the gap in his teeth. Herezah hated him.

Lazar stood, fully composed again. His expression gave the impression of a gathering storm. "Do not rebuke Her Majesty in my presence again, Salmeo. If you have something to say to her, say it in private. If you insult Her Majesty again in front of me, I shall draw my sword against you. Now leave, eunuch. I'm going to take a cool bath. Please excuse me, Valide," he said, bowing softly to Herezah and striding to the connecting chamber, throwing off his shirt as he did.

Herezah just had time to glimpse his torn back, a reminder of what she had helped perpetrate on this man she adored. She couldn't decide in this moment of distress whether the recent intimacy with Lazar meant more to her than his referring to her as Majesty for the first time in their lives and his thrilling support for her. A year ago she was sure he would have sooner drowned himself in the Faranel than taken her side in any matter. Now he offered to kill for her. She felt her desire for him increase just thinking about it. Hurriedly she retied her veil, straightened her clothes, and began folding the blanket that had been tossed aside.

"Go, Salmeo. We shall discuss this later," she said, her own composure regained, and not a moment too soon.

Boaz entered, talking over his shoulder to Bin, who halted at the entrance to the Spur's suite.

"My Lion, what a surprise," Herezah said, continuing her slow folding of the blanket. "Did you wish to speak with Lazar?"

"Mother," Boaz replied, with a dutiful peck at her cheek. "You look flushed, are you well?"

"Oh, I'm fine. I was just straightening out Lazar's chamber. You men are so messy."

"You don't have to do that," Boaz said, frowning. "We have servants to—"

"No, but I like to. I know he's getting the best care, and because of it, he is now fit to do your bidding, son."

"Where is he?"

She shook her head absently. "I believe he's bathing. I've only just arrived and sent that wretched Pez scampering. My

Elim escorted the dwarf but should be back any moment. Would you like me to leave with Salmeo?"

He looked at the bowed bulk of the eunuch. "No, this involves you as much as anyone else. Salmeo, you may go."

The great black man straightened and made to leave but not before Herezah glimpsed the triumph sparkling in his dark, cunning eyes. She closed her own momentarily, knowing the eunuch now had something very dangerous over her. When she opened her eyes, the head of the harem was gone.

Lazar emerged, tendrils of wet hair licking at his shoulders. The fresh shirt he'd donned was damp from a body that he hadn't dried terribly well. "Zar Boaz." He bowed. "Valide." He bowed to her separately, suggesting he was seeing her for the first time this morning, for which she was grateful.

"Sorry, Lazar, I don't mean to disturb you," Herezah began, "I, er, sent Pez away. He was barking like a dog."

"I'd already asked him to leave my bathing chamber. Forgive me, Zar, for not being here to meet you."

"Lazar, anyone who can persuade my mother to keep house for him has my admiration. You need not apologize. She seems to be a charming farisque for you."

"My farisque?" Lazar arched an eyebrow. "I would never level that term at the Valide. She is too generous to me."

Herezah laughed. "How many farisques do you know, son, who keep house and have nails in this condition?" she said, holding up her elegant hands.

The Zar smiled at the levity but only briefly, and Herezah realized that he was not here on a social visit.

"Zar Boaz, for you to come unannounced must mean something urgent is afoot. How can I help?" Lazar asked, flicking the water from his face.

"I have grave news. The Galinsean fleet is anchored off the Isles of Plenty. They could be upon us in just a few days."

Lazar's brow furrowed and Herezah could tell he was instantly focused, their indiscretion and what it might mean forgotten for the time being. "How many ships?"

"Thirty at least, I'm assured. The royal pennon flies atop one."

"Does that mean your father is here, Lazar?" Herezah asked.

Lazar looked thoughtful but could not hide his worry. "Possibly. It could also be one of my brothers, of course, although . . ." He didn't finish, but his frown deepened. "There will be more coming. And they will all anchor and take stock for a while."

"You're sure?" Boaz insisted.

Lazar nodded slowly. "Galinsea never goes to war lightly and only if it is convinced it can win outright. It will make sure by use of numbers, an ability to wear us down by attrition if necessary." He shrugged. "They would be here understanding that they may dig in at the Isles of Plenty for several months."

"Months? Why? We're at their mercy."

"The King is cautious. He is a master strategist, Zar Boaz. He will make no hasty move. He will weigh up every possibility. Right now he'll be sending out spies, posting lookouts, setting up the lines of communication between where they're anchored and Romea. He has no reason to rush, trust me. He already knows that the mere presence of the galleys will be sending the Percherese into panic."

"Then time is of the essence. Lazar, you cannot be found here," Boaz urged.

It was the Valide's turn to frown. "What do you mean?"

They ignored her. Lazar shrugged softly. "I can be gone immediately, Highness."

The Zar nodded. "The sooner the better. We are fortunate that they held off long enough for you to be well. Will you brief Ghassal before you leave? I'm planning to meet the royal ship."

"Let me finish dressing and I shall brief you on how best to handle King Falza."

"Fret not, you have schooled me well these last few weeks. I feel I know your father and his weaknesses."

"He has plenty. But he should not be underestimated and we are depending on my memories of two decades ago," Lazar reminded him. "The one stroke of luck of having any of the royals here is that my father and brothers speak Percherese. Not well, be warned, but sufficiently that they can communicate."

Boaz nodded. "That's a relief, then. Without Ana or yourself, I was fretting as to how we'd achieve any sort of diplomatic conversation."

"Will one of you please tell me what is going on?" Herezah asked, her eyes darting between the two of them.

Boaz turned to his mother. "If Lazar is found here, we suspect that he will either be taken by the Galinseans or possibly killed. Either way, we cannot risk that he be discovered—not yet—although they know by now from Marius that he is alive."

Herezah fixed Lazar with a stare. "So what do you plan? To flee?"

Boaz answered for the Spur. "No, Mother. He is following my orders and will be leaving shortly for the desert. He has to find Ana, has to secure the heir of Percheron."

"Then I shall go with you," she demanded.

Both Spur and Zar shook their heads and spoke in synchrony. "No!"

"Absolutely not, I forbid it," Boaz continued. "We nearly lost you once. And anyway, we need you here for diplomatic reasons. I have no wife to wait upon them. You are the highest ranking woman in the palace. I need you."

"Lazar is not well enough to travel into the desert. He's only just—" Herezah knew she was clutching at straws but she wasn't ready to give him up, not when she had come so close to getting what she most desired.

"Valide," Lazar said gently. "You have been more than generous and a nurse who holds no equal in my mind. But I am fit enough to do my Zar's bidding, to fulfill my duty and promise to him. I will return to my home and I shall write a letter to my father, which I would ask you to pass on to him, Highness."

Herezah curtsied to her son. "I shall be in my chamber if you need me, Boaz," she said, and fled, not even looking at Lazar for fear of losing her composure.

An awkward pause hung momentarily in the air before Boaz spoke. "My mother, it seems, has grown fond of looking after you, Lazar."

The Spur felt himself blush. "I, er, appreciate her ministrations but I'm well enough now to return to my own abode. Thank you for your generosity, my Zar." He cleared his throat. "Has Pez spoken to you of Ana?"

"Only that he believes she is alive."

Lazar nodded. "With your permission, Majesty, I would like to take Pez with me."

"Really?"

Lazar nodded. "I think he will be a great help to me in finding Ana quickly."

"His magics," Boaz said. "Yes, of course, by all means."

"He is staying out of sight at my house but will need to take a few things from his chamber. We will rendezvous at a given point this evening."

"How will he reach you?"

Lazar could hardly tell his Zar that Pez would fly, so he lied. "I shall make arrangements for his safe dispatch to the rendezvous point, but I think we need to have excuses in place for him." Lazar deliberately found a casual tone. "People like the Grand Vizier or the girls in the harem will be confused as to why he's been sent away so soon after returning home safely."

Boaz nodded. "Yes. I shall think on this. What else do you need?"

"Nothing, Majesty. I shall have a letter delivered by Ghassal for my father. I hope it helps reassure him that he has no basis to declare war on Percheron."

"It is a slim chance, Lazar. He is here with his fleet, eager to sack the city no doubt, which is all the more reason for you to press on with your plans. Ana and my heir must be secured."

Lazar nodded. "Then I shall take my leave, Highness, and return shortly for the final briefing."

8

Herezah was fuming, unable to settle down. She'd snapped at everyone who'd ventured near her in the harem and had finally sensibly retired to her own wing, banishing all callers.

Elza appeared not long after, looking understandably nervous.

"You certainly have a death wish, woman," Herezah hurled at the cringing servant.

"The Grand Vizier has sent a message that he needs to speak with you, Valide. I have told him you are not seeing anyone today but he insists that it's vital."

Despite her mood Herezah could not tolerate any matter of importance slipping by her. She banged down the cup she had been drinking from. "Very well. Get me dressed."

Shortly afterward she had moved beyond the harem proper to a private salon where she accepted guests. The Grand Vizier was shown in, escorted by one of the Mutes.

"Your own personal guard, Tariq?"

The Grand Vizier bowed, smiling. "I'm sure you've heard the news, Valide. I'm just taking precautions. You don't mind?"

"Why would I?"

"Indeed. You look flushed, Valid. Are you well?"

"If one more person tells me that, I shall have his head cut off," she fumed, angrier that her emotions were on such public display than for any other reason. She needed to rein them in now; knew it was not at all like her to be so transparent. But then she'd never held Lazar before, never so much as touched him. Little wonder she was flushed; she could still conjure how it felt to hold his sex, taste his mouth. The memory of Salmeo's cunning smile haunted her and she wondered again how he would make her pay for his knowledge.

"Forgive me," the Grand Vizier said, offering a short, clipped bow. "I don't mean to pry," he added.

Those words gave her the answer she was searching for. If there was nothing to pry for, then Salmeo had nothing over her. If she was honest about this episode, then Salmeo had no secret, and she had nothing to hide from anyone, not even her son. Would it really matter to Boaz? It's true that he might well have objected to finding her draped over Lazar or been angry if they'd progressed to the point of lying down together when he'd walked in on them . . . that might have provoked a strong reaction. But even so, Boaz might well be shocked but not necessarily unhappy that his Spur and his mother were lovers. He might see it as welcome respite from years of acrimony. Herezah smiled beneath her veil as a tentative plan formulated.

She looked up to see that the Grand Vizier was watching her carefully. "Something is wrong, isn't it, Valide?"

"Yes, something is. You must forgive my distraction, Grand

Vizier. I'm sure it's meaningless in comparison to what Percheron faces. Please continue," she said, amazing even herself at conjuring up contrived tears.

"Oh, Highness, please. Do tell me, can I help at all?"

She shook her head, looked away. "I'm so sorry." She sniffed, making a show of composing her emotions. "It's of a personal nature. I've been embarrassed this morning and I imagine there will be ramifications."

"Embarrassed?" Tariq said, frowning. "By whom?"

"Grand Master Eunuch Salmeo. He does like to have his little sticks with which to beat us harem members. I'm afraid he has a large club to hold above my head as of this morning and I'm just confused as to how best to handle it. Again, forgive me, Tariq, this is not your problem. You have far more important duties than allowing me to cry on your shoulder."

The Grand Vizier was at her side in a second. "Valide," he said softly. "Salmeo wields far too much power. He is dangerous. And you are the last person who should be in any way under his thumb."

"Oh, but I am, Grand Vizier, and there's nothing anyone can do."

"Share the problem, Highness. I am sure I can help you to find a solution. Nothing you say could shock me," he soothed.

"Are you sure of that?"

"I'm positive."

"Come out onto the balcony. Elza likes to eavesdrop."

He followed her eagerly, shaking his head at the Mute not to follow. She wrung her hands absently. "Oh, can I offer you some refreshment? Forgive my manners. My mind is certainly addled this morning," she said, affecting a soft laugh of confusion.

"No, I need nothing, Valide. Now tell me and let's sort this out."

"It's a delicate matter, Grand Vizier. I'm not sure how to approach it, other than to be direct."

"I appreciate candor, Majesty," he replied, clearly keen to put her at her ease.

Herezah hesitated only for a blink. The Grand Vizier leaned forward and she hesitated no more, took a deep breath in mock fear, ensuring that he understood her reluctance. "Spur Lazar and I have become lovers. We didn't mean for it to happen, Tariq, but over these last few moons that I've cared for him, something special has developed between us. Today, Salmeo interrupted us at a most delicate moment."

The Grand Vizier rocked back on his heels, obviously shocked. Herezah saw the disbelief in his gaze. "I know you find it hard to put us two together but—"

"Hard? Impossible, more like, Majesty. Anyone could be forgiven for believing the two of you detested each other enough that you would happily stick knives into the other's gut. I understand you have a long-held fascination for the man but it was also my belief that you enjoyed punishing him."

She shrugged, even allowed a coy smile to play on her lips. "I know. It's a shock for me, too. But there's no explaining love, is there, Tariq?"

"Love?" There was an audible intake of breath. "Are you serious, Majesty?"

She had turned away from him as she spoke but now looked back over her shoulder, a contrite expression on her face that she knew her eyes would reflect. "It's probably wrong and I've tried to hide it through that opposition toward the Spur you speak of, but I've always felt this way. The fascination you mentioned was always genuine." She smiled inwardly to see that the Grand Vizier was, for once, rather lost for words, and waited for him to rediscover his voice.

"How serious is this affair, Valide? Where do you expect it to go?"

"Nowhere, Tariq, absolutely nowhere," she replied, lacing her tone with resignation. She flounced into a seat. "That's part of the problem. It was never anything that could go anywhere; we both knew it, but it was ours. And in this palace, Tariq, you of all people should know that shiny, bright moments are few and far between. We kept it to ourselves and we enjoyed it for as long as we could. It was not meant to be shared with anyone else and certainly wasn't intended to hurt anyone—how could it?"

Tariq shook his head. "I don't see who you can offend."

"Exactly! But Lazar is a private man, a mysterious man, as we've all discovered," she said, dismay now in her voice. "To be found like that by the chief eunuch—of all people—has distressed him. It distresses me. Salmeo will find a way to use it against us. To blackmail me, perhaps."

"With your son, you mean?"

"Well, yes." She nodded sorrowfully. "I don't want to hurt Boaz. He loved Joreb."

"I don't think he'd expect you to remain celibate—you're still so young and . . ." He struggled for the right word, couldn't find it, and hurried on. "And anyway he has only the highest respect for Lazar."

"I know, but it's the manner in which Salmeo will see to it that Boaz learns this secret. You know how cunning he is."

"I do. Hmm, well, this is a prickly situation, Valide. You've quite taken my breath away. I don't mean to offend you, but the Spur always seemed so smitten with Ana. Surely you noticed?"

Herezah felt her temper flare. "Noticed? Of course I noticed. I'd have to be as dim as the dwarf not to notice, Tariq. But that's it, you see. Because I refused his advances, he used Ana against me."

The Grand Vizier's mouth opened and shut. Again she waited. "I noticed he was very cool toward the Zaradine on our journey," he finally said. Herezah nodded. "And he chose you over her. He risked his life to save us."

"To save *me*, Tariq. Your life is expendable. Do you believe Lazar cared whether you lived or died? It was me he came for, fought for."

"You're right. I never understood why."

She demurred with a soft sigh. "Well, I think you do now. He's told my son it was about duty, and it's true that he has never come to terms with leaving Ana behind, her being the Zaradine and so close to Boaz's heart," she lied smoothly. "Did you know that Boaz is sending him back into the desert to find her?"

"I did, Valide, and I think it's important that Percheron have its Zaradine safe, particularly if an heir exists."

"So that's my dilemma, Tariq," she said, ignoring his sentiments and bringing their conversation back to her needs rather than Ana's. "I'm frightened."

"Well, we can't have that, Majesty. At this level you should fear no one but your Zar and his enemies."

"What do you suggest, Tariq?" she asked eagerly, already knowing, already counting on him suggesting the very solution she had been leading him toward.

"I think perhaps I should talk with your son. Man to man. He is not very approachable right now and I respect his reasons for it, but I shall find a way to let him know what has occurred.

I will even suggest that the Grand Master Eunuch is threatening to use this against you. If the Zar knows and doesn't overreact—and in fact turns a blind eye—I see no future for Salmeo's cunning in this regard."

Herezah's stomach unclenched. No man was any match for her guile, not even the Grand Vizier. She smiled gratefully. "Oh, that's such an inspired notion, Tariq. You are clever! Thank you. I would be so, so grateful if you would do that for me."

Instead of smiling graciously as she'd anticipated, the Grand Vizier frowned. "How grateful, Highness?"

"Pardon?"

"How will you show this gratitude?"

"Zarab save me! What are you asking, Tariq?"

"Not what you think, Valide. A simple matter of exchange. I do you one favor, you give me one in return."

Her eyes narrowed above her veil. "What is it you want, Tariq?"

"I want your son gone from the palace."

"Gone?"

"Away from the Galinsean threat."

"Oh" she said, understanding with a fresh frown. "He refuses to flee, you know that."

"That's a dangerous situation. Until we have confirmation of an heir, your son is being flippant with the Crown of Percheron."

"Flippant?" she asked, surprised by the Grand Vizier's attitude. "I am proud of his courage. He is prepared to die for his realm."

"And what good will that do any of us, Valide? If he dies we have no Zar and the fabric of our society is destroyed. As long as Boaz lives, as long as there is a threat that he can sire more heirs of the royal bloodline, Galinsea will not prevail."

Herezah was shocked by Tariq's attitude; she had always assumed him to be a coward. And it surprised her even more that she could appreciate the sense of what the Grand Vizier was promoting. She had expected the exchange of favor to be something of a far more personal nature—riches, land, perhaps even use of her body for his own relief. But certainly not a maneuver that protected Percheron's Crown. "What do you suggest?"

"I had made arrangements for us to go upstream into the foothills but he ridiculed that suggestion."

"He would see it as cowardly. To be honest, I thought you were protecting yourself, but now I realize that's not your intention, is it?" When he gravely shook his head, Herezah believed he could have no other agenda. "You have spent enough time in the company of my son to know how seriously he takes his position as ruler. On his very deathbed, his father impressed upon the boy his role—how he had been chosen because no one else was better suited to rule than Boaz. He is still so young. His head is filled with idealistic notions of being a grand, wise, and much-beloved Zar."

"I'm approaching this the wrong way—is that what you're saying, Valide?"

"Precisely. You need to come up with a plan that plays to his sense of the heroic. Boaz has been such a studious, serious boy all his life. He reveres Lazar, most likely because of the Spur's devil-may-care attitude. Did you see how the tale of how Lazar fought all those attackers fired Boaz's imagination when he heard it?"

Tariq considered the Valide. She could all but see his mind working, accepting that what she was advising was true. "Have you any advice on how we might encourage the Zar to place himself in safety, then? Perhaps even where he may agree to go?"

Herezah paused. Suddenly a new thought occurred to her, a notion that was so neat in the way it dovetailed into her own plans, she nearly hugged herself.

"Valide? You are smiling," Tariq said. "Have you an idea?"

"I do, Grand Vizier. And it's perfect. I shall suggest to my son—and you will support this suggestion with vigor—that he accompany Lazar on his quest to secure the heir. In all truth, Boaz is safer with Lazar than anyone else. And the Spur would never put him in danger, so I imagine he will find ways to leave Boaz behind once he knows where Ana is. Boaz has never been out of the palace grounds, save for one or two trips to the bazaar when he was quite young. That's probably why Ana intrigued him so much; she was so daring. He will relish the opportunity to travel alongside the Spur into the desert and on the hunt for his wife. It has the right balance of the romantic and the heroic to appeal to him."

"Valide, that is a masterful plan. I think he might actually go along with that."

"Then you keep your promise to me, Grand Vizier, and I shall do the same for you."

"Just one more thing."

"Yes?" She had been turning to leave.

"I intend to go with the Zar."

"What? I can't make that happen."

"But you will try."

"Why, Tariq? Why would you want to go back into that place?"

"I am no use here without a word of Galinsean to my name, Valide, and should Lazar leave Boaz behind, the Zar will need someone at his side. I can't protect him physically with a weapon but I can protect him through wisdom. We will, of course, have to take some of the Mute Guard."

Herezah nodded. It was of no consequence to her where the Grand Vizier went and in fact this played even more to her advantage. "You speak to him today, Tariq, and clear this business of my union with Lazar. Then I will attempt what you ask."

He bowed. She acknowledged his obeisance with a nod, relishing the idea that she would not only be the highest-ranking royal left behind in the city, but that without the Grand Vizier, her role might be even more critical. She watched Tariq make to leave. She would force herself not to be scared of the Galinseans. They didn't seem to be keen to raid the city yet. Perhaps diplomacy would prevail. She shivered with delight, suddenly remembered Boaz's news, and said to the Grand Vizier's back, "By the way, Tariq, have you heard that the dwarf has turned up?"

9

Maliz was fuming. He slammed the door behind him as he entered his official chambers in the palace. Pez back! How could that be? How could the dwarf have survived alone in the desert, when three people of sound mind barely returned in one piece? He had hoped they were well rid of the freak, who seemed to have a curiously strong friendship with the Zar, the Spur, and the Zaradine, even though he spoke such gibberish all the time.

Maliz had been suspicious of the dwarf for a long time now but he had watched him carefully for more than a year and not once had Pez given him any reason to believe that he was involved with Lyana's rising. At first he'd thought the dwarf might be Iridor, and certainly Iridor had come into being again or Maliz would not have been called from his slumbers, but the dwarf was too stupid, too frustrating with his moods and idiocy, to have anything on his mind except his own lunatic thoughts.

No, Iridor was wily and cunning. Lyana's messenger paved the way for her arrival, discovering ally and foe alike, passing on messages to other disciples of the Goddess, and warning them of their enemies. Pez did nothing except drool, make bodily odors and noises, and apparently amuse most, although he certainly didn't amuse the Grand Vizier. Who was Iridor? The old priestess at Lyana's temple had claimed that Salmeo was Iridor! She had clung to her loyalty to the last—a brave woman indeed. And although Maliz laughed at the suggestion, he had also taken precaution, made sure he "accidentally" touched the great eunuch on several occasions to reassure himself that no magic flowed through the head of the harem. Boaz had flitted through his mind as a possible candidate but the same "inadvertent" touches had revealed that no magic ran through the Zar. Salazin, all the Mutes, in fact, and great numbers of the Elim had been checked using the same ploy. No luck. Iridor evaded him. The demigod was always male; so Maliz didn't have to concern himself that it could be Herezah or Ana or indeed any of the women of the harem, or the palace servants. He had even taken to roaming the streets in a jamoosh, brushing past countless unsuspecting Percherese, in the vague hope that he might stumble upon Iridor, but so far his travels had brought him no closer to his goal.

He had kicked himself upon realizing that Kett, the young eunuch who had niggled in his mind seventeen moons ago, had been the one called the Raven, the bird of omens. He wondered what message the blackbird had brought. If only he had listened to his instincts as he normally did, he might have had the opportunity to interrogate the black servant. But he had been so distracted by events that he had not paid attention to Kett until it was too late. That had been a costly mistake. But it was no use crying over it. None of it explained Iridor.

Again he was brought back to the dwarf and all of his supporters. Ana he had touched—she had no magic that he could feel or sense. Lyana couldn't have risen anyway because Maliz had not felt anything akin to the usual surge of power. He was sure of that. Apart from that moment in the desert when he had been awoken and felt a muted response to something magical, anything that might have prompted him to have the stirrings of Lyana's awakening amounted to nothing but confusion. As for Lazar, the Galinsean Prince had not permitted himself to be touched; that made him a suspect but it didn't fit, not with all the sickness and heroics.

Maliz frowned in frustraton. Iridor and Lyana's magics were not closed to him. He was connected to them; they had never been able to hide from him, but this time, although he sensed their presence, he could not lock his focus onto anyone in particular. He would need to go back over everything. Surely he had missed some crucial clue. But his immediate focus now was to keep Boaz's body safe. The Zar's harem was to be the demon's playground and no Galinsean war was going to stop Maliz having what he wanted.

Regarding the Valide's problem, he was baffled by Herezah's claims of being in love with Lazar. That the Valide had finally followed through on the yearning that was transparent to all was not so much of a shock, but that the Spur had not only welcomed such attention but actively sought it didn't fit the picture that Maliz had of Lazar. Tariq's memories told him only of the traditional rancor between the head of security and Joreb's Absolute Favorite. It didn't make sense, but then the relationships between mortals rarely did. They were a contrary bunch, prone to unexpected divergences from original pathways regarding their desires.

Ah, how this strange plot thickens, he said to himself. He would go along with the Valide's needs because it suited him. He didn't relish another trip into the desert with all of its inherent dangers, especially as he was still vulnerable in Tariq's body until Lyana's rising brought forth his full powers—and immortality. But Galinsean invasion posed a far greater threat to himself and the Zar whose body and status he wanted too badly to waste.

Maliz knew he needed a plan. He must find the dwarf and satisfy himself once and for all over Pez's madness.

Pez was with Lazar at the Spur's house. They were sharing a kerrosh that Pez had brewed as the soldier readied himself for travel.

"Are you going to tell me what else is on your mind, other than racing off into the desert to find Ana?"

"Apart from war, you mean? Or on top of the fact that the father I haven't seen in almost two decades might be leading that war? Or—here's a good one—how about the fact that Percheron may well be decimated on account of me!"

"Stop it! I don't mean any of that. I mean, what has made you so angry this morning?"

"I don't know what you mean," Lazar said, stuffing a few items into a sack.

"I've known you long enough. You're the most irritable person who stomps this realm and yet I can see genuine angst written on your expression."

"Don't pry, Pez."

"Why not? What secret could you have from me when you shared the deepest held secret of all?"

"And you didn't hold on to that one at all well."

Pez glared at him. "I held it for those two decades you speak of. I divulged it to the one person you personally sanctioned to have the knowledge upon your death. You alone chose to tell the next person."

Lazar put a hand in the air to stop the dwarf's tirade. "All right. I'm sorry."

Pez rubbed his hands, reached for the cup with the dregs of his drink. "Ooh, not like you to apologize over anything, Lazar. Something has pricked you. Tell me."

The Spur sighed. "Herezah made her move," he said baldly.

The kerrosh Pez had sipped spluttered back out of his mouth in shock at Lazar's claim. "How bad was it?"

"About as bad as it could get. She wasn't taking no for an answer and I was cornered and in no fit state to do much about her advances. Worse, I felt sad for her."

"Sad? Herezah?" Pez queried, aghast. "I don't usually put that sentiment together with that woman."

"She has taken very good care of me. Without her efforts and determination I might have taken a lot longer to recover."

"True."

Lazar ran his hands through his hair with frustration, growling as he did so. "It was so humiliating. I can fully understand how Joreb fell under her spell, Pez, that's the truth of it. I was helpless not just because of my condition but simply because I'm a man. That close to such generous invitation, my resistance broke."

"You've managed to resist for so many years," Pez commented, an overlay of disgust in his tone.

"I've never been at her mercy as I was this morning."

Pez blinked slowly. "How far did it go?"

"Far enough."

"And the mortification happened why?" Pez asked, frowning.

"Salmeo walked in on us."

Pez's eyes widened. "I understand now," he finally said. "How was it handled?"

"I have to say the Valide was magnificent in her temper but I don't believe it was anger at being discovered so much as being interrupted," Lazar admitted wryly.

"And you?"

"Sheer relief, if I'm honest. I was a lamb to the slaughter and the blade was poised. It's not as though I can thank the man. I hate him with all my heart. But he saved us a worse misery. He had come to tell us that Boaz was on his way."

Pez made a whistling sound. "So it was going to be bad either way." Lazar nodded. "But whereas Boaz might be shocked or dismayed, Salmeo will simply use the knowledge."

"Of course he will. Salmeo's whole power base revolves around knowledge and disinformation about others. He will make Herezah pay, certainly, but how he plans to use this against me remains to be seen."

"Herezah gets all she deserves, Lazar. I can't feel a moment of pity for that woman. Don't tell me you do?"

Lazar shrugged. "Not pity so much as I realize how magnificent she could be if she were a real queen."

"Like your mother?"

"Yes. She reminds me of her, but Herezah has to use cunning to survive. Her shaky throne extends only around the harem. My mother commands real power from a real throne and over all her subjects. She's terrifying," Lazar said ruefully.

"So what are you going to do?"

"Nothing. We face much bigger trials and tribulations than Boaz worrying about who his mother lies with. I'm ready. Stay out of sight of the palace. We don't want anything getting in the way of your coming with me, especially the Grand Vizier. We'll meet tonight at the rendezvous point."

Pez nodded and Lazar locked hands with his friend in farewell.

"I hear Pez is returned to us, Majesty," Maliz said lightly. "You must be so relieved."

Boaz was signing parchments. "I can't believe how the gods have smiled upon us in returning him to Percheron."

"How extraordinary that he survived the desert." Maliz watched Bin slide another document before the Zar, whispering its contents.

Boaz nodded, signed as he replied. "I don't care how it came about, I'm just glad he lives. I'm not sure he'll thank me when, through his haze of madness, he realizes I'm sending him back."

"Back?"

"He's going with Lazar on the hunt for Ana."

Maliz reined in his natural desire to take Boaz by the throat and shake him. Did the Zar know something about the dwarf that was eluding him? "How come, Majesty?" he asked, his tone nothing but polite.

Boaz scrawled the final signature and handed the paper to his assistant. He stood. "He's company for Lazar, he's amusement, I hope, for anyone who comes across them—he may make a gift for this Arafanz, who knows. He's another pair of eyes, however reliable or not they may be." Boaz shrugged. "He's dispensable, although I hate to admit that. So few can be spared from the city's cause."

Maliz sensed the Zar was feeding him placations. There was something too neat about this. The dwarf, Lazar, Ana . . . the connections were too strong in mind. He could not probe further, though, at this stage, he decided; that would have to be done more covertly. "Excellent; if there's anything I can do to help regarding this clandestine trip, just ask, Majesty. Now, there is something private I need to discuss with you."

"You can speak freely in front of Bin."

"Er, no, Majesty, I cannot. This is a delicate matter of a personal nature—not to you or me, Highness," he assured, "but to someone close. I would rather you make your decision later about who might be made privy to the information."

"That will be all," Boaz said to his assistant, who glowered at the Grand Vizier. Maliz couldn't care less. He waited for the young man to be gone.

"What is this about, Tariq?"

"The Valide, Your Majesty."

"My mother . . . what has she been up to now?" the Zar asked wearily.

"Were you aware, Majesty, that the Valide and the Spur have struck up a sexual relationship?" There was no easy way to say what he needed to—Maliz knew it would be best to be blunt with the young royal.

"Is this a jest, Tariq? Because—"

"No jest, my Zar. I speak the plain truth. The Spur and your mother are lovers. They have been for a short while, since she has been caring for him."

"Lazar?" Boaz asked, choking back amusement. The older man nodded. "I cannot believe it. You've been in the palace all these years, Tariq, you surely appreciate the only barely controlled animosity between those two?"

"Apparently not so hostile after all, Majesty. The ins and outs of it are irrelevant, my Zar. I'm telling you this for a completely separate reason and not for shock value or titillation. Who your mother spends her private hours with and shares her body with is of no concern to me, so long as it doesn't spill into the realm's business."

Boaz straightened his expression. "Quite right. And?"

"Well, it seems they were disturbed in their . . . well, shall we say disturbed from their privacy earlier today."

"By whom were they discovered?"

"The Grand Master Eunuch, my Zar." Maliz watched the royal's top lip all but curl into a sneer.

"I see."

"Your mother, who has been discreet to date, and mindful of not wishing to offend your sensibilities, my Zar, is now extremely fearful that the head of the harem will use this information to either blackmail her or leak it to you in a manner that has serious ramifications."

"He is certainly an opportunist," Boaz responded in a rare show of naked thought.

Maliz kept his tone even. "I cannot agree with you more, my Zar."

"Did my mother ask you to speak with me, Tariq?"

Maliz adopted a tone of indignation. "Of course not, Highness. She would probably howl for my punishment if she knew I was so much as breathing a word of it to you. But my role is to be your ears and eyes around the palace. It occurred to me this union would only really offend you if you happened upon the information by chance and were in some way embarrassed by it."

"Yes, indeed. But I really can't put the Valide and the Spur together. This is a shock."

"A shock, yes, but perhaps not an unwelcome one, Highness."

"What do you mean?"

Maliz shrugged softly. "I shouldn't be presumptuous."

"Tariq, you have promised me honesty. That is why I have permitted you far more access to the Zar and his thoughts than my father ever allowed. I'd suggest you don't become coy with me now."

"Forgive me, Highness. That is not my intention but I wonder sometimes whether my candor is too forward."

"Not at all. Say what is on your mind."

Maliz nodded. "I'm sure I'm not the only person in the palace to privately believe that the Spur has held a deep admiration for Zaradine Ana." He saw Boaz open his mouth but hurried on, determined now to craft this delicate path he had promised the Valide he would lead her son down. "And I am the first to lay my hand against my heart and assure you that the Spur acted with only the greatest courtesy and duty toward your wife on our ill-fated trip. He kept a distance from all in the royal party but fought so courageously for us all when it mattered that I am surprised he lives to fight another day."

"I'm sure you are," Boaz commented.

"Indeed, Highness. And his very choice when a terrible scenario was laid out before him was the choice of a man utterly loyal to his duty. In this the Spur was above any criticism. And so, as much as anyone believes he holds a bright torch for the young woman who is now your Absolute Favorite and Zaradine, I also believe it is based on a loyalty. He discovered her, he purchased her, he brought her to the palace and even took her punishment

rather than see the young woman flogged for her indiscretion."
The Zar nodded but was frowning, obviously unsure where
Maliz was heading. "The point is, Highness, it seems the Spur's
ardor has always been directed elsewhere and yet his dutiful behavior toward your new wife has often been misconstrued. Perhaps in an effort to conceal his true feelings toward your mother,
he has allowed others to continue believing he has feelings for
the Zaradine."

"I'm fairly certain Lazar doesn't care what others think."

Maliz smirked behind his beard. "Every man has his level, my
Zar. Some, like the Spur, have a greater tolerance for gossip and
innuendo."

"And all of this boils down to the fact that you believe I should
be quietly grateful that the head soldier of our realm is secretly
making love to the Valide, and when this secret finds its way out
via the Grand Master Eunuch—as it surely will——that I place no
importance on it and thus give him no weapon to use against myself, my mother, or the Spur."

Maliz realized that once again he had underestimated the
young man who ruled Percheron. "Precisely, my Zar. If we are
to curb Salmeo's influence, we must do so using his own cunning
ways."

Boaz sighed. "I can't imagine why we've wasted so much time
discussing this. I have crucial state business on my mind, Tariq,
and this sort of petty palace stuff holds no interest."

"I understand, Majesty, but again it is my role to keep you fully
informed. I could not know that you would take such a pragmatic
view—the Valide is your mother, after all."

"She has no reprisals to fear from me."

"That's excellent, Highness. I believe she wishes to speak
with you today. She asked me if you were available for a meet-

ing. Perhaps Bin could set it up, although I understand that you must be very busy with your preparations and it may be easier after the Spur and the dwarf have left. When do they leave, incidentally?"

"Later today."

Time was short. "I shall take up no more of your time, Highness. Thank you for allowing me to have this private conversation."

Maliz quickly sent a handwritten message to the Valide informing her that he had kept his side of the bargain and that her son had barely twitched an eyebrow during their discussion. He suggested that she be humble but not too prickly about the liaison. *Be forthright, Majesty*, he wrote. *He will be surprised by this approach and realize that you are not asking his permission so much as treating him with the respect he deserves.* The Grand Vizier ended his communication with a warning that the Spur and the dwarf were leaving after midday and that she should meet with the Zar immediately.

After the Elim runner had been sent to the harem, Maliz went in search of the dwarf. He found him in his chambers, humming to himself. Maliz knew he had arrived silently but still Pez had spun around, shocked. Could the dwarf sense people?

"The donkeys are flying high today," Pez wailed, jumping up and down.

"Calm down, Pez. How are you?"

"My nose hurts. I feel sick. I want to be sick," he groaned, and began to retch.

"Ah, not on me, I hope. Stay calm, dwarf," Maliz said, wondering if Pez, whose eyes were rolling back in his head, could hear him.

But apparently he could. "Don't touch me!" the dwarf began shrieking repeatedly.

Maliz ignored the dwarf, looked behind him to ensure they were alone and quickly covered the distance between himself and Pez. The dwarf was cornered, but he opened up his lungs and began unashamedly screaming. Maliz knew the Elim would be here in moments. He just had to lay a hand against the dwarf. He reached forward and Pez grabbed his hand and bit it hard. Maliz squealed and withdrew hurriedly, but the next moment he pretended with one hand to reach for the dwarf's shoulder, and whilst Pez swatted and kicked and prepared to bite again, Maliz used his other hand to swiftly grab the little man's neck . . . and squeeze.

Pez screamed louder than Maliz thought possible; he felt sure his ears would be left bleeding and his hearing impaired by the shrill sound. As he had anticipated, the strong arms of two recently arrived Elim were suddenly pulling him back.

"Grand Vizier!" one exclaimed. "What has happened?"

The other was bent, soothing Pez, who refused to stop his caterwauling.

Maliz shook his head, hoping to rid himself of the terrible ringing in his ears, before indignantly shaking himself free of the Elim's grip. "He collapsed, you fool. I was seeing if there was anything I could do."

"He hurt me!" Pez wailed. "He keeps trying to hurt me."

"Is there any truth to what Pez claims, Grand Vizier?"

"Don't be ridiculous! I take offense at that question!" Maliz pointed at Pez. "I was passing by when I saw him lying on the ground."

"Passing?"

"What is your name?"

"Amooz, Grand Vizier."

"Well, Amooz . . . " Maliz bristled. "I'm not in the habit of explaining my movements to the palace servants."

"I understand, Grand Vizier, please forgive me. Pez takes some time to calm when he becomes worked up like this. Perhaps you would be kind enough to let us handle him now. Thank you for trying to help. He is contrary at the best of times and only newly returned to the palace; we fully expect him to be disoriented for a number of weeks to come."

Maliz straighted his robe in a further show of ire at being manhandled. "Next time I see him writhing in agony, I'll leave him to his struggles, shall I?" He did not give the Elim an opportunity to respond, but turned on his heel and stormed out, his mind reeling at the magic he had felt simmering in the palace's jester. Whether he was Iridor or not, Maliz had not had time to test. But it mattered not. Pez—mad or not—was dangerous and Maliz would no longer take any chances about whether or not the dwarf was Lyana's messenger. The dwarf had to be dealt with swiftly.

Pez allowed himself to be gradually soothed and taken to one of the Zar's private gardens. The Elim left him there, unsure of what else to do for the dwarf, although Pez heard Amooz say as they left that he would be sending a message through the palace hierarchy about today's incident.

Whatever recriminations might come, they would come too late, Pez knew. The Grand Vizier had taken him by surprise and seized his chance; he had laid his hand on Pez and the little man couldn't be sure what conclusions had been drawn. He had done his utmost to cloak his powers whilst trickling some shepherding magic directly at Maliz in the hope that the counterattack might unexpectedly sidetrack the demon. Pez could not fully conceal his magic—not from the touch of the demon—but he hoped something he'd done had baffled Maliz. It's all that he had standing between him and death, for he could outwit Zarab's disciple for only so long. If the Grand Vizier finally decided that Pez was Iridor, he could have the dwarf killed in a multitude of ways, from a seeming accident around the palace to shameless murder at the hands of an accomplice.

Pez wept at his own stupidity for leaving himself vulnerable. How could he have left himself so open, especially now, when the hour of their greatest battle was virtually upon them? Naturally news of his safe return would grab attention from those who had a vested interest in his well-being—either positive or negative. He should have known Maliz would come looking, unable to believe the dwarf could survive the ferocity of the desert. Pez was furious with himself. Had he endangered them all? Was it too late to find Ana, to secure Lyana's rising? He dearly wished that Ellyana would pay a visit, but she was more elusive than ever.

He thought about how Ellyana had manipulated him. From the moment they had met, she had seduced him with her words, cajoled him into doing precisely what she needed. She had still been controlling him as recently as the disastrous trip into the desert. That awful demand—he had never understood its cruelty and knew now he was never meant to. And where was Lyana? She had not even told him who Lyana was for this battle and Pez admitted openly to himself now, for the first time, how much that hurt him. They had always traveled so closely, he and Lyana could tap into each other's thoughts, but in this cycle Lyana was keeping him in the dark, keeping them all guessing about one another. He was convinced that the new Zaradine had her part to play; he just wasn't sure what her part was, and sadly, as much as he wanted to believe that Ana was the Goddess, too many signs were saying she was not. He bent forward, cupped his head with his hands, and let the tears flow freely. They couldn't lose. Not again. Not this time. He had never felt this lonely or abandoned in all of his memories either as the dwarf or as Iridor.

"Pez?"

He jumped. "Highness! And how high can you jump?" He yelled his nonsense out of habit.

"I was told you may still be here. What happened?" Pez looked around furtively. "I've come alone," Boaz assured him.

Pez motioned for the Zar to close the door, which he did. "Are you sure no one is there?" Boaz shook his head, frowning. Pez sighed softly. "The Grand Vizier attacked me."

"Attacked? Are you sure?"

Pez grimaced. "Well, he grabbed me by the neck and pinned me down. How else would you describe it?"

Boaz's frown deepened. "I did hear from the Elim that you were found struggling beneath him but I can't imagine why someone so phlegmatic as Tariq would assault you."

"Ah, you are of course referring to the new Tariq, not the one who served your father? That Tariq was rather easily excited."

"And this one?" Boaz asked.

"Is, apart from outward looks, an entirely different being . . . don't you think?"

Boaz's mouth twisted wryly. "He's certainly akin to the vestren."

"Except that even though the snake adapts its color to suit its surrounds, it remains a vestren."

Boaz looked faintly amused. "And Tariq?"

"Is quite simply changed. He is not adapting to a new role, Highness. He is not the man we all once knew."

Boaz sighed. "Where is this going, Pez? What are you saying?"

This was a dangerous question to be asked. Pez preferred honesty with the Zar . . . and Boaz deserved it, but how in Lyana's name could he convince the young royal that a demon had possessed the Grand Vizier's body? He had to try, though, because Maliz's attack today changed everything. Now Pez desperately needed his Zar's protection. He began carefully. "You have witnessed the Lore at work, Majesty."

Boaz frowned, confused. "Yes."

"So you have no choice but to believe magic exists."

"I still shake my head at that incident on the night of Ana's choosing, Pez. I don't understand it at all."

Pez nodded patiently. "Nevertheless, you've felt its touch upon you, and not just once, but again when you drew upon my powers during the execution of Horz."

Boaz nodded and Pez could see how uncomfortable this discussion made the young Zar. "You believe, don't you, Boaz?"

"Against all my upbringing and will, yes, I believe in magic," he said sombrely. "I could hardly refute it after being at its mercy."

"Then would you believe me if I told you that I thought an impostor roamed the Stone Palace?"

Boaz's head flicked up, his eyes wide with astonishment. "What sort of impostor?"

"One using magic."

"Against you?"

Pez shook his head, his stare intent, his expression serious. "Against all of us."

"I'm lost," Boaz said, opening his palms. "Who is this impostor?"

Pez held his breath. Then risked it. "He is Tariq."

Boaz stared at his friend, aghast.

At least he isn't laughing or dismissing me, Pez thought as he watched the young royal try to digest what had just been thrown at him. He took his time, the intensity of his stare not lessening. Pez held his gaze firmly.

The Zar spoke in a hushed tone when he finally addressed Pez. "You think the Grand Vizier is wielding a magic and that he is not the Tariq we have known for all these years." It was not a question but a bald statement.

Pez nodded, too scared to say anything. He knew how much he was asking for the Zar to go along with this notion.

"How did you reach this conclusion?"

"The same way you might, Majesty. He is behaving so differently it's not possible he is the same man. Consider his physical state—the change is remarkable, even the stoop has gone, and that's not physically possible for a man headed toward his eighth decade. How about the way he looks? Where is the forked beard hung with gems? Where are the bejeweled sandals? The ostentatious garments? And consider his approach to life. He is no longer the grasping, sycophantic, excitable courtier but suddenly a rational, sober, even modest counselor." Pez's voice took a tone of plea. "Perhaps in isolation none of these things matter, but together they surely prompt questions. Boaz, he is the man you once detested more than Salmeo. Now he is the first person you turn to for advice—and no, Majesty, this not jealousy speaking. This is fact." He returned to his former, more grim tone. "Consider the way his mind works. He was once shallow, an order taker, frightened of his own shadow. Now he leads.

Now he thinks for himself, for you! Now he walks with the air of a man who to all intents and purposes feels invincible."

Boaz stopped him with a hand in the air. "Pez, listen to yourself! Do you know how far-fetched this sounds?"

The dwarf nodded. "I am only sorry I haven't had the courage to share my fears with you before today. But I didn't think you'd listen. I'm not even sure you can accept this now."

"Who else have you shared this with?"

"Only Lazar."

"And surely Lazar laughed in your face?"

"Quite the contrary, Majesty."

"He believes this?" Boaz asked, unable to hide his dismay.

Pez knew he had gone far enough with this conversation. Boaz would tolerate only so much. "He is deeply suspicious of the Grand Vizier."

"And still he saved his life," Boaz said, his tone disdainful.

Pez shrugged. "Lazar is honor bound, Majesty. He would leave no man of Percheron to die in the desert, no man of any nation, in fact."

"And what do you expect me to do with this outrageous information?" Boaz demanded, anger erupting now.

"I ask only that you keep it in mind, Highness. Don't dismiss my claim that the Grand Vizier meant me harm."

"But tell me, why would he want to harm you?"

Pez wanted to tell Boaz everything—about the death of Zafira, the rising of Iridor, Lyana's battle—but instead he said merely, "He suspects that I am not the fool I appear to be."

"And he would be right! Are his suspicions enough to condemn him as a magical impostor? You are suggesting, are you not, that someone else walks in Tariq's body?" Pez could only nod. Boaz sighed, exasperated. "Pez, I am facing war with Galinsea. I don't know what I'm doing. I never lived through war alongside my father, so I have no experience to draw upon. It is taking every ounce of my resilience to stay brave in the face of this threat, in the loss of my wife, in the role as Zar. Please don't heap any more onto my shoulders."

Pez nodded apologetically and meant it. "Protect me, Boaz, that's all I ask. Keep the Grand Vizier from me. Perhaps use the Elim's complaint to forbid him from being near to me . . . just for a while, until this all blows over."

Boaz nodded. "I shall do that for you, Pez, but I think going into the desert again will achieve the distance you request. Are you sure about this trip?"

"Absolutely. I know exactly where Arafanz headed from our camp. It's all we have," Pez lied.

"How will you ever find the trail."

"Lazar will find it."

"You are very faithful to Ana."

"Why wouldn't I be?"

The Zar shrugged. "It's right that you are but your friendship with Ana, and, indeed, with Lazar, seem on a level with the friendship you and I share."

Pez looked at the Zar, astonished. "And that bothers you, Highness?"

"I just wonder sometimes . . ." Boaz hesitated, but Pez sensed the Zar felt himself to be in too deep to withdraw the statement.

"Yes?"

"Well, I'm wondering if a terrible choice were upon you, who you would choose."

Pez looked at Boaz, shocked. "Do you mean would I choose you over Lazar."

"For instance," Boaz replied, his firm gaze unwavering.

The dwarf was unsure how to answer his Zar. There was definitely a correct answer required here and he had to give the obvious one that the Zar wanted to hear. "Boaz, I would choose you. Although I'm deeply hurt that you would need to ask. May I ask, Highness, what precisely is bothering you about my friendship with Ana and Lazar?"

"I'm not sure. I wonder how far you'd go to protect a friend of yours."

"I have so few, Boaz, that if any of you were threatened in any way, I would do anything to protect you." Pez felt his initial surge of irritation turn to anger. He didn't understand Boaz's convoluted attack at all.

"You would lie?"

"I have lied for you many times."

"Ah, but you have lied only to others who think you are insane. You would not lie to Lazar or Ana about me."

"No, but that's because they love you. They are loyal to you. We all are."

"But you would protect one of your few friends at any cost?"

"Yes!"

"That is all I asked," Boaz said, infuriatingly calm. "Now, what about the impostor?"

Pez shrugged. There was nothing more to say. He had tried and he had failed to convince the Zar that his Vizier meant no good. Iridor must face Maliz alone—it was always so. "We'll worry about that once we have Zaradine Ana safely back by your side, Highness."

Seemingly satisfied, the Zar nodded and the atmosphere between them switched from a sense of being at odds to conspiratorial. "Pez, did you hear about the Spur and the Valide being discovered this morning?"

Confused by the switch, Pez nevertheless grinned. "I did." He waited, needed to see how Boaz handled the news and precisely how much he knew.

Boaz was suddenly back to being a young man, barely out of childhood, sharing an amusing conversation. He screwed up his face, as if smelling something bad. "I can't believe that Lazar has apparently been lusting for my mother all of this time."

Pez clamped down the surprise that rose instantly; where had that notion come from? He kept his expression open. "Neither can I," he replied truthfully.

"So you didn't know either?"

"This is the first I'm hearing of it. Lazar did tell me about an incident this morning but we didn't have time to discuss it."

"Hmm," Boaz mused.

"Does it anger you, Majesty?"

"Anger me?" Boaz asked, surprised. "No, I don't think so. I'm just shocked that Lazar hid his ardor so well from all of us who are close to him."

"Indeed."

"If anything, I suppose I should be quietly glad, to tell the truth."

"Because of Ana?"

Boaz's eyes narrowed as they regarded Pez. "You know me too well, dwarf. Anyone else would leap to the conclusion that I'd just be glad the bitterness between them was done with. I did warn Ana before she left that she would be scrutinized, that her behavior had to be exemplary."

"And it was, Highness. You have no cause for anxiety on that. Lazar behaved impeccably at all times as well, and I think any quiet concern you may have held in this regard is unfounded," he lied, unhappily.

"So I hear. I would share my concern only with you, Pez."

"Of course. And I would speak of it to no one."

"Leave now, Pez. If you are worried about Tariq, best you are gone from the palace to your rendezvous point with Lazar. I have a meeting with the Spur and the Grand Vizier shortly."

"We shall bring her back, Majesty," Pez said.

Boaz reach out and hugged him. "If it's true that she carries a son in her belly, then you must bring them both back to me." There was something in Boaz's voice that stirred a curiosity in Pez but he couldn't think about it now. He had to escape the palace, be gone from here, into the relative safety of the desert. Percheron would have to hold its own without its Spur or its royal buffoon. They were facing a far greater battle.

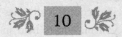

10

Ghassal of the Percherese Protectorate was providing the Zar with thrice-hourly reports. Boaz had just learned that all was quiet at the Isles of Plenty. The Galinsean fleet was anchored, the sailors relaxed, and there was still no sign of which royal of most interest was aboard the ship.

The threat of war felt all-consuming and yet something more dire had been nagging at his mind for months. It was a matter he had given himself plenty of time to think on; to see it from every angle and to be sure that the decision he had secretly reached was the right one . . . the only one. "Send in my mother," he said to Bin. "I shall take quishtar with her on the balcony."

"Yes, Majesty."

Herezah was shown into the chamber and dutifully bowed. Boaz took her hand. "I'm sorry to have kept you. I needed to bid Pez farewell. Not that he understands." He gestured to the balcony. "Come, let us talk outside. I hear you wish to speak to me on a matter of importance."

"I do, son. Thank you for seeing me at such short notice."

"Make yourself comfortable," he offered once they were outside, soaking up the cool drafts of air soaring up the hill from the bay.

"I prefer to stand, if you don't mind?"

Boaz shrugged. His mother looked nervous and he could understand why, considering what she was here to discuss with him. He would let her anxiety build a little further. It was valuable to have her coming to him so humble. "All is quiet with the Galinsean fleet. I wonder what they're waiting for?"

"Do you believe the Galinseans are eager for war, Boaz?"

"They're here, aren't they?"

"No. They're at the Isles of Plenty. There's a significant difference. It's not a declaration of war. To me it's a declaration of strength; it's them making clear that they will not be dismissed. If they were irrationally seeking war, we would already be dead. Someone is giving us time to make diplomatic contact."

Boaz nodded. "Now, why don't I think like that?" He meant it lightly but his mother took his comment seriously.

He saw her visibly relax as she slipped into her role as counselor. "Only a woman does. Women do not take pride in having their sons and daughters slaughtered in the name of a realm. Trust me, a mother will always seek a peaceful solution if precious lives can be saved." The servant arrived with a tray of quishtar and its accoutrements. She smiled at Boaz. "I'll pour, darling. Send him away."

Boaz obliged. "Do you think I should go to the Isles of Plenty?"

Herezah began her elegant ritual pouring of the quishtar. "No, that would seem too humble. But someone should. Someone senior should make contact. We achieve nothing by staring at each other across the waters. They are obviously being very patient, biding their time, but I don't think we should make them wait too long before initiating discourse." She handed him a beautiful porcelain cup from Joreb's collection.

"Thank you," he said, taking the quishtar and sipping. "I shall think on what you say." He appreciated her wisdom—she was at her best when playing politics. He decided to put her out of her misery swiftly. "So, Mother, you are here to plead your case regarding your liaison with Lazar. Let me say now that—"

"No, Boaz. I am not here to do any such thing," she interrupted politely but firmly.

He was blowing the steam from his quishtar but looked up at her sharply. Her veil was removed and there was no sign of nervousness in her expression. Had he misread her? "I thought—"

"Yes, son. I suppose you would and I shall certainly explain myself on that score but I wasn't aware that I needed your sanction on whom I choose to spend my time with. Let me add, though, that I do appreciate your blessing and seek it now."

Boaz looked back at her, stunned. She was not here to cringe or ask for his indulgence, not even here to plead for his help against Salmeo? "I must say I am surprised about your new relationship."

"But not disappointed, I hope?"

"No," he had to admit. "I didn't think you and Lazar cared that much for each other."

"Boaz, I loved your father but that love was founded on pragmatism—as was his regard for me. We were an exceptionally good choice for each other and we were happy considering our situation. If I had not belonged to the harem, if I had been able to choose a man to spend my life with, having not known you or your father, I would have chosen Lazar. That's the truth. But I couldn't have him, and as you know all too well, the harem is the most frustrating prison of all. I took those frustrations out on Lazar, not realizing for a moment that he was harboring similar feelings."

Boaz shook his head. "I can't believe it. You are both so hostile to each other."

"Love and hate are separated by a hair's breadth, son. I hope you never have to discover this at a cost to your own heart. I was never disloyal to your father and it's only now that I can indulge my own desire, now that I have reached the right status and am no longer important to the palace hierarchy. You have a wife now and she is, we suspect, already pregnant. My years as Valide are numbered." He thought she was being overly dramatic and made a soft sound of disgust but it seemed Herezah was earnest, as she ignored him and continued: "It is time for me to take my pleasures instead of being so focused on aiding you. You will always have my undying support but I must step back now."

Boaz could barely believe what he was hearing. "You want to retreat to your chambers, to have no official role?"

"I didn't say that, son. But I will no longer expect or demand any official duties, other than whatever you require of me. I genuinely nursed Lazar—none of that was a ruse. And as I did so I realized how much I have felt for him. I presume he experienced a similar epiphany. I'm just sorry that we were discovered in the manner we were and by whom."

"Salmeo will not be permitted to use this knowledge against you."

She smirked. "Oh, that's easy to say, my Lion, in the safety of this palace. The harem is a different realm, sometimes, all of its own. He will find ways but I shall survive, as I always have. Please do not let this play on your mind. I have a far more important case to plead, my Zar."

Boaz shook his head, his expression wry. What a day this was turning into, revelation upon revelation. "And what is that?"

"The people of Percheron are understandably scared, Boaz. Some are hoarding food, whilst others are fleeing to the hills. If I'm aware of it in the closeted world of the harem, I know you are aware of it in the wider community of the palace."

"There is nothing I can do. They are frightened and rightly so. I can't imagine that if the Galinseans do take the next step toward war, many Percherese lives will be spared."

"That's not the point."

"Mother, I cannot stop our people taking precautions or feeling so unnerved."

"Yes, you can. You can lead by example."

Boaz's initial expression of surprise quickly slid into scorn. "You dare accuse me of being a coward. Why do you think I'm still here, I—"

"Wait, Boaz! You misunderstand me. Hear me out." She reached for him, clutching his arm firmly as any mother would her son. "Your approach right now suggests a frigidity. It's as if you don't know what to do." She soothed his immediate bristling, her eyes soft with understanding. "I know it is not like that at all, but the people don't know what's going on. There is confusion; there is lack of information, and when that occurs, a city can become rife with gossip and misinformation. Do something."

"Like what, storm the Galinseans?" he asked, his tone filled with disdain.

"No. Much more subtle. Go after Ana. Scream from the

rooftops that Percheron has an heir. Tell your people that Ana has been abducted while performing her role as emissary to plead Percheron's case with Galinsea. Tell the people why war is coming. Explain everything! Let them understand that our Zar has been busy trying every diplomatic tool to keep the people of Percheron safe. Remind them that no blood must be shed without trying every peaceful means first. That is precisely what fires a nation's collective spirit, Boaz. This protective silence doesn't work."

"Go after Ana?" He could barely believe his ears. Not because of the audacity of her suggestion—and it was bold indeed—but because of how exquisitely it answered his dilemma. Here was the answer he had been searching for . . . the final piece of the jigsaw puzzle he had hoped would somehow slot itself into place.

"Yes! My darling, let them see you in full-blaze anger at what has occurred. A Zar, riding off into the desert to reclaim his new bride from the monster who has stolen her, and his heir who is the new jewel in the Percherese Crown. Oh, my Lion, it is the very stuff upon which realms are built!" Herezah's chest was heaving with the passion she was pouring into counseling her son.

Boaz felt his spirits lift and soar. *Ride alongside Lazar. Into the desert to save Ana.* His personal plans aside, the very notion of freedom, the desert, riding with Lazar, provoked a spike of intense pleasure. Leave the palace and go on a rescue mission, a crusade to return the heir and the Zaradine to their rightful place in the palace. It was perfect, but he schooled his expression into one that was thoughtful as he pretended to consider his mother's advice.

"And, Boaz," Herezah pressed, "this alone would strike a

new chord with the Galinseans. They have held off this long, I suspect, because they're confused. They know a diplomatic mission was being sent. This action of yours will confirm that things went wrong in the desert and that you are now attempting to put things right. The Galinseans will respect your courage and join your outrage that some upstart, hiding out in the desert, has stolen a royal . . . a Percherese royal on her way to Romea, no less. They aren't so dull that they don't understand the critical need for the royal structure. If renegades can behave like this in Percheron and get away with it, then Galinsea might be next—or so the thinking will go."

In his mind Boaz was already thundering along on his camel, white robes flying! "But . . ." he stammered for effect, "I can't leave the Grand Vizier in charge of Percheron at this delicate time. I don't trust him completely anyway," he said, Pez's claim haunting his thoughts.

"No, absolutely not the Grand Vizier! In fact, I would take Tariq with you."

"What?"

"That would demonstrate a very clear determination on your part. It shows Galinsea that you are prepared to leave your realm all but unprotected, having taken your Spur and your Grand Vizier—your two most senior advisers—despite war threatening. You have left yourself vulnerable because something greater is at stake. The very fabric of the land is under siege. If a royal can be stolen, abused, jeered at, what hope is there for our societies?" she demanded, her zealous gaze impaling Boaz. She shook him. "Send a letter to your counterpart in the Isles of Plenty, stir his rage that such a thing could be perpetrated against any royals of any realm by a peasant."

"But who is left to deal with the Galinseans?"

"Listen to me, Boaz. I am a loyal subject of Percheron, and, my darling, I will do anything . . . anything for you and your throne. You know that?" He nodded. "I am royal. I was the First Wife and Absolute Favorite of the former Zar and now I am the Valide to the present one. I speak Galinsean, of a fashion. I will defuse this tense situation—for a while. I will go to King Falza. I will open talks, take the diplomatic route, keep the Galinseans occupied."

Now Boaz felt bewildered. His mother's suggestion fitted his desires so neatly he found it irresistible. But he could not vacate the throne his brothers had died to give him—the throne his father had handpicked him above all others to occupy—without being sure of the right course of action.

"You?"

"If you'll have me," she said humbly. "I will be guided entirely by you. But get Lazar away from here. We know he's in danger and we also know he's the only person who can actually find Ana for you. Get the Grand Vizier away so he does not interfere. He has delusions of grandeur, son, and it's fine to let him be your voice when you require it, but he should not have any notion that he is the Zar by proxy. Just take him with you. He's another pair of eyes, another cunning mind. I think the situation here in Percheron could benefit from a woman's touch. My very presence makes us seem so much more vulnerable, and, my Zar, that might be our ultimate defense. The Galinseans will not deem it terribly brave, or royal, to strike against a woman. That's why Lazar suggested Ana in the first place. Trust his judgment. Get away from here and keep yourself safe, but secure that heir. I give you my word, they will not attack us yet."

"And will you also give me your word, swear in blood, that this is not one of your devious plans?"

"Give me a blade. I shall swear it in blood before you."

Boaz stared at his mother, his pulse racing. He believed there was no guile. This plan was either mad or inspired, but he suspected Herezah was suggesting a wise course. He was crippling Percheron with fright through what looked like inaction. He did need to take decisive action and he couldn't help but feel motivated by his mother's fervor. And, in traveling with Lazar into the desert, he could also lay to rest his demons and produce the heir that everyone in Percheron would surely celebrate.

"Bin!"

The Valide stepped back from her son, veiling herself. He could tell she was unsure of whether he was going to have her removed and incarcerated on the accusation of insanity or whether he was going to take action in the direction she proposed.

"Highness," the man said as he entered and bowed.

"Is Spur Lazar here?"

"We heard he's on his way up from the gate, my Zar."

"Bring him in as soon as he arrives. Don't stand on ceremony."

"Very good, my Zar."

"And, Bin. One more thing. I am going on a journey into the desert. Speak of this to no one, but make the necessary arrangements yourself. Time is short. I leave this afternoon."

Beneath her veil, Herezah smiled.

Lazar entered and Herezah's heart skipped a beat. Memories of touching him only hours earlier—her lips hungry on his—streamed into her mind, stirring a deliciously intense tingling in parts of her that had long been in need of awakening. She sucked in a breath softly as he strode toward the royal couple. Her former patient looked suddenly strong, dressed in his traveling clothes. He stood tall and broad; there was color in his cheeks, his hair was still wet and she could imagine the smell of his freshly washed body. Herezah re-created in her mind the prickly feel of the stubble on Lazar's chin against her smooth cheek and that breathtaking moment of response when she had caressed the part of him she had held in her hand. As he bowed she looked longingly at the top of his head, from which flowed the classically golden Galinsean hair she had washed so many times over the past few moons. He straightened and she allowed his proud bearing—every inch a crown prince—to impress her as she regarded the sad pale eyes, the aquiline nose, the lips so perfectly defined amid his clean-shaven face. It had been a long time since she had felt so strongly aware of her body's needs; right now, in his company and unable to satisfy her immediate surging desire, she felt weakened.

"I am ready to leave, my Zar," he said.

"Lazar, there is a change of plan," Boaz said, and Herezah, dragging herself from her musings on the Spur, was pleased her son was being direct and firm.

"Oh?" Lazar said, his eyes narrowing.

"I have decided to go with you."

The Spur's expression changed from instant surprise to dumbstruck. The silence lengthened.

"And," Boaz continued, "as you know, I am sending Pez. I fear for his safety here and he is contrary enough to be uncontrollable. If we lose him in the city or he creates any havoc during any diplomatic discussions, it could be dangerous." He held his hand up and Herezah was surprised that the Spur wasn't remonstrating. Perhaps Lazar was still too shocked about learning that the Zar was coming with him as well. She listened to her son's rationale for sending Pez. "You and he get on in the same friendly way that he and I do. He feels calm around you. And I give you my permission to leave him with whomever you must in order to complete your task for the Crown."

"I'm sensing there is still more, Highness," Lazar said, his tone icy but polite. "Pez is the least of my worries."

"I am also bringing the Grand Vizier. I—"

Lazar's interrupted. "Forgive me, my Zar, but this is turning into a caravan as cumbersome as that which caused the abduction of the Zaradine in the first place. If our party had been your wife, myself, and Jumo, as I originally intended, we would have made it across the desert to Romea without losing Jumo to quicksand because we were trying to feed such a vast number, or losing your wife to a madman."

"Are you blaming me for Jumo's death and Ana's loss, Lazar?" Boaz asked, his tone brittle.

"No, my Zar, not at all. But I advised you then and I give you the same advice now: the desert is hostile," Lazar replied carefully. "I cannot protect so many and we are vulnerable in numbers. I can perhaps look after Pez but not four of us."

"Lazar, I watched you cut down a dozen men in moments!" Herezah exclaimed, unable to stop herself from deriding his modesty. "It's vital for Percheron that the Zar is seen to be doing something."

The Spur's gaze, repressed fury now evident in it, slid from the Zar to his mother. "Valide, is it your idea that your son risk his life in the desert?" Lazar asked, his rage now directed at her.

"It is not my mother's idea at all," Boaz interrupted before

Herezah could answer. "The Valide is here because I have just told her of my plan. And also to brief me about the new liaison that seems to have erupted between yourself and her."

Lazar's mouth opened and Herezah smirked behind her veil. Though Lazar had probably feared Boaz would learn of what had occurred this morning, he must have anticipated that the news would come from Salmeo, not from her. Now she had him. He would not go against the Zar's wishes, not feeling so threatened.

"Our liaison?" he spluttered.

"Lazar, don't be embarrassed," she leaped in, keeping her voice smooth, calm. "The Zar understands. In fact, I think he might even give our new union his blessing. I wanted him to be the first to know and I didn't want the Grand Master Eunuch to have anything dangling over either of us. You know, do you not, how cunning he can be." Lazar nodded, seemingly stunned. "I am sure this news makes Boaz happy, in the sense that you and I no longer have to take out on each other quite so publicly our frustration at not being together. Now that the Zar and Ana are married, about to give us an heir, we need them both to feel unharassed by our bickering." She conveyed through her pleading stare that she had good reason for this humiliating revelation and that Lazar must go along with her ruse.

Lazar took a steadying breath, then shook his head briefly. "Zar Boaz, I do not wish to talk about this here and now. I am preparing for a dangerous journey and there are far more important things at stake for Percheron."

"I couldn't agree more," the Zar said.

"I wish to strongly counsel against your accompanying me into the desert, Highness. No Zar has ever undertaken such a perilous journey, and whatever your decision I humbly beg you to reconsider sending the Grand Vizier. He was an encumbrance last time and he will be so on this occasion. He serves no value on the journey—he is awkward on the camel, he is senior in years, he is another mouth to feed, he cannot swing a sword, and he is hostile toward Pez. If I must have the dwarf alongside me, I beseech you to reconsider sending the Grand Vizier."

"Lazar, I am going to share something with you now that is private. I do not fully trust the Grand Vizier to run the realm in my absence, but that is precisely what he will try to do the moment I am gone."

"Then don't leave, Highness."

"I must. I realize that until we have our heir, I am endangering Percheron's Crown by making myself an easy target for the Galinseans. Until my son is secured, Lazar, I must protect myself for Percheron's sake. At the same time, I refuse to cringe and flee, so I shall protect myself by removing myself from the city. I intend to show the people that I am fighting back in a different fashion, by helping rescue the Zaradine and our heir. I hope it will bolster my people's courage, instill a fresh wave of pride in their Crown."

Lazar murmured something beneath his breath before addressing his Zar. "Highness, if you leave and you take the Grand Vizier with you, who is going to be the representative who will deal with the inevitable delegation from Galinsea? Your enemy is being exceptionally patient, Highness. It surprises me and it reveals that they, too, are unsure of this war. That means we have a chance to arrest any escalation—but it needs to be handled with diplomacy and subtlety."

Boaz nodded. "Exactly, and why I shall ensure only the most capable of people with a definite understanding of politics. It's important that the royalty of Percheron open negotiations."

Lazar looked momentarily baffled but Herezah watched with satisfaction as dawning understanding moved across his face, his eyes widening, mouth slackening. "The Valide?" He couldn't disguise his alarm.

"She is well suited to the task. I have thought this through, Lazar. Galinsean pride would not allow them to go to war with anyone but the Zar himself. My mother's mind is as agile as yours or mine. And she can act more vulnerable than any man, plus you, more than most, should acknowledge her powerful skills in charm and seduction." Herezah smiled inwardly as Boaz's last barb hit Lazar hard. Lazar clamped his mouth tight, and stared at his Zar, his pent-up fury visible but under control.

"May I, Boaz?" Herezah asked. The Zar nodded. She stepped forward, her eyes softening, and she saw how much Lazar still disliked her. He would not forgive her easily for either this or her previous cunning, but he was clearly mindful of his debt to her. She would trade on that. "Lazar, don't you see we have to keep Boaz safe? I agree that he should not be put in any danger. Perhaps you could leave him somewhere that is relatively safe whilst you press on toward Ana? No, Boaz," she said, turning at her son's sound of disgust, "Lazar must have some say in this. He is leading this journey again, and after the last attempt I can understand his anxiety and reluctance. We must respect his knowledge and fears." She turned back to Lazar, her eyes glittering, hoping he was taking in her silent messages. "But if Ana needs help being carried, you have more hands if Boaz is there. If you need more eyes to scan the dunes, you have them—and this time you don't have your trusted Jumo at your side. Furthermore, I'm sure news of our Zar's journey would impress your father, Lazar. He would at least hold off on any engagement with our army until Boaz was ready to accept defeat or fight."

"You claim to know the Galinsean royal mind well, Valide," Lazar replied, cutting through her smugness.

"I have known you for long enough, Lazar. You have been our silent teacher."

"I am not my father," he growled.

"But you know what we say is true," Boaz joined in, his words sounding final.

Lazar bowed. "Zar Boaz. I will give my life for you, but not for the Grand Vizier. I can be no more honest than that."

"Or blunt," Boaz replied. "He can take his chances, Lazar. I feel sure we will be successful in this venture and that you will keep us all safe."

Herezah watched the Spur's jaw grind before he spoke. "There is nothing more to discuss, then, my Zar. I shall arrange our departure for early this evening. We will meet at the same location from which we left originally."

"We will be there. We will travel so lightly you'll hardly notice us, Lazar."

"I'll make the necessary arrangements. Here is the letter for my father. Valide, I imagine you are now the best person to give this to. It is a private message."

Herezah noticed he could barely hide a sneer as he handed it to her. "Good luck, Lazar. I hope you will allow me to say farewell properly."

Lazar refused to answer her, bowing instead to the Zar. "I shall take my leave, Majesty."

But Lazar didn't leave immediately. Suffused with anger, he left a message with Bin that he would be in his old sick chamber and wished to speak with the Valide if she would meet him there.

He strode through the palace toward the harem, veering

off in the direction of the wing where his former rooms were located. Once inside, he prowled around his old quarters, as restless as one of the great cats he had watched roaming up and down its caged enclosure in the royal zoo. Memories got the better of him. He left the chamber as thoughts of Herezah's seduction assaulted him for the second time today, stepping out grim-faced onto the balcony and dragging in a lungful of sea air in the hope of clearing his mind. The task ahead was fraught with danger; he really needed to be focused on Ana and Arafanz, not Herezah's petty manipulations. He waited for an hour, lost in his thoughts.

"Thinking about me?" a voice drawled as arms came around his waist.

It was unlike Lazar to allow anyone to creep up on him, and he rounded on her angrily, as much for his vulnerability as for his anger at her actions.

He pulled her arms from his body roughly. "What game are you playing at now, Herezah?"

"Lazar!" she breathed. "You are exciting when you are stirred like this."

He batted away her playful hands. "Have you finally gone mad?" he demanded. "What is in your head, convincing your son to go into the desert? You are aware that Arafanz is likely to want the entire royal family, and those that serve them, dead?"

"How can you possibly know that?" she asked, her friskiness temporarily banished.

Yes, how can I know that? he asked himself, annoyed that he'd let that information from Pez slip.

Herezah gave him the answer. "Did that madman threaten us further after he'd sent us off like dogs running in the desert?"

"Did you think he was just playing some sort of game? Did you not imagine that he would strike you down in a blink? Of course he told me! His very intention is to kill the Zar."

She frowned, arrested by his claim. "He stole Ana to lure Boaz?"

"Quite possibly."

"I thought he'd taken her for himself."

"I believe his intentions are aimed squarely at the Crown. And now you've just handed him the Zar of Percheron on a platter. I had a slim chance, Herezah, of finding and bringing back the heir of this realm. You've dashed that tiny chance now. You've not just burdened me with Boaz, inexperienced, needing day-and-night protection because of who he is, but just in case it wasn't enough of a challenge you've also lumbered me with an old man who brings nothing but more trouble. Plus there's Pez. How am I supposed to launch a rescue mission when I'm babysitting the Zar of Percheron?"

He was just short of shouting, knew he was getting through because for only the second time in all the years he'd known her, Herezah looked frightened. The first had been when she was facing death at the hands of Arafanz's warriors. Now she looked genuinely fearful of him.

"I . . . I thought it was the right thing to do. He is in greater danger here, surely?"

"The right thing for him?" Lazar mimicked. "Or for you? Now you get to play queen for a while!" He twisted back to face the sea, his disgust at her at clearly visible on his face, mixed with anger.

"Is that what you really think?"

"Tell me, Herezah, because I'm all ears as to what else could possibly inspire you to send your precious son to almost certain death!" he spat.

"I won't be spoken to like this."

"You *won't*? Or you'll have me flogged, burned, have my throat cut? I think not, Valide. Not when there's a Galinsean war fleet just itching to pull into Percheron's bay, and when our only slim hope—and that's all it is, let me assure you—of holding off war is me alive and well."

"You have an inflated idea of your importance to this realm," she hurled at him.

He surprised himself by laughing. "Is that so? Valide, without me the heir of Percheron is lost. And that means the society you know and love is finished. How do you fancy living under Galinsean rule? You'll be well and truly out of the harem—that I can promise you. But you may not like serving King Falza and he will be sure to turn you, especially, into a proper slave. No gowns, no servants, no bathing, no feasting. You'll work so hard you'll weep. Your skin will itch from lack of cleanliness, your so beautifully groomed fingernails will be filthy and broken. But let's look on the good side. You'll certainly have at least one meal a day and you'll never have to fret about the men in your life." He leaned close. "You'll have them queuing at the door and they won't have to ask your permission."

She shoved him away, breathing hard. "I do not have grand notions of ruling alone. Believe me Lazar, this was not my idea."

"Not your idea? I know it wasn't Boaz's inspiration. His mind doesn't work like that. Only yours does!"

"You forget, you arrogant Galinsean swine, that my being Boaz's proxy shifts focus away from our dalliance."

Her words hit like stones. "Swine? I'll remember that next time you're throwing your body at me. Let's be clear right now, Herezah; there was no dalliance, as you call it. There was a woman, filled with lust like a dog in heat, who took advantage of her position and a man's gratitude for her kindness, a kindness so rare in his experience with her that he was surprised into giving over a measure of trust. You may recall, through your haze of salacious desire, that this *dalliance* was one-sided."

"That's not what my hand told me." She sneered, glancing toward his crotch.

His lips thinned. "Valide, it seems you have not known enough men. A shehazzah from the docks who preys on drunken sailors with little coin could achieve the same effect, so long as I didn't have to see her face or smell her. Her hand is no different from yours, just dirtier . . . perhaps more experienced."

The sound of the slap across his face seemed to echo off the walls. For a moment, whilst he saw stars, Lazar was certain the Elim would come running to see what had created such a terrible noise.

He didn't cover his cheek with his hand, though. He turned and stared back at her, eyes glittering with such fury and threat that Herezah looked down.

"Lazar, I'm sor–" But she was not permitted to finish her apology.

"You will never raise your hand to me again, do you understand that, Valide? The next time you think about striking Galinsean royalty, be prepared to die for the privilege." She looked up at him, visibly trembling. "And I never want to feel your touch on me again. It revolts me."

"Lazar! I was just trying to protect you, I swear it."

"Protect me? From whom?"

"From Boaz. He suspects you of holding unhealthy feelings for his wife."

"You lie!"

"I do not! Ask him yourself if you dare. Didn't he warn you before you left on the desert journey? He certainly warned your little Ana to be very careful how she conducted herself. And you were both certainly cautious. You are transparent to me, Spur. I have never allowed myself to dream that you might fall under my spell as you have Ana's. But I am under yours, and call that idiocy if you must, but it prompted me to hide your sad devotion to her behind the ruse that you and I are lovers."

He continued to stare unblinking, shocked by her mangled rationale but determined not to admit to his true feelings. "You really believe you are helping me, don't you?"

"Boaz is a man of passion, Lazar—and he's too young to be as rational as you or I. He has been carried away by his ferocious love for the same woman who has seemingly stolen your heart. No," she said, a finger to her lips as she spoke softly, "do not deny it. It matters not anymore, for she can never be yours. The fact is, Ana carries our heir. And I will do everything I can to ensure that Joreb's line continues to rule Percheron. That baby is more important than you or I, than Ana . . . than Boaz himself. The boy must be brought under our safety."

"And if it's a girl?"

She shook her head. "I've had Yozem, my crone, do a foretelling. I used some of Ana's hair." She shrugged. "I stole a wisp as she slept. It is a male, Lazar. It is our new Zar—Boaz is not interested in any other son than that of his union with Ana."

"What do you gain by sending him into the desert with me?" He could still feel the sting of her slap, wondered if she'd left her livid mark upon him.

"To keep him safe, too."

He gave a harsh laugh of helplessness. "Safe?"

"Tariq said if we—"

"Tariq? What's he got to do with this?" he demanded, no longer lost in the sneer.

"This was his idea!"

His voice turned to a hiss. "The Grand Vizier put you up to this? Why?"

She looked at him as though he was being especially thick-skulled. "For the same reason, Lazar. He wants Boaz kept safe, away from the city, far from any Galinsean blade."

"Herezah, if you believe that, you are a fool."

It was her turn to show offense. "I am no fool, Spur. If not for Boaz's sake, why would he put himself through the danger of traveling through the desert?"

"Did Tariq specifically ask you to do this?"

"Of a fashion."

The pulse at Lazar's temple throbbed as he grabbed her arm. The hiss had become a growl. "Did the Grand Vizier tell you that he wanted to be on this journey?"

"You're hurting me," she warned through gritted teeth. He squeezed harder. "Yes, damn you! Yes! He insists upon it."

Lazar let her go, and twisted away from her. He needed to think but there was no time. He understood her motives finally but suddenly they were irrelevant; there was so much more at stake now.

"Lazar!" she called to his back. "Wait, I—"

He turned and sneered. "Farewell, Herezah. Enjoy the chance to punish Salmeo in your new role."

Herezah had left her son almost immediately after Lazar had taken his leave of Boaz. In the meantime, the Grand Vizier had been summoned and given the news that he would accompany the Zar and the Spur into the desert.

"I know this is a shock for you, Tariq, but we think it's best if all the senior male counselors are removed as well. I want to ensure that the Galinseans have only the Valide to discourse with."

Maliz knew it would surprise Boaz when he took a philosophical approach. He shook his head. "No, my Zar, I am not shocked. I think the idea is clever. I completely agree with your view that Falza would not consider it manly to make war upon a seemingly helpless woman. It's that damned Galinsean pride that may well save our skins."

"So you're not upset?"

"It matters not if I were, Highness. We are making vital decisions now for the good of Percheron."

"Tariq, you constantly surprise me. I imagine the desert is the last place you might wish to go, but I would appreciate your wise counsel alongside myself and the Spur."

Inwardly, Maliz smiled. Herezah had done her job so very well. "My Zar, it would be an honor to stay close to you and serve you however you see fit. I thought you said Pez was going along as well."

Maliz watched the Zar hesitate before replying. He wondered what that meant. "Er, yes, he is."

"So it's a party of four."

"The Spur reckons that is three people too many."

The Grand Vizier obliged with a soft ghost of a smile. "I imagine he would. What can I do? Shall I make arrangements for Pez as well as us?"

And again he noticed a slight hedging in the response from

the Zar. Why was his mentioning Pez making Boaz feel uncomfortable? "My Zar, I have to tell you that I believe your royal jester is frightened of me."

Boaz nodded. "The Elim mentioned there was an incident this morning."

"A misunderstanding, Highness. Pez decided I was attacking him when I was simply checking that he was all right. He had fallen down."

"Pez can misconstrue anyone's intentions, Tariq," Boaz replied. Maliz sensed that the Zar was choosing his words with care.

"I shall do my utmost to make friends with him on this trip."

"I think it would be best if you kept your distance, Tariq. In fact, I may have to insist upon it. Pez is highly agitated. I've seen him and whatever actually happened is of little consequence. He is disturbed and distressed . . . and that makes him difficult to handle. We cannot risk his jeopardizing our journey. But I cannot leave him in the palace. He can disrupt delicate talks and he is best under the control of myself or Lazar."

Maliz was delighted—now that his place on the caravan was secured and his plans were taking shape, he felt the time was right to deal with the dwarf and his suspicions.

"I shall be careful to give him a very wide berth, then, Majesty, as you request."

It was no request, of course, but still he watched the Zar nod. "That's good. We need Pez calm for this journey."

"Where is the jester now, Highness? I shall keep a distance."

"No need to worry yourself. He is at Lazar's house and safe."

"Then let me hurry to finalize everything in my office and with my palace staff, Highness, in order that I can accompany your karak to the meeting point this evening."

Maliz left and hurried back to his official chambers in the palace. He wasted no time summoning a runner, scribbling a note, and giving the servant instructions as to where the note was to be delivered.

In very little time two strangers were admitted to the Grand Vizier's chambers.

Pez, keeping to himself at the Spur's house, had been deeply lost in thought at Lazar's hastily scrawled message.

Tariq, the Spur had carefully written, *is up to something. He apparently insisted he come along, conscripted the help of the Valide to push his cause . . . and has been successful. What does this mean?*

Pez had been trying to work it out ever since, pondering every possible angle as to why Maliz would run the risk of this second foray into the desert and a potential clash with Arafanz.

"It has to be Ana," he muttered to himself. "He must sense the same potential I always have."

His mind drifted as he considered every possible scenario. How had the demon settled his attention on Ana and why? Astray in his meandering thoughts, Pez allowed himself to feel too secure in Lazar's private sanctuary. His Lore sense was too preoccupied; he missed the stealthy arrival of two men, never saw the blow coming.

He awoke groggily to find himself trussed like an animal for slaughter and to see eyes he recognized, despite the disguise of the jamoosh, staring intently at him.

"Hello again, Pez," the Grand Vizier said. "Now I know you must be feeling rather ill—that's a very nasty blow you took—and whether you understand me or not, I am going to do the polite thing and warn you that you have been given the root of topriz. Do you know what that is?"

Pez stared back, silent.

"I'll tell you anyway," Maliz said calmly. "It is the essence of a plant that curiously loosens the tongue. Not many people know of it—its use has died out, you see—but it was very popular a few centuries ago in wartime to help release information from captured enemy soldiers."

Pez's head was throbbing. Nausea began to overwhelm him but he didn't dare draw on the Lore to help himself. Instead he began to recite the names of all the root plants he could think of.

The Grand Vizier smiled. "Mad? Or somehow impossibly feigning it?"

Pez began to weep. "My arms hurt." He was hoping it sounded especially childish, as if he couldn't concentrate on anything but the pain.

"I know, but it won't last too long. Time is short. The Spur will be back soon, I imagine. But I have him watched right now, I know his every movement."

Pez knew the Grand Vizier was looking for any signs that he was being understood, so he sang softly over all the man's words.

"I'm going to be sick," he warned, belching.

"Go ahead, Pez."

Pez ignored him. He thought about screaming but figured it would be useless; they'd just hit him again. He realized both the other men were not far away and there could be more outside.

Instead he began to count, in Merlinean, in multiples of eight.

"Pez, who is Lyana?" the Grand Vizier asked reasonably.

Pez belched several times amidst his counting. He really did feel as though he was going to be ill all over Lazar's floor. Blood was trickling into one eye, too. They must have hit him hard enough to open his scalp, perhaps even crack his skull. It hurt enough. Was he drifting again?

"I think you are Iridor and I want to know who Lyana is," Maliz pressed.

In reply Pez spoke louder, managed to break wind twice during his recitation of the Merlinean numerals. He thought about changing into Iridor but that would achieve too little in return for giving the demon proof of what he searched for. In remaining Pez and helpless, he could keep Maliz hunting and desperate. He was glad his body and mind were stronger than the drug.

His captor looked up, frustrated, and nodded, and Pez couldn't help but wonder what that signal could mean. It didn't take long to find out.

11

Boaz had summoned all of the Pecherese officials and dignatories—anyone of status who answered to the Crown—
and now they were all crowded into the Grand Hall of the
Stone Palace, their agitation evident, whispering amongst
themselves.

The young Zar realized that they were anticipating this to
be his declaration of war and they feared the words that would
almost certainly signify their own deaths. They believed that
the Galinseans would prevail, that no Percherese male would
be left alive—he could sense this notion in the room, see it reflected in their stricken gazes.

Boaz bit his lip, vexed that the Grand Vizier was not present. At least the Valide looked stunning, and this gathering was
primarily for her benefit. The announcement that Percheron
was not going to war tomorrow would bring an equal measure
of surprise and assurance for many present.

At this thought his gaze fell upon the large, dark bulk of Salmeo. The eunuch looked smug, no doubt fully confident of his own safety. Boaz was certain the Grand Master Eunuch had already set up his own escape route for when the time came to flee. How unlike Salmeo was to the Elim he ruled; those warriors would gladly give their lives rather than yield their courage. The chief eunuch, by contrast, wouldn't think twice even about the women—girls, in fact—that he would leave behind to face the abuse of the Galinsean soldiers.

Boaz blinked as the fat eunuch's gaze met his and he watched with a grinding hate low in his gut as Salmeo's tongue slipped out, wetting his lips in that habitual way. Then the Grand Master Eunuch's head nodded, a soft smile of acknowledgment lifting the rope scar along his cheek. And Boaz felt deep satisfaction that his mother would finally have status beyond Salmeo. What recriminations she might be able to make in this new role against the eunuch would be her business, and Boaz, for one, would turn a blind eye. He looked forward to seeing the effect of his announcement on the Grand Master Eunuch's face, for no one in this room would feel the reach of the Valide's temporary new status more keenly than Salmeo.

He began. "Brothers . . . and Valide," he said, bowing his head once to his mother. "I have asked you here this morning to share crucial news regarding Percheron's future." He held his hand up for silence as alarmed mutterings rose. "Let me assure you that the Crown is doing everything within its power to avoid war," and then he began crafting the explanation for his departure to the desert in such a way that anyone listening could be forgiven for thinking it was more like a victory address than a prewar speech.

Anyone that is, except Salmeo. He alone felt the undercurrent of this announcement and what it could mean.

The Grand Master Eunuch had come to this gathering out of courtesy. He had been asked because of his position and, no doubt, because of his contacts across the realm that could be used to spread the word of the heir he was hearing so much about. But he had no intention of fighting it out to the last, of bravely dying for the harem. Zarab's Fire! He would not put himself at the mercy of the Galinseans, who would likely take genuine glee in further punishing the senior royal eunuch and the keeper of so many beautiful girls.

No, Salmeo was canny enough to know that remaining in Percheron, should the situation escalate to war, would be suicide. And his escape plans were well advanced. He had hoarded and stashed coin at strategic points for easy access and had supplies already in place along the river. He intended to escape by royal barge initially, then switch to a sturdy riverboat that had been positioned at a secret location. He would travel with two well-armed and capable accomplices—not Elim—who would be responsible for his needs and for rowing him to relative safety. Horses and covered cart would be waiting to whisk him further from Percheron, headed northeast to begin with, then south.

Extraordinarily enough, he might actually be heading in the direction of home. Whether he got back to his village was left to be seen and he didn't much care if he did or not. That place wasn't truly home anymore but simply the country in which he had been born before being captured by slavers. He had been taken at the age of four with his father and older sister, seven at the time. The children had watched their mother's throat slashed open with such force it had nearly taken off her head when she'd fought back against the attackers. He wondered at the luck of his two older brothers to be playing in the cave network above their village at the time of the raid. And he had watched with wonder the fight go out of his father—a huge, proud man, leader of his tribe—as the slavers had systematically begun killing a child of the village each time he refused to cooperate. In the end his father had had no choice but to capitulate to their demands; the three members of their family had been selected to go with the caravan back to Percheron. The slavers had not been Percherese, of course, but that mattered not to the young boy—Percheron was the destination and that made it the culprit in his shocked, immature mind.

Salmeo's father had died of an infection from one of the wounds he had sustained in the initial brawl following the attack on the village, although his youngest son knew the truth, had watched as the chieftain deliberately pushed his chained hands into the decomposing bowels of a large dead animal their captors had forced him to lie next to. Salmeo could still remember the powerful stench of rotting meat, could still recall the moment when his proud father had smeared those huge hands, now dripping with the creature's waste, into his wound, his eyes full of apology to his son.

"Look after your sister," were his last coherent words to Salmeo. The chieftain had begun his slow descent into death during the course of that night, and two days later their captors had left him on the path, still bound, to die alone in terrible pain. He mercifully had slipped into a delirium by then, but Salmeo had looked into his father's blood-filled eyes and seen the flare of pride that the chieftain had somehow beaten the slavers. That moment of despair for Salmeo but triumph for his proud father had shaped the boy. Just a few years later, when a cleric was proclaiming him "of age" and Salmeo realized what was to happen to him, he had sworn that he would rise above being simply eunuch; he would carve his own position, his own base of power. He might bow to a new royal, but privately he would never give loyalty, and everything he would do in the future would be for his own gain. He hated the world for what it had done to his family; he especially hated the Percherese and their pampered Zars. Salmeo smiled; now, almost five decades later, he had been true to that promise. He had even killed his own sister, slipping out from the palace before she was to be bedded by a man who had recently purchased her. He had kissed her gently good-bye and strangled her as she slept, for fear that she might become a plaything for a filthy Percherese. She had certainly been beautiful enough to catch the eye of a wealthy man and she had been just ten, ripe and already long-limbed and graceful as a ferez deer. He remembered brushing his fingers over her lids to cover those once laughing liquid eyes, dark as the feathers of a crow she had once kept as a pet. She was a chieftain's daughter and she had been forced to be a servant, but she was bed slave to no one. He had seen to it.

In his own particular way, over the years, he had stayed true to his oath, disrupting the life of the royals as best he could. He had been there when Zar Koriz had infamously died by the banks of the river after eating the poisonous bloatfish. No one knew that the Zar's fine knifework had been flawless in removing the deadly fish liver but that a young, fleet-footed Salmeo had ensured that a little of the liver was tossed back into the food and eaten by the Zar. And Joreb? Oh, he had bided his time. When the Zar had chosen to display his prowess on the horse and had come uncharacteristically unstuck, Salmeo had seized the chance he had waited on for decades, and poisoned Joreb.

A tiny amount of drezden added regularly to the Zar's food had worked wonders; the physics, too frightened for their own lives, had not picked up on the poison trail and had never made the connection that the Zar had been murdered. This recollection made Salmeo think about his most recent use of drezden. Such a pity, he thought, that someone had been wary enough to spot his favored poison in the Spur not so many moons ago. He had gotten away with it, regardless, but the death of cringing Shaz, the young inflicter who had known too much, had been necessary. Again Salmeo's patience had been rewarded. He had waited for the chaos of the first Galinsean delegation to distract everyone at the palace and then it had been so easy to contrive a drowning for the hapless Shaz. It had been reported back to his masters, of course, that he had drunk too much liquor one night with his winnings from a game of krosh, either falling into the harbor or being pushed by disgruntled losers of the game. Either way Salmeo's secret was safe. Another loose end tied off.

Salmeo actually smiled at his own cleverness, although the expression died on his face as he came out of his private thoughts and registered the last few words of the Zar's most recent sentence. Had he heard right? It seemed the Zar was mindful that not everyone would believe what he had just said and was reinforcing the point.

"Yes, brothers, you heard me correctly. I am leaving our realm in the very capable hands of the Valide, who has my authority to rule by proxy until I return. Forget that she is female, that she is my mother, that she belongs to the harem. From today, she is your Zar and you will obey her. She has my instructions and I trust her implicitly not only to follow them but to rule well in my stead. Anyone found to be defying the Crown

Valide, as she is to be addressed, will face death upon my return. So, my brothers, I implore you to help her through this highly difficult time. Do as I say and spread word through Percheron that I go in search of the filth that has defiled my wife, stolen the heir of Percheron, and insulted my reign. I will bring him back for your pleasure and let the people decide his fate. His name is Arafanz . . . let everybody know."

Salmeo didn't hear any more. He couldn't care less about Ana, or the heir, or which renegade was insulting whom. But he did care about his own huge neck and how it was threatened right now by the woman staring down from the dais, directly at him, and clearly smiling behind her veil.

Pez was gasping for breath. Physical pain was not something he had had to face much of during his time in Percheron and he had always felt safe in the knowledge that the Lore could protect him anyway. Not now, it couldn't, not with Maliz bending over him. He knew that if asked, he would not even be able to describe the pain racking his small misshapen body.

The Grand Vizier had screamed at him throughout the shocking agony he had inflicted upon Pez, but though his body now lay slumped, broken, slashed in places, and even partly dismembered, he had given the demon nothing but nonsense. He had wondered, amid the exquisitely bright pain, how he'd become so brave. He'd had nothing but willpower and the memory of Zafira's courage under the same torment. But it was that thought of Zafira that had urged him to utter the few words he did. Perhaps some small good could come out of his death.

The blood loss had to be enormous. He could feel himself floating. He wished he could let go and simply float away but

Maliz ensured the pain was sufficient to bring him back to the nightmare.

"Well!" the Vizier said, holding up Pez's little finger, bloodied and hacked from his hand. "That's the last of them," he said, throwing it aside to land near the other nine, discarded on Lazar's tiles.

"What did he say?" a new voice asked.

"Not that it's any of your business as a hired thug, but he told me that the Valide was made pregnant by the Spur in the desert but is hiding it well. I'm being led to believe that Lyana is connected to the Valide . . . does that make sense?" he asked, the sarcasm bitter and cutting.

"None of it. But I think he's dying."

"That's the point." Maliz sneered.

"You never said anything about killing the royal's dwarf."

"I'm not sure I ever mentioned killing you either," Pez heard the Grand Vizier reply and assumed he had dragged a blade across the man's throat, for fresh blood gushed over Pez before the man collapsed on top of him with a strangled groan.

He heard, rather than saw, the Grand Vizier stand up from his grisly work as the man's accomplice ran in.

"Are you going to kill me or get paid twice as much?" the demon demanded. "Your friend's always been a liability. Finish the job and have his share." Maliz was only barely controlling his anger, Pez realized, and inwardly he found a dull spike of humor as he understood that the demon was confused. His mind was likely racing back to the desert, wondering how true the dwarf's claim might be. Pez hadn't admitted knowing anything about Lyana but the mere suggestion of intrigue was leading the demon's overactive mind to make assumptions.

Pez didn't hear the second thug reply but he presumed

money spoke louder than the threat of death because the dead companion was suddenly being dragged off him. Pez played dead himself. He couldn't be far from it anyway.

He heard a guttural roar before feeling a rib crumple inward as the Grand Vizier kicked him, no doubt in deep frustration. Fortunately his head was turned to the side, so Maliz did not see him squeeze his eyes tighter as a new wave of pain coursed through him. He prayed to Lyana for a quick death.

"Wrap him in that rug and toss him into the sea. Get someone to clean up this mess. No evidence of bloodshed. Be quick!" the Grand Vizier said with obvious disgust. "What a waste of my time!"

The burly accomplice began to roll Pez into the blood-soaked rug. It took every ounce of the dwarf's determination, holding the face of Lyana in his mind, not to scream out in agony.

"What did you want from him?" the man asked. "Everyone knows he's a half-wit."

"Feebleminded or not—I needed to know which."

The man laughed, the sound dull through the rug. "You believed he could be sane?" he asked incredulously, and chuckled again.

"Not after what I just did to him, no," Maliz said, his tone as sharp as his hidden blade. "Get rid of him and your friend here." Pez heard what had to be a pouch of gold hitting the floor. "There's plenty more of that if you keep your mouth shut. If you don't, you'll be dead before you have a chance to spend the first karel. Be warned."

He didn't hear anything further. Presumably the Grand Vizier had left. Within minutes after being heaved onto the shoulder of the paid thug, Pez felt himself falling. He was barely conscious now but just aware enough to realize he had obviously been tossed over the side of Lazar's balcony. As he fell into the sea he had only a moment to send his undying faith to Lyana with his apology for failing her once again. Death had come sooner than expected.

Although the rug absorbed a lot of the impact, he felt the last of his intact bones sigh and give way just seconds before he began to drown and Lyana welcomed her most beloved disciple to her dark and icy depths.

And as Pez's drowning began, the skies overhead darkened with uncharacteristically heavy clouds that momentarily obliterated the sun, plunging the city into gloom. At the same moment many Percherese would later swear an earthquake began as a series of tremors, adding yet more terror to the already besieged land. The initial cracks that had curiously formed down the great giants who guarded the harbor now widened alarmingly and some believed their precious icons were preparing to crumble and crash into the sea.

But the giants were not disintegrating. Instead they bellowed in anguish to the only person they knew would hear.

Lazar, sitting on a horse, awaiting the arrival of his Zar, seething that Pez was not present as they had arranged, had looked up, surprised, as the heavens darkened without warning. A minute later he was overwhelmed by the outpouring of grief that hit his body so hard he had to dismount, half falling to the ground as Beloch and Ezram groaned into his mind: *Iridor dies!*

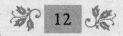

12

Ana was leaning comfortably against Arafanz's chest as he reached his arms around her to hold the reins, guiding the camel on its plodding journey across the sands.

She had fully lost track of how long she'd been at the fortress now, but her taut, swollen belly told her that enough time had passed to be nearing the end of her pregnancy. And although the passage of time had been vague for her, she was aware of the subtle change that had washed over her during her confinement. Curiously, for the first time in her life she felt at peace. Since the day in the cave when the glittering pillars had welcomed her, Ana had felt as though she belonged—not to anyone in particular, but to this period in time, to this place ... especially to the desert. If not for the quiet pain of losing Lazar for the second time, Ana would say she was happy ... truly happy.

That early, horribly insistent nausea of her pregnancy had

passed and her baby had begun to move inside her a couple of moons earlier. Low in her body she had felt the faintest of flutterings. At first she thought she was imagining it but it recurred, becoming stronger. Consciousness? Her baby had become a person! The fluttering that she had convinced herself was a tentative unfurling of a hand had now evolved into something more dramatic—akin to an awakening. This baby seemed to be constantly on the move, one moment low, the next high in her chest. She was explaining it now to Arafanz.

"Feel here," she said, taking his hand and guiding it to her belly in what was a familiar gesture.

"Ah, that feels decidedly like an elbow," he replied, genuine pleasure in his voice.

"Very good. I forget you're an old hand at this."

She couldn't see him shrugging but felt it. "I didn't take enough notice of Razeen growing in my wife's belly. I regret it deeply. Now that I share this baby's growth with you, I realize it is something magical, something every father should participate in."

Ana sighed. Even though she had quipped that she still felt like a child herself, this child coming into her life made her feel suddenly very grown up. And in truth she was thoroughly enjoying this maturity. It helped that the enforced separation from the harem and everything that had become so familiar to her gave her enormous pleasure as well. She felt at peace. "That's a good way to describe it. My child seems to know precisely what to do and when. It's a magic only it understands."

"The baby and your body are one, Ana. Don't forget that your body also knows what to do. It possesses its own knowledge of how to nurture the babe, keep him safe, nourish him. I am sure he hears your voice and knows you already." He paused, adding a moment later, "To be a mother is to be closest of all to Lyana."

She snuggled farther back into the security of his chest, privately amazed by how comfortable the two of them had become when they were alone together. "Yes. I wish I understood what she wants from me."

He leaned his chin on her head. "We shall see what your role is in due course, although I say again that it is the son you carry that is of most interest to Lyana."

Ana didn't think so but kept her own counsel as she wondered at which point over the past few moons she and Arafanz had become close friends. All animosity had disappeared. Now they ate together of an evening, took regular walks, and especially enjoyed these rides alone. She watched from the rooftop of the fortress as he continued to train his men for the coming battle and he was always aware of her presence, acknowledging her with a glance, a brief wave, sometimes that rare smile. They were actually never long apart these days. But the knowledge of what Arafanz planned for the palace and all attached to it sat like a festering sore in her thoughts. She picked at it often, felt it bleed along with her sorrow for Boaz and all his dreams for Percheron. Yet she hated herself for allowing it to scab over so easily when Arafanz permitted his caring to shine through and charm her. These quiet times alone with him away from the fortress were special; when it was like this, she didn't see him as Lyana's zealot but simply as a man, with all the usual frailties and desires. She sensed he was allowing himself to cleave far closer to her than he knew he should. There had been moments when what was disguised as simple, polite gestures—a guiding hand, a helping arm, moving a wisp of hair from her face, or more recently, briefly massaging her back when she mentioned how much it ached—felt tender, meaningful. Right now, her leaning in so carefree a way against his broad chest, his chin resting casually atop her head—anyone could be forgiven for thinking them lovers. If she was honest, this shift in their relationship frightened Ana. She loved Lazar—that would never change—but it scared her that she could harbor such intense fondness for someone else.

There! She'd allowed it out into her mind. She was attracted to Arafanz in spite of the darkness she attached to him; she would be lying to herself if she admitted anything else. The attraction, she knew, had a lot to do with her longing for Lazar; the two men were very similar. But Arafanz had qualities of his own that she found irresistible, especially his vulnerability. For all his arrogance and unswerving faith in himself . . . Arafanz was mortal. He was prone to all the same temptations of his men, even though he had convinced himself he was impregnable to any attack, especially any weakness in his heart. She sensed, rather than knew, that Arafanz was in love with her. He had never voiced anything along such lines but her intuition told her he only barely controlled his feelings. She wanted to hate him as completely as she had when she had first met him but she had seen a different side to him that she enjoyed. And now, with the birth of her child almost upon her, Arafanz had become her closest confidant—the friend she trusted.

He gently squeezed her shoulders. "Are you all right? You're very quiet."

"I was just thinking about us."

"Us?"

"What is this relationship between us, Arafanz?"

His hands stopped working. "I don't understand."

"You do. You're being coy. And there's no need to because

there's only us. You are my captor and yet you go to such lengths to give me freedom. You are my enemy but you are also my close friend. When we met, you treated me with scorn and yet why do I feel something else blossoming between us? Is this a deliberate ploy or can you not help our bond either?"

His large hands returned to massaging her neck through the linens of her sand veil. It felt wonderful and she wished she could ask him to pay attention to her lower back, which was particularly painful today. She hadn't yet mentioned the soft bands of pressure that came now and then, moving up and down her belly. She had to assume these were early warnings of what was to come when her son was ready to enter the world.

Arafanz's voice was thick with emotion when he finally replied. "I want to be impartial about you, Ana, but that is not as easy as it seemed to be before I'd met you. Ellyana should have warned me."

"Is that why you kept me locked up and remote?"

Again he didn't answer immediately. "You are too insightful. Yes, I didn't want to know you. I just wanted to follow my cause, keep to my set path. We have been building toward this for too many years—since the day you were born in fact—before, even."

Again the mention of his knowing of her birth staggered her inwardly. But she kept her poise. "Is that why you punished those men?"

"Not entirely. I did need to show you how committed we are to Lyana."

"Not entirely?"

"I was angry. Hurting you, threatening you, did help to make me feel immune to you."

She gave a soft anguished groan. "It's so wrong. I wish we could give those men their lives back."

"They gave them willingly."

"To Lyana perhaps. But you made them sacrifice their lives for no gain in the cause to which they pledged their lives."

He held a long silence this time before clearing his throat. "You shame me."

"You didn't need me to do it. You've felt the shame anyway."

"You know me too well."

"I hardly know you at all."

"That's where you're wrong, lovely Ana," he said, stroking her aching back.

She arched it, unsure whether her reaction was from pleasure or fright from enjoying it, an attempt to escape his touch.

He was about to say more when the skies deepened above them. "What—" Arafanz began.

And Ana shrieked as a sharp pain seared through her belly, and her baby—she knew it was the child even though her head told her it was impossible—opened a passage into her mind and spoke to her in an ancient tongue. "Iridor dies. It is not his time." The voice was beautiful but anguished and it tore at Ana's heartstrings.

Disoriented, Ana overbalanced, while Arafanz, in an effort to prevent her injuring herself, slid off the beast with her, toppling below and breaking her fall as they hit the soft sand.

"Ana . . . Ana!" he shouted, terror infusing them both.

She hadn't realized she had screamed Lyana's name just before they fell but she could hear it echoing off the rock face.

"Please," Arafanz begged, scrabbling out from beneath her, "tell me what is happening. Have your pains begun?"

She didn't know what to tell him. She shook her head in silent fear as tears leaked out of her eyes and dampened her hair. *Surely Pez was not dying?*

Arafanz was hovering above her, his face a mask of worry. "Speak to me. What has occurred?"

"It's Iridor," she gulped. "I think he's dead."

As he sank, the rug unraveled about him and Pez finally found himself floating free in the depths of the Faranel. It was soundless and dark and it would not be long now, for he didn't have the strength or ability to do anything but give himself to the water. The burning in his lungs distracted him from the throb of his fingerless hands.

As he began a final prayer to Lyana, knowing he had but moments, for there was truly was no more breath in his aching lungs and his chest was racked with pain from broken ribs, he saw a vision floating toward him. It began as a soft green light that strengthened into a shimmering brightness, so bright that it was almost unbearable by the time the figure was clear enough to make out.

Ellyana drifted fully into view and gave him a heartbreaking smile. Her luster seemed to dim the terrible pain and the exquisite desire to give up his last and most precious air. She was young and dazzlingly beautiful. He felt suddenly safe in her cocoon of luminescence.

"I am dying," he said, shocked that he could speak.

"Not yet, dear Pez. This is not your time."

"But how can I live?"

"If you were going to drown, believe me, the Faranel would have claimed you by now. Maliz should have finished you off himself; if he had, we could not interfere. This is his mistake.

He will rue this day." She smiled again. "You must trust me now."

"I always have," Pez replied, entranced by her shimmering beauty and the realization that he was no longer struggling for breath, no longer cold or even frightened.

"That's not true. You privately question my motives."

"But I do obey you," he qualified.

"Because you know in your heart that I am not your enemy."

"Then what are you?"

Her brilliance intensified. "You already know. I belong to Lyana—I am an extension of her. A messenger, you could say, a disciple, her servant. As are you. We must trust each other. There are too few of us to not believe."

"It's not easy when none of the few you refer to know what is going on," he admonished softly. "Iridor, above all, should know."

"It is this factor that will help us prevail," she soothed, floating before him, her golden tresses stretching out in tendrils and waving gently in the water.

"So I am saved? I know she commands the waters," he said, mesmerized.

Ellyana smiled. "Lyana *is* the water. She is the sky, the wind, the sun, the desert."

"I am to live, this is what you're here to tell me?" he clarified.

She nodded, her hair weaving patterns in the currents as fish darted amongst the silky strands. "There is a condition."

Pez's heart sank. "Why am I not surprised?"

"It is not my doing. Maliz has destroyed your body, my friend. That is certainly dying. You must leave it behind and emerge from these depths as Iridor. You will be whole, but you must understand that you can never return to the being you were before. You are no longer Pez." Her tone was sorrowful and Pez appreciated that she grasped how deeply her news must hurt him. His body had been hardly attractive and his face had not been pretty but they were what his goddess had given him; the dwarf's body belonged to him and made him who he was. Iridor had chosen him, not the other way around.

She could read his mind, it seemed. "Surely you would not choose death over life?"

He didn't answer straightaway; he needed to let the soft grief that her revelation provoked dissipate slightly. She let his silence lengthen, happy to drift nearby, bathing him in her bright sea-green glow. "Not if by living I can serve Lyana longer," he finally spoke.

She smiled. "Iridor still has his role. There are lives to be saved and a battle still to win."

He fixed Ellyana with a baleful stare. "Then what are we waiting for?"

The sun reemerged and the skies lightened instantly. Lazar looked back at the city and its return to its more usual sparkling landscape. He had no idea where those angry clouds had come from, and though they had seemed unnatural, he knew anything connected with the weather around Samazen time should not surprise him.

He realized his head hurt from the voices and from the dire revelation they had brought. His emotional thoughts about Ana, about Herezah's behavior and how easily he had been compromised by her, and especially about his father's potential presence only made his confusion and pain worse. He looked out across the Faranel and wondered if the King was doing the same. Was he thinking about the son he despised and yet would honor by massacring another realm? When had it come to this? Had it been only such a short while ago that he had been wandering through the city he loved, looking forward to a spicy ratha at the famous emporium? It felt as though he had lived a lifetime since that messenger had burst through its doors and interrupted his breakfast with the grim news of Zar Joreb's death. The excellent, totally controlled, and unemotional life that he had so carefully shaped over so many years had changed in that instant. And not just changed because of the delivery of that news, he thought; his life had dramatically twisted and turned to leave him near death, forever scarred, deeply in love and more shattered than he had ever felt.

And now stone statues—seemingly lifeless sculptures—were talking to him! And had just delivered chilling news. He couldn't believe the dwarf had perished, and whilst he dithered, wavering between shock and disbelief, Beloch spoke again.

Lazar, Iridor lives.

Relief flooded his body, and in his desire for information, it seemed suddenly natural to be having this conversation with a stone statue. *What happened?*

We do not know. But we felt him dying.

And now?

He has survived the attack.

He is completely safe?

As Iridor only. He is no longer the dwarf.

Lazar felt his gut twist. *Where is Maliz?* he demanded.

We are not connected to him, only to Lyana's disciples.

But he made you, Lazar insisted.

Beloch gave a sound that was part sigh, part moan. *His evil touch is upon us, yes, but we do not feel him and he cannot feel us, hear us, sense us.*

Where does this magic you possess come from?

The giant gave a sound of amusement. *We used his.*

His? You'll have to explain that.

Ellyana taught us. She told us how to use the darkest of his magic and twist it, knead it . . . mold it, you could say, into something he could never understand.

I'm not sure I do either. Is that why she asked me to stop by you when I was being rowed to Star Island?

I'm impressed you remember.

It was only a fleeting moment of consciousness. But I remember you towering up above us and her whispering to you.

Maliz used a sinister magic to turn us to stone. It remained inside with us. Ellyana showed us how to release it, use it to begin to break the bondage of the stone. That night she was thanking us for our steadfastness.

Did you use it to reach me?

Yes.

And he can't sense it.

He wouldn't recognize the magic anymore. It is like the Lore, completely beyond his comprehension, although he can sense its sinister power.

The Lore is wild, I'm told.

It is. As is your magic.

It was Lazar's turn to be amused. *I have no magic, Beloch.*

Does it not strike you as odd to be talking to me now? Do you believe anyone can do this?

No. But I presumed the magic was all yours. All one-sided.

You are wrong.

Lazar couldn't imagine what the giant was referring to,

wasn't ready to pursue the conversation until he'd had time to think it through. *So I can talk to you when I want?*

We are only ever a whisper away. You are only now learning how, though. Until now, we could only reach you at times of great stress . . . the drezden fever, especially. Hold on to this. Remember how it feels.

Lazar, bewildered, changed the subject. *So I continue with this journey.*

Yes.

What about Pez?

There is no Pez anymore, and Iridor has his own journey.

Lazar wanted to shout, hurl something at the giant. Beloch used the same irritating, cryptic manner of speaking that he recalled Ellyana employing.

You must release us very soon, Lazar.

I told you, I don't know how!

Think about what we have discussed today. You alone can do it—must do it!—or Percheron is lost.

Lazar, still distracted, was impressed to see that Boaz arrived not in a karak, flanked by a host of guards, but covered head to toe in a white jamoosh with only two other people at his side, one of them his mother, similarly disguised.

"We thought it best to leave the palace unobtrusively," Boaz explained. Lazar could hear the tinge of excitement in his voice.

"You were wise to do so, Majesty."

"Let's drop my title from now on."

Lazar nodded, again impressed by the Zar's wisdom. "And we should change your name. What should we call you?"

"I have always liked the name Fayiz."

Herezah squirmed. "Oh, Boaz, that's so common."

"Victorious," Lazar translated. "It is a good sentiment and a strong name," he assured Boaz, ignoring the Valide.

"It's a favorite name of mine, so I like to think of it as destiny that I can use it," Boaz said, his eyes shining.

"Well, my Lion, you are our destiny."

"No, Mother, my son is our destiny. He will be called Fayiz if we find him."

"When we find him," Lazar countered. "I do not mean to return empty-handed."

The Spur couldn't imagine that it was possible for the Zar to swell any larger. He was bursting to be on his way. "I have picked out a horse for you, Fayiz," he said, giving the young royal a wry grin. "It's not as fine as you are used to riding, nor is it a stallion, but we will give ourselves away if we are on magnificent animals. She's hardly a nag but she will do you proud." He nodded toward the chestnut filly.

Boaz seemed untroubled by the horse's lack of pedigree, moving to stroke her muzzle, whispering to her.

Herezah spoke up. "Lazar, it is all very well racing off into the desert with the ruler of Percheron, but how can we ensure his safety?"

"We can't, Valide. But it was never my idea to bring Boaz along. With all due respect, my Zar, if you give me the option, I would leave you behind without a moment's hesitation."

"Mother! The decision is made. Please do not fuss or ask any more irrelevant questions," Boaz snapped.

Herezah pasted a suitably chastened expression on her face. "My son, I will worry for you until I see you safely delivered back to us."

"I know," Boaz said, all aggression gone. "And in the meantime you will serve me well in looking after the realm. You know what to do."

Herezah looked up and nodded, her gaze firmly fixed on the Spur when she replied. "I will make haste to meet with King Falza, or his representative, immediately." Lazar flinched, felt his lips thin in an effort to suppress any overreaction. "And assure him that I have firsthand experience that his son is alive and well," she added, her tone laced with innuendo.

"Valide—"

"Mother," Boaz interrupted, glaring again at his parent. "Lazar, please. We are too far down the path now to worry about petty matters. Mother, do not inflame the situation with your intimations. I have already told you what I want said to the King of Galinsea. Follow my orders or don't take on the role of Crown Valide."

Her eyes glinted with amusement. "I shall do only your bidding, my Lion. Be safe. Do I get a farewell kiss, Lazar?"

Boaz sighed as Lazar bristled and snarled, "Farewell, Valide. Give my saluations to my family." He turned briskly to the Zar. "Where is the Grand Vizier?"

"Coming. He sent a message that he is minutes behind us."

"And Pez?"

Boaz frowned. "I thought he would already have met up with you."

Lazar felt his anxiety deepen. He had somehow impossibly hoped that Beloch had been wrong. "I have not seen him."

The Zar gave a sound of exasperation. "Both Tariq and Pez late?"

"Coincidence, no?" Lazar muttered.

"They detest each other, Lazar. I'd hardly say they were deliberately in tandem."

"You may be surprised," Lazar added but turned away as further confusion flared in the royal's gaze. He would achieve nothing by making snide bites at the Zar, who was wholly oblivious to what was being played out around him.

"Mother, Ghassal will see you back to the palace. He will be your right-hand man throughout my absence and has orders to protect you with his life. You will do as he says whenever you leave the palace—is that understood?"

"Of course."

"Then wish me luck, Mother."

"Come home safely, Boaz."

Lazar couldn't help but wonder if Herezah meant that. She had at last her chance to rule by royal authority—could there be a more perfect scenario for this woman?

As she bowed to Boaz, a plain karak arrived, bearing the Grand Vizier.

Boaz looked over his mother's bent shoulders. "Ah, Tariq, we were wondering where you were."

The Grand Vizier all but tumbled from the silk screens. "Forgive me, Majesty. I had to finalize a lot of irritating but necessary state business."

Boaz gave a look of contrived sympathy. "We are leaving now, so instruct your entourage to get back to the palace before it draws attention."

Lazar noticed that the Grand Vizier had the good sense to look suitably admonished once he had taken in the surrounds and realized that even his Zar had arrived without the fanfare of a karak and bearers.

"Again, forgive me, Majesty. My legs are not as young as yours and I knew we needed to make haste."

"Tariq, you seem younger each day," the Valide gibed, before inclining her head once more to her Zar and throwing a final glance toward Lazar. She turned and began sauntering back down the hill, seemingly carefree and in no hurry—as though she had nothing more important on her mind than what flavor sherbet to choose that evening.

Lazar couldn't help himself. "I do hope you've made a wise decision, Fayiz."

Boaz nodded, looking equally concerned.

"Fayiz?" the Grand Vizier queried.

Lazar turned his attention from the retreating and graceful back of the Valide. "And you shall be called Garjan."

"Garjan?" Maliz repeated. "I don't know that word."

"It's very old, very colloquial Galinsean," Lazar said, realizing too late that his couched insult could backfire should the demon recognize the word's true meaning: *of evil import.*

"Oh? How does that translate to our language?"

Lazar nodded. "It means 'wise one' and is usually directed at our older citizens who have earned great respect."

The Grand Vizier smiled. "Indeed? How appropriate. Garjan—yes, I like its sound. So we move in disguise now?"

"We do," Lazar replied. "Do we go on without Pez?" He directed the question to Boaz, but kept his eye on the Grand Vizier.

"We'll have to, although I'm not sure how he'll catch up."

"He knows the way; he also knows the meeting point where we pick up our camels."

"From the Khalid people? I hear some accompanied you on the last trip." Boaz sounded irritated.

Lazar nodded, ignored his Zar's vexation. "They have agreed to supply our beasts directly. Otherwise we would need to make a couple of stops, once to make an exchange with my usual supplier and then to meet up with the desert people. You will like them and must forgive their fleeing that terrible night. It was the wisest course of action; I would have ordered the same if I had been in a position to. Pez will find us, I'm sure," Lazar added, unable to resist needling at the Grand Vizier. "Did you see him at all this afternoon, Garjan?"

"Yes, I did," the Grand Vizier snapped. "Annoying as ever. Turning somersaults down the main palace hallway and dribbling a great volume. He really is impossible at times."

"Oh? When was that?"

The Grand Vizier looked even more annoyed. "Moments before I left."

"And he seemed well?" Lazar persisted.

"If by *well* you mean was he animated, then I would have to say that yes, he was. He was his normal, thoroughly insane self," the Grand Vizier replied testily.

Lazar nodded his thanks, hiding his burning desire to grab his sword and cut the liar down. With the Grand Vizier's blatant lie, he now knew for sure that Maliz was behind the attempt on Pez's life. But he remembered the dwarf's warning that the demon could not be killed by conventional means and also that the supporters of Lyana must never reveal themselves. He swallowed his hate and instead said, "Well, brothers, shall we?" as he gestured toward the horses.

"Iridor?"

"What?" Ana said groggily.

Arafanz gently swept the hair back from her face. "I thought the baby must have begun its labor but I remember now that you said Iridor."

She felt weepy. "I know."

"You are trembling. What just happened? Tell me while I find us some shade," Arafanz said, his concern genuine. He lifted Ana effortlessly. Her arms clung around his neck as he walked her over to the rock face, which gave a measure of shade in its shadows.

He tenderly placed her down. "Let me fetch some water."

Ana stared, her gaze unfocused as she tried to imagine the scenario playing itself out in the city of Percheron, where she knew Pez must be.

Arafanz was back, crouching at her side and urging her to sip from the water skin. She obliged, not because she was thirsty but because she knew it pleased him to feel useful and it bought her some time to think.

He began carefully. "Ana, I know you see me as your enemy but the truth is we are on the same side, you and I. Will you tell me what has happened?"

She gazed into his anxious face, so close to her own; she noted that he had trimmed his beard today and for the first time saw that his eyes had golden flecks in what she had always thought were deep brown. He was close enough for her to be aware that his breath smelled sweetly of clove. His age remained very difficult to determine; he was not old, not by any means, and yet the lines in his face gave clues that this man had already lived a life that was more than twice hers in years. Not immediately aware of her own action, surprising herself with her tenderness toward her captor, Ana touched his cheek in a gesture that could not be mistaken for anything but affection. Her hand lingered, and although he initially hesitated, she watched now as the man who had imprisoned her, who had so frightened her, now nestled his face against her hand and closed his eyes. His response could not be mistaken for anything so innocent as a simple gesture of friendship.

"Don't, Ana," he begged, his voice suddenly hoarse.

"I'm sorry," she whispered, moving to pull her hand away, but he stopped her, covering it with his own, pushing her hand still harder against his cheek as he turned and kissed her palm. She felt his close beard graze her skin, his soft lips adore her.

His reply was taut and tense. "I say don't but I am lying to myself. I can't resist you," he groaned. "You make me weak. I want to avoid you and yet I struggle not to see you each day now."

"I noticed," she said softly, terrified by what he was building up to saying. She realized she had long suspected him guilty of harboring feelings toward her that conflicted with his role as her keeper.

He opened his eyes. "Ana, I—"

"Shh," she pleaded. "Don't say any more. Let this lie unspoken between us. It has no future."

To Ana he looked sad enough to cry; instead of doing so, he pulled back from her and offered the water again. She took the flask simply to have something to do with her hands and as a distraction for them both. She berated herself for feeling instantly bereft at his withdrawal. Was she truly heartless—no different from Herezah or Salmeo? How else could she find herself in the position of having three men in love with her? And worst of all, she held each in a separate place within; there was a fondness for Boaz, an irrefutable attraction to Arafanz, but there was a deep, abiding love for Lazar. Lazar alone owned her heart, yet their love seemed doomed.

Arafanz's voice was more even when he spoke again. "If we

cannot speak of my affection for you, will you tell me what just happened? Why you just became so upset?"

"Do you trust Lyana?"

"With my soul!" he declared.

"Then continue that way. She has chosen not to share her plans with any of us and I imagine there is good reason. I am not Lyana. I have no idea of my part in this struggle but I did feel something bad happening just now and Iridor came to mind."

"You are connected to him?"

"Presumably. Of course I could have imagined it."

He shook his head as he sat back, scratching at the newly trimmed beard and again she was struck by how often he reminded her of Lazar. "No. Something did happen. Did you notice the skies, did you hear the roar?"

"What roar?"

"You didn't hear? I don't know what it was—I think it was the wind."

"The Samazen?"

"Possibly, but it came and went as the skies darkened and then lightened again. Is Iridor dead?"

Ana didn't know, wasn't sure she was remembering what had actually happened. She had felt pain, she thought. "Did I faint?"

"For a few moments, yes. You recovered swiftly."

"I can't remember what occurred. I just heard his name in my mind."

"Is that all? What would prompt you to claim he was dead?"

She shook her head, baffled. She would think it through later when she was alone, convinced she would recall exactly what had taken place. The fear that something had happened to Pez would not leave her, though, and for once she wanted to return to the fortress.

"I . . . I don't feel too well."

Arafanz smiled sadly. "Let's get you back. All we have to do is point Farim in the opposite direction. Remember that—she will always get you to the cave or to the fortress from the cave."

"I'm sorry we didn't make it there today," she said, meaning it. This would have been their first return since the Crystal Pillars had spoken to her.

He nodded. "I'm afraid we will not risk you out in the desert again. I sense the child is due. We must take care of you now." He began guiding her back to the patient Farim.

"Arafanz!" she called, a sudden notion all but taking her breath away. "Do you mean to steal my baby from me?"

His expression had never seemed so desolate to her. And she knew that expression, had seen it several times on the man she loved. She had to stop seeing Lazar in her mind's eye. "I once threatened your baby to your Spur. I was lying, of course. The son you carry is not yours, Ana. He belongs to Lyana and the new Percheron."

"So do I," she countered, her breathing shallow, suddenly angry.

"He belongs on the throne."

"And I will be Valide." It came out as a threat.

"Ellyana never said anything about—"

"Oh, to Zarab's Fires for Ellyana!" she yelled.

Arafanz stepped away as if slapped. He looked genuinely shocked. But Ana hadn't finished. "I'm tired of Ellyana and her manipulations and what she's told whom and what she hasn't told someone else. She is using us all as pawns. I used to admire her. I wanted to help her. I felt . . . I felt as if we were connected somehow."

His eyes narrowed. "And now?"

"I despise her! Zarab have her! She feels more like my enemy now and she brings nothing but heartache and gloom to us all. She's convinced the few people who mean anything to me that they're involved in the struggle between Lyana and Zarab and yet all she's doing is leading us to our own demise. We'll never experience the satisfaction of Lyana's coming because we'll probably all be dead—you included!"

His expression smoothed. "I am not afraid to die in Lyana's cause."

"How did you become so fanatical, Arafanz? You must have had a life once, somewhere away from here? Be sure it's not Ellyana's cause you die for," she snapped, knowing her words were ridiculous but wanting to hurt him, wanting to injure him into seeing how he was being manipulated.

"They are one and the same, Ana. If you despise Ellyana, then you despise the Goddess herself."

"I don't," she said, her voice breaking, treacherous tears rising. "I don't despise Lyana. I want to serve her, I just don't see the point of constant suffering as a means of being her servant." Her hood and veil had fallen away and her hair was being blown softly by the gentle breeze beginning to stir across the dunes. He stroked her hair now, his gaze helplessly filled with affection, and again she saw a shadow, a reminder of Lazar. She was glad she was likely not to survive this struggle; she felt sure that she would begin to see Lazar in every man she ever spoke to, so desperate was she to see him again.

"You are so much more than her servant. Wait and see, Ana.

She has a role for you that is yet to be explained. And your son will be a good ruler for Percheron—can you want more?"

"Yes! I want to be his mother in more ways than simply the vessel that carries him. I want to nurse him, watch him grow, witness his personality forming itself."

"See if he's like his father?"

She blushed brightly. "Perhaps he will be like me."

"Perhaps." Ana heard the end of their conversation in Arafanz's comment. "Come, this wind is strengthening and the camels sense it. We must return."

"It is early for the Samazen," she pondered aloud.

"Nothing is how it should be," he said. "We have all been warned that this time it is different . . . even for the desert winds."

"You are the difference, maybe?"

Farim knelt for her and Arafanz helped her position her cumbersome body on the saddle, luxuriously softened by blankets and cushions. "Not me. I certainly add a fresh aspect to the fray but I am not directly involved in Lyana's battle. My role is to put a new Zar on the throne—one who is Lyana's disciple." He paused, then added, "Fresh blood, you could say," and she thought she saw guilt spark in his eyes before he looked away, cleared his throat.

"Then who? What is the difference?" she begged.

He shook his head. "Look to the other men who love you, Ana . . . and who love her, too. Perhaps the secret lies there."

13

Iridor flexed his wings to let them dry. *So this is me from now on?*

Yes. You can be only Iridor.

I miss my old form already.

But you are so beautiful as an owl.

I was beautiful on the inside as Pez, too.

She regarded him gravely before looking around them one last time at Star Island. *This is a lovely, lonely place. I'm glad I could see it once more.*

Once more? He shook himself.

I shall not return.

Are we close, Ellyana?

She nodded. *I sense that we are drawing to the end. Have we done enough? I cannot tell you.*

But what have we done? he asked, surprised. *I feel as though all we've done is hide.*

Ah, but you see all that hiding has nevertheless revealed so much. We know who our enemy is and now you must be very careful. Maliz has declared himself.

Iridor instinctively looked down toward his clawed feet, talons sharp on each toe. All that was still Pez recalled in horribly clear detail how Maliz had savagely cut off each of his fingers, snapping them first for maximum pain before removing them with his small, keen blade. But it was the casual way in which the demon had cast aside the small, gnarled fingers that had bothered Pez the most. The horror of Maliz's cruelty would stay with him always. Nevertheless, he had beaten Maliz. And Maliz did not know it yet.

What now? he said to Ellyana.

You have your own journey. You alone know the next stage of it.

He sighed. She was obviously not going to help him. *I shall find Lazar.*

She nodded but then again he felt sure she would have nodded if he'd said, "All right then, I think I shall fly to the moon." *Be careful,* she warned. *The demon must not know of your presence. It is the only surprise you have left now, my friend.*

I understand. Will I see you again? He wasn't sure he cared.

She shook her head and shrugged. *Who can know?*

Well, he began awkwardly, hating the coy manner in which Ellyana handled every question. *Thank you for saving my life.* It was the least he could say.

As I said, it was not your time, no matter what Maliz thought. But I cannot rescue you again, you understand?

He nodded, not understanding at all. *Farewell, then, Ellyana.*

Lyana guide you. May her light forever shine upon you.

He swallowed. Her farewell sounded ominous. In a practiced move and in a hurry to be gone from Ellyana's gloom, Iridor leaped from the rock on which he had been standing and flew out across the Faranel. He didn't look back. There was nothing to look back for. Ellyana was surely already gone and so was life as he had known it. All he could do now was fly toward his destiny.

Boaz had talked and talked during the entire journey about everything from how to ride a horse bareback to his favorite foods and Lazar could forgive him his excitement. The young man had never been beyond the city's gates in his near seventeen summers. By the same age Lazar had been spending more time outside of Romea than in it. What he felt sure he could never convince the young Zar of was the fact that no matter how many cities beyond Percheron there were, none—in Lazar's experience—could match her beauty. No, Boaz would have to find that out for himself. He was grateful to the youngster for his ebullient conversation and especially for the fact that Boaz didn't seem to need any responses from his two mostly silent companions. Lazar felt the frisson that had passed between himself and Maliz at the beginning of their trek. He knew the Grand Vizier had lied about Pez and obviously the demon had no idea that the dwarf had survived his attempt at murder. Lazar made a silent promise to never be off guard around the Grand Vizier—not anymore. It had gone beyond the threat of touch. Maliz would likely stick a knife in him if he came to the decision that Lazar was a risk to his cause.

" . . . and I'm just wondering if we shouldn't get the city stonemasons to take a closer look."

"Pardon, I'm sorry. I was just thinking about the next stage of our journey," Lazar replied into the silence that his Zar had clearly left for him to fill.

"I was talking about Beloch and Ezram—haven't you noticed they seem to be crumbling?'

"I have seen cracks appearing."

"Cracks?" Boaz repeated with feeling. "Lazar, I think our precious giants are going to collapse. There must have been some sort of tremors beneath the sea."

"I don't think so." Lazar seized a fresh opportunity to bait the Grand Vizier. "Some people are saying the giants are returning to life, breaking free of their stone prisons." He smiled briefly at the Zar to ensure that those listening could see he was speaking fancifully.

Although Boaz began to laugh at the suggestion and offered an answer, Lazar no longer heard him. He felt, rather than saw, the Grand Vizier turn and stare at him. Lazar kept his eyes fixedly on the landscape ahead.

"What makes you say that, Spur?" Maliz said, cutting across his Zar's amused retort.

"Forgive me, what did you say?" Lazar replied absently, feigning the look of someone dragging his thoughts back from elsewhere.

"I wondered what prompted you to say such a thing."

Lazar frowned. "About the stone giants, do you mean?"

Maliz nodded, tight-lipped.

"Oh"—Lazar shrugged—"it's just something I heard in the streets. People jesting to cover their fear that some sort of earthquake is going to shatter our fair city."

"I see. And what do you think?"

"Me? I don't think about them much," he lied. "Although I would hate to see the giants perish."

"Why?"

"Well, they're icons. They are precious art from our history. They reflect a time and a style."

"Perhaps it's time for a new style? We have a new Zar after all."

"Perhaps," Lazar said, tired of the banter and deciding he would not bait the demon again. "I think they're wonderful but then I'm a lover of history."

"Do you know the story behind those icons you speak of, Lazar?" Boaz asked. Not waiting for the Spur to answer, he continued: "The legend goes that a demon called Maliz made a terrible bargain with Zarab—"

"Yes I know the story," Lazar admitted, not at all keen for this conversation to continue and now deeply regretful that he had been stupid enough to provoke it.

"I don't," Maliz said, a glittering gaze fixed on the Spur.

"Oh, then let me enlighten you, Garjan. I didn't think I'd ever teach you anything!" Boaz said, clearly delighted. "The legend says that Maliz was actually a warlock, but he gave his loyalty fully to Zarab in return for life eternal."

"And what was the bargain?" Maliz asked, his gaze not leaving Lazar, who had deliberately turned away and pretended intense interest on the landscape ahead, which was turning from the greenish scrub of the foothills into the golden wilderness of the desert.

"Oh, well, he had to rid the land of the Goddess Lyana."

"He was obviously successful," the Grand Vizier replied, a mordant grin noticeable beneath his neatly plaited beard.

"He banished her and her supporters—the giants, the magnificent winged lion, the dragon and other creatures that no longer roam the land were—"

"Turned to stone?" Maliz finished, and Lazar felt his sneer.

"Yes," he heard Boaz say, his voice filled with enthusiasm.

"My, my, what a tale. And you believe this?"

Boaz laughed. "I want to. I like the romance of it."

"We're here," Lazar interrupted, determined to end the conversation before it dragged them all to a place he certainly didn't want to visit.

"Ah," Boaz said, untroubled by Lazar's rudeness. "I see the camels."

"And our Khalid again, my Zar," the Grand Vizier added. "I recognize Salim."

Lazar bristled. "Use only 'Fayiz' from now on, Tariq. They will recognize you and me, of course, but no one must know who travels with us. And if we meet any strangers besides the Khalid, we must rely on the names we settled on. No bowing, no titles, no special treatment for Boaz."

"Surely the Khalid wouldn't hurt the Zar?"

"We don't know what they might do and we don't know who they talk to. For all we know, the Khalid led Arafanz to us."

"I hadn't considered that," the Grand Vizier admitted.

"No, and I don't think it's true, but regardless, no one is to know Boaz is with us."

Maliz nodded. "I understand and shall be careful. But I don't speak their language."

"It is not necessary, probably even best—that way you can keep a distance and they won't feel offended. What about you, Fayiz? Have you learned any Khalid in your studies? I know you're a great linguist."

Boaz nodded smugly. "As a matter of fact, I have a little Khalid—only a smattering, mind, but perhaps enough to follow a simple conversation."

"Be friendly by all means but don't get involved with them."

"All right. But how am I supposed to fit into this traveling group?" Boaz whispered. They were close to the Khalid now; the men were waving.

Lazar frowned, considering. "You're Tariq's sister's grandson and you're training to be in the Protectorate."

"That sounds perfect," Boaz said, grinning. "This is fun."

"Oh, for the sense of invincibility that only youth can experience," Maliz drawled, and Lazar actually threw a wry smile his way.

"Lazar!" Salim came running toward them.

"Who is this?" Boaz asked.

"The leader. A good man," Lazar murmured, then raising his voice, he spoke in the language of the desert people. "Salim! Salutations."

The man caught up with them and put his hand on his heart as the Spur dismounted. "Spur Lazar, it gladdens my soul to see you alive."

"We were fortunate," Lazar answered in the Khalid tongue.

"You have forgiven me?"

Lazar nodded. "Nothing to forgive. I would have instructed my men to do the same if I'd been in your position."

The man completed his welcome, his hand moving first to his forehead, then to his lips, and settling again on his heart before he bowed low. "We would all have been dead. He was after the beautiful young woman, I am assuming?"

Lazar flicked a glance toward Boaz. "I have no idea of his intention but Ana is why we have returned."

Salim's eyes narrowed and there was a wryness to his tone. "I imagined you would."

Lazar cleared this throat, relieved the Zar was not privy to this conversation. "Salim, you remember Tariq?" Lazar said as the Grand Vizier came alongside.

"Of course, welcome back to the desert. You are a brave man."

The Grand Vizier nodded politely, not understanding a word but no doubt understanding the sentiments being expressed.

"And this is Fayiz, who is training to be a member of the Percherese Guard. He is Tariq's sister's grandson."

"A fine young man. Not far off my own son's age, I imagine."

For the first time since Zar Joreb had died, Lazar suspected, Boaz bowed in greeting.

"I have something for you, Lazar," Salim continued.

"Apart from my camels?"

The man grinned, his teeth white against his bronzed face. "This is a gift. But you will have to pay for the camels."

Lazar returned the smile. "What gift?"

Salim called over his shoulder. Another man walked toward them, a bird perched on his arm. Lazar noticed that its eyelids were stitched and the bird appeared understandably nervous. "A new falcon?"

"We caught him yesterday, whilst we waited for you."

"He's for me?" Lazar said, disbelief evident in his tone. He was deeply touched by the gesture. As a child, he had always wanted his own hunting bird but somehow his father had never gotten around to teaching him falconry skills. His father had never gotten around to much at all in terms of teaching his headstrong, eldest son, he thought.

"He is called Jumo," Salim said proudly, "and we have branded a sign—a sword—onto his beak. Throughout the desert this sword now denotes you because you are such a fearless fighter. No one will ever dare steal this bird now that he has your mark. You must keep him close and pet him as we showed you. That is how you will make him yours. He is a ferocious bird with enough courage to match your own and he will train well. He will be brave, like his namesake, and he will make you proud."

Hearing this man of the desert speak so proudly of Jumo had caused helpless tears to well, threatening to spill down Lazar's face. "I don't know what to say," he managed to croak, fighting through the emotion.

The Khalid quickly grasped Lazar's sentiments. "Nothing to say, other than that you will accept him and let me help you train him."

"That's a promise."

"Then he is yours to keep. Remember: a man and his bird should not be parted. Jumo will die of grief if you should die; that's how close the bond will be, must be."

All Lazar could do was nod, relieved he hadn't disgraced himself in front of Boaz or the demon. "I am without words. Thank you, brother." He held out his hand, palm up. The little man placed his palm down above Lazar's and they gripped fingers. It was a gesture, a bond of brotherhood, that encompassed all men of the region, be they from cities or desert, from Galinsea or from Percheron.

The Khalid smiled.

"Lazar," Boaz inquired, "what has occurred?"

The Spur sniffed back the emotion and explained quickly to the Zar and the Grand Vizier what had taken place.

"Are you going to the fortress?" Salim asked.

"Yes."

"Then we are coming with you."

"There is no need."

"I know. But my son may be there and you can use our help. We will not run this time. We will stand firm with you."

"Only you. I can't risk more."

Salim nodded. "Do you know how to get there?"

Lazar realized they'd arrived at the point he'd dreaded. He was glad that neither Boaz nor the Grand Vizier could understand this conversation. "I was hoping you might lead me." His tone was sheepish but he made sure his body language didn't betray him to the avid listeners.

The Khalid looked momentarily stunned. "I know only the rumors . . . a rough direction to the west."

Lazar thought of Pez, prayed he would find them somehow. "We head west, then. I have some ideas, too," he lied, praying Pez would make contact soon. "Come, Jumo," he said, liking the sound of hearing his friend's name rolling off his tongue again. The falcon gave a brief, soft whistling sound and Lazar felt an instant bond.

They left their horses with the Khalid in exchange for camels and would exchange the beasts back for the horses upon their return. Salim and Lazar never discussed ownership of the horses should the Percherese not reemerge from the desert, as if to talk of it might invite bad omen.

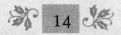
Herezah awoke with a start and a hammering heart. She had dreamed of herself laughing with King Falza, who looked very similar to Lazar. He had been enchanted by her witty retorts and gracious attention. She had impressed him with her hospitality and charmed him with her tinkling laugh and engaging personality. He had just leaned across to his general—although who knows what that fellow was doing in her dreams—to discuss the withdrawal of the Galinsean fleet and Herezah was imagining her son returning to a peaceful city because of her ingenuity, when the door burst open. In stomped a squattish, paunchy woman of indeterminate age but definitely well past her prime, with washed-out brown hair piled on her head and held in place by a clip studded with gems. The woman's face was powdered, adding to her pale, floury appearance, but her skin was oily and she wore a light sheen about her forehead and nose.

"Angeline!" Falza exclaimed.

The wife? Herezah had smiled, for the woman reminded her of mounds of rathas before frying, an entire pyramid of them rolled together to form one huge wobbly ball of ratha.

The Queen of Galinsea had yelled at her husband in guttural Galinsean, of which Herezah was able to understand only a minute amount. She made out the word that meant "to lie" and something about livestock. Perhaps it was the word "pig"? She couldn't be sure. Falza was on his feet, yelling straight back at her in Percherese—which was curious but helpful—and then Pez cartwheeled into the room and urinated on the ratha mound's silks. The dream turned decidedly dark at this point as the Queen of Galinsea had withdrawn a bow and arrow—of all ridiculous weapons—and carefully taken aim.

"No!" the King had yelled.

"Not you, my darling," she had said quietly, suddenly in perfect Percherese. "You are too precious to our realm. But I can't let you jeopardize our plans," and she had swung the bow to point squarely at Herezah and let loose with her killer arrow, catching the Valide in the throat.

Herezah exploded into consciousness, breathing raggedly, hardly daring to believe at first that it had only been a nightmare. Gradually her breathing evened. The dream had lost much of its clarity and she'd already begun to forget the fear, telling herself it was just a silly dream as Elza came bustling and curtsying into the chamber.

"Good morning, Valide. Are you well?" the servant asked, throwing open shutters.

"Distracted," Herezah replied. "Where is my tea?"

"The lemon infusion was too sour, Valide. I have sent it back and ordered a pot of pomegranate tea instead," Elza offered, and Herezah could see the woman cringing, awaiting the inevitable tirade. But she couldn't be bothered with trivia anymore.

"Get me my silk wrap."

Elza threw it around the Valide's shoulders as Herezah stepped into soft slippers. "Pack up my chamber, Elza. We're moving."

The servant could not hide her astonishment. "Where to, Valide?"

"Crown Valide, please, Elza. You are the person who takes care of my most intimate needs and you must set the tone for the other slaves."

"Yes, Crown Valide, forgive me."

"We're moving into the palace proper. I don't plan to take audiences with visitors, having to run from the harem every hour of the day!"

"No, Crown Valide, but has Grand Master Salmeo given his . . . er, his permission?" Elza stammered.

"His permission?" Herezah said, her tone sharp enough to cut ice. "Elza, have you any notion of what my new status means?"

"Yes, Crown Valide."

"Then you should know I don't need anyone's permission to do anything, save the Zar himself—and he is not here. I rule in his stead. I will not be imprisoned in the harem and I owe no fealty to Salmeo outside of its walls. Even inside them I reckon a Zar by proxy or a Crown Valide—whichever you choose to think of me as—has far more status." Herezah wasn't convinced that the servant agreed with her on this last point; she looked doubtful despite the polite cutsy. "So get things organized. We move out this morning—I think the Peacock Suite will suit me. Now go away and make the arrangements. I shall dress myself, but have the Zar's private secretary meet me in the salon just outside the harem immediately."

Elza's anxiety was naked on her face but she disappeared to her duties as bid. Herezah quickly dressed herself in some day clothes and hooked a thick veil across her face. Bin wouldn't even be able to tell it was her, if not for her voice. She hurried to the appointed chamber and soon enough the Elim who had escorted her announced that the secretary had arrived.

Bin bowed low. Herezah was familiar enough with him to do feel relatively at ease, although this new one-to-one situation would test that comfort.

"Thank you for coming so quickly," Herezah began, deciding this was one fellow she needed on her side, and politeness and appreciation toward him would go a long way.

"It is my role now, Crown Valide, to serve you."

She inclined her head. "Bin, I wish to set up a meeting with the Galinseans. I presume my son briefed you that this was something he wished."

"He did. Do you have a plan for how you would like this to unfold, Crown Valide?" He noticed her frown and continued. "Do you prefer me to make arrangements for you to visit the Isles of Plenty, or that we request that someone from the Galinsean hierarchy visit the palace first? Or perhaps you have some other ideas?"

"The Zar cautioned that we are not in a position to make demands of the Galinseans," Herezah replied. "But then again I am not inclined to set off across the bay aboard a ship." She looked again to him for his guidance.

"It is not my place, Crown Valide, to tell you how you should behave—"

"No, but I am asking for your advice, Bin. In the absence of my son, the Spur, and, I suppose, the Grand Vizier, it is down to you and me to make these decisions. I could consult some of the more senior dignatories around the palace but the Zars of Percheron have always prided themelves on resolving political issues within these very walls. I don't wish to dilute my son's powers by seeking their aid."

"The more input, the more muddied those matters become, you mean, Crown Valide?"

"Exactly."

"And next they'll be offering advice you have not requested," he added.

"Quite," she said, pleased that she was dealing with someone with a sharp intelligence. Bin had always seemed so young to her. He was barely older than Boaz and she had been worried by her son's choice of someone so young for such an important role, but now she was seeing the wisdom of his selection.

"The way I would recommend, then, Majesty," Bin began, for the first time addressing her by the title that most pleased her, "is that we suggest a meeting of the royals on neutral territory."

"Ah." Her eyes gleamed. "Where would you suggest?"

"Outside the Bay of Percheron in close-by waters of the Faranel. They belong to neither Galinsea or Percheron but are easily accessed by both royals from their present locales. You would only have a day's travel at most, Highness, and the Galinseans would face a similar journey. Galinsea would be permitted one ship, yourself the same. We would need to talk with Ghassal regarding the meeting specifics, on which vessel it would take place, and so on. Ghassal has specialist lieutenants who are in charge of our fleet, Highness, and they would advise us best in this matter."

"Excellent," she said. "Thank you, Bin. Can I leave it up to you to pursue this matter? I would like to set up this meeting during the next couple of days."

His eyes widened. "Then I must move quickly, Majesty. Is there anything else for the time being that I can help with?"

She was about to say no but nodded instead. "I am moving into the Peacock Suite and will take all messages there from now on. Please organize a salon where I can receive visitors who relate to state matters." He nodded. "I no longer want the escort of the Elim. I do not belong to the harem for the time being. I wish you to set up a guard from the Mutes."

She watched the secretary's nostrils flare briefly, but to his credit, Bin simply nodded. "Of course, Crown Valide. I'm sure the Zar would want all resources put to work for you."

"And because I do not understand the special sign language that you and my son use with such ease to communicate with the Mutes, I wish you to instruct them that no one from the harem is admitted to see me merely on the grounds that I am one of its members. Until the Zar of Percheron returns, I am his representative in all matters and in stature. It would not be fitting for me to be receiving any instructions from Grand Master Eunuch Salmeo, for instance," she said carefully.

Bin didn't blink. "Of course. That is how it should be."

She smiled behind her veil. "Thank you, Bin. Perhaps you could get a message to the harem for me as you leave?"

He was already bowing, having heard the polite dismissal. "I would be happy to do so."

"In that case ask Salmeo to visit me in the Peacock Suite at fifth bell."

The secretary nodded. "It will be done, Crown Valide," he assured her, departing quietly. Herezah knew her orders were now in good hands.

Alone once more, the new Crown Valide remembered her nightmare and experienced a vague notion of residual fear but the situation and details of the dream had vanished. She could barely remember what had so disturbed her, as she absently moved her hand to her throat, and why she made that gesture was lost on her. Instead, she dismissed her faint dread as being nothing more than nervousness about what lay ahead and busied herself in preparation to charm a king.

This was their first full day on camels and the memories rushed back to Maliz. There were moments, like now, when he regretted his interest in Boaz. Perhaps he should have chosen some other bright young thing to inhabit for the next cycle, but then, he reminded himself, Boaz did offer marvelous status and wealth and access to women. Of course there was always Lazar, but somehow Maliz didn't think even he could persuade Lazar to invite him into his body. As it was, he realized that Boaz would have to be coerced. He wouldn't be tricked as easily as Tariq but Maliz was sure there would be a weakness that could be exploited. He just had to find it . . . and fast.

There was no weakness, as far as he could tell, in the wretchedly arrogant Spur. He was increasingly convinced that the Spur was not just a follower of Lyana but an important disciple. He had long ago decided that Lazar was connected with Lyana's struggle, but now he believed this Prince, masquerading as a soldier, was intrinsic to this cycle. He had no idea what the Spur's role might be, though; there had never been this person in any previous battles. It was frustrating because there was no magic of Lyana within Lazar—Maliz had touched him to be certain—and yet Maliz could not let the thought go. Right now Lazar remained useful but his time would come, too.

He cast a glance the Galinsean's way, noted how proud the Spur looked atop his tall camel as he whispered sweet words softly to the falcon perched silently on his arm.

Yes, indeed. His time would come, too.

Lazar felt the weight of the Grand Vizier's gaze fall upon him but he did not glance his way. It was obvious Maliz was measuring him, wondering what Lazar knew. And Lazar had only himself to blame for this fresh interest; he had baited the demon with innuendo. Well, the demon needed him for now. As long as he was leading them toward Ana, and in turn another step closer to Lyana, Lazar knew he was safe. After that, he was expendable and it was likely that Maliz would act upon that fact.

He stroked Jumo, already feeling as though the two of them belonged together, and wondered how, in Lyana's name, he was going to find Ana.

Boaz was having similar private thoughts, although his were more sinister.

He was not wondering how they would find Ana, so much as when. He held no doubt that somehow Lazar would lead them to the Zaradine. And when he got to this fortress they spoke of and finally confronted the man who had stolen his wife, he would take great personal pleasure in killing him.

And then he would kill Zaradine Ana . . . but take no pleasure in it.

15

I ridor flew. He was not ready to consider himself entirely Iridor, even though he had to accept that from here on the owl shape was all that was left to him. There would be no more cartwheeling in palace corridors or belching at opportune moments to achieve the personally amusing silence his bad behavior could provoke. There would be no more accidentally on-purpose treading on toes or screeching so loudly that he could terrify the Elim guards. Pez the dwarf no longer existed, other than in his mind.

No body would ever float to the top of the sea and alert the palace to his fate. Neither would the body, as Maliz had planned, sink too deep or be pulled out to deep sea. There was no body; it had disappeared in the single instant that he had transformed into Iridor and then, with strength he didn't know he possessed, lifted himself free of the water, and despite soggy feathers flown far enough to dry out on a rock. Later he had flown to Star Island, amazed that his bird form had suffered no ill effects from his trauma, whilst Pez's body had taken such punishment.

But there was no more time for sorrow. Ellyana had ordered him to leave his grief in the Faranel's depths and to emerge from the water a new individual. It must have sounded appropriate to Ellyana but to Iridor the words were hollow, all but meaningless. How do you leave yourself behind? How do you suddenly stop sadness? It is not a tap that can be twisted on or off at will. But it was Lyana's will that he return from certain death as the owl—he had no choice if he wanted to live, wanted to go on fighting in her name. And though he had chosen life in front of Ellyana, privately he had chosen revenge. He wanted to see Maliz not so much suffering—as he had made Pez suffer—but destroyed.

He had to find Lazar and knew the Spur would be heading in a westerly direction into the desert. They would have met up with their camels and probably with the Khalid by now. He estimated the royal caravan would have been traveling for a full day now and would be approaching the second night. It was important he reach Lazar at some time this night, for he needed to direct them on the fastest route to the cleverly disguised fortress. Arafanz had not positioned himself that far from Percheron in fact; certainly deep enough into the desert that his presence drew no stray visitors, but though his fortress was cunningly positioned away from the traditional slaving and trading routes, it was within easy striking distance of the city. No wonder the leader of the assassins felt so confident of his own success.

Iridor flew harder, ignoring fatigue, hunger, fear. Lazar needed to know that it was time to veer north, into the area known as the Empty Quarter.

It took Iridor the rest of that day, resting only a few hours in the hottest hours of the next day before flying through the early evening and night—before he first spotted the dark, snaking shape of the camels moving ponderously. From the height at which he was traveling, they were at first just a dark smudge on the relentlessly burned yellow landscape. As he flew slightly lower and got closer, Iridor could recognize the Khalid. He was sure it would be Salim and his men again. The Khalid didn't care to travel without hawks or falcons but Iridor knew the hunting birds would be hooded for the night, so he dropped as low as he dared, skimming just above the desert sand, hoping none of the men would seem him. He could feel the heat of the earth searng into his belly. It was the summer heat, the sort to invite the Samazen to come and play in the desert. He would stay a relatively far distance from the men whilst daylight lasted and hope to see Lazar during the dark.

He had been too frightened to use any sort of mindspeak. It didn't matter that Maliz was nowhere near; his experience in nearly being revealed had scared him off from reaching out with the Lore.

By the time dusk had arrived, the fires were going, decent food was being prepared—they still had fresh meat at this stage, of course—and he could hear the low voices of men carrying across the darkening silence. Iridor flew soundlessly to alight atop a low dune, remaining in the shadows.

Now he just had to remain patient and pick his moment. The Spur was sitting quietly, removed slightly from the rest of the group, as was his way. There were seven other men and most had their backs to Iridor. They were all dressed so plainly, with blankets around their shoulders to keep out the desert chill, that he could not tell which was Boaz. He hoped Lazar wasn't taking such a large party toward the fortress. Arafanz would know of it long before they came within sighting of the cunningly concealed structure.

Lazar . . . it's me, I'm here. He spoke across the sand directly into the Spur's mind.

There was silence from Lazar although he suddenly looked agitated, Iridor noted. Worse, one of the group suddenly stood up and a commotion ensued.

"What was that for?" It was Boaz's voice that he heard.

Lazar! Iridor tried again.

The man who had been hopping around—and now Iridor could see had dropped his mug of quishtar—had his head cocked slightly to one side and was scanning the dunes as if looking for him.

In surprise, Iridor dropped his body low and flat. He heard Lazar's voice, uncharacteristically loud. "What are you doing, Tariq?"

Tariq! So Maliz was here. In his haste and the trauma of his near death, he had forgotten Lazar's warning. Iridor felt a tingle of fear pass from his body through to his wing tips.

"What is it?" he heard Boaz's irritated voice again, then he recognized Salim's voice asking Lazar something in the desert language.

He peeped over the dune and saw Lazar stand and bark various orders. Iridor picked out the Zar, who had cast off his blanket in surprise at the Grand Vizier's behavior. He heard Lazar speak to Boaz briefly, as if he were a mere servant and not his Zar. To Salim he said something low, angry, that Iridor couldn't make out. But to the demon he spoke clearly, loud enough that his words carried to Iridor hiding in the dunes.

"Tariq, are you all right?"

Finally Iridor locked his keen gaze on the Grand Vizier. He could feel his tendrils of magic reaching out in an ever-widening arc. Iridor dragged in every ounce of his Lore, gathered it up into a tiny ball as best he could, and buried it deep inside himself. Maliz must not, under any circumstances, know of his survival, let alone that Iridor was now present. He felt sickened that he had been so careless. He should have checked, should have waited and watched the group for a longer time. He couldn't bear to look and dipped behind the dune again, listening intently.

"Tariq!" It was Lazar again, doing his best to distract the demon.

"I'm sorry," Maliz said finally. "I thought . . ."

"Fayiz, go help make a new brew," Lazar said, disgusted.

Iridor wondered who Fayiz was. He had to be one of their group, rather than Khalid, because Lazar was speaking Percherese.

"Are you burned?" Lazar asked, obviously to the Grand Vizier. Iridor hoped he was.

"I thought I heard something," Maliz replied. Iridor knew better. The demon had more likely felt a rush of magic wash over him.

"I heard nothing," Lazar replied matter-of-factly.

"I think we should do a search of the dunes."

Lazar laughed. "And which of the twenty or so in the immediate vicinity did you mean?"

"All of them," Maliz replied, and his tone was not respectful.

"Tariq, believe me, the Khalid are more attuned to the sound of the desert than you could ever hope to be. Had something disturbed them, they would have reacted faster than you. Swords would already be drawn."

"I insist, Lazar."

"Out here, Grand Vizier, you insist on nothing. There is only all of you and there is me, your superior. Fayiz, hurry up with that quishtar," Lazar growled. "Now, I suggest you settle back down. I heard nothing, other than the sigh of the desert, and I am thirty years younger than you."

Inwardly Iridor had to smile. There was nothing more biting than an angry Spur Lazar. He realized now that talking to his friend was going to be impossible unless they met in person. He would have to be patient. In the meantime he would hunt. He needed nourishment, even if it was desert rat. Silently he flew away into the deep of the night.

Lazar's heart was hammering. That had been close—too close. Maliz was drinking the fresh brew but Lazar could tell the demon was far from relaxed. He noted how he pretended to gaze at the flames of the fire, but the dark, shrouded eyes were constantly scanning the dunes for any sign of the owner of the magic that had disturbed him.

As much as the manner in which Iridor had announced his arrival had terrified Lazar, he could not escape the heartfelt sense of relief to hear his old friend's voice in his head again. He wanted to shout his delight either aloud or across the strange mindlink but he dared not do either.

Iridor would be sensibly watching now from a safe vantage, he was sure. At some point Lazar would have to excuse himself, although he suspected the demon would now watch his every move. He'd need an excuse to disappear. He could claim he needed to relieve himself but that would not permit him to be gone long, and no one would care or notice if the Grand Vizier followed, as he almost certainly would. No, he needed a far more compelling excuse to get away from the main group and be left private enough to speak with Iridor face to face.

Suddenly he realized that Boaz was talking to him; Lazar hadn't been paying the Zar any attention. Was he imagining it, or was Boaz acting strangely? He knew the young man was excited to be away from the palace, and to be out amongst men alone was an additional treat. But something suddenly niggled Lazar's mind about the royal. He felt that Boaz was not being truthful with his Spur—this camaraderie and determination to hunt down Ana's captor felt somehow contrived.

Lazar had known Boaz all of the youngster's life and Boaz was nothing if not a cautious and serious individual. He was measured in all that he did—that was part of his charm and part of the reason his father had chosen him to succeed him. It also explained why he had risen so well to the challenge of ruling. He was well beyond his years in maturity and Lazar had never seen him behave any differently.

Boaz was a passionate person—Lazar would certainly acknowledge that—but now there seemed to be something else burning in him. This coming to the desert to stalk Arafanz was odd. Lazar felt sure that if Boaz was forced to make a choice between the good of his realm or Ana, the young Zar would follow duty and choose Percheron. And the city was where the most senior royal should be—and Boaz knew that—for he had the Spur to hunt Arafanz, to find his Zaradine. No. This curious decision felt contrived, and although there was certainly a feeling of zeal, Lazar didn't understand what was driving it. Boaz might be courageous but he was not a fighter and he was far too sensible to put his role as Zar into any threatening situation. Boaz knew his role above all was to protect the status of the Zar. Without an heir, this was even more paramount and all this talk of finding his heir—a child who could be dead, could be killed on the journey home, could be a girl!—was not worth endangering the Zar. That was the Spur's job. This whole situation gave off a bad smell. Why had Herezah and the Grand Vizier encouraged Boaz to risk his life so carelessly?

Lazar had to find a way to speak with his friend Iridor.

Salim innocently provided an answer, sidling over to the Spur. "You look far away in your thoughts, Lazar."

"Sorry. I'm thinking of what's ahead of us, whether I'm taking us all to our deaths."

"It is out of your hands," the desert man said, his eyes raised to the skies. "You can only do what your heart and your head tell you from the knowledge you have."

"More desert wisdom?" Lazar asked wryly.

Salim grinned. "This is our last night in safe Khalid territory."

Lazar nodded. "I know. Your men will need to leave us tomorrow. Are you still sure you want to come? There's no guarantee we'll find him—in fact, I'd say our chances are remote—and your own life is at risk . . . think about the rest of your family, Salim."

"I do. My son means everything to us. We are incomplete without him. If I knew he was dead I would let him go, but I don't know that, and until I have proof, I must continue my search. Would you ever stop looking for Zaradine Ana if she were your daughter—in fact, whether or not she was your daughter, would you halt your search simply because it was impractical?"

Lazar shook his head, ashamed that he had not made the comparison himself or comprehended that anyone could feel the same depth of love for another person as he did.

"You love her, Lazar, don't you? But not as a daughter."

Lazar nodded again, slowly, sadly this time. "Even though we speak a private language, you must never repeat that claim in this company. It would mean my death. Our love is forbidden and she is married to the Zar. Promise me you will never repeat it in this company."

Salim looked at him, a bemused expression creasing his face. "The Vizier and a servant boy aspiring to being a soldier?"

"Even to them, never speak of it again. Yes, I love her more than life."

"Then you do understand now why I must find my son." Lazar nodded. "But that is not what I am here to tell you. I sense tension in the camp between you and Tariq."

"You could say that. I don't want him here—he's a liability for all of us. Watch him, Salim. He's unpredictable and I would be lying if I didn't tell you that I think he's dangerous for us. Just look at his odd behavior of just moments ago."

"I think I know what he heard," Salim said, offering a low chuckle.

Lazar was sure his heart skipped a beat. "What do you know?" he asked, worried afresh for Iridor.

"I know who is here, hiding in the dunes." Again the man smiled conspiratorially.

The Spur felt all his breath leave him. How could he know? "Salim, I—"

The desert man spoke over him in a rush of glee. "I thought we'd give you some real Khalid entertainment to wish you well and to bless our journey."

Lazar held his tongue, surprised at what he was hearing. He frowned in query.

Salim continued, "A few of our women have come. They

will provide some traditional dance and music as a welcome to you, Spur Lazar–it is actually for you rather than your companions. We want you to know that we hold you in high esteem. And our women want to wish you Lyana's speed."

He wasn't sure whether to be appalled or touched. Salim sensed his confusion.

"Do not worry, Spur. We are far enough away from the fortress and his men. They will not trouble themselves with us in this region. The Khalid are always singing and dancing and making music, and we look like any small family group."

Lazar was not thrilled by the prospect of noise and activity suddenly invading what was meant to be a caravan of stealth, but he realized that this distraction might just give him the opportunity he needed to speak with Pez. He had to take the chance.

"I am honored, Salim. Please invite your women forward."

Salim beamed. "Thank you, Spur. I shall fetch them."

Lazar looked across to where the demon sat, watching, no doubt wondering what the two had been talking about in the desert language. "Tariq."

"Yes?" The demon's voice was not friendly.

"I have found out what you heard."

"What do you mean?"

"We've found the source of what may have disturbed you. Although I must say you do seem overly jumpy, Tariq, spilling an entire pot of precious quishtar."

"What is it?" Boaz asked, his tone betraying that he was already wearying of playing the inferior youth.

"A group of dancers has been brought to entertain us."

"Surely not in my hon–"

"No," Lazar hastily corrected. "In mine. But they're keen to dance for all of us."

Boaz grinned. "Well there you are, Tariq, all that leaping about and anxiety for nothing. However, I can easily forgive your jumpiness after what you went through on your last visit into the desert."

"Indeed, Fayiz," the demon said drily, his gaze fixed firmly on Lazar as he replied.

There was no doubt in Lazar's mind now. Maliz was certain that Lazar was hiding something. But by the same token, Lazar took a measure of comfort in the fact that the demon now knew his own secret was threatened. Lazar was certain Maliz couldn't know how much he knew, if anything at all, but a new understanding had settled between them without a word being exchanged. They had just put each other on notice that suspicions were now clearly in place.

16

The beaming men of the Khalid had arranged cushions around a central large square of sand, with the fire burning in the middle. Lazar chose the spot farthest from Tariq, his mind racing as to how he might now use this situation to escape. He prayed the owl was paying attention because they wouldn't have long.

A drum sounded in the darkness, becoming more insistent as out of the night, illuminated by burning torches, came a dozen women in the traditional festive dress of the Khalid. They wore bright colors of crimson, scarlet, purple, emerald, and ultramarine, their midriffs exposed and gauzy fabric veiling their faces, hung from chains wrought in gold. Around their wrists and ankles they wore bells, which they jangled now in perfect synchrony to the drum's rhythm. As unwelcome as this disturbance had seemed moments earlier, Lazar couldn't help but be fascinated by the sudden explosion of color and sound and movement. Some of these women were young, many just girls, but others were clearly in their middle years. And yet age did not seem to matter. They all looked magnificent as they ran on tiptoe around the fire, fabric floating in their arms, making a swirl of bright color. They split into two groups and danced, encouraging the audience to clap as they hit a frenzied but supremely fluid movement, their hips tracing a pattern in the air. Lazar had seen similar dances many times—this was the traditional female dancing of the whole region after all—but there was something very special to witness it in this setting as an act of gratitude and blessing.

The men of the Khalid clapped loudly and Lazar noticed that Boaz was entranced by this spectacle. He wasn't so sure about the Grand Vizier, even though Maliz had the good grace to fix a smile to his face.

The rhythm of the drum slowed and new instruments joined as a few male musicians emerged from the dark. The stringed lerz offered the tones so traditional to the Percherese and indeed Galinseans. The haunting sound of the zuva and kruel wind instruments echoed into the still night, and in spite of his mood, Lazar felt the music lift his spirits. And as a young man—younger than Boaz—picked up the rhythm with the spoon-shaped wooden flaks and the fresh percussion took the piece to new heights, another figure stepped out from behind a dune.

She was dressed in the brightest of yellow silks, her bronzed belly taut as her hips moved at what looked like an impossible speed, in an impossible direction. Even though she was veiled, Lazar could tell she was beautiful, and he realized, as all the other women withdrew, that she was not as young as he'd first thought. Her shape was perfect but the way she moved it suggested maturity.

Salim had moved to sit near him.

"She is captivating," Lazar breathed.

"Her name is Ganya—it means 'beautiful.'"

"Most appropriate. Whose family does she belong to?"

"To mine. She is my eldest daughter." When Lazar turned in surprise, the man grinned, nodding. "It's true. She is widowed. Very sad, for she hasn't been blessed by children."

"But she looks so young."

"As I said, no children," Salim replied wryly.

The rhythm of the drums changed and both men gave their attention to Ganya. She had moved to stand directly before Lazar, a jewel studding her navel and gold chains glittering across her body. The firelight made her dark eyes, filled with invitation, sparkle. Lazar cleared his throat and beside him Salim gave a chuckle as his daughter began rotating one hip in synchrony with the beat. Her left foot was planted firmly on the ground, while the ball of her right foot was responsible for creating all the movement. She truly was magnificent as she bent backward to show perfect poise, perfect balance, and a dazzling display of control as her pelvis began a series of sideways thrusts.

"She's incredible," Lazar murmured.

"She is asking for your sword," Salim whispered.

"Why?" He couldn't tear his gaze from her.

"Oblige and she will show you."

Lazar stood, drew the sword.

"You must give it to her," Salim urged as the desert folk began to whistle and clap loudly.

Lazar stepped into the ring and held out his sword with both hands. Ganya's eyes glistened with mischief, but she didn't break a step as she pointed to the hip that was still moving at fascinating speed.

"Place it on her!" Salim called with delight.

It would surely fall off, Lazar thought, but he was intrigued. He stepped closer and balanced the sword, and to his disbelief Ganya didn't slow down as he'd anticipated. If anything, her dance increased in speed and complexity as she moved off around the circle, still leaning precariously backward to balance the sword perfectly. The sinuous undulation of her hips remained unbroken, her left foot still anchoring her even though it guided her now around the fire, whilst her right foot continued to do the trickier work. Lazar watched in amazement. His sword didn't even look like it was going to fall off her hip bone as she made her way around the fire, never once betraying the frantic rhythm that the musicians commanded.

The women began to add their voices to the fray and what was initially a low sound escalated into a cacophony, just short of a scream. Ganya fell to her knees, the blade never losing its balance. And as the voices rose, the volume increased as the musicians used stunning dexterity to coax the most complex and rapid tunes on their instruments. And Ganya began to move her shoulders backward, shivering in tandem with her hips, and all the while the sword remained horizontal, secure. Back she went, farther and farther, the music and voices a frenzy of excitement until Lazar was sure she would have to stop, but still lower she pushed, and as her shoulder tips finally touched the sand behind her and brought her dance to a theatrical close, so, too, did the music and voices stop dead. Though it had appeared magnificently effortless, Lazar could see her sucking in deep breaths of air to slow her pulse.

Everyone clapped and cheered, including Lazar. He noticed even the Grand Vizier had a fresh new gleam in his eye. Who could resist such a raw sexual display? But the dance went beyond that, Lazar was sure. This dance was telling the men that it was a woman who was in control, a woman who actually controlled the sword, a woman who was ever balanced, always strong, and yet would submit—but only when she chose.

It was both subtle and magnificent. He wasn't aware that he was licking his lips nervously when Ganya finally stood up, still breathing hard. No woman had drawn such a purely lustful reaction from him since the day an experienced, very expensive, and extremely pretty prostitute called Vadia in Romea had introduced him to the pleasures of the flesh. Vadia had enjoyed him and his innocence so much she'd urged him to share the night and the next at no further charge. The Prince had spent several evenings, in fact, tumbling around her chamber and marveling at this exciting new pastime in his life. He had convinced himself that nothing in the world could match the pleasure offered in Vadia's bed. And her early death at the hands of a drunken, vicious lord had sent the young Lucien into a mood so dark, so dangerous, that even his seemingly uncaring parents noticed. His mother doubled the guard around him but that precaution didn't stop the Prince slipping his minders after careful planning and endless patience—nearly a year—to steal into the lord's love nest, where he kept a mistress, and slashing his blade across the man's throat.

The guards suspected it was the work of Lucien but kept faith with him and said nothing; in fact, they'd sworn to a man that the Prince had never left their sight that night. The lord in question had been heartily disliked by most in the palace and particularly by the soldiers for his memorable behavior at the infamous battle of Black Rock, where too many fine young Galinseans had died after this same lord broke ranks. And so the soldiers had closed their own ranks around the Prince, who vowed privately never again to take a man's life in such a cowardly fashion.

Since Vadia, there had been plenty of women in his life and two who truly touched his heart. Only one of these could he now honestly say he loved with his very soul, would gladly give that soul for. And that was Ana. But even after all these years, Lazar maintained privately that only Vadia had ever made him feel as though he were invincible. The very sight of her sweet body and full breasts could make his throat go dry. Ganya, for whatever reason, was having the same effect on him now . . . and it amazed him.

He watched the rise and fall of her belly; she was still breathing deeply from her exertion and the cheering and whistling was finally dying down. Lazar wasn't sure what drove him to do it, but he stepped closer and held out his hand. Ganya's slim brown arm snaked up from the sand and clasped it. He pulled her gently to her feet as he took his sword from her hip.

In the language of the Khalid he murmured for her hearing alone, "I could believe my weapon is magically stuck to that marvelous pelvis of yours."

Ganya reached for the fabric covering her face and unveiled herself. The audience fell quiet. Lazar was unsure of himself; he was not used to any woman unveiling herself in public, but Salim grinned broadly and he was reassured.

"Perhaps there is somewhere else upon my body you would like to put your weapon?" she asked, eyebrow arching with her innuendo.

Lazar's throat felt suddenly gritty, as though he were unable to speak. He swallowed but still no pithy response came. He could tell she was around Herezah's age, probably moving into her fourth decade of summers. Not only did Ganya have a superb body but she possessed dark, exotic looks. Her large black eyes had a query in them, awaiting his answer, whilst her full lips pouted slighty, bemused that he was so hesitant.

"I'm not sure I understand," he finally stammered, annoyed with himself for sounding so hesitant.

"I have no husband. I invite you to lie with me," she answered, her expression now bold, her tone spiced with sensuality.

Lazar felt himself blush in the firelight. Not since Vadia had any woman been quite so unabashed with him. Even Herezah, so obvious in her desires, was made to look coy beside Ganya's candor.

Music struck up around them as people began to sing and dance. Lazar and Ganya had not been forgotten but they were no longer the center of attention, although Lazar was aware of the demon's cold stare boring into his back. And it was at this notion that the idea fell into place.

"Are you permitted?"

She laughed. "Permitted? The Khalid women make these decisions on their own, Spur Lazar. And I am a free woman. Since my husband died, I can take whomever I choose."

He gave a grimace. "Sounds like there have been many."

"There have been none," she assured in her smoky voice. "I am simply telling you that I can lie with whomever I choose. You are not married?"

He felt a presence at his side and glanced around to see Salim and the Vizier approaching.

Salim answered his daughter. "His heart hurts for someone, Ganya, but the Spur is unmarried, to my knowledge."

"Ah," she said, amusement sparkling in her eyes. "I can ease that pain." She and Salim both laughed softly.

Lazar had not ever before been propositioned in quite so

direct or confident a manner. He was excited and yet slightly unnerved by Ganya.

"What are you talking about, Lazar?" Maliz asked, irritation at not being able to understand in his voice.

Lazar turned and regarded the impostor. Ganya was his chance! She provided the opportunity to get to Iridor. He allowed the hint of a lascivious grin to crease his face. "Seems as though I'm the lucky one, Grand Vizier," he answered. "I've been offered a proposal I'm not sure I can turn down."

It obviously didn't take much for Maliz to read the body language and appreciate the sensuous atmosphere that hovered around the dancer or understand the Spur's innuendo. "They're offering her to you?" There was a note of envy in the Grand Vizier's voice.

Lazar shrugged now. "She alone makes the offer, Tariq. Salim here tells me it would be impolite to refuse."

"All part of the desert hospitality, I suppose?" Maliz finished archly.

"I suppose. I for one will not turn her down. Would you?" He grinned again, fiercely this time, then lifted his eyebrows in query.

"No, Spur. I certainly wouldn't. Enjoy." The Grand Vizier moved away.

Lazar, his heart hammering, quickly returned his attention to the Khalid pair beside him.

"Well, Spur?" Ganya said, her voice husky.

"How can I refuse such delectable Khalid hospitality?" he asked, palms wide in resignation.

Ganya gave a knowing smile. "Follow me," was all she said.

Salim clapped his hands and laughed. "I should tell you, Lazar, that Ganya is our tribe's lajka."

Lazar frowned, watching the woman move away toward the dunes. "Lajka?"

"Our dreamer," the man qualified. "She sees things. She is very special. You should be honored that she has chosen you."

"Indeed. Salim, I want you to make sure that we are left alone."

The man nodded, his expression saying that Lazar was stating the obvious.

"No, really, I need to be left entirely alone with Ganya. Do not let the Grand Vizier follow me under any circumstances, no matter how much he protests." Now Salim was frowning. "He will try, my friend. Tell him Ganya will bring bad luck down upon him, threaten him. Restrain him if you must."

Salim nodded again, looking slightly bewildered.

Lazar moved quickly toward Boaz. "Fayiz, I am going with this woman. Look after Jumo."

"What?"

"Make no fuss, my Zar," Lazar whispered, "It is important."

"Lazar! Is this dangerous?"

"No! But keep Tariq occupied as best you can. I don't want him following me."

Boaz nodded, confusion creasing his brow. "I trust you."

Lazar inclined his head with thanks and strode to catch up with Ganya. The Khalid folk began to clap and whistle as the pair left the light of the fire.

I hope you're paying attention, Iridor, Lazar thought, *because this is our only chance.*

Iridor watched keenly as his friend spoke to the person he had to presume was Boaz, who, except for his tall and slight build, looked almost unrecognizable in desert garb. He could see that Lazar was breaking from the main pack, following the magnificent dancer into the darkness. That must be the sign, he realized. This would be their chance.

He took off from the vantage of the dune and flew a long way around toward the direction in which Lazar headed, careful that he didn't risk exposing himself.

rafanz was sitting by her side. "Should I fetch someone? The old man who took care of your bathing has delivered babies in his time."

She recalled old Soraz with a soft smile as she took Arafanz's hand. "Don't look so worried. Lyana will take care of me. It is too early. These are warning pains, that's all—at least I think they are. And if the baby comes early, he will come with or without anyone's permission. Let us face that when it happens. He knows what to do and my body will guide me." He bowed his head and Ana felt her heart go out to him. When he was like this—so tender, so caring—he was irresistible. "It is kind of you to bring me to your room."

"I want to be able to watch you. You scared me today."

"Are you sure you want to give up your bed? I could easily—"

He lifted his gaze to hers. "Ana, I could sleep on the hard

ground for all the difference it would make to me! I am mindful, however, that you should be in a real bed, not this desert pallet."

"Perhaps you forget that I, too, am of the desert, Arafanz. I spent the first thirteen summers of my life sleeping on the ground."

"We are more suited than we give each other credit for, then," he replied in an attempt to lighten the leaden atmosphere.

Neither of them smiled.

"Do you regret your part in this?" she asked gently.

He shook his head miserably. "No," he answered with vehemence. "But I regret yours."

"What do you mean?"

"I wish you weren't involved. Why couldn't you be like the Valide, for instance? Then it would be easy to carry out my task and to feel nothing for you."

"How *do* you feel?" The question tumbled from her mouth before she could censure herself. She regretted her rashness immediately; she was opening up a pathway to him that should remain closed.

His gaze fell again and he looked to Ana like a wounded animal awaiting the fall of an ax. "I feel despair."

Ana knew what he meant but tried to backtrack, twist his meaning. "You're frightened of what's ahead."

"No," he said again, "that's not it. I am not frightened of what's ahead, other than losing you."

"Arafanz, there is no—"

"I know, don't say it. You've undone me enough. These past few months have allowed me to glimpse how life might have been."

Ana smiled in spite of herself. "Do you truly believe anyone lives like this out in the desert?" she asked, gesturing about the dimly lit but nonetheless attractive chamber.

His mouth twitched in an attempt at a grin. "It is unusual here, I admit, but I sense you have enjoyed your time nonetheless."

"I would be lying to you if I said anything other than I have never felt more at peace with myself." She looked away, hoping the conversation might end.

But Arafanz persisted. "Happy?"

His gaze was fierce; his eyes had a burning intensity that seemed to make the brighter flecks in his irises glow as if they were illuminated. They demanded that she answer truthfully. "Yes, I'm happy but—"

Arafanz leaned forward and coverered her mouth with his own. She was so shocked by his sudden movement, and then absorbed by all the sensations his lips exploring hers provoked, that she could not pull away. As Arafanz deepened his kiss, Ana's addled thoughts swirled guiltily toward Lazar. She realized she could never confuse the two men. With Lazar there was such hunger, such longing in their intimacy. With Arafanz she felt only tenderness . . . and a surge of sorrow. This needed to stop—now!

One of the candles that Arafanz had lit around the room suddenly guttered. Ana broke apart from him and immediately both of them looked at the smoking wick, an ominous sign.

"We mustn't, please, Arafanz," Ana said, feeling instantly fearful.

"Do you subscribe to such childish superstitions? That was only a draft." He smiled.

She ignored his question. "This is not right," she replied instead, embarrassed by his amusement as much as relieved that the spell had been broken. And gone with it was the dangerous moment of abandon and enjoyment.

"Apologies, Ana. I hate myself for being so weak."

She shook her head sadly. "It is not weakness. It is life, Arafanz. It is normal to have feelings for another—you cannot expect yourself, or your men, to be celibate, especially cast together like this and in a battle we neither understand nor choose. But you and I are not normal, are we? We are pawns. We are being moved around and used. Our lives matter not in the great scheme of this battle. We do her bidding for the greater good and then we die." She grimaced again as a fresh contraction, soft but urgent, rippled through her body. It was uncomfortable, but now was not her birthing time, she was certain of it.

Arafanz wore a wounded expression. "It doesn't have to be like that, Ana. Perhaps—"

"What? You take my son from me, you deliver him to Percheron, and you ride back to the desert for me . . . is that what you think? We can just pretend none of this happened? What of your struggle? Your men? Boaz? Did you think the Zar will accept his wife and Absolute Favorite living in the desert with a rebel who declares war on the Percherese people?"

Once again he held her gaze with an unflinching stare, all injury gone from his face now. His voice was brittle when it came. "But this is not about Percheron, or the Zar, duty or the battle for Lyana's supremacy, is it, Ana? Your reluctance is not even about your son, or the desert, or your conscience. This is about Spur Lazar, isn't it?"

She had nothing to gain from lying to him. "I love him, Arafanz. I have since the day I met him—the first moment I spied him from the window of our hut in the foothills, standing so proud, so deeply unhappy. I don't understand what has happened between you and me. But it cannot flourish. I would be insincere to you if I allowed this to continue."

"I should have killed him when I had my chance," he said sourly.

"You don't mean that. You let him live for good reason. As you said, you both fight for the same cause, even though Lazar does so unwittingly."

"Be very sure, Ana. If Lazar tries to stop me in my mission, I will kill him."

"I know you will try."

He nodded. "Then please forgive my indiscretion."

Ana reached for his arm. "Arafanz, wait. Please." He looked back at her and she could see pain in his eyes that he was trying to hide. "My heart is not hardened toward you. I need you to know that. In a different life, a different situation, I would live in the desert with you and I would not regret a day of it. We were meant to meet. But we were never meant to be lovers."

"Are you referring again to the omen of the candle . . . the hidden message; perhaps Lyana speaking to us?"

His sarcasm bit but she ignored it. "I do not refer to the candle, but Lyana has spoken to me."

"The pillars?"

She shook her head. "No. Have you heard of the Raven? The bird of omens?"

He frowned, shrugged. "It means nothing to me. What is it?"

"It is a he. This time he was Kett, a slave at the palace, and now I realize poor Kett was destined to join the harem."

"And what does this Kett have to do with me? Do I have to meet him?"

"Kett is dead. He drowned alongside me."

"Ah, I know now to whom you refer. Why are you telling me about him?"

She looked up, fixed him with a stare. "Because he told me about you."

"What?"

"He told me to find the rebel—yes, that's what he said. I'm only properly remembering it now; it was meaningless to me at the time of his death. Find the rebel, he urged me. And now I know that you are the rebel. We were predestined to meet, to know each other, but he said nothing about your importance to me or that we should be together. The truth is, Arafanz, I have my journey and you have yours. They are interwined but not in the manner of lovers. Whatever your role is, it is very separate from mine."

He nodded. "Finding myself so attached to you is painful, but it's true, I cannot be deterred from my life's mission. I despise all that Percheron has become, Ana. Fat, lazy, carnal, and without a guiding faith that means something. Zarab's way is indulgent, rather than nurturing. The Percherese have become soft. Crime and sin are rife. Have you seen the moneylenders and marketeers selling their wares outside the temples? Do people pray anymore? Do they hold true to a faith that guides them, inspires them, ensures they look behind them and offer help to someone who has fallen down?"

"I have no fight with your spiritual path, Arafanz. I uphold your faith and your desire to bring Percheron back to Lyana's Light. But I fear the bloodshed and death that you accept to achieve that. I could never go along with that reasoning, that the end justifies the means."

He smiled, stroked her cheek fondly. "You speak as though you are several decades older than you are."

"Boaz is a good Zar. Given the chance and the right support, he could be Percheron's greatest ruler. He has modern thinking but he is respectful of the old ways, the ancient thinking. He is a man of Zarab because that's how he was raised and yet his mind inquires toward Lyana."

"All very admirable, Ana, but—"

"Give him a chance. He has sat his throne for barely sixteen or seventeen moons. He learns fast, he is his own man. Let him grow into his role—"

"No! Your son will be Zar. He will outlaw Zarabism from the first day of his rule. And the present royal family and all the palace hierarchy will be put to death. We will start again through this baby," Arafanz said passionately, pointing to her belly. "I will set the terms of his rule and I will choose who acts as Zar Regent until your son is of age."

"When you are like this, it is hard for me to feel anything for you but contempt."

"Then you are fortunate, Ana." He kissed her hand and stood. "I wish I could feel that way toward you. Now rest. Your son must arrive healthy or all is lost."

Lazar led Ganya as far from the campsite as he dared.

"You obviously want privacy." She smirked when he finally pulled her around the back of a smallish dune. It was so dark he could barely make her out, for there was little moonlight tonight. "What did you have in mind?" she asked as he felt her arms around his neck.

"Ganya—"

"Shh," she said, placing her lips on his.

Ganya's arousing dance was suddenly back in his consciousness, her tongue working in treacherous tandem with his own lustful thoughts, winning an instant response from him. Helplessly he kissed her in return, his mind fleeing toward Ana as his arms felt the warmth of Ganya's naked back, her belly pressed hard against his. He begged Lyana to forgive his using this woman in such a manner. One of her hands reached down but Lazar pulled it away before gently pushing her back. "Don't," he said. His words came out as a plea.

"Don't?" she echoed, amused. "And yet your mouth says otherwise."

"I cannot," he groaned.

"Do you not want me?"

"More than you can imagine, Ganya. But what I need is your help."

"Help?"

He sighed. "It's so complicated, too hard to explain. I need you to trust me, as your father does." He could just see her brow creasing in confusion, and he hurried on, whispering, "As hard as this is to believe, I suspect an owl is going to arrive any moment and I don't want you to be startled."

"An owl, you say?" She laughed. "Well, this is a first for me."

"Ganya, please trust me. You are a beautiful, incredibly desirable woman and in different circumstances . . ."

"You would have thrown me to the ground and enjoyed me, I know," she said, an edge to her tone. "What about this owl? And what does it have to do with me?"

"He has nothing to do with you. He is a friend. I need to speak with him but I had to get away from the campsite. I used you. I'm sorry."

"You are going to talk to an owl? Are you some sort of good-looking madman?"

He shook his head. "This is a matter of life and death. You need to trust me."

"You've said that three times now. So, what happens when this owl arrives?" she asked. Her words went along with his story but her sharp tone goaded him.

"I told you. We will speak, share some knowledge. Actually, it's more likely he'll change into the form of a dwarf."

"Have you any idea how ridiculous you sound?"

Lazar sighed. "Frankly, yes."

"I put my claim upon you, Lazar. You accepted. In the way of the desert that agreement is binding. Don't humiliate me or lose the high esteem that my people hold for you."

"Help me and I will honor our agreement. But time is short."

"What do you want from me?"

"Just don't make a fuss when he arrives. Keep a lookout for anyone who may steal up on us. Garjan is my enemy. He especially must not know about the owl."

"And who is this all important bird, Spur, that would cause you to cast aside a chance to make love with me beneath the stars?"

Lazar took a breath. "His name is Iridor."

He heard her gasp as she yanked herself from his grip. "You dare to take Iridor's name in vain! It is wrong of you to make a jest like this."

"Ganya, wait, please. I warned you." He heard the beat of wings. "Watch."

Right enough, the owl appeared as if on cue.

"Don't scream, I beg you," Lazar beseeched.

But Ganya made no sound at all, just a soft moan of disbelief, tinged with awe. "How can this be?'

"It is him," Lazar assured her, hoping with every ounce of

faith that Lyana had guided him to this point. That she would not betray his instinct to be honest with this woman.

"How can I be sure?"

"The desert isn't normally home to snow white owls, is it?"

Ganya was silent.

"You follow the Goddess, don't you?" he asked.

"With every beat of my heart," she whispered.

"Then by his presence you will know what is occurring here."

"She is rising," Ganya answered. Her tone had lost none of its wonder.

He didn't really know what to say; he hardly believed it himself. "I told you Garjan is our enemy. I need to talk with Iridor but Garjan can sense the owl's magic. It is dangerous. I need to think."

Iridor had listened as Lazar spoke with the woman. He'd been listening from slightly farther away earlier and had taken his cue to arrive at the moment he did for maximum impact. Lazar had obviously put his trust in this woman, even though they were strangers. And now Iridor waited, frightened to talk to Lazar for fear of discovery but helpless to know what else they could do. He needed to give Lazar instructions. He sat still, sensing the woman's gaze fixed upon him.

"Lazar," she whispered, "what do you mean, he can sense the owl's magic?"

"The owl is here to give me a message."

"Who are you," she demanded, "that Iridor himself talks to you?"

Iridor could hear Lazar holding his rising irritation in check. "We are friends. I am helping his cause."

"Then I am his friend, too," she answered. "Can I help?"

"I don't think so. The magic can be traced. We need to speak but it will draw the wrong sort of attention."

"You use magic to speak?"

Of course, Iridor thought, equally frustrated. *How else is an owl going to talk to a man!*

"He speaks to me in my mind. No, wait!" Iridor watched Lazar take her arm as she prepared to stomp away in disgust. "I speak only the truth to you, Ganya. I have no reason to lie."

"How can I trust you?" she asked.

Iridor was surprised, even bemused, despite his fear, to see Lazar dip his head and kiss the woman in a long, deep embrace. Finally Lazar parted his mouth from hers. "That's why. If you sense any guile in that, you may leave and tell whomever you wish about what you've seen tonight. If you felt only sincerity, then trust me."

Iridor's exceptional eyesight saw Ganya smile at Lazar's words. "Did my father not tell you I was the tribe's lajka? There is an aura about you, which I don't understand. But I don't mistrust it either. And I think I can be more than a sentry for you."

"What do you mean?"

"If I hold the owl and I hold you, too, and go into my dream state, I might be able to surround you both with my own protection. I cannot maintain such a protection for long but it will stretch to a minute perhaps, enough for you both to communicate."

Iridor watched Lazar hesitate, then nod. "Anything's worth a try. But then we will have no one standing guard."

"Risk it!" she said, taking his hand.

Lazar turned to his friend and Iridor glided down from the

dune and watched as Ganya helplessly fell to her knees, still holding Lazar's hand. "Iridor," she murmured, placing her other hand over her heart. "The Khalid welcome and revere you."

"Ganya," Lazar growled. "There is no time for this. It has to happen now."

Iridor hopped over to the woman and allowed her to pull him close so that his back nestled against her. She wrapped an arm around him and once again took Lazar's hand. "Ready?" she asked.

"Do it!" Lazar replied, urgency in his voice as he cast an anxious glance around him.

"I must find my quiet place and then I will slide into a trance. I won't be able to see or hear anything around me, not even you. I cannot guarantee—"

"Ganya, please. Let's try," Lazar urged.

She nodded, bowed her head. The trio were bound in silence for several tense moments. Suddenly the air felt thick around Iridor. He could no longer feel Ganya behind him or her arm around him but he was aware of her as a smothering presence about him. He took a slow, deep breath, and put the threat of Maliz to one side.

Lazar, he said gently. *Can you hear me?*

I can. How are you, old friend?

The very short version is that I am stuck as Iridor now. The demon found me. Pez, as you knew him, is dead. Tortured and drowned. But Maliz learned nothing; he is no closer to Iridor or Ana . . . or you. But you must be careful about everything you say or do. He is frustrated and is in a dangerous frame of mind.

I don't know what to say, Lazar said softly into his mind.

There is nothing to say. I am gone as you knew me. What is im-

portant is Ana. I cannot tell you the way. I can only lead you there, but if the Khalid carry hawks, I'm in danger.

One hawk is certainly with us, Lazar confirmed. *Let's just figure out tomorrow's journey and we'll worry about the rest of it as we go forward.*

All right. Travel all of the next five days in a firm westerly direction. We will need to meet the night of that fifth day to reassess our plans. I'll be watching you that evening for any sign that you can get away. As for how we avoid Maliz sensing our conversation . . . I don't know. We may just have to place our faith in the Lore and hope it's enough.

We know it's not.

We have nothing else. Use Boaz to divert him.

Boaz? What reason do I give?

I have shared my fears with him. Not explicitly that his Grand Vizier is Maliz but that he's an impostor, using magic, and means us harm.

If Lazar was surprised at this news, he didn't share it. *We'd better stop. Ganya's cloaking—if it's working—cannot last much longer.*

I shall fly ahead to stay well clear of your birds. I'll probably be a day ahead.

Be careful, Pez.

Iridor smiled sadly within. *Call me Iridor now. Our one advantage is that Maliz has no idea I've survived.*

What about Ana? Can you not reach her through the mind?

Right now I am nervous about how vulnerable that makes us. Who knows what powers are being used by Arafanz? And with Maliz in our amidst I am fearful of revealing us all.

Risk it. We have to risk everything.

All right. When I feel far enough ahead, I'll try.

Lazar broke the chain with Ganya and pulled her hand from around Iridor. "Go now," he said, and the great owl took two hops and flew into the night.

"Ganya," Lazar whispered. She moaned softly. "Ganya, it is done."

She opened her eyes and took a deep breath. "And you were safe?"

He grinned in the darkness. "It seems so."

"It worked!" she said.

"Perhaps. We could have just been lucky."

"That won't get you out of our bargain, Spur Lazar."

"I have no intention of reneging. What you did was brave."

She shook her head. "What I did was for Lyana. I am not going to think about what I just experienced until later when I'm alone and have silence and solitude to understand it. Iridor!" She gave a soft laugh of awe.

"You believe it was him, don't you?"

"I do. I felt his presence. And you, Lazar, who are you in this struggle?"

The question hurt. "I don't know," he said sadly. "But I seem to be in the thick of it."

"I saw other things just now. Things about you."

"What did you see?"

"Pain, mainly."

Lazar sighed but said nothing.

"Let me help you lose that pain, if just for a short while," she said gently, huskily. "There are no consequences with me, Lazar. I listened to your heart speak. The name of a woman echoes around it. Although I cannot make it out, I know she is young, vulnerable."

She pulled him close and he nodded, his face buried in her neck, her long hair shrouding him.

"I love her but I cannot have her," he groaned. "And I fear for her. She is in mortal danger. She is why we make this dangerous journey."

"I understand. You carry many burdens and much grief within you, Lazar. You do not love me but you can have me. I offer you a transient but safe sanctuary."

Lazar picked up Ganya effortlessly, and in a relative cocoon of privacy between two dunes, he released his sorrows.

18

"Lazar has been a long time," Maliz said sourly.

"You can't rush these things," Boaz replied with annoying calm. The Grand Vizier grimaced. The youngster had certainly rushed his copulation with Ana and still managed to sire a child. "Besides, it's good for him," Boaz confirmed.

"And how do you think your mother will feel?" Maliz asked.

"I can't say. But what she doesn't know can't hurt her, eh?"

Maliz could hear the edge of disdain in the youngster's voice, as if he were speaking to the old Tariq. Why would the Zar be pleased about this situation?

"So you're happy that the Spur has left his Zar alone and unguarded whilst he attends to his own carnal needs."

"Oh, Tariq, please," Boaz hissed. "Firstly, I am not alone. Secondly, we have not left Khalid territory yet and Arafanz presumably has no gripe with the tribe; if he did, they'd already all be dead. I see no reason that I need a guard right now. Thirdly, what Lazar does with his nights is his business, not yours."

"I just think we should—"

"What? Go take a look? Go check to see if he's all right? Whether lying down with the beautiful dancer is as good as it sounds? For Zarab's sake, Tariq. He's a man, he's doing what every unattached, red-blooded man in his prime does. The woman offered herself. Let's leave my mother out of this. She is a grown woman and she has made her own decision regarding the Spur. She knows their 'relationship' will be plagued by problems, not the least of which are his freedom and her enforced attachment to the harem."

"So you're comfortable with his dalliances?"

Boaz laughed. "Tariq, if you think Lazar has given his heart to the Valide then you are far more naive than I. You know their history. What happened between them has certainly surprised me but it cannot last. Lazar, by his own admission to me many years ago, has no capacity to love a woman in a single-minded fashion."

"In the way that you do, is that what you mean?" Maliz baited. He hadn't meant to antagonize but he didn't like the Zar's condescending tone.

"Perhaps."

"How you admire the Spur! You advocate the notion of a man spreading his seed among many women and yet you do not."

"Consider my position. I can hardly subscribe to any other way of life."

"But—"

"But how I choose to live within that way of life is my own choosing. I am, after all, who I am. The fact that I choose to be monogamous at this point is a personal preference. I have absolutely no gripe with any other man following the Percherese way—Lazar, or, indeed, yourself included. My mother knows this. My mother would accept this. She is hardly in a position to do otherwise, wouldn't you say?" Maliz opened his mouth to respond, only to be cut off again. "But that does not mean I wish to grind salt into a wound, Tariq. If my mother hears of Lazar's desert dalliance, as you put it, I could only assume that you helped her to discover this news, and if, Tariq, it should upset her, then I would blame you for her angst . . . not Lazar, who, if nothing else, is discreet."

Tariq's head bowed in acknowledgment of the artful rebuke, but Maliz was not yet prepared to accept that rebuke quietly. "And I wonder, Majesty," he muttered, "how you might feel if you were in the same position?"

"And what is that supposed to mean?" Boaz challenged, all politeness gone, his anger evident by how quickly his hand moved.

"Majesty," Maliz whispered, spluttering, "people will see your hand at my throat and they won't understand. You are meant to be Fayiz, a soldier in training."

"Don't forget your place, Vizier," Boaz growled, but he let go of the man he threatened. "I enjoy your new sardonic style, Tariq, and by all means let it be a fresh weapon you wield against others, but don't use it against me. Ever."

Maliz rubbed Tariq's bruised neck, trying not to cough. "Forgive me, Majesty. I was simply trying to understand your incredible devotion to this one woman."

"Are you mischief making, Tariq, or do you have something to tell me?" Boaz demanded.

Maliz stared at his Zar, disguising his shock. The Zar's violent and highly emotional response was unfounded. "Let me just fetch myself a cup of water, Fayiz," he said, still rubbing his throat.

Boaz nodded his permission and Maliz moved over to the skins, poured himself a small cup of water, and took his time swallowing it whilst he thought about what he knew. For all intents and purposes, Lazar was much too fond of Ana, and although he worked hard to hide it, everyone, down to the servants, had noted his helpless devotion to the girl. Their distance from each other on the previous trip into the desert had certainly been contrived—he could work that much out. What he hadn't considered yet was how much of these same signals Boaz was picking up from a distance. Maliz already knew he should not underestimate the Zar. The youngster might still be trying to grow a decent beard, but he had a mature head on his shoulders. Could the Zar be aware of the doomed couple's unwise fascination for each other? Maybe the Zar was insanely jealous, given his feelings for the Zaradine, and was just sensibly keeping a lid on his emotions. But it surely wouldn't take much to lift that lid. Boaz's outburst was testimony to those emotions beginning to escape . . . his physcal threat alone demonstrated the depth of his anger. With some careful management, perhaps Maliz could make use of all that pent-up rage.

He wandered back to the Zar and sat down.

The Zar cleared his throat. "Tariq, you must forgive—"

"No, Majesty, I have nothing to forgive," he whispered, checking to see that no one could eavesdrop. "The error was mine. It is true that I am jealous of the Spur. I always have been. I resent him not only lying with the most beautiful woman in the harem—your wife aside, of course, Highness—but now he casually plucks an exquisite ripe young woman from the desert and has his way with her, too, barely a day after kissing the Valide farewell."

Boaz gave him a sympathetic shrug. "Tariq, Lazar did not kiss my mother good-bye. I was there. He was his usual detached and distant self. If my mother suffers delusions that Lazar is going to suddenly become an affectionate, demonstrative, and monogamous partner, I would counsel her otherwise. The fact is, Grand Vizier, the Valide is far too smart to put any sort of constraint on a man she can barely call her own and who has operated under his own set of rules since I was old enough to know him. You have no need to fret on the Valide's behalf. And you insult Lazar—and indeed me—if you think Percheron's lauded Spur can be controlled by his physical needs. Let's face it, Tariq, you and I both know Lazar does not need a tribeswoman to arouse his desires in the middle of a dangerous crossing of the desert when he could lie down with just about any woman he chooses at any time."

Maliz smiled inwardly. This was the opening he needed. "Yes, of course you're right . . . but that, I hasten to add, was my very point, Majesty." He sighed. "Anyway, I had no right to talk to you in such a familiar manner and I beg your deepest pardon."

He watched Boaz frown. "What do you mean?"

"Highness?" Maliz's tone was all innocence and regret now. "Explain what you mean by that being your very point."

"Er, perhaps not, Highness. I have already overstepped my mark tonight and I wish not to inflame your senses. What I think is not necessarily always wise to share. My years make me more cynical than most, Highness. I must learn to keep my thoughts to myself."

"Don't play coy with me, Tariq. Now you're treating me even worse than you did when you were being honest with me."

"Highness, I beseech you. I am a loyal servant of Percheron. I have only your interests at heart."

"And that is precisely why I am giving you the chance to explain yourself, Grand Vizier."

Maliz allowed Tariq's expression to turn into one of dismay and fear. "Zarab save me, Highness," he hissed. "I just want to spare you heartache."

"What exactly are you talking about?" Maliz heard the dangerous edge to the Zar's voice now. He had pushed him hard enough. It was time to let Boaz, who was teetering on the edge, choose whether to step back or fall into the abyss.

Adopting a tone of injured innocence, Maliz replied: "Why, Lazar and Ana, of course."

Boaz rocked back. "What about them?" he asked, glaring through his frown.

"I know that I told you Spur Lazar had been exemplary in his treatment of the Zaradine."

"The Valide said the same."

"In all respects he was, my Zar, except . . ." Maliz dropped his head and now moved into his ruse that was half truth, half lie. "There was an occasion—it was one of the nights after the manservant Jumo had died. Lazar was deeply withdrawn and hostile to everyone. He refused to eat, and sat alone, well away from either the royal party or the Khalid."

"The Valide told me she delivered food on one of these nights and Ana accompanied her."

"That's right, Highness. It was this same night!" Maliz replied eagerly.

"Go on."

"Well, it was much later, into the early hours of the morning perhaps, when I was disturbed from my sleep. I don't know what woke me—I have to presume it was a sound and yet I don't remember hearing anything." So far it was the truth. Maliz still pondered over that curious moment in the desert when he had felt something akin to the awakening he had been searching for, was still in fact searching for—the awakening that would bring him fully into his powers and tell him Lyana had risen. He saw the frown of irritation on his Zar's face and knew it was time to hurry on with his tale. "I got up, and lo and behold, there was Zaradine Ana stepping back into the campsite."

He watched Boaz suddenly sit upright. "What do you mean, *back* into the campsite?"

Maliz shrugged. "Well, I was told by the Zaradine that she had needed to relieve herself. Naturally I believed her. She was, after all, pregnant and sickening."

"Was anyone with her?"

"No, Majesty, she was alone. We were alone. All was silent and still."

"Then what is your point, Tariq?"

Maliz waited for the fresh gust of exasperation from the Zar to dissipate and then let another few moments pass as he feigned reluctance to speak.

"Tari—"

"Majesty . . . " He cut across Boaz's words softly, putting a sad tone into his voice to enforce the lie. "I didn't return immediately to my tent. I sat outside, drank some water, got lost in my thoughts. A little while later I saw a figure rounding a dune—precisely the same dune that Ana had emerged from behind. The man moved silently—stealthily, you could say."

"Lazar?" Boaz asked, and Maliz heard the catch in the Zar's throat.

He nodded miserably. "It seemed so innocent at the time.

It's only now that I am piecing together what could have happened. Majesty, I have no proof. This is speculation and that's why I was reluctant to say anything."

Boaz ignored his protestations. "Do you believe my wife had been with the Spur?"

Maliz shrugged with as much contrived embarrassment and reluctance as he could muster. "I cannot say. All I can tell you is that it is very possible, Highness, that they were alone and all their careful avoidance of each other is a ruse. I say that with deepest respect to yourself and Zaradine Ana. She is pregnant by you and so clearly fond and loyal to you, Majesty, that this is all—simply speculation. I could be reading the situation entirely wrongly; it may have been pure coincidence. I would counsel you that it is unwise to jump to any conclusions."

"But you have made me arrive at a conclusion, Tariq, or you would not have begun this conversation. Nothing you say is ever said by chance or without careful thought."

"That is true. But I am very mindful that two hops don't make a leap, Highness. It is always dangerous to make assumptions until the information has been verified. In this instance we cannot verify anything unless . . ."

"Unless what?" Boaz demanded, and Maliz suppressed his smile in the darkness. This was too easy!

"Unless, of course, you already have your own personal suspicions about Spur Lazar."

Boaz swung away but Maliz didn't miss how the young ruler balled his fists, his body tensed with anger.

"Go and find Lazar. It is time he returned to the camp," Boaz said in a dull tone. Maliz heard the repressed fury in the young man's voice. He wanted to laugh out loud. Instead he followed the Zar's orders and duly went in search of the rutting Spur.

Lazar had just finished tying on his sword belt.

"Do you ever go anywhere without those weapons?" Ganya asked lazily from the sand, where she had finally sat up.

"I bathe with them," he said smiling to hear her deep chuckle.

"I enjoyed you, Lazar, but I have to wonder what was driving all that passion. It felt like anger, not lust."

Lazar gave a glance of remorse. "It's not you, Ganya. You are nothing short of delicious . . . and especially generous," he replied, offering her a helping hand. She took it, allowing herself to be pulled up to her feet, and set to re-dressing herself. "And you are very beautiful too," Lazar added, hoping he hadn't hurt this woman's feelings. She really was spectacular in every way.

"Beauty is transient. I like to think I excite a man in other ways."

"You do excite me on many levels."

"Not enough, though, perhaps?" she queried, eyeing him with her head cocked to one side.

He sighed. "I cannot offer you anything."

"I don't remember asking you for anything," she replied. Suddenly she shivered. The temperature had dropped.

Lazar offered her his cloak, which she gladly allowed him to place around her shoulders, turning her back on him to make it easy. He kissed her neck as he fastened the garment.

The moon emerged to light them and Lazar knew it was time for them to return to the campsite. "Percheron is on the brink of war, Ganya. Stay here; stay safe and forget this night. I could be dead within weeks."

She spun within his embrace to face him. "Don't die, Lazar. And don't trust those who are seemingly closest to you."

He stepped back, looking at her quizzically, his hands resting on her shoulders. "What does that mean?"

Ganya shrugged. "I don't know. I saw something, sensed something—I'm not sure. But there's a threat from someone you trust."

"I trust no one," he replied.

"You trust the owl, you trust the girl you seek, you trust the men you travel with . . ."

"The girl's name is Ana and yes, I trust her with my very soul. Iridor will not betray me. I trust only one of the people I travel with."

"Who is the young man in your group?"

"No one," he said hurriedly. "A friend's son, training to join the Protectorship."

"You don't trust the older man you're with. But you aren't close to him, either. Consider my warning, Lazar—someone close to you will betray you."

Lazar felt a chill pass through him and was reminded why he never visited seers. "Is that all you can tell me?"

"Ana is definitely in danger. I cannot see her but you and she are connected. I followed that connection and I could sense that the threat against her is very real." Ganya hesitated, then pressed on. "Did you know she is pregnant?"

Lazar dropped his head. "Yes. She is Zaradine Ana. That's why I can only love her from afar. Her baby is the Zar's child."

Ganya didn't seem at all surprised by his confession. "It is an heir."

"You're sure?"

"Even she knows it is a boy."

"What else do you see? Please tell me."

"I have told you everything. I can only sense certain things—besides I only glimpsed her through you and so can only learn from what you know or feel, or direct me toward."

"The main thing is that she is safe."

Ganya nodded. "For now. Listen, Lazar, there is something else I want to suggest."

"Why do I already believe I won't like it?"

She smiled. "Perhaps you will."

"Lazar!" They both started at the sound of the voice calling from the darkness.

"It's Garjan," Lazar said, annoyed by the interruption.

"The one you don't trust?" she asked, her eyebrow arching.

"Yes."

"I know who he is, Lazar. My father told me that you travel with the Grand Vizier of Percheron."

"Does anyone else know?" She shook her head. "Well, as none of the people who were with your father last time are among us now, I would be grateful if we could keep it between us."

She nodded. "He will find us any moment. I want to tell you something. I think I should come with you."

"No, absolutely not. Definitely, no!"

"Listen to me," she urged.

He pulled away. "No, Ganya! I will not risk your life as well as that of your father. We are all probably walking into Arafanz's trap, into our deaths. No!"

"Lazar, I can help you. I can allow you to talk with Iridor. I can protect you both from him." She pointed into the darkness in the direction of the Vizier's voice.

"You know?"

"I know only that you fear him. I don't know why and I don't care. But my skills kept you safe. Trust them. Trust me."

"I shall think about it," he agreed, seeing that she had no intention of backing down.

"Don't leave it too long to decide, Lazar. My father will send us all away tomorrow morning. Now kiss me, make it look real when he comes upon us."

Lazar grabbed her and kissed her deeply. A moment later the Grand Vizier hoved into view.

"Ah, there you are, Spur! Did you not hear me?"

Lazar broke the kiss, winked at Ganya, and moved into Percherese. "I was otherwise occupied, Garjan, can you not see?"

"You certainly took your time," Maliz replied, his tone acid.

"I never rush a woman. And this one is far too delectable to hurry."

"Fayiz needs to ask you something," Maliz said, loading the name with ridicule.

Lazar sighed. "We're coming."

"I was told to find you and now I'm going to escort you." Maliz's tone was officious and presumptuous.

Lazar spun on his heel, his effort to sound lighthearted in the afterglow of his lover's embrace vanishing. "If you ever presume to tell me what to do again, I'll break your neck in a second and there won't be any warning." It was all bluster, since he had been warned that he couldn't kill Maliz, and yet he was surprised to see the Grand Vizier swallow, his lips pursing as he turned and stomped off.

"Hurry up, Lazar," he called over his shoulder.

The Spur's eyes narrowed in thought and he stared hard at the back of the fleeing man.

"Lazar?" Ganya pulled at his arm.

The spell was broken but the niggling notion that he had stumbled upon something stayed with him. "Yes," he replied. "It is time to go."

19

Herezah was restless but thoroughly enjoying the new-found freedom of her new suite of rooms beyond the harem. An Elim guard moved with her at all times, which heightened her sense of importance. Since her new status had been declared, she had ensured that she was veiled, conservative in her dress, and guarded in her movements. She would give no one any ammunition at this point; she would be the model regent. But she knew her absence from the harem and her superior status would be galling to Salmeo, hopefully even frightening him.

She intended to make him pay for his indiscretion and his quietly spoken but not very well-concealed threat. Had he not disturbed them, things might have turned out differently between her and Lazar.

A bell jangled softly. "Come," she said, and Bin entered. "Ah, Bin, what news?"

He crossed the floor and bowed. "We have heard back from the Isles of Plenty, Crown Valide."

"And?" she asked, impatient.

He took a breath. "King Falza of Galinsea is aboard one of the ships. He has accepted your invitation."

She clapped her hands. "Thanks to Zarab! When?"

Bin's expression turned sheepish. "He would not say, Crown Valide. He said he would send a message soon enough."

"Soon enough?" she replied angrily. Then she reined in her critical tone. Bin was her eyes and ears in the world outside the palace. She needed him loyal and keen. And although she was not used to apologizing to anyone other than Boaz, she did so now. "Forgive me, Bin. That was ungracious of me. I realize you are merely conveying the information you have."

He looked surprised at her apology, bowing in acknowledgment. "I can confirm, Crown Valide, that there are now five more war galleys and we suspect more are on the way."

"The Spur warned there would be more and still Falza waits. He must surely know we are no match for their might."

"I'm sure he does. Perhaps he is toying with us?"

"Well, let us face the beast that threatens us, Bin. I shall go mad sitting around in the palace awaiting death."

"What do you mean, Crown Valide?"

"I mean that I shall take control of this situation as best I can and I will present myself to Falza. He can hardly refuse me."

"Crown Valide, I must—"

"Bin, I do hope you don't plan to contradict me?" The servant stared at her, wide-eyed, before slowly shaking his head. "Oh, that's good. You must not worry about me. We are all in this precarious situation together. My role right now is to do everything I can to protect Percheron. If that means throwing myself on the mercy of a foreign king, I shall not hesitate. I mean to return this city intact to my son when he reemerges from the desert with his heir."

She watched Bin stand straighter at her rousing words. She was right. Percheron needed a fearless leader right now. "Prepare a statement for our people, Bin. Let's let them know my intentions. Have it ready by eighth bell for me to approve."

Bin swallowed. "As you wish, Crown Valide. When, er, when do you intend to make this visit?"

"The day after tomorrow, I think . . . if we haven't heard from our Galinsean rival by then. Thank you, Bin. Send in Elza if you see her on your way out. I must make plans with her for readying me for this expedition."

The morning had dawned and brought with it a dry, hot wind. Lazar was eager to depart to get in a few hours' travel before it intensified.

Salim approached. "I hear you and Ganya enjoyed each other's company last night."

Lazar glanced at his Khalid friend. "She is very special, your daughter. Who looks after her in your absence?"

Salim shrugged. "She belongs to our people. She is our lajka—everyone would fight to protect her."

"I see," Lazar said, nodding. "It is time to send your people on their way, Salim. We must make our own way west now."

"How do you know in which direction we are to travel?"

"You will have to trust me on this. And I am going to pretend to my companions that you know the way."

"I? Lazar—"

"Please, Salim. Just do as I say."

The Khalid stared at him through narrowed eyes, their

gazes locked momentarily before the desert man nodded. "Ready your people."

Lazar turned immediately to start hurrying along his Zar and the Grand Vizier. "Are you set?" he said to Boaz, although he could already see that the young Zar was ready to leave.

"Yes," Boaz replied crisply, and Lazar did not miss the chill of his tone.

Lazar called out to the Grand Vizier. "Tariq, we're leaving now. Your camels await." He returned his attention to Boaz. "I'll see you over there."

Boaz did not respond.

"Highness," Lazar said, moving close to the Zar so he could speak quietly. "Is anything wrong?"

"No, why? Should there be?"

Lazar noticed the Zar gave him no eye contact, was busying himself picking up his sleeping roll. "You seem a little out of sorts, Majesty."

"Do I?" Boaz asked, fixing him with an imperial gaze.

"You slept well?"

"I got more sleep than you, Lazar," Boaz fired back. There was none of the usual amusement in his tone.

"I hope you understood that I was with that woman because I was given no choice. It was expected."

"Yes, I worked that out for myself."

"But you're upset about it?"

"No, Lazar, you're the one who thinks I'm upset. I feel perfectly calm."

"Forgive me, Highness. It's just that you don't seem nearly as happy as you were yesterday.'

"Perhaps the gravity of our journey and what must be achieved has fully registered with me," Boaz said. Still Lazar detected a note in his Zar's voice that he had never before heard.

"Fair enough," he said. He would have to work out the hard way what was prompting this suddenly odd behavior in the Zar. "I shall meet you at the camels."

As Lazar walked toward the beasts he could see an argument in full swing between Salim and his daughter. He wished he could avoid being pulled into it, but he could see they were both waiting for him to arrive. Salim shrugged helplessly, embarrassed, as the Spur drew close to them.

"Lazar!" Ganya began, her eyes filled with anger. "I've told my father that I will be joining this caravan and that—"

"No, Ganya, you will not," Lazar interrupted. "It's too dangerous."

"But last night—"

"Last night was last night. I will not risk your life. I explained that."

"It is my life to risk!"

"Risk it somewhere else, Ganya. Right now you are too precious to your people for me to allow you to come."

She looked at him, the hurt in her expression obvious. But the fight went out of her stance and he could see that she had heard the tenderness in his voice.

"My love," her father began. "What we do is more than dangerous. It's suicide." He gave a short, humorless laugh.

"And yet you and Lazar press ahead!"

"Lazar must find this woman who belongs to his Zar. I must find your brother. You have nothing to find."

"Father, this should be my decision, not yours. And not his," Ganya argued, pointing at Lazar.

"Is there a problem?" Maliz's voice broke into the debate.

Once again Lazar was irritated by the manner in which the demon crept up on him. "Just a difference of opinion," Lazar said, hoping the Grand Vizier would move on.

"Oh? Can I help?"

"I don't think so," Lazar replied, glancing across the sand toward Boaz, hoping the Zar would understand the look for help and find a way to distract his Grand Vizier without it appearing odd. Instead, Boaz looked away, moving toward his camel.

"Yes, you can help," Ganya began breathlessly, ignoring Lazar as well. "Lazar, translate this or I will somehow communicate to him—and your younger friend, fiddling with his camel's straps—that you raped me. Somehow I sense you would mind the boy knowing this, no?"

Lazar stared at her incredulous. "You cannot mean that. No one would believe you."

"And you could lie in the translation anyway," she said.

Their gazes locked, each of them neither angry at nor amused by the other. The standoff lengthened.

"You know I can help you with your friend," Ganya pressed, careful not to mention the owl or his name. "You both need protection. And your cause is more important than any of us."

Lazar nodded, although his expression told her he didn't fully agree with her final statement.

"Spur, I really must insist you explain what's happening," the Grand Vizier said, his exasperation spilling over.

"Tell the Vizier what I say," Ganya urged. "And trust me as I now trust you."

Lazar was hopelessly cornered and could see he would get no help from Salim, who was gently shaking his head.

She began, looking at the Grand Vizier. "Tell this man that I am not allowing my father to walk into danger without receiving all the right help we can possibly give him."

Lazar reluctantly turned to the Grand Vizier and gave a quick version of what Ganya expressed.

"Ask her to explain that, please," Maliz asked, more politely now.

"What did he say?" Ganya demanded, and Lazar translated through gritted teeth. She nodded. "Tell him I am this tribe's lajka and my father is the elder of our desert people and we are risking his life for the benefit of your Zar's wife."

"This man has no authority out here," Lazar said to her.

"Tell him all the same. Let him think that I consider him important."

Lazar did so and the Grand Vizier nodded. "I understand. How can we further minimize danger, then?" He glared at Lazar, who, frustrated, continued to act as interpreter.

After listening, Ganya replied, "By allowing me to join this party!"

Maliz heard her demand through Lazar and to his credit looked thoughtful. "Forgive me, but last night you danced for and lay with the Spur. I don't see how your presence adds anything more than . . . er, shall we say *entertainment* for him."

Her eyes narrowed as she regarded the Grand Vizier. "That may be, sir, but do you know what being a lajka means?"

Maliz shrugged at the question when Lazar posed it. "A fortune-teller, isn't it?"

Lazar told her the Grand Vizier's response. Father and Spur looked down as Ganya straightened, her expression instantly indignant. "It seems you need enlightening, sir. A lajka is a seer. A tribe is fortunate to find one of their own with the sight."

"Forgive me," Maliz said, a new respect in his tone that Lazar communicated. "Make sure she understands," he said to the Spur, before adding for her benefit, "I am indeed ignorant. And have you seen something?"

"Yes," she said, turning a fresh glare on Lazar. He could see where Ganya was taking this, and much as he didn't want another life to defend, especially one so precious as this one, he also knew this woman was likely the only real protection that he and Pez had against the demon.

"Last night as I 'lay' with the Spur," she began, loading the word with the same derision the Grand Vizier had, "I saw the way forward for you."

"What?" This had Maliz's attention. "What does she mean, Lazar?"

"I believe she's about to explain," Lazar replied.

She nodded. The man's reaction needed no interpretation. "Ask your Spur; it's easier than asking my father."

The Grand Vizier's gaze moved between the two men. "What does she mean?" he demanded.

Boaz sidled up to join the small group.

Lazar sighed. "She means that last night, in touching me, she could 'connect,' for want of a better word, with our mission. She knows what we seek and she can sense the direction we need to follow."

"But don't you know where we are going?"

"I know only that Ana was stolen and taken in a westerly direction," Lazar lied. Ganya was right. Warming to his task, he decided that if Salim was comfortable with Ganya's risk, then who was he to tell her how to live her life.

"And she knows differently?" Maliz queried.

Lazar nodded. "I'm slightly in awe of her, in fact. She gave me very clear directions for us to follow."

"She sees this?" Maliz spluttered, unable to hide his incredulity. "What sort of magic is this, Lazar? Do you expect us to believe it? Or is this some excuse you and she have cooked up so that you can have a warm body next to you during the cold desert nights?"

"Garjan." Boaz spoke up. "It is fortunate that these people do not understand us entirely, although I wouldn't hesitate to admonish you in front of them, whether it gave away our secret or not. Do not ever again let me hear you speak with such disdain to my Spur. He is my chosen guide and leader. In him I place all my faith. I place my life. You can neither protect me, fight for me, nor guide me to my wife. Lazar can. I demand that you show him respect." He said this all in a friendly way, taking such a subordinate tone that Lazar felt a whole new surge of admiration for his Zar. The young man was a born politician. If Joreb could see him now, he would smile from his tomb.

Boaz didn't wait for his Grand Vizier to respond. He turned directly to Lazar. "Can she help us find Ana?"

"Yes. But she is one more mouth to feed, one more life to protect."

"Then don't protect it," Boaz said more heartlessly than Lazar thought he was capable of. Neverthless the Spur kept his expression impassive as the Zar continued. "Tell her she is welcome to come with us and we will pay her people handsomely for the use of her skills. I presume you will have the dubious chore of a nightly meeting with her, Lazar, and you have my permission for that and the privacy it would require. As long as she takes us closer each day to the Zaradine, she can have whatever she wants. Come with me, Garjan."

"Thank you," Lazar replied softly, angered by Boaz's lack of care for Ganya, but still impressed that he'd managed to say all that he did without his tone ever changing from one of respect to his Spur. He ignored the Grand Vizier's scowl and turned to the patient Khalid pair. "We have discussed the matter, and if you insist on coming along, it must be your decision alone. I can offer no special protection."

"I didn't ask for it," Ganya replied curtly, flouncing away to fetch her few belongings.

Salim looked wryly at the Spur. "It seems my daughter is more fond of you than she cares to admit."

"Salim, I cannot—"

"I know. I will talk to her. But she will insist on accompanying us. I know that look. Her mother taught her well."

Lazar twitched a grin. "She can see, that's the thing. I won't refuse her help."

"Then we give it gladly. It means we get closer to her brother with each day. But, Lazar, don't hurt her. She is lajka, yes, but first she is a beloved daughter of mine."

Lazar nodded. "I didn't tell my people the whole truth. Ganya and I do not need to . . . well, you know," he said, shrugging. "She only needs to hold my hand or touch a shoulder to use her powers."

Salim laughed. "That won't stop her, Spur. She has chosen her place in the sand. Now she intends to lie in it."

"I know," Lazar admitted, embarrassed, "I just wanted to assure you that I won't—"

"You miss my point, Spur," the Khalid said, still amused. "I would be more disappointed if you didn't. This is what she wants. So long as you are honest with her—I am her father, I want her happy. If being close to you keeps her happy and she can help me find my boy, then the winds are calm—as we say in the desert."

"Your winds may be calm, Salim. Mine are blowing hard."

The Khalid chuckled. "The boy seems to speak his mind," he said casually, nodding toward Boaz.

"He is young, brash. Wanted to know what we were arguing about and then had the nerve to say his piece. He's lucky he didn't get a cuff around the ear for it," Lazar answered, moving toward his own camel.

Salim fell into step with him. "And yet you seemed attentive to his words, nonetheless."

Lazar gave his friend a sideways glance.

"I know, Spur. Shut up, Salim, and just trust you . . . and I do." This time the Khalid strode ahead, throwing a rueful glance back at his companion before he began barking orders to his people.

ord had come back from the Galiseans but it was not
as Herezah had anticipated.

"They said what?" she demanded.

Bin swallowed. "Crown Valide, it is difficult for us to comprehend precisely what the Galinseans are communicating. You
understand that we are working through interpreters on both
sides."

"Don't be fooled, Bin. King Falza, I'm assured, speaks
Percherese, no matter how haltingly he might convey it. He
is toying with us if he wants us to believe he needs to speak
through vague translation. Don't believe it. Tell me again what
was said."

"The messenger reports this message, Crown Valide: King
Falza will meet with the Crown Valide of Percheron via an-
other party. They wish this meeting to take place within the
Stone Palace complex. I am taking our own interpretation now,

Crown Valide, when I say that they understand that you may prefer not to have a Galinsean war delegation in the palace proper. Thus the King has agreed for the parley to occur on the Daramo River aboard barges."

"Aboard barges? He dares to tell us where and when and how?"

Bin looked nervous but remained steadfast. "Crown Valide, I'm not sure we're in a position to argue. It appears to me that the Galinseans are paying you quiet respect."

"Does it indeed?" she snarled, but his rationale caught her attention, impressed her with its insight. "Well, you're right in one respect: I don't have a choice. Set it up for tomorrow. The furthest point of the river, mind," she warned. "Is he sending this party alone?"

"An emissary—if we may call this person by such a title—plus one servant. You are permitted the same."

"I am *permitted*?" she repeated.

Bin stared at her, wide-eyed. "I am telling you only what has been communicated, Crown Valide. I would send many Elim if it were up to me. But you will be strong, Crown Valide, and the people of Percheron trust you to represent them with courage."

Bin's words appeased Herezah. He was right. She would show fortitude and she would not feel threatened but would instead be courteous and magnanimous in her dealings with the barbarians. "Fine. Set it up. Advise everyone you need to. Tell Elza and anyone else who needs to get me ready. And send for Salmeo but don't show him in immediately. Let him cool his heels outside until I'm ready to see him."

"Yes, Crown Valide, as you wish."

"Oh, and Bin?"

"Yes, Crown Valide?"

"Do we have a name for this *party*?"

"Yes," he said, and Herezah noticed his trepidation.

"Well? Don't stand there gawping at me, boy. What is his name?"

Bin took a breath. "It is a she, Crown Valide. Her name is Angeline."

It was Herezah's turn to suck in a breath. She swung around, momentarily speechless. Her voice finally pushed through the shock. "The Queen?" she asked, fright layering over her initial astonishment as her dream came back to haunt her.

Bin nodded. "So I am told, Crown Valide."

The smell of violets accompanied the swish of silks as Salmeo swept into her salon. He bowed, but only slightly, unable to pay the same kind of homage he was forced to give the Zar to a woman he saw at best as his equal, at worst as the most important slave of his harem. Although, if the Zaradine were alive, Herezah would be relegated to only second most important. This thought pleased him as he straightened.

"I thought it was urgent when you called for me, Valide."

"Did you? I lose track of time in this new role, Salmeo, but I have ordered some refreshment if that will console you."

He noticed the slight sneer and the lack of apology for keeping him waiting for nearly a bell's length. "And please call me Crown Valide. It is my proper title, as desired by the Zar. We must respect him in this," she said, her tone not quite hiding its sardonic edge.

A servant arrived with a tray and quickly laid out a jug with cups as Salmeo reined in his fury that had been stoked through the long wait in the corridor, his own Elim staring balefully at him and even the wretched Bin showing no apology in that impassive expression of his. "My apologies, Crown Valide—I shall certainly adhere to your wishes, although I would respectfully caution that we mustn't get too used to the royal title. After all, your son will be gone only weeks and then it's sadly back to the harem for you and for Ana."

"If she's alive," Herezah commented, unfazed by his words of caution.

"Indeed. But you are alive, Crown Valide, and I would hate for you to feel any more unsettled than you already have since returning from the desert."

"It's my welfare that you care about—is that what you're saying, Salmeo?" she queried, laughing.

He hated her calling him by his name, rather than by his title. Salmeo wasn't even his real name. His real name—Yokabi—meant "chieftain" . . . "king!" . . . "power!" Salmeo had been forced upon him by the slavers when he had refused to reveal his true name, given to him by his father, branded on his mother's back as proof that she had birthed a new king. He let none of these angry thoughts show on his well-arranged, calm expression.

"Crown Valide, I hope you will never question our longstanding relationship. We have known each for too many years." Salmeo could see by the way her eyebrows arched that Herezah understood precisely what his couched warning meant. But she clearly wanted him to say it in raw words.

"Are you threatening me, eunuch?"

"Threaten? Me, Crown Valide?" he asked, feigning injury. "Absolutely not. I am simply reiterating my loyalty to you. I will keep to myself what has passed between us certainly these past sixteen or seventeen moons, and I hope you will do me the same courtesy." He giggled softly. "We are, after all, a sister and brother of the harem. It is a world separate from the palace—we have our own rules, Crown Valide, our own ways."

"We must protect each other. Is that what you mean?"

"Precisely, Crown Valide. I'm glad we understand each other," he lisped, satisfied.

"I may understand you, eunuch, but you have to realize that my loyalties are being guided—no, demanded—in a new direction. I am now directly responsible for the security and well-being of our realm. I am, to all intents and purposes, a queen, and I must act as autonomously as that role requires. I cannot be limited or swayed by the needs of the harem. I have moved beyond its boundaries."

"For now, Crown Valide," he counseled carefully. "Soon you will be back within its confines—and then what?"

"Well, Salmeo, I'm not sure it has to play out that way ultimately. I have plans, you see?" *No, he didn't see, but he understood*. "Right now I'm not at liberty to discuss those plans with you because they involve Crown business, and whilst my life must now revolve around the Crown, Grand Master Eunuch, yours unfortunately revolves entirely around a group of slave girls who are learning how to sexually satisfy my son."

He understood so well, in fact, that in the few moments whilst she spoke, gazing at him over the top of her veil with eyes that smiled savagely, Salmeo made his decision. For far too long had he kowtowed to this woman—this cunning, disloyal whore who wasn't worthy to stare at his feet, let alone stare into his eyes with such loathing. He was unacceptably vulnerable to her—and Salmeo knew the Zar would welcome any excuse he could legitimately use to rid the palace of the present Grand Master Eunuch. No. There would be no waiting for Herezah to make her move. It seemed more radical measures would need to be taken . . . and swiftly.

"Pardon? My apologies, Crown Valide," he said evenly.

"I asked if you were paying attention to me?" Herezah demanded.

"Forgive me, I felt momentarily light-headed. The heat, you know, and the long wait. May I take a drink?"

"Of course," Herezah replied, leaning back against her chair, which was beautifully wrought and gilded with gold, as she watched him struggle forward against his own bulk to pour himself a cup of grape cordial, its cloying sweetness cut with lemon juice and chilled water.

It was an excuse, of course—a play for time—but he nevertheless welcomed the refreshment of the drink as it slid down his throat.

"Better?" she asked, clearly uncaring of whether he was feeling any brighter.

"Much," he lied.

"I was just telling you that tomorrow we are expecting an official visit from the Galinseans."

Salmeo smiled. "Is that so?"

"Yes. Apparently King Falza is sending his own emissary for a parley."

Salmeo didn't reply but pasted a quizzical expression onto his face to give the impression that he was, at least, vaguely interested. But to his mind the parley was evidence enough that the Galinsean patience had worn thin. "And how can I assist you, Crown Valide?"

"I need someone we trust more than any other to be my guard and servant. I am permitted only one person. It will be Elim, of course, as he'll need to guide the barge."

"One of the Mutes, perhaps?"

"Salmeo, I don't care who listens in on this. I'm fighting for our lives and I'm past being secretive about what might be said in royal company. I want you to select your best man. Strongest, most fearless."

"All Elim are strong and fearless, Crown Valide."

"Does that include you, Salmeo?" she asked in a biting tone.

"I am not Elim, Crown Valide."

"Well, I choose you anyway."

"Me?" He was taken by surprise but his smile was entirely genuine when it stretched across his mouth.

"I hope your size doesn't preclude you from being able to steer me to my destination aboard the royal barge, Salmeo."

Again he allowed her viciousness to slide past him as though he hardly heard her taunts. His tongue unconsciously flicked between the large gap in his front teeth. "It would be an honor to be at your side, Crown Valide."

"Good. Not that you have any choice in the matter, Salmeo. But I'm not asking you to accompany me because I need companionship, because I enjoy your presence, or out of any misplaced sense of friendship between harem members, eunuch. I want your slippery, cunning mind listening in and advising. We can use Percherese, and the Queen will struggle to follow when we speak quietly and quickly between ourselves."

She was extraordinarily misguided in thinking this was the way to repay his years of confidentiality. All of a sudden she viewed herself as a queen—feeling secure as a royal on her new throne—insulting him and baiting him in one breath whilst begging for his help with the next and expecting it to be given. He was not befuddled by her superior attitude, nor was he intimidated by her deliberate discourtesy; instead Salmeo could plainly see that Herezah was unnerved by Falza's move and suddenly needed the sort of help only the Grand Master Eunuch could provide. Except he'd run out of patience with this harem whore. He might even have helped her to escape had she taken a different attitude toward him. But now he couldn't wait for tomorrow to arrive. "I understand, Crown Valide," he said, arching his fingers. "Perhaps you would be kind enough to send one of the Elim with details of where you want me to be and when."

"Yes, I'll do that. Expect my runner, Salmeo. That will be all." She looked at Bin for him to follow. Herezah stood briskly and departed her salon for her personal chamber before the Grand Master Eunuch could even struggle to his feet and effect a bow.

Salmeo smiled and recalled something his father had said to him many years ago in an effort to soothe the youngster over their capture by the slavers. He remembered his father, manacled, chained, for all intents and purposes humbled; and yet in his eyes a fire burned when he spoke to his son and said: "*The lion does not turn around when a small dog barks.* You are that lion, Yokabi, while your slavers and those who will compel you, claiming superiority over you, are merely the dogs. Never forget that."

He had not forgotten it and he would not ignore that advice now.

They had been traveling for almost the whole day, and as much as Boaz was thrilled to be away from the stifling atmosphere of the palace and in a world he barely knew existed, the novelty of the desert was already wearing thin. It was unspeakably hot—so

arid that it sapped all desire to move—and if not for the ponder-
ous but soothingly rhythmic progress of the camels, he would
have wondered how any traders moved forward across this wilderness. He had already lost all sense of time, had been able to
isolate his mind from everyone around him in this single day of
mostly silent, slow travel. The hours in the saddle, the cocoon-
like protection of the veil of his turban, and the turning inward
that the desert naturally prompted had pushed him deeply into
his own troubled thoughts.

According to Tariq, Zaradine Ana had cuckolded him—and
apparently she'd managed to do this under the nose of the
Valide. It sounded impossible, for his mother, in particular,
would have been itching to find any fault with Ana. But Valide
had not said a bad word about either the Zaradine or the Spur.
And even if he accepted that Lazar was suddenly his mother's
favorite person, Ana would never be accorded that privilege.
And how odd for Tariq to *suddenly* remember something so
blatantly damning, especially at a time when it was obvious that
the Grand Vizier's dislike for the Spur had reared to the fore
again. For a while it seemed that Tariq's obsession with Lazar
had quieted to the point of no longer being an issue. But it was
back; and they were baiting each other again. Was Tariq making up this terrible story? But then Boaz was reminded of an old
Percherese saying: *if you can hear the river, the water is flowing,*
meaning no rumor or story was without some truth. So perhaps Tariq was not lying; perhaps the fright of their traumatic
journey had caused him to temporarily forget what he saw that
night in the desert. The deeper Boaz plowed into his private
musings, the darker his thoughts became, the more silent and
insular his world felt. Without Pez, and with Ana and Lazar's
treachery, he was truly alone. Joreb had always impressed upon

Boaz that a Zar walks alone, no matter how many favorites and wives he might have, no matter how many sons and daughters. How right his father had been.

He looked up and saw Lazar directly ahead, striding alongside his camel, falcon on his arm. The two Khalid, Salim and his daughter, also walked beside their beasts. Boaz hadn't been concentrating. He slipped off his camel, which managed to make him smile despite his mood, with what sounded like a grunt of thanks. Lazar heard it, too, and slowed slightly to let Boaz and his camel catch up.

"How are you feeling? A bit light-headed?" Lazar asked, concern in his tone.

Boaz shook his head free of his bitter thoughts. "Yes, er, I am, to tell the truth."

Lazar nodded. "It's normal. Don't fight it. I can remember the first desert journey I undertook. I think I went mad for a while. It's not the loneliness or the silence. It's the heat and the dryness of the air. If you allow yourself to lose too much moisture, your mind starts to play tricks on you." He reached for his saddlebag. "Here," he said, dribbling some water into a smoothed bowl that Boaz had seen the Khalid use. Lazar's movements were as fluid as the liquid nectar he was collecting in the bowl, without missing a step or losing a drop to the parched sand. "Drink regularly. We have plenty for the five of us and no one is more important than you."

"Do you mean that?" Boaz asked, gratefully swallowing from the cunningly crafted lip of the bowl. He licked droplets of water from his lips so none could escape.

"Your importance, you mean?" asked Lazar. Boaz nodded. Lazar gave him a glance of query. "Of course I do."

"It's just that I thought the desert made all men equal."

"All *men*, perhaps, Highness, not Zars," Lazar said, winking.

Boaz didn't smile but felt his heart ease slightly. He missed Lazar. Why was he thinking such dark thoughts about him? This man had been loyal to his father and was equally loyal to him. It was wrong to mistrust him.

"Have another bowl."

"No, really, I feel quenched."

"Only your mouth is telling you that. If you're going to walk with me, you need more. Please, trust me."

Boaz did as he was asked, relishing the cool liquid as it slid down his throat. "I don't know how you ever managed that journey across the desert alone. You wouldn't have been that much older than I am."

Lazar chuckled softly, a sound Boaz knew was shared with few, if any. "I was driven by an urge I barely understood—one I still don't."

"What was it?"

"It was over a woman," the Spur said. He sighed softly, stroking the falcon briefly. "And you're the first person I've ever admitted that to."

Boaz was intrigued. "What was her name?"

"She was called Shara and was a sweet, bright, gentle soul."

"You loved her?"

"With all my heart. I would likely be king-in-waiting for Galinsea right now had we been together."

The pause that followed Lazar's admission felt so suddenly fragile that Boaz filled it with a lighthearted comment. "And no doubt eyeing Percheron as potential plunder."

"Not at all. As soon as I laid eyes on Percheron, it owned me. I don't believe, even as king-in-waiting, I would have felt any differently toward it. I know I would have worked toward our being friendly neighbors."

"What happened?"

"To Shara?"

Boaz nodded. This was better than the dark silence. The heat was suddenly easier to bear.

"She died."

"Oh, forgive me. An accident?"

"No," Lazar answered quickly. His tone was final. "She just died. But she broke my heart and it has taken many years to mend."

"Is that why you've never taken a wife?"

Lazar nodded slowly. "Yes. At first it would have felt like a betrayal and then I just got used to myself and being alone. I had Jumo for company. I didn't want anything more for the last couple of decades."

"But now you do?"

Lazar turned to him and Boaz saw a flash of something spark in the Spur's eyes before he narrowed them. "What do you mean?"

"Well, my mother, of course!"

"Ah!" Lazar made a rueful sound, as though he hadn't even considered Herezah. Boaz frowned as his Spur continued: "Your mother and I are not meant to be. That was a mistake. Nothing happened, in fact—"

"That's not what she says."

Lazar nodded. "I know. I think your mother would like to read into a situation something far more than what actually occurred."

"So you are not lovers?" Boaz queried, astonishment rippling through him.

Lazar checked that they were not being overheard. "No, we are not. May I be candid, Majesty?"

"Please."

"Your mother made an advance that I was not in a position to refuse. Or perhaps that's unfair. I should have been more firm in my refusal but she had me cornered, Majesty, and without going into detail, it was a delicate situation. She had been so generous and kind that I was a little unprepared for her."

"I see. She paints an entirely different picture."

"I imagine she would. Let me confirm that I hold no feelings for the Crown Valide, other than deep appreciation for how she helped me back to better health and no little admiration for her courage in facing the Galinseans alone."

"Then who did you think I meant just then, may I ask?"

Lazar looked back at him, bewildered. "Pardon, Majesty?"

"Just a moment ago. When I asked about whether now you feel ready to take on a woman, you seemed to react favorably to the suggestion."

Lazar did not answer immediately. He cleared his throat before he finally replied. "No, Highness, that's not what I meant. It's not that I'm ready to take a woman into my life. All I was trying to explain—and perhaps I should never have revealed it—is that I've been very blinkered in my approach to women over the years. But since I've been sick and my own mortality has come into question, I realize that hankering after a lost love is a cold and pointless existence."

"In this you are right. That's why the Percherese encourage a man to enjoy many women, to take many wives." Boaz saw Lazar bite back on whatever response was leaping to his lips.

"Indeed," was all he said. "Do you feel any better for the water?"

"It's amazing but yes, I do. You were right. I must take liquid at more regular intervals."

"And then your mind won't play tricks as I've warned. I was convinced I was being chased by the devil himself, I can recall. Another time when the heat and silence had gotten to me, I began to believe all sorts of nonsense about people I had liked, people who'd been generous to me my whole life."

"Such as?" Boaz asked, his interest piqued.

Lazar shrugged. "I believed for a while that Shara died to spite me. I believed my parents hated me and I was sure my father was sending a party to hunt me down. My friends I suspected of treachery—these are people I had known all my life and who had been nothing if not the most loyal of companions." He sighed. "I'm only telling you this because the desert can twist your mind if you aren't strong, if you don't take all the right precautions against its weapons."

"And water is a good weapon?"

"It's the most potent one in your arsenal. Here, keep this bowl. Drink on the move, every hour. I think we should get back into the saddles. We can do another few hours before sundown."

Boaz nodded. "Lazar, what about Pez?"

Lazar looked gravely back at him. "Do you have any idea why he would not have come to the meeting point as arranged?"

"No idea at all. He told me he would be at your house, in fact."

"He was," Lazar said tonelessly. "It's where I left him and he was counting the minutes almost to leaving."

"Yes, he was eager."

"Do you know why?" asked Lazar.

"He told me he was nervous about Tariq, of all people. He was keen to get out of Percheron and into the desert away from him."

"Did he elaborate as to why he was so uneasy around the Grand Vizier?"

Boaz glanced at the Spur uncomfortably. "I'm sure he's told you, so you don't have to act ignorant. He said he believes that Tariq is . . ." He paused to shrug, suddenly embarrassed.

"Go on."

"Well, he seems to think the Grand Vizier is an impostor, that he wields a magic." Boaz waited for Lazar to scoff but his Spur only gazed at him awkwardly. "And the fact that you don't so much as scorn such a ridiculous sentiment truly troubles me."

"Why?"

"Because it is ridiculous."

"Is it?"

"Oh, come on, Lazar. Don't tell me you agree with him."

Lazar remained silent momentarily, looking straight ahead. Boaz cast a glance in the same direction and saw only the same featureless golden wilderness stretching endlessly ahead of them, heat rising from the sands, making the whole landscape shimmer and trick the eye.

"Zar Boaz, this is not easy for me to say to you because I realize it must sound paranoid at best, and at worst you will consider me as insane as Pez would like to have everyone believe he is. However, I don't know anyone more steady than Pez, and I trust him implicitly." He had turned on the last word to stare at Boaz. "Yes, I do support his notion," he added, "no matter how mad that makes me sound."

"Magic?" Boaz repeated, incredulous.

He watched Lazar cast a glance backward as though fearful of being eavesdropped upon.

"You've experienced magic in your own life, Highness. Its presence should not shock you."

"But we're talking about Tariq!" Boaz urged.

"Except we don't believe that person to be Tariq, Highness," Lazar uttered softly.

"We? Listen to yourself, Lazar."

"I know how it sounds. It took me a while to accept it as well."

"Who do you think he is?"

Lazar ignored the question. "Surely, my Zar, you can see the outward changes if not accept the more sinister nuances in manner, temperament?"

"I do accept he has re-formed himself into someone I can respect now, rather than detest."

"Is that not enough to set the alarm bells ringing, Majesty? A man doesn't 're-form' himself at close to seventy summers."

"I rather meant that he was not honest with my father."

"And the man he truly is—that's the man we now see here today, is that how you see it?"

"Yes," Boaz said. "That's precisely what I meant."

"Then what did Tariq gain for more than two decades by acting with such guile when he was in a position to be this man with your father?"

Boaz realized he had no answer for that. Instead he gave a disgruntled sigh to cover his lack of response. "I'll think on what you say," he finally said.

"I would appreciate it, Highness, if you would not allow Tariq to know my suspicions, for this is not the time or the place to be challenging the Grand Vizier. We need to be as cooperative with one another as possible."

"I do agree with you on that, Lazar."

"Thank you. I had better go speak with the Khalid, get everyone mounted up. I see Tariq never did give his camel a rest," Lazar said sarcastically, drifting back down the line of beasts and leaving Boaz with yet more questions swirling in his mind.

21

As early as it was, Herezah winced at the ferocity of the day's warmth as she squinted out toward the sea from her balcony. Today was the single most important day of her life. How she handled herself during the course of the next few hours would shape how she, the first Crown Valide in almost two centuries, would be remembered by history.

She was already daydreaming of her triumphant smile as her son returned to a Percheron that had been secured by her negotiations. People would laud her courageous, single-handed effort to broker a peace for the realm whilst the Zar was engaged in an equally brave hunt through the desert for his abducted Zaradine. It would make inspiring reading in the history books. Herezah fed off this notion of grandeur and respect as a means of quelling her increasing nervousness. Her meeting with the Galinsean Queen was in three hours.

That the Queen's name was Angeline was all Herezah knew

about her; she had no idea about her personality or how best to play to her. Herezah didn't like the unknown, and her lack of clues to the Galinsean royals was the only reason she had permitted—indeed demanded—that Salmeo be present. It had probably been unwise to unsettle the Grand Master Eunuch in the way that she had. It certainly would not aid their relationship, which was now clearly at an end. But she hadn't been able to help herself. For the first time in their history, the roles had been reversed, and for once Herezah had held the upper hand. She had found the lure to intimidate him irresistible. He would, of course, make her pay. Salmeo was an interminably patient man and she knew he would wait for his best opportunity to humiliate her, likely when—and if—she was returned to the harem.

Herezah never intended to return to the prison. After tasting the freedom of her role as Crown Valide, how could anyone expect her to go backward? Perhaps Boaz, in his bid to modernize Percheron and its ways, might accede to her desire to dissolve her position, allow her to join the palace community as some sort of ambassador for the royals. She knew this was wishful thinking but it was nice to dream. More likely, he would grant her permission to move from the palace into a guarded house, perhaps in the lower foothills, or he might build her a beautiful villa overlooking the sea. She would agree to be surrounded by Elim but she would be free of Salmeo and free of the harem.

She had lived without love all her life. She could easily live alone and lead the life of a chaste, quiet woman if necessary. So today she would parley for peace; she would impress the Galinseans with her diplomacy and intelligence and she would promote neighborly relations. She would be everything Boaz wanted her to be and she would do everything Lazar didn't think she could do. And then, with her son's permission, she would withdraw to a quiet life with no political aspirations and no intrigues. If they returned Ana—as she hoped they would now—then the Zaradine could be the most senior and important woman in the harem. Ana already had the harem women eating out of her palm. They all adored her.

Herezah turned at the sound of Elza's arrival.

"Your tea, Crown Valide," the servant said, bowing. Before Herezah could ask, Elza said, "It's pomegranate and lizuli leaf."

"You think I need calming?" Herezah asked, watching the woman set down the tray.

"The palace is abuzz with your task today, Crown Valide. I hope you don't think it impertinent of me."

"No, Elza, I don't. I would be lying if I said I wasn't apprehensive," Herezah replied politely, turning her gaze back to the balcony but not before catching the frown of surprise on her servant's face.

"May I fetch some food to break your fast, Crown Valide?" Elza asked hesitantly.

"No. I have no appetite this morning. But you can bathe me. I want my hair curled today and pinned. Tell Salmeo I want the emeralds—the full set, hair, ears, nose, fingers, wrists, ankles, and navel."

"Yes, Crown Valide."

"I will be wearing the cream-and-emerald silks today."

"Thank you, Crown Valide, an excellent choice," Elza replied.

"And send in Bin. I want to go over the arrangements."

This time Elza simply bowed and departed silently.

Salmeo was shown in, and despite his mood, he made a sound of genuine appreciation at seeing the Crown Valide, who stood, like a vision from a dream, bathed in sunlight streaming in from her balcony as Elza made final adjustments to her mistress's robes.

"Elza, enough! It is hot enough without your forcing me to stand in the light and bake my skin brown!"

"Crown Valide," Salmeo said lightly, bowing low. "You look incredible."

"Thank you, Salmeo. I really needed to hear that," she replied. Salmeo read the same surprise he felt at Herezah's tone and courtesy in the glance Elza threw him. He continued to smile. "I have brought the royal emeralds, as requested, Crown Valide. May I help you with them?"

"Please," she said, and again he felt a spike of startlement.

"How are you feeling today, Crown Valide?" he inquired, his tone light and conversational as he opened the first of the flat boxes.

"Filled with anticipation. Anxiety, determination, excitement."

Salmeo could barely believe this was Herezah. He glared at Elza to dismiss her. "I can look after the Crown Valide from here, Elza. Go see about your other duties," he said. It would not do for Herezah to be too honest in front of the lowest slaves. "Let's start with the earrings," he said brightly.

Before long, Herezah's body was glittering with green gems, and her tall, slender frame carried her robes and the royal jewels immaculately. If she didn't impress the Galinsean entourage, Salmeo couldn't imagine what might. Even Ana, for all her ethereal beauty, was no match for Herezah when the Crown Valide set her mind to flaunting her alluring stature together with her all-too-sharp mind. "Allow me to dress your hair, Crown Valide, with this final piece."

"It's the emerald circlet, is it?" she asked.

"Yes. It will make you feel every inch a queen."

"I'll need it," she admitted ruefully, and their gazes met in the mirror she sat in front of. Salmeo cocked his large head to one side. She puzzled him today. He could almost forgive her. Almost. But not quite.

"There," he said girlishly, giggling. "You are finished, Crown Valide, and I defy any man or woman, any king or queen, not to be dazzled."

"You're most generous," she said, distracted. "Can you operate the barge alone?"

"It is the small one that the Zars have used for private trips rather than the one we use for ceremonies. So yes, of course, it will be straightforward."

She nodded. "I'm going to have to rely on you to serve refreshments to our guest, Salmeo. I know this is below—"

"Don't mention it, Crown Valide," he assured her, probably surprising her as much as she was surprising him. She actually believed he might contribute to this parley—be a genuine aid, a true confidant. Well, those days were behind them both. She had made sure of that with her high-handed treatment and underhanded threats. "I am looking forward to seeing how we can surprise the Galinseans with our hospitality." He smiled broadly. *Oh yes, indeed, they were certainly going to leave an impression on their royal guest.*

It had been many years since Herezah had traveled aboard the royal barge. There had been a time when Joreb had loved to be out on the water, fishing, playing, entertaining his wives, but especially spoiling Herezah with the freedom that the river afforded her. But in his later years Joreb had lost interest—his appetite for more perverted pastimes with her overrode those simple pleasures of yesteryear. His preferred outdoor physical activity as he aged was riding his beloved stallions or riding her. His health dwindled, his girth increased, and his coloring lost that glow, turning sallow, whilst his breath turned bad. His once faithful adherence to frequent bathing turned disloyal and there were times when Herezah felt the need to hold her breath and count just to get through the few minutes it required the old Zar to spend himself inside her. But what never diminished in Joreb was his sharp mind, and this was something she had always appreciated, always learned from.

She'd forgotten just how beautiful the royal barge was and how elegant a means of travel it offered on the pristine river waters. Salmeo was quiet this afternoon, she noticed, not his usual effeminate self, whispering and lisping at her. Instead he was silent and withdrawn. She could hardly complain, for she, too, had turned inward, appreciating the quiet as the great black eunuch steered them gently forward. They would not travel very far from the main palace area. The Galinsean party would be accompanied first by their own soldiers, who would hand responsibility to unarmed Elim near the palace at a predetermined docking spot. There Angeline and her single servant would alight on a barge and travel upriver, carefully watched but not followed and not accompanied by anyone. No Percherese guards were permitted near either barge. It was intended that Angeline and her companion join Herezah on the royal vessel via a special bridging platform that would be placed between the two craft.

Herezah rehearsed her welcome in her mind. She kept recalling her odd dream and the vision of the large woman in a voluminous dress unsuitable for the Percherese climate, her overly painted face having its makeup leached by the wind and the sun as well as by her own perspiration as her size and the oppressive summer warmth took their toll.

By contrast Herezah imagined her own appearance as cool and calm. Her silks were so lightweight she could barely feel them and her hair was pinned expertly by Elza and clasped by the emerald circlet, a massive teardrop jewel resting on the middle of her forehead. Herezah's complexion was slightly olive and flawless—she had worked hard to maintain it and required no paint on her face, save some lip color in a shade of soft ruby. She knew she had never looked more exotic or more dazzling, not even on the day she married Joreb. Today she felt like a queen. Today she would act like one.

"What if she doesn't like the food we've brought?" she said, thinking aloud, not meaning to say it.

"Fret not, Crown Valide. I don't imagine much eating will take place this afternoon."

"The wine is chilled?"

"A perfect temperature. I brought your favorite—a georkian from the north, sweet and plummy and filled with young fruity freshness. Your counterpart will enjoy it, I promise."

"And so will I, Salmeo," she replied. "Although water mine. I need a very clear head."

"I will prepare your goblet with special care, Crown Valide. She will never know the difference."

"Thank you." She hadn't meant to thank him. In fact, she'd made a pact with herself that she would never show any sort of servility to Salmeo again.

"I see them ahead, Crown Valide," Salmeo said quietly behind her. "I shall stop the barge now and anchor us."

"Go ahead," she said, mesmerized by the sight of the other

barge drawing inexorably toward them. She could see no one clearly yet and was glad that she was veiled.

Salmeo, surprisingly swift and light on his feet, finished anchoring and tying up the royal barge. Then he drew alongside Herezah and awaited their guests. "I don't see her," he said.

"She is under the awning. Her servant is older than I imagined."

"Perhaps like you she felt more comfortable with someone she could trust. No warriors are required here, Crown Valide."

"You're probably right. Old or not, he is certainly handsome, perhaps that's the reason she chose him."

"I doubt it. Right now her concern would be receiving good counsel. No doubt this man has been chosen because he can listen in to the conversation, advise her appropriately. Remember, Crown Valide, Queen Angeline will be just as nervous as you."

Herezah didn't turn but she received this as sage counsel. Salmeo was right. Presumably the Queen was not in the habit of acting as an emissary. Although Herezah was entirely unconvinced that Angeline was nervous, considering she held the upper hand, she accepted that Angeline was likely to feel some trepidations.

"I appreciate your wise words."

She didn't see him blink in what appeared to be irritation.

The second barge was almost upon them but still the Queen remained in the shadows. Herezah regretted now that she herself had chosen to stand away from the awning of the royal barge; she was no doubt being studied by her counterpart. She had no choice but to hold her head high and her shoulders back, to ensure that the first impression she gave to those watching was one of bedazzling beauty and regal stature. She lifted her hand to the side of her face and in a simple movement dropped her veil. If she was on show, then she might as well let Angeline see her for all her magnificent beauty. Herezah tried not to let the heat burn at her resolve to stand tall but it quietly niggled at her mind that the frumpy, large woman from her dreams had not yet emerged.

The boats were close enough to each other now that Herezah could properly make out the features of the servant who steered the barge for Angeline. He preferred to stand at the front, unlike Salmeo, who worked from the back. He was not especially tall but he was a broad, striking man with a pronounced jaw, no beard, and a mane of hair.

Finally he brought the barge to a standstill and Herezah could at last see a figure within the deepest shadows of the craft. The person remained seated, however, and Herezah found herself squinting in the sun. She wished with all her heart that she had thought this through more clearly. She should have been the one with the sun behind her; she should have been the one to take her time. It was too late now. Salmeo was already quietly setting up the platform that would act as a bridge. She noted that the Galinsean servant did not move a muscle to help. In any other situation she would have been delighted to see the fat eunuch huffing and puffing over a menial task but at this moment she felt only indignation on his behalf.

She made a point of showing that indignation the only way she could without giving offense. "Thank you so much, Grand Master Salmeo," she said loudly enough for both Galinseans to hear her and his title. Swallowing hard, Herezah took a deep breath, her back to her guests, before she turned and fixed them with a bright smile, one that showed off her perfectly white teeth, not often seen in and around the palace.

"Queen Angeline," she said toward the shadows. "Won't you please step aboard our royal barge? As you can see, I am alone but for the company of Grand Master Salmeo, who is the head of our harem."

She waited, saw the movement at the back of the second barge as a figure stood. Herezah held her breath. This woman was neither frumpy nor stocky. The tall, straight-backed, square- shouldered Queen of Galinsea finally emerged and the Crown Valide found herself swallowing softly this time, her throat dry, as someone who surely was the epitome of royalty glided toward the front of the barge.

The woman wore an uncomplicated robe, almost sheath-like in its airy, lightly woven texture. No silks or rich colors for her. She was a picture of simple elegance in the palest of silver gray, a color that matched her once golden, now softly silvered hair. As she drew closer still Herezah could see that the gown also matched her intensely light eyes, which were so gray they were startling. Lazar had indeed inherited his famous light-colored eyes from his mother. In fact, the startling likeness that this woman had to Lazar took Herezah's breath away. The set of their mouths, that penetrating gaze, the very stature of this woman screamed that she had birthed Prince Lucien of Galinsea. It was hard to tell her age. Perhaps heading into her seventh decade if Herezah was harsh—but looking at the woman's hands and relatively unlined face, she was more likely in the early summers of her sixth decade.

Herezah tore her gaze from the beautiful woman and forced herself, against all her inclinations, to bow with every ounce of grace she could muster from all those years of training. "Queen Angeline," she said as smoothly as she could in the little Galinsean she knew, "you are most humbly welcomed."

"Thank you, Crown Valide. But let us speak Percherese—you may find it more comfortable."

Herezah felt her stomach clench. Was that condescension or was she being paranoid? She straightened, looked the Queen directly in her light eyes, noticing at the same time that Angeline had not so much as dipped her head to her. The Galinsean did not see Herezah as even close to her equal. Herezah's paranoia deepened. Was that a disdainful look the Queen was giving her? She switched from her halting, quaint Galinsean to Percherese. "Of course, thank you. I was not sure whether you were familiar with our language, Queen Angeline."

Herezah saw the faintest of smiles touch the Queen's lips. "Did Lucien not mention that Galinsean royalty know all of their neighbors' languages? And call me Majesty, it's easier, isn't it?"

Herezah had to look briefly away for fear of revealing the fury that was rising swiftly through her. Such arrogance! It was very easy to see whose mother this was. "Er, Salmeo, perhaps you could aid our royal guest?" she suggested, for want of something to say that diverted her from the Queen's question.

Angeline replied directly to Salmeo. "That's all right, eunuch. My companion here will assist. Luto?"

The man dipped a short bow before offering a thickly muscled arm to his queen, helping her with care to step across the small bridge onto the royal barge. Herezah watched Salmeo bow graciously as the Galinsean royal boarded, sneering inwardly that he did so without any of the usual struggle.

"Perhaps you'd care to join me under the awning, Majesty? We've set up some chairs and your servant can stand in the shade over there?"

The Queen nodded. "Luto will stand in the shade, but beside us, if that is no problem for you?"

Herezah held the steely gaze momentarily before glancing at the stocky Luto and acquiescing. "Of course. Whatever pleases you." She watched the man show his queen to one of the chairs before moving back just a few steps to stand, his arms crossed beside her. "You certainly remind me of our Spur, Queen Angeline. I can see from where he takes his handsome looks."

Angeline considered her with a mild, almost disintersted gaze, ignoring the compliment. "I have received word that my son is not in Percheron. And the only thing that assures me that this is no ruse is that I received that information in a letter written in his own hand."

Herezah was shocked by the confrontational nature of the Queen's inquiry. "Majesty, it is no ruse. Your son, Lucien— Lazar, as he is known to the Percherese—has accompanied my son, Zar Boaz, into the desert to find Zaradine Ana. Lazar alone knew how to find the impostor or he would be here now."

At this the Queen smiled genuinely but without warmth. "I doubt it. Lucien, it seems, will go to any length to avoid his mother. I know you Percherese think the Galinsean race is barbaric, not especially kind to women. You'd be surprised by how much power we wield in our own homes."

Herezah wasn't sure how to respond. She had no desire to get involved in any Galinsean royal-family squabble, nor did she understand what had happened to divide mother and son. But she had to remain focused on Boaz's desires for Percheron. "I can see that by the fact that King Falza is comfortable to send you in his stead. He obviously respects you enormously, Queen Angeline. The main point, Your Majesty, is that your son is alive and he is well. I can assure you of this, and your own dignatories would have done the same, I trust. He suffered a small setback when he was trying to cross the desert to Romea, of course—"

"Yes, I heard he was leading your emissary's party to Galinsea. We are quite intrigued to meet this young woman who seems to have everyone in a stir, including your son."

It was as if Angeline knew all of her personal weaknesses. Herezah reined in her anguish. "She is a remarkable person, yes. Very beautiful, immensely intelligent, too." If only Ana could hear her, she wondered privately.

"A rare combination . . . as you and I would both know," the Queen replied, and Herezah accepted the compliment even though it was said almost disdainfully.

"Indeed, Majesty. Ana has certainly captivated the Zar."

"And has she won through the stone heart of my son, or am I imagining things?"

Herezah caught her breath. "Queen Angeline, what could you mean by that?"

"I don't speak in riddles, Crown Valide—I always say what I mean. And I know my Percherese is fluent enough. Let me say it like this: is my son in love with this girl?"

Herezah was momentarily speechless. She opened her mouth to say something and then closed it.

"Ah, my question is too direct, then? I wonder why it should offend."

"No, er, Majesty, I'm not offended—more astonished that you would ask such a thing. This young woman is, after all, a Zaradine. My son's wife. My son's Absolute Favorite. To covet a Zar's wife, let alone the Zaradine, is treachery." Herezah spoke Ana's title with as much weight as she could.

"That's meaningless to me, Crown Valide—we are but ignorant Galinseans." Angeline's last two words were loaded with irony. "I can't imagine why my son, who has not only snubbed his right to the Galinsean throne but has steadfastly ignored his realm, and furthermore allowed us to believe him lost to us for almost two decades, would suddenly rush across the desert to reach Romea."

Herezah's tone was icy when she replied. "He put Percheron before any personal prejudice, I imagine, Majesty."

"And does that not sound stupid to your own ears, Crown Valide?" the silver-haired Queen demanded.

Herezah actually gasped, stung by the woman's words. "Stupid? No, I do not consider him stupid, Queen Angeline. I consider him only truthful. The fact that your crown prince chose Percheron as his realm over his own is something you should take up with him, not his adopted people. Here he has found only respect and affection. Lazar is revered by those who know him. He is loved."

"Yes, indeed. That's my very point, Crown Valide," the Queen replied, entirely unmoved by Herezah's admonishment. "My question is about love. Does he love this girl?"

This time the breath caught in her throat but Herezah fought the choking sensation and forced out an answer. "No, Queen Angeline, I do not believe so," she lied, wishing she could have faith in her words.

"Let me assure you that Lucien's veins may run with Galinsean blood, but his soul is Merlinean. And we Merlineans never forgive. Never. He would not have traveled toward Romea on any account—not even for his adopted Percheron, I'd wager—unless, of course, this girl is very, *very* special. Lucien the young man was vulnerable through his heart. I have no reason to believe as an older man he would be any different."

Herezah had managed to recover sufficiently to answer with a firm tone. "To be honest, I have never seen any evidence in the near two decades I've known your son that he is vulnerable to anything or anyone. Lazar has no longtime partners and is not engaged in any meaningful relationship, to my knowledge. He belongs to no one. He is an island. As for Ana . . . well, Ana is certainly special to the Percherese Crown, Majesty. She carries my grandson in her womb. She carries an heir to the throne of Percheron and if I read my son correctly, I would say she carries the next Zar in her belly. Lazar knew what was at stake for all of us and I believe he felt some guilt, you might say, for being the cause of potential trouble between our realms. And he alone knew how to get us to Romea the fastest way across the desert."

"Us?" the Queen asked, seemingly ignoring Herezah's impassioned speech.

"I was on that journey, Your Majesty. I was set upon by the impostor that our two sons now hunt. I am a mother to a king," she said, deliberately stripping her voice of any rancor. "And you are the mother to a king-in-waiting, whether or not he renounces his throne. Your son is royal. We are both creatures of the same cloth—although we wear it differently."

Angeline actually laughed. "Golesh!" she said, and at Herezah's frown, she translated. "It means congratulations, Crown Valide, or, more to the matter, that you have scored your point. It is a compliment I give you, although royal sons or not, you are not a queen but, more accurately, a king's mother."

Herezah took a moment to calm her fury but refused to be baited. Either this woman was deliberately trying to provoke her or Angeline was simply too impressed with her own power, her own status, to care how she sounded or whom she offended. Herezah glanced toward Salmeo and nodded. "Can I offer you a cool drink, Highness? I have our finest sweet wine on board."

"That would be acceptable," the Queen replied, nodding once.

"Thank you, Salmeo," Herezah uttered softly through near-gritted teeth.

"And so," Angeline began, picking up the threads of their original conversation, "my son is in good health, you say?"

"As I began to explain, he suffered after the desert trip. An old illness brought about by a poisoning attempt sometime before."

The woman's eyebrows arched. "And I understood from Lucien's friend Jumo that this threat likely came from within the palace."

"The man who confessed was duly executed hours after he admitted to the attempt on Lazar's life. Fortunately your son is strong, both mentally and physically. And with good care he returned to health. Unfortunately, the debilitating poison remains in his body, it seems, and can still affect him. His exertions in the desert made him weak. But we have nursed him back to good health and I am confident he will remain well."

"And so I hear he chose to save you over the Zaradine. Is that not odd?"

"Why, Majesty?"

"Well, she is the Zar's wife. She carries his heir. Presumably, she is more important than a mere Valide."

They had been making small headway but now Herezah openly bristled. "I'm not sure you fully comprehend how the Percherese hierarchy works, Majesty. The Zar takes many wives—dozens, if he chooses to—but he has only one Valide. She is precious for her singularity." Herezah worked hard to keep any smugness from her face.

"And how many wives does your son have, Valide?"

It was not lost on Herezah that the Queen had just dropped the royal part of her title. She fumed inwardly, though outwardly she held herself upright and kept her expression bland. Joreb's voice rang in her mind, urging her to remain steady, to not allow her personal feelings to sway her ability to broker a peace. Her voice was mercifully steady when it came. "One."

"Just the one?" The Queen shrugged. "So, in fact, Zaradine Ana had no rival and thus holds equal importance to the mother of the Zar, both of you being singular in your respective roles."

Herezah blinked slowly. "I suppose you could view it that way."

"And the fact that she carries an heir—the next Zar, in fact—in her belly possibly gives her just a little more importance . . . a little more weight to her status?"

"I don't—"

The Queen made a noise of disdain as though she had tired of the point. "It is irrelevant anyway, Valide. Lucien chose to save you for his own reasons and you have nursed him back to health and now he's making amends for saving you over the Zaradine and is out in the Empty somewhere hunting down the impostor."

"That is right, Majesty."

The Queen shrugged lightly again. "Then we are on the same side. I cannot condone the behavior of this Arafanz simply because Galinsea and Percheron have a traditional enmity. The fact is, we are both royal families and we cannot let some upstart renegade threaten either realm. In this we must stand side by side, shoulder to shoulder. If we can help with his destruction, we will."

Herezah felt her churning insides go still with relief. This offer of working together was a revelation given their realms' long and bitter history. Her hopes soared. She even gave a tentative smile. "Our thoughts precisely, Majesty. I trust you'll forgive that your son is not here to present himself to you, to prove that he remains in Percheron of his own free will. I don't want you to think that the Crown of Percheron ordered his death. Far from it. Zar Boaz loves Lazar as a brother."

"Where is Jumo?"

"He is dead, Highness. He died in the desert."

"Ah, pity. It never sat comfortably with me that we feigned an inability to speak Percherese. We made it very difficult for him to make himself understood. It bought us time, however, to send our emissaries to find out just what had happened in Percheron."

"Yes, Masters Lorto and Belzo."

"Indeed. Neither actually spoke much Percherese, as I'm sure you discovered. But it gave us all the time we needed. What Jumo never did explain, however, was why my son was being flogged at the behest of the Zar, whom you claim considers himself a brother to Lucien."

Herezah felt the snakes inside her stomach twitch again. She didn't want to have to explain to the queen that once again Lazar's decision had been connected to Ana. Her mind raced as to what else she might say but she knew she was ensnared in her own web—she could not risk dishonesty at this delicate stage. She took a moment to gather herself as Salmeo unobtrusively laid out two golden goblets, dripping with the icy water that had been used to chill the wine. He withdrew silently, just a waft of violets reminding Herezah that he was even present.

"Perhaps Master Luto would care to sip your wine first,

Majesty?" Herezah knew it was the courteous offer to make, whether the Galinsean Queen felt herself threat-free or not.

"That won't be necessary," Angeline replied. She reached forward but surprised Herezah by picking up the goblet that Salmeo had placed before the Crown Valide. "This is a much better test," she said, smiling humorlessly before sipping. "Your turn, Valide. You may now drink from the other goblet."

"Pardon me, Crown Valide," Salmeo suddenly said softly in the pidgin Percherese of the harem, one of the oldest languages of the realm and known only to the members of the harem.

"Yes?" Herezah said, her tone brittle, irritated to be interrupted by the eunuch at such a fragile juncture.

"One of the Elim has just gestured to me from the riverbank. It looks urgent. I'd better find out what it is. They wouldn't interrupt us unless it was very important."

She couldn't see the Elim he spoke of, of course, but they were meant to be hidden, so she agreed. She couldn't imagine what could force the Elim to butt into these delicate negotiations, though. Perhaps word from Boaz? "Hurry," she said, frowning.

"Is something wrong?" Angeline inquired.

"Forgive us, Majesty. Salmeo speaks only the harem language," Herezah lied. "He has been called ashore. We believe it may be an urgent message from the Zar or perhaps your son. My apologies. As you can see, Salmeo is already hurrying across the riverbank." Herezah followed the Queen's gaze and was impressed as well as puzzled to see the speed at which Salmeo was moving his immense bulk away from them toward the palace.

"Hmm. And leaves you alone. Do you feel vulnerable, Crown Valide, or does this riverbank possess many dozens of eyes that make you feel safe?"

"I'm sure neither of us came to this meeting today with anything other than peace on our minds, Highness. Whoever may be watching us will not risk that potential peace. I have no idea who may be hiding, but like your people, I imagine the palace has organized a close watch. I'm sure you expected as much?"

"I'm sure I did," Angeline said, sipping her wine again. "This is an interesting wine, perhaps a little bitter in its aftertaste."

"Bitter?" Herezah frowned. "It is my favorite," she added, a little surprised, and took a large sip. She recalled expressly asking Salmeo to water her drink, and if anything, her wine was especially luscious and rich, which meant that even watered down the Queen's wine should be delicious. The Galinseans must drink pure syrup if Queen Angeline found the sweetness to be lacking.

"Of no matter. It is nicely chilled and I am enjoying it on this warm day," the Queen replied, sipping again.

"Queen Angeline," Herezah began in earnest now, placing her goblet back on the table between them, "may we discuss the Galinsean fleet's presence so close to Percheron. It is our understanding that the fleet is here because you might have believed us insincere in our intention to send our own emissary as arranged."

Angeline said nothing. She drained the contents of the goblet as though indifferent to anything the Crown Valide had said.

Nevertheless, Herezah took her silence to be an agreement. She continued: "I hope that Lazar's letter to you explained the full extent of our trauma in the desert and why the journey to present ourselves had to be aborted? Not only was our entire Elim guard massacred but the Zaradine—the very emissary you awaited—was abducted by this madman." She noticed Angeline flinch and look away from her, which seemed odd. Herezah glanced briefly at Luto, who had not seemed to notice anything strange, and was giving Herezah his full scrutiny. She refused to let it threaten her. "Zar Boaz is determined to cooperate with you in any way that he can. We are not a warlike people; we have no wish to engage in any conflict with our neighbors. With your son alive and clearly in Percheron because he chooses to be, Majesty, I'm charged by the Crown to ask you how we can appease any offense that might have been mistakenly given by Lazar's manservant Jumo. At the time he told you of Lazar's death, Jumo was not fully informed of all the circumstances. The secrecy surrounding Lazar's survival from the poisoning was for his own protection and was masterminded by a priestess of Lyana's sisterhood. She feared for his life, understandably, and took it upon herself to secret him away to an island where she kept him until he healed—seemingly against his own knowledge for he was too frail, his mind too befuddled by the poison, for her to let anyone know that he lived. She saved his life, of this we are sure, but her secrecy has endangered all of us. From the Zar down to the lowliest palace servant, Majesty, we all believed Lazar dead and grieved over it. I fully comprehend your wrath. As a parent—especially as a mother—I can understand your need to avenge what must have sounded like a senseless death. But now that we've . . ." Herezah trailed off, shocked, as the Queen suddenly began to moan, struggling for breath in great groaning gasps.

Luto was at her side in a blink. "Angeline!" he cried. "What occurs, my love?" The granitelike expression on his face was gone. Suddenly he was all tenderness and concern.

Herezah was shocked that the Galinsean guard spoke to his queen with such familiarity. She realized instantly that queen and servant were lovers; suddenly the lofty Angeline was not as superior as she behaved but prone to the same base instincts of any mere mortal. But there was no time to dwell on this. Herezah could see the Queen was in desperate trouble. Angeline had begun grasping at the fabric of her robe in an attempt to pull away her clothes, vainly believing it would bring more air into her lungs. Her eyes stared wildly, bulging, begging her lover to help her.

"What is happening?" Herezah whispered, kneeling at the Queen's side opposite Luto and trying to calm Angeline. But to no avail. The Queen began to thrash uncontrollably as her lips turned blue. Spittle escaped those lips and ran freely down her perfect chin. The once immaculate hair looked as though it belonged to a crazed woman, falling around her ears in wild, sweaty strands.

Herezah could see they were losing her. She must be choking but she had eaten nothing. In her helplessness, Herezah stood up and screamed for the Elim. In seconds men came running from all directions, but by the time the first man had leaped aboard the barge, she could see the light dying from those once intensely gray eyes, now glassy with fright and bloodshot from her exertions.

Herezah noticed the white-knuckled grip of the Queen's manicured hand around Luto's great fists, and as a tear leaked from Angeline's eyes—the only way, it seemed, that she could communicate a farewell to her beloved—she watched the fight for life go out of the woman. Angeline gave one last mighty gasping spasm and died before them, her legs kicked out at an odd angle, her body slumped backward, the sightless eyes staring upward.

"Zarab save us!" Herezah exclaimed, distraught at what she'd witnessed.

Several moments of frigid silence ensued before Luto finally moved. He gravely unwrapped the Queen's fingers from his own and kissed her hand gently as he tenderly closed her eyes and placed her limp hand in her lap. Then he stood and faced the Crown Valide. "Calling on Zarab is pointless, woman. Your aimless god will not save you or your people from our wrath, slave," he said imperiously in Percherese.

Slave? Herezah felt herself repeat it silently, mouthing the word as if testing it.

"I would slay you here and now if you were worthy. But never let it be said that a Galinsean king cut down an unarmed woman, a Percherese whore at that."

"King?" Herezah stammered. "But—" Her mind felt addled by all the shocks.

"I am King Falza. I wish you and the slave son you bore, who dares to call himself royal, dead."

A unanimous ringing sound was heard on the barge and along the riverbank as two dozen Elim drew their vicious, curved blades.

Herezah looked around wildly. This was not how the meeting was supposed to go. This was not how her daydream had unfolded. "Wait!" she commanded the Elim, turning in full circle so all could hear her. "Stay your weapons." Herezah moved to face Luto again. "You are truly King Falza?"

"Do you doubt it?"

"I don't understand."

"You don't have to."

"She . . . Queen Angeline called you Luto."

"A private pet name."

"I need proof."

"You demand nothing of me, whore. That I grant you life alone to breathe before me is a wonder to me. You have slain my queen."

"I did no such thing!" Herezah whispered, terrified for her life now. "Why would I? What in Zarab's name could I gain from it?"

"Then why? How is she dead?"

Herezah held her face in her hands. "I don't know, I don't . . . was she ailing?"

"Did she look unwell to you?"

Herezah shook her head. "She looked magnificent; she looked to be at the very peak of health," she answered dolefully as her mind raced to achieve some comprehension of what was unfolding here. "All she has drunk is some wine."

"You offered me a sip, slut! You tried to kill *me*!"

Herezah believed she was addressing the much-feared King Falza of Galinsea. "King Falza, as far as I knew, you were Luto the faithful servant. I offered you a taste of the Queen's wine in an honest demonstration that I meant her no harm. I wanted to prove to her that we wished only to broker a peace. She ate nothing, drank only her wine . . ." Again Herezah's voice trailed off as she tried desperately to make sense of the situation. "King Falza, if I wanted you dead, I could order my Elim right now to dispatch you. I could have done that to the Queen at any time," she said, building her argument as she went along. The truth was, she didn't believe the Elim had ever meant to show themselves, nor could she command them to kill.

"You barely touched your wine. Did you even sip it?"

There was nothing for it. She grabbed her wine and inelegantly drank the entire contents of her goblet, the ruby liquid spilling down the side of her mouth and staining the bright cream silk of her gown. Herezah slammed the vessel down, not bothering to wipe her mouth. Her heart pounded as she frantically awaited any telltale signs of poisoning. "There, King Falza," she said, her chest heaving with the effort of controlling her fright. "Have you already forgotten that Queen Angeline chose the cup she drank from? She deliberately took my goblet and left hers for me to sip from." And as the words were spoken, realization hit as hard as if someone had stepped up behind her and clubbed her with something hard and blunt.

The same dawning comprehension had hit Falza. He stared at her now, his eyes glittering with hatred. "It was meant for you, slave!" he hissed. "Your own servant was trying to poison you! He didn't imagine that my Angeline would be cunning enough to switch goblets."

Herezah felt the blood drain from her face. Salmeo had meant to kill her today. He had served her a cup of poison and had been prepared to stand by and watch her die.

"That's why he ran away," she whispered. "There was no urgent message. He knew she was going to die." Herezah felt as though her head were going to explode with rage. Instead she took three steps to the side of the barge and hurled up the contents of what little was in her stomach, hot acid burning her throat, anchoring her in the reality of what had just taken place. She retched again but it was a dry heave and she used the sleeve of her gown to shakily dab at her mouth, uncaring of the mess on her silks. Straightening slowly, the silence around her deafening, Herezah turned to once again confront the Queen's body.

"Lay her out," she whispered. The most senior Elim glanced at her, uncomprehending. "Lay her out, Zarab strike you! Don't let her stiffen in that position," she shrieked as the the tears came. Not a trickle but a flood of despair and grief, years of anguish over her helplessness in the harem, her fear for Boaz, her intrigues to keep them both alive, to help them achieve her dream of becoming Zar and Valide. Tears flowed for her hopeless obsession with Lazar, and over Ana, who had stolen both his heart and that of her son within a moon of meeting both, whilst she had struggled for years to win even their respect. And tears ran in chest-racking gasps for Queen Angeline, whom she had despised within just a few heartbeats of meeting but who, she now realized, was going to bring the realm of Percheron to its knees with her untimely death.

And behind it all—behind so much of her pain—no, all of it, for he had personally bought her from the market when she was just a few summers old and set her destiny as a whore slave—was Salmeo.

"You really had nothing to do with this, did you?"

Herezah realized she was on her knees, next to the prone corpse of Queen Angeline, holding the dead woman's hand. King Falza was now crouching beside her, speaking to her in a new tone, one laced with disbelief. She looked him directly in his green eyes and for one of the rare times in her life wanted to be entirely honest. She didn't care what happened anymore. Her life was now forfeit.

"You had no idea about this," he added, searching her tearstained face.

Herezah could only shake her head dumbly. "Kill me, Your Highness. Take one of these blades and strike me down. Pour all your rage into the blow, but use me. It is all I am good for now. Zar Boaz wanted only peace and I was arrogant enough to believe I could broker it for him, little realizing the enemy was not the Galinseans but a snake in our own courtyard. I beg you to forgive the Percherese. They are innocent of the Queen's blood."

He stared deeply into her eyes and she hoped he read the honesty. She would not have been surprised had he stood, grasped a knife, and smote her; she would even have begged the Elim to stay their own hands, to allow the King safe passage back to his ships after her death. Her death was the only bait she could throw at him to bargain for the security of Percheron.

"Very noble, Crown Valide. However, I need you alive. I want you to tell my son—whom I suspect, from what you didn't say, you hold close to your heart—in whichever manner you can communicate, that he and the rest of the royals and their entourage have three days to leave Percheron. You might like to let your Zarab-loving son know that he is probably better off in the desert if he values his head. Be warned, Herezah, my warships will take control of your harbor as the sun goes down in three days. And at sunrise on the fourth day I will enter Percheron and sack it. Anyone who defies me will die. Any royal or any noble or dignatory connected to the palace will die, come what may. I suggest they flee now with their lives and not much else. As to your people, I shall spare no man, woman, or child who does not give fealty to Galinsea. Percheron will be an annex of our realm. And tell my son his mother's body will be kept for him to pay his respects to and that his king awaits him."

Without another word, Falza bent and effortlessly picked up the slim frame of his dead wife. He crossed the bridge to the barge and laid Angeline on the deck beneath the awning. Herezah wanted to believe she heard him stifle a sob but his grave countenance gave away nothing as he somberly untied the barge, turned his back on the Percherese and pushed off the bank. The barge rocked momentarily and then felt the pull of the river's journey toward the Faranel and gave itself over to the smooth waters that would take them back to sea.

Elim helped her up from her knees but Herezah's gaze didn't leave King Falza's back. She watched him steer the barge carrying his dead queen until the river was empty again. And then she wept.

22

Lazar had been following Iridor's directions implicitly and they were on course for Arafanz's fortress. As the night of the seventh day set in, the group had fallen into an almost constant but relatively comfortable silence as Lazar remembered what had happened on the previous journey. Ultimately everyone settled into the routine. The desert alone was in charge; all of them, royal or peasant, had to kneel to the might of the sands and its ferocious sun.

Maliz had certainly left him alone but he was still puzzled by Boaz, who seemed sulky and uncharacteristically withdrawn. Ganya was animated, however, and was certainly exacting her price for helping him to stay in touch with Iridor. She had no shame and it would be no different tonight after his talk with Iridor. They awaited the owl now.

"The man you call Tariq observes you closely."

"Do you think he wants my body?" Lazar asked playfully

despite his mood. He enjoyed hearing her throaty laugh.

"I know I do," she replied, rubbing herself against him. "I shall miss these nights of ours when this journey is done. But I suspect you won't." She laid a hand against his mouth when he opened it to speak. "No, don't answer that. It needs no response. I understand our arrangement."

He obeyed her request, remaining silent.

"Tariq means you harm," she added.

"He always has."

"Lazar, pay attention. I don't mean with fists or blades— with those he is no match for you, and he knows it. But he will hurt you in other ways—by more sinister means."

"What have you seen?"

"Not much. But he is a darkness in your life—he troubles you. In fact, he frightens you."

Lazar looked down, knowing she was right, amazed that she saw so much. "He is not a good man," was all he was prepared to say.

"He is worse. He is very much your enemy—and enemy to Iridor."

"I know."

"And still you allow him to travel with you."

"There is a saying about keeping friends close but enemies closer still."

She nodded. "I have heard it. And there is truth to it. But he is no help to you. It would be better for you to arrange his death—by accident, if necessary."

Lazar sighed. "I wish it were that easy."

"Why is it not? Who here can trouble you? My father and I? A boy who dreams of being a soldier?"

"What do you see in the boy?"

"Goodness, but there is something troubling him—a darkness in his heart. He hides it."

Lazar nodded.

"But answer me: why can't you just kill Tariq?"

"It is more complex than you imagine."

"Tell me."

"No. It is dangerous for you to know."

"Dangerous? I am not frightened of an old man. I want to know who he is and why you are so careful about him."

"Don't be fooled by appearances, Ganya, and stay clear of him."

The owl arrived, preventing any further discussion. He flew without hesitation to land next to Ganya, who knelt and welcomed him, laying her hand gently on him. Lazar obediently knelt beside her and offered his own hand. They gave Ganya a few moments to find the silence within that she needed, her speed at moving into a trancelike state not failing to awe Lazar.

We are here, Iridor said without preamble.

Here! Lazar couldn't hide his shock.

That's why I told you to stop at this point for the night. I would say an hour's ride north now and you'll be able to see the fortress.

How is it guarded?

Lazar, I won't lie to you. There are dozens and dozens of men. All of them prepared to go to their death to defend a personal honor that is somehow wrapped up with Lyana. I don't understand it either, he said, acknowledging his friend's deep frown of consternation.

Lyana?

Apparently. I know too little. From the brief time I watched them, I didn't detect anything that told me they worshipped her. It was only when Arafanz ordered the death of his own men that day at the fortress, in front of Ana, that I realized they were shouting battle cries in honor of the Goddess. I can't make sense of it.

Is that why they stole Ana?

Who knows. Arafanz is hardly an ally, though. Don't be fooled. He intends to kill Boaz.

I don't care about Arafanz, anyway. He can die on the end of my sword. I'm here only for Ana.

Well, you're going to see her very soon. I flew ahead yesterday, tried to glean whatever fresh information I could.

And?

The baby must be due any day. I heard her talking about pain.

Lazar sighed. *She's early, then. We are approximately eight moons since she left Percheron. This adds a fresh complication. I thought it would be hard enough with her heavily pregnant but it's going to be far more dangerous if the baby is born.*

Or worse if she is laboring for it.

Lazar frowned more deeply still. *We have no choice. I want her back!*

To return her to Boaz, of course, Iridor finished gently.

Lazar glared at him. *Of course.*

Good.

What's that supposed to mean?

Iridor sighed softly in his mind. *You must let her go, Lazar.*

I have! She's married to the Zar. I have no hold over her.

That may be, but she has a hold over your heart. Don't deny it. Once you rescue her from the rebel, you must—

The rebel?

That's how he sees himself. Lazar, whatever happened between you and Ana is—

Enough! What else can you tell me about this "rebel"?

Iridor didn't respond immediately.

Well, come on, time is short. What can you tell me that can help us?

Nothing. He sends out riders at random and in no set direction. Guards are everywhere. There is nothing I can tell you that can prepare you. I don't even know how to suggest you access the fortress, other than to do so under cover of darkness. I will be your eyes.

Lazar nodded. *I will die if I must to save her from the clutches of this "rebel."*

Iridor remained silent.

Lazar's eyes narrowed. *There's more, isn't there? There's something you're reluctant to say. Nothing you tell me can surprise me. Nothing can hurt me more than I've already been hurt.*

Are you sure?

Lazar stared at the owl, suddenly unnerved. *What do you know?*

Lazar, Iridor began plaintively, hesitantly.

Tell me! What are you hiding?

Ana is Boaz's wife, Iridor said. *You've already accepted this.*

Well, thank you for reminding me of that critical piece of information, Lazar said, unable to hide his sarcasm. *What is your point?*

My point, Lazar, is that Ana does not belong to you. She never has!

A new voice entered their minds. *But in his heart she does,* Ganya said to Iridor. *Ana has always been his.*

They both flinched at her interruption, shocked that she could enter their private discussion.

Lazar felt light-headed. Her few gently spoken words drew a rush of emotion within him. It felt as though she were looking into his soul; he hated that she could hear his treacherous thoughts, see his beguilement written all over his troubled heart. *We did not realize you could join us,* he said.

Neither did I. But there is so much emotion emanating from you, Lazar, that it is not hard to follow. It is a beacon, guiding me into this private domain of Iridor's magic that I protect with my own. Forgive me for speaking out of turn but Iridor continues to protect you from yourself, Lazar. He hides the truth through reluctance to hurt you.

What is she talking about? Lazar demanded of the owl.

You must tell him, Ganya urged.

The owl's head swiveled and its grave countenance fell upon Ganya. Iridor's voice sounded uncharacteristically cold when he replied. *Then he will not like hearing that either she or the rebel, or both, have given their heart to the other. I saw Arafanz embracing Ana early this morning on the rooftop of the fortress.*

Lazar felt his world spin. He allowed his thoughts to explode in accusation. *You lie!*

No. I am very sorry to say that I do not, Iridor replied sorrowfully. *I have seen them together.*

Then she is being forced against her will.

It did not appear that way to me, Lazar. Ana is a free spirit. As young as she was when we first met her, I believe she did love you. In your absence there is no doubting her fondness for Boaz. And now, with neither of you in her life, she has moved her affections to Arafanz. Whether he is coercing her is beside the point. You must understand that Ana does not struggle beneath his touch. I would be lying to you if I said she behaved in any other way than to "suffer" it happily.

Lazar broke their link, flinging Ganya's hand away as he stood and stomped a few paces from them. He was breathing hard, trying to make sense of what he'd just heard.

We should leave him, Ganya said to Iridor. *I—* She sounded embarrassed. *I can't help but sense the personal war that goes on inside his heart.*

He has loved her since the moment he clapped eyes on her but he denies it so much it is like a disease that consumes him. It festers and wounds.

I know. Perhaps Lazar is more comfortable with feeling wounded by the world and constantly angry at it.

Ganya, you have more insight than a hundred people twice your age.

She smiled at the owl. *But we need him strong, do we not?*

Indeed. The heir to the throne is in Ana's belly. I don't know what Lyana requires of us but I sense we must do our utmost to rescue the Zaradine and her child. Lazar alone has the ability to do so.

He's that capable?

Ask your father.

The Spur is watching us, she said furtively.

That's because he knows we are talking privately about him.

Lazar could sense that Iridor and Ganya were discussing his anger, but he didn't care. Iridor's news had ripped through his mind like a fiery arrow, igniting rage as it moved through him. But the resulting fury was burning with a cold flame now. All the heat had gone and what was left was pure and cold wrath.

He returned to his friends and grasped Ganya's hand, instantly feeling the reconnection to Iridor in his mind. He knew Ganya would listen to all that they shared as though some sort of unspoken permission had been granted. It mattered not to him, and he began by addressing them both. *Whatever Ana's personal choices might be is irrelevant. I am charged by the Zar to do everything in my power to return the Zaradine and her child to the Stone Palace, whether she likes it or not. I am prepared to die in the effort to carry out my duty.*

Naturally, Iridor said, a fraction disdainfully, and then added more softly with a sigh, *Lazar, I had to warn you in case—*

Don't think on it again. I'm sure your eyes did not deceive you. Ana is young and emotionally vulnerable. In light of all she has faced in her time at the palace, we shouldn't be surprised if she attaches herself to anyone who has a kind word for her. Arafanz clearly never had any intention of hurting her, and he is likely manipulating her emotions. His own words felt intensely hollow and it didn't surprise him that neither Iridor nor Ganya gave him any response. He pressed on doggedly through their silence. *All right, we face him tomorrow. I shall have to think on our approach. Salim and I alone will attempt to breach the fortress.*

What about me? Iridor asked.

Lazar shook his head. *You have done all that has been asked of you. You cannot do any more.*

But this is my role.

Not to die.

Lazar, you must understand—

Not to die! he reiterated. *You have suffered enough. You have guided us here. Now it is time for you to hide. We will not speak again until this is over and he is dead.*

Lazar knew Iridor understood which "he" was meant. Arafanz was a dangerous distraction, but neither of them had lost sight of the true enemy who walked among them.

You must do nothing rash. Remember, Lazar, he cannot be killed by conventional means. Leave it to Lyana. They both heard and ignored Ganya gasp at the mention of the Goddess. *This is her battle.*

You don't even know who she is! Lazar countered.

I must remind you that I don't wear this guise for entertainment. The fact that Iridor is present is testimony to the fact that she is also within our midst. Let's forget Ana for the moment, let's just focus on the Goddess, whom we struggle for. Trust me, whether I know who she is or not, Lyana is incarnated.

Then where is all his blazing power you have warned me about? Lazar watched the owl's feathers ruffle, the movement akin to a shrug.

I cannot say.

If Lyana is alive, walking amongst us, he should be full with his magical powers. Why doesn't he use them?

I cannot explain it. But I trust her and you will have to do the same.

Unless, of course, Lyana is somehow hiding her existence well enough to not prompt his powers in full, Ganya offered. Lazar noticed that her brow was furrowed in deep thought.

He knew Iridor did not appreciate the woman joining in, but they were making use of her magics and that was all that was protecting them right now. It was only fair that she joined her thoughts with theirs. *What do you mean?* he asked.

Ganya answered him mildly but looked at the owl as she spoke. *Iridor insists that Lyana is incarnate.*

She is, I tell you, Iridor said, exasperated.

And I believe you, she said. *That is how the old stories go. Iridor's rising heralds the imminent arrival of Lyana but also provokes the search by Maliz. It is how it has always been. Perhaps she is with us.* Ganya's voice was dreamy. *But maybe she hasn't been born yet?*

Lazar felt his blood turn thick and cold, moving sluggishly through his veins, whilst his insides seemed to turn to stone. He was sure he was holding his breath. Iridor must have felt the same way; there was only a chilled silence emanating from him. Ganya's notion hung between them, echoing through their minds.

Lazar knew in his very soul that of course she was right. Ana was not the Goddess—she never had been. But she had been chosen to give birth to Lyana. And in the meantime she would keep Maliz confused and guessing as her protective shield around the baby masked Lyana's presence.

It is the child, he said, knowing that if he'd had to say the words aloud, he would have choked on them.

Iridor sounded equally shaken. *The baby. Of course. How crafty, how perfect.*

And then Ganya proposed a fresh thought to traumatize them. *But how a newborn goes into battle with Maliz is beyond me.*

Lazar was still stunned by the revelation, could not think straight.

The secrecy surrounding her might explain why everyone's convinced this is a boy, Iridor said, picking up the thread of thought.

Lazar nodded. *Herezah had the old crone, Yozem, do a foretelling. She has pronounced it a boy—so cunning . . . as you say, the perfect foil.*

Lazar! Ganya said, squeezing his hand. *That's the point. You must hide the child. This attack on the fortress is not just to rescue Ana but to protect the child.*

Lazar looked uncertain. *I understand that but—*

Listen to me, Lazar, Iridor began earnestly, *if Ganya is right—and I suspect she is—you must hide the fact that the child is a girl. Let everyone think it is a boy, the heir. Let Ana believe it is a boy, if need be. But don't let anyone—no one, I tell you—see that it is a girl. Perhaps we can fool him. Maybe this is the role you've wondered about. Possibly this is what Ellyana has always had in mind for you. Forget about Arafanz. You must guide Lyana safely out of that fortress and into hiding.*

To where? Lazar yelled into their minds. *What am I supposed to do with a newborn child?*

Her mother will know what to do, Ganya counseled sagely.

Exactly, Iridor said, but Lazar heard a note of desperation in his voice. *Arafanz is not the issue. He is going to do what he is going to do. You are not responsible for him. Just get mother and child out of there and away from Maliz. Let him come into his power at her birth. Let him rage, filled with magic that he cannot use in the way it is meant. Let him kill us all if he must, but never let him know where she is or who she is. He will never hear about the baby from me.*

Nor me, Ganya said, her eyes open and sparkling as she turned to Lazar.

This is madness. We don't know anything about the child yet. You're making assumptions. You could both be wrong, Lazar spluttered.

And yet you agree deep down that Ganya is right, Iridor said quietly. *I felt your reaction. You were as shocked as I was but you heard the truth in it.*

Let us wait. There are many bridges to cross before I have Ana safely under my care, before I can think about her child.

Someone is coming, Iridor suddenly spat. He broke the link and launched himself into the darkness. Lazar looked at Ganya with momentary shock before they fell against each other, kissing passionately as they dropped to the sand.

Who is it? Lazar asked, only realizing now that their link was still open—probably not closed in their haste.

My father, she said into his mind, and at his embarrassed astonishment, she giggled softly.

23

Ana's pains had become a distant rumble, reminding her that the birth of her child was near. By her calculations she was past eight moons, but she had no say when the baby was coming—it alone was in control of her body now and she would just have to pray that Lyana made this newborn strong enough to survive not only its early birth but the hostile desert into which it was being born.

She rubbed her taut, swollen belly and smiled. She herself had survived the Samazen. It eased her troubled thoughts that if she had lived alone through such a vicious event, her child had a fighting chance with the fierce protection she was ready to provide.

Arafanz came up behind her and hugged her gently. "Are you all right? You've been looking wan."

"I'm fine," she said, shrugging deeper into his arms.

"I've brought you some broth. Old Dazeel is fretting for you. Don't refuse it, or he'll use my guts to belt his robes."

She allowed him to guide her to a small table and stool, both of them sharing gentle amusement that quiet, seemingly ancient Soraz, who cooked so carefully for her, would do anything so dramatic or cruel. "He told me the other day that he'll deliver my baby for me and I wasn't to worry, that he keeps his blades very sharp."

Arafanz actually laughed. "I know. He's already put me on very loud notice that the moment your time arrives, he is to be called."

"I don't mind. He said he's delivered some babies over the years. That's good enough for me."

"I was going to ask you about that," he said, gesturing for her to begin eating. "I wondered if you'd allow me to attend you as well."

Ana looked up from her bowl. "That's a bit awkward, don't you think?"

He shrugged. "I don't mean to embarrass you—"

"No, that's not it. It's the abduction, the killing of my people, the threat to murder my child's father, the hate for the Percherese. Need I go on?"

He shook his head. "Are we not friends?"

She looked at him sadly. "No."

"What are we, then?"

"I don't know. I am close to you. I feel for you. But putting it into words is impossible. In a way," she said, sipping modestly from the ladle provided, even though she didn't feel like food, "I hate you."

"And yet we are bonded, are we not?"

She nodded. "Every moment with you that I spend hating you, I enjoy."

Now he smiled softly.

"Will you take my son from me immediately?"

"I must."

"He cannot survive without me."

"I have organized a wet nurse. He will be well nourished and I promise you I will get him safely to the city and placed upon the throne at the Stone Palace."

"Where you will kill his father."

'Yes." Arafanz's eyes glittered. "Your child will rule Percheron. He will smash the temples and rebuild them in Lyana's honor. Zarab's name will be erased, his memory dust in the people's minds."

"Why not put any child on the throne? Why bother with mine?"

"Because I believe in bloodlines. I believe only a ruler's son should inherit the throne."

She nodded slowly. "I see. And who will raise my son?"

"I will appoint people."

"And then you will come back here to me?"

"Of course."

"Then it will be to place a death shroud over my body and commit me to the depths of the sands."

"I will have you watched in my absence."

Ana spooned more soup into her mouth and swallowed slowly. "I know you will. But I will find a way to kill myself, Arafanz, if it means swallowing my own tongue or willing myself to death. You know it can be done."

"Ana—"

"This is why I hate you. I don't want my son to be born yet. I hope he holds on. I hope Spur Lazar comes for me, as he always has before."

"And kills me?"

Ana put down the ladle and wiped at a single tear that was threatening to escape. "If killing you is the only way to keep my son and to save Boaz, so be it."

"Perhaps you will get your wish."

She turned to gaze into his sad, dark eyes. "How so?"

"A vulture roost has arrived. They are following potential carrion."

"I don't understand."

Arafanz stood. "I think your precious Spur has arrived in my desert. A group is on the outskirts of the fortress now, freezing through the night around the smallest of fires in the vain hope that I will not know they are close. But the birds have given them away. There are no animals to die out there, save camels. And with camels come men. This is not a trading route, Ana. There is no reason for any man to be in the vicinity unless he's lost or . . . is trying to find you. I suspect it is the latter."

Ana tried to keep her expression impassive but she knew the hope that flared inside was mirrored on her face. "Lazar is here?"

"I cannot say for sure. But men are here. I will bring you the body of your Spur and present it to you."

"Arafanz, wait! I beg you."

"Are you going to petition me to save the life of the man you truly love, Ana? Do you think I am so dim that I can be beguiled by all your talk of duty, of your son's father, of the great young Zar?"

"I have tried to be honest with you."

"Have you? Tell me, Ana, what is the most important thing to you?"

"My child."

"I think you lie. I think another holds that claim. If you had to choose between the Spur or the Zar, whose life would you spare?"

She faltered before whispering, "The Spur's."

"Louder. I can't hear you."

"Lazar's."

"Why?'

"Because I love him," she said, lifting her chin and staring at him defiantly. "And killing him or killing me will not change that, Arafanz. I do not love you. I can never love you. You have too much hate in your heart." She watched his jaw grind, understood that he was wrestling his emotions back under control.

"I am simply doing what Lyana asks of me," he finally replied.

Ana stood and upended the bowl of soup across the table, sending the ladle clattering to the ground. "She has not asked you to kill Lazar!" she yelled at him, unable to control her emotions. "He is no enemy of Lyana."

Surprise registered on the desert man's face and she guessed he hadn't thought she had such fire within her. "Be careful, the baby."

"The baby! The baby? Arafanz, I would sooner murder my own child than allow you to have him and use him for your own ends. Lay a hand on a single strand of Lazar's head and I swear to you on all that you consider holy I will refuse this child his passage. I shall use my own will to prevent his birth. He will die in my womb and his royal blood will be on your hands. Try explaining that to Ellyana as her wicked, complex plans unravel. Do not use me. Do not use my innocent child. Do not so much as rough up the robe Lazar wears, or take the consequences. I will find a way to carry out my threat. Now leave me!"

Whether Arafanz left to get help, frightened for the birth of her son, or whether he turned his back on her because he accepted that she would never love him, Ana did not know. What she did know, though, was that the fragile, tender relationship that had quietly emerged between them since her abduction had been shattered. It lay in pieces on the threshold of the chamber in which she stood, breathing deeply to regain her equilibrium and to steady her excitement at the news that Lazar was coming.

"May I speak candidly, my Zar, in the absence of everyone else?" Tariq said, looking around at the emptiness. Boaz and he had been sitting silently around the tiny fire since Salim had excused himself.

"You normally do," Boaz replied mildly.

"Are you feeling all right, Majesty?"

"Why do you and Lazar keep asking me that? I am perfectly well."

"You are withdrawn, mostly silent, not at all the enthusiastic Zar who set out on this journey. Is it something that we have done or said?"

"Perhaps I'm looking forward to seeing my wife, and the child she carries . . . and concerned that we all might not survive this adventure."

"It could be that, my Zar, but I suspect it is not," Maliz said.

"You know me that well, do you?"

"I think so," the demon said, worrying at the embers of the fire with a stick to throw out more heat.

"It must be the desert that makes you so reckless, Tariq. I don't remember you being quite so direct in the palace, or so aggressive."

"You think I've changed personality?"

"I think you've changed entirely," Boaz answered truthfully, taking advantage of the opening that the Grand Vizier had provided. He was determined to get to the bottom of Lazar's concerns and Iridor's warning.

"Indeed? How so?"

"Everything about you. This is not the Tariq who served my father."

"But we have been through this before, Highness. I thought I had explained it to you."

"What you actually think, no one would know. What I think is that you believe you have beguiled me with clever words. I am young, Grand Vizier. But I am not stupid."

"My Zar, please let—"

"No, Tariq, don't. In fact, let's start with your name, shall we? Is it really Tariq?"

"What can you mean?"

"The words are plainly spoken. Tariq—the man I knew and despised—has gone. The person who replaces him I rather like but I'd prefer honesty because he's too different and suddenly I feel apprehensive."

"What is it that you suspect, Your Majesty?"

"Let's speak candidly, as you suggested, shall we?" Boaz didn't wait for a response. "Magic does not frighten me as it does so many. I believe it exists around us. For the most part it doesn't affect any of us but a few it may touch, now and then. In fac—"

"And have you ever been touched by it, Boaz?" The Grand Vizier's voice was somehow deeper, and incredibly seductive.

Boaz blinked. "I . . . I have not," he said, determined to keep control of this conversation. "But I believe in it."

"Why?"

"Don't question me, Grand Vizier. Remember your place."

"What is it you want to know?" The man sitting opposite Boaz suddenly seemed to be closer and, yes, his voice was definitely deeper. Even his expression had lost that usually disinterested, almost amused look that the Grand Vizier normally adopted.

"I want to know who you are. I want to know your real name. I want to know what you truly want."

"Are you sure?" The voice had dropped even lower and Boaz felt a coldness wash over him. He felt genuinely alarmed for the first time in the Grand Vizier's presence.

"I insist," he said, forcing bravado to the surface, refusing to cower beneath the disturbing expression that seemed to be claiming Tariq's face. He knew he was probably imagining it—the fire, the cold, the empty expanse, the loneliness, the paranoia and anger over Ana all playing their part—but it looked as though someone else was pushing through the Grand Vizier's features.

"Tell me, Zar Boaz, if you could have anything in the world, what would you like most right now?"

The dramatic switch in subject threw Boaz off balance. He looked at Tariq, dumbfounded, but aware that the Grand Vizier's eyes were taking on a mesmeric quality.

"Answer me, Boaz."

Boaz registered that Tariq was also not paying him the usual respect, calling him by his name; somehow it didn't seem to matter right at this moment. "I want Ana alive."

"Not your child? Is he not your first priority?"

"He should be."

"That's right."

"I don't know the child. I love Ana." It was not a lie. What he intended to do with her was his own business.

"What about duty?"

"The Crown already has my life. It's not as though I can renounce it. Ana is the only thing I can choose for myself, personally."

"Are you sure she loves you? Be honest with me, Boaz. I intend to be deadly honest with you." Tariq chuckled deeply. "Does she love you as singularly as you do her?"

Boaz fought the truth, felt himself trying to wrestle his answer away from his lips, but it was determined to escape, as though it was being dragged from him. "No."

"You are not sure?"

The young Zar felt himself perspiring. What was he fighting? How was Tariq compelling him to be so honest? "I know she loves me, but not in the way . . . not in the same way she loves . . ." He trailed off, trying to swallow the words, too frightened to say them aloud, too frightened to accept the reality of it.

"In the way she loves Lazar? Is that what you're struggling to say?"

Boaz felt as though he was choking. A whimper escaped him. "Stop it, Tariq! Whatever you're doing, stop it!"

"Oh, but you asked for honesty, Majesty. And I'm paying you the honor you deserve by allowing you to glimpse the real me. That's what you wanted, isn't it?" the Grand Vizier demanded. "I'm showing you how to be honest."

"Yes, I want honesty," Boaz choked out. "I'm dying."

"No, you're not. I'm just making sure I have your full attention. You're right, my Zar. You've found me out, although how you have does intrigue me. I have to wonder what help you've had and from whom."

"What are you talking about?"

"Nothing that concerns you. Boaz, how do you feel about being cuckolded?"

"How dare you!" Boaz instinctively tried to stand but realized he could no longer move.

"Ah, yes, I knew that would touch a nerve. Boaz, you are a Zar. How can you tolerate that a mere soldier—a Galinsean at that—makes a mockery of you, your title, your Crown, your very manhood?"

"You have no proof! You—"

"I don't need it. Your very reaction tells me that you suspect Lazar and Ana are lovers."

"You lie. You put that notion before me. No one has ever suggested it."

"And still you overreact. Curious. A secure man would laugh in my face, although I'll grant you that Lazar is certainly a handsome, obviously desirable man. It now seems that both your wife and your mother are opening their legs for him."

Boaz, unable to move his limbs, helpless in his fury, began to splutter. "What do you want?"

"I want to make you the most revered and feared Zar in the history of Percheron. The Galinseans will pay fealty to you in time to come. Trust me."

"And how do you intend to do that?"

"I have access to powers that you can barely dream of." Boaz felt the sinister magical hold over him lessening, found he could breathe properly again. "Revenge, Zar Boaz!" Tariq continued. "I want you to take revenge."

"Me?"

"What if I told you I could provide it?"

"What are you talking about? Who are you?"

"Time is short. They'll be back soon. My name is unimportant. It's what I can do for you that is. It's what we can achieve together that counts."

"Let me go! I order you!"

"Tell me you'll test my theory."

"What?" Boaz felt the world right itself. Suddenly all was normal. He was looking once again into Tariq's slightly amused, thoroughly normal face. He could almost believe he had imagined the previous few minutes of fright.

"Test Lazar. Find a way. If I'm right, come talk to me. I will help you."

Boaz stared, uncomprehending, at the Grand Vizier. Before he could respond, however, the person in question strode into view. Behind him came the Khalid folk.

"Leave me, Tariq," Boaz demanded, feeling a hollow victory in wresting back some superiority over the Grand Vizier. Tariq merely smiled at him before nodding and withdrawing.

"Sorry we took so long, Fayiz," Lazar said sheepishly. "Is everything all right?"

"Yes, Spur," Boaz said, forcing a smile, careful to keep his tone deferential in front of the Khalid. He picked up Jumo the falcon from his perch and handed him to Lazar.

He saw Lazar frown at him as he accepted the bird, now hooded for the night. "Where's he going?" he asked, nodding toward the Grand Vizier.

Boaz shrugged. "Probably to relieve himself now that you're back. I hope you enjoyed yourself?"

Again Lazar frowned, looking over his shoulder to see that Salim and Ganya were settling themselves down to sleep near their camels. "Zar Boaz, you seem so unhappy. Is it about my time with the desert woman? You understand why I must go with Ganya, don't you? She is leading us to the fortress."

"So you say. And what has she told you after tonight's passion?" He could see how the words inflamed Lazar; how the Spur took a steadying breath to ignore the irritation reflected in his face by the firelight.

"You seem angry about this arrangement. Would you prefer that I stop seeing her?"

"It's of no consequence to me whom you lie down with, Lazar, so long as it doesn't encroach on my sensibilities."

Lazar's gaze narrowed and Boaz felt the full weight of his intense stare. "Forgive me, I'm not sure I understand what you are saying, Majesty," he replied softly. "Do you refer to the Valide? Because I thought—"

"This has nothing to do with my mother, Lazar."

"But something is troubling you. I would be grateful to know what it is before tomorrow, when we face Arafanz."

Boaz opened his mouth to respond but found his words frozen in this throat. "We're here?" he finally asked.

"One hour's ride northwest, according to Ganya."

"I see. So you will want me to remain hidden from now on?"

Lazar nodded. "Tomorrow only Salim and I will leave the camp. I am leaving you with Ganya and Tariq. If anything should happen—anything at all that doesn't seem right—you are to get on your camel and ride. Take Ganya with you. She will be able to sense the way back." He sat cross-legged opposite the Zar. "I want no heroics. Forget me. I have my role. Yours is to stay safe."

"What about Tariq?"

"Take him, by all means, but do not slow yourself down because of him. I mean this, Zar Boaz. You are all that matters, not Ganya and not the Grand Vizier. As it is, it galls me that I might put you in this position of fleeing alone."

"You didn't put me here. I chose to be here."

Lazar nodded. "And I still don't fully understand why. However, your choice aside, I am still responsible for your safety."

"What is your plan for tomorrow?"

"I have no plan." Lazar shrugged. "I can only assess the situation once I am faced with it. Whatever happens, I intend to return the Zaradine and your child to you unharmed, Majesty."

Boaz swallowed, doubt creeping back to challenge his suspicions. If Lazar was so treacherous, why was he still behaving so loyally, acting so concerned? But Tariq's taunt niggled. *Test him*, he had demanded. "Are you feeling confident?" he asked, buying himself time to think.

Lazar shook his head ruefully. "I have to believe that I will bring Ana out of there alive, at whatever cost."

"You're prepared to die," Boaz stated baldly.

"Of course."

"Why?" Lazar's head snapped up from where he'd been watching sand sift through his fingers. He stared at Boaz with a look of frank disbelief. "I don't mean to shock you, Lazar, but doesn't it strike you as odd that a Galinsean prince—the heir to the throne, no less—is prepared to lay down his life on behalf of a mere odalisque, a young woman and former goatherd's daughter?"

"Zar Boaz, she is Zaradine. She is Absolute Favorite. I—"

"She is not me! I can understand your loyalty to the Crown . . . to my father and subsequently to me. Many can't, considering your background. But I do. I don't comprehend why you'd give your life for one of my women, however."

"Perhaps because she carries your heir," Lazar said. Boaz

noted that all incredulity had left his Spur's voice, and was replaced with a wintry tone that was filled with warning. But he refused to be daunted, not now that he had started on this path.

"People could be forgiven for reading far more into your apparent loyalty."

"Apparent loyalty? Zar Boaz, please explain what precisely you're not saying. We are facing immense danger and I would rather do so knowing I have your full support. If there is something you want to tell me, or ask me, I will listen or answer truthfully as required."

"Will you, Lazar?" Now the Spur looked at him, aghast. Boaz continued: "You see, I just don't know if you are being entirely honest with me where Ana is concerned. You've never made a secret of your attachment to her. Initially we all put it down to the fact that, having sourced her in the foothills, purchased her, and brought her away from her family at such a tender age, you felt responsible for her, as an uncle might a young niece. But the Protectorship you offered her and the risk you took on her behalf struck me as beyond avuncular. And then you dove into waters to rescue her from drowning, and cradled her in your lap and fought to breathe life back into her; but I heard from the Valide and the Grand Vizier that you were positively cold toward Ana throughout the journey to Romea. My mother assures me you all but ignored my wife. It doesn't add up."

He watched Lazar's jaw grind. "And your point, Your Majesty? What is it that you want me to explain?"

"I want your assurance that this tremendous risk you take with your own life is on my behalf and not on Ana's."

"I risk my life, Zar Boaz," Lazar growled, "for the heir to

Percheron so that life in your realm might continue long after yours is dust. It is for Percheron that I have been loyal to Joreb, his son, and his son's son."

"But you are a king in your own right!"

"I am a prince, that is all, Highness. My father still sits his throne. And I renounced my right to the throne of Galinsea; I chose to be Percheron's Spur. I did this before you were chosen as Zar and long before Ana came to your harem. I am first and foremost a loyal subject to Percheron."

Boaz nodded. At any other time he would have felt ashamed of his behavior. He despised his own insecurity where Ana was concerned. But his own deep suspicions, mirrored by the taunting words of the Grand Vizier, haunted his thoughts. He had not imagined Tariq's hold over him earlier. There was magic at work, as both Lazar and Iridor had warned. And if that were true, perhaps there were other truths to be unearthed. Out of the corner of his eye he saw Salim get up to take a drink. And he knew what he must do next.

"Forgive me, Lazar. I think I am mistrusting of everything and everyone right now."

Lazar glowered, but he said nothing other than, "Get some sleep, Zar Boaz. Tomorrow is almost upon us." Boaz could hear the disappointment in the Spur's voice.

"I must relieve myself."

Lazar sighed and settled himself down on his sleeping rug. "Don't stray too far."

Boaz moved silently across the sand, ignoring Tariq, who seemed to be snoring lightly around the embers, and only glancing at Ganya, who was seemingly already asleep as well. He found Salim hidden behind the camels, chanting quietly to himself.

"Forgive me," Boaz said softly, realizing the man was praying.

Salim's eyes opened. "You speak Khalid?"

"Very little." Boaz shrugged, holding his thumb and index finger barely apart.

The man smiled. "A little is all you need."

"I can't sleep. Do you mind us talking?"

The man shrugged.

Boaz sat down and leaned against one of the camels. "Lazar told me you and he go tomorrow."

"It will be dangerous." The Khalid pointed behind him to where Ganya slept and back to Boaz. "You two must be safe."

Boaz nodded, then tipped his head toward Tariq. "Lazar doesn't care about him."

The man's grin widened. "Neither should you."

"I know that Lazar cares only for the girl, Ana. I haven't seen her. Is she that lovely?" He struggled to make himself understood whilst hating the deception he was employing.

But Salim grasped what he was saying. He nodded, smiled widely. "Ana, beautiful!"

"He must care for her a lot," Boaz replied, running sand through his fingers in the same distracted way he'd watched Lazar do. He wanted to give the impression that he was merely a youngster making conversation. It was also a way to hide his shame.

"Dara," Salim said, "plenty."

Boaz grinned, loading the expression with a playful wickedness and further despising the insincerity of his methods as he touched his heart and sighed, a question in his eyes.

Salim echoed the gesture, placing his own hand over his heart. "Dara, dara," Salim repeated, obviously believing it mattered little to share this with a lad who clearly idolized his Spur, wanted to emulate the ways of the senior soldier.

"He has given his heart to her?" Boaz queried in halting Khalid.

Salim put his finger to his lips and nodded.

It took every ounce of composure but Boaz forced down his rage, smiling with resigned fury at the poor Khalid.

He didn't have to shake Lazar awake. The Spur, he was sure, only ever dozed; in fact, his falcon, sitting on a stake in the sand, took more exception to being disturbed.

"Lazar?" Boaz whispered.

"Yes?"

"Tariq feels unwell."

"So what?"

"I said I'd go with him."

"Why?"

"Because I know you won't. I told him you insist none of us wander off alone. He needs to relieve himself and it may take some time. I'm awake and not tired; I'll go with him. You two can't be left alone for longer than a few moments anyway before you're at each other's throat."

"I'll come, it's all right," Lazar grumbled, rousing himself from his blanket.

"No. It is unnecessary. We're just behind that dune." Boaz pointed, lying. "I'll let Salim know as well. He's still awake."

"You have a few minutes before I'll arrive to make Tariq feel even more uncomfortable than he already is."

Boaz shrugged and began walking over to where Tariq slept. The five of them camped the same way each evening. Salim and Ganya always lay next to the camels; Tariq and he usually stuck fairly close, and Lazar always wrapped himself in his blanket in a lonely spot well away from the four of them.

"Grand Vizier," he hissed at the man's ear.

"What's wrong?"

"I've told Lazar you're not well, that you need to relieve your bowels and that I'd come with you because he won't let anyone move too far alone from here."

"Why?"

"I'm ready to talk."

The Grand Vizier clearly needed no further encouragement. He groaned softly as he slowly rolled over and pulled himself to his knees, clutching at Boaz for a helping hand. If Lazar was watching—as Boaz was sure he would be—he would see the Grand Vizier stagger slightly, leaning against his Zar as they disappeared toward the darkness of the dunes.

Boaz shivered in the cold of the night as his anger settled into something hard and unshakable. His friends had betrayed him. Two people he trusted implicitly: Lazar, whom he loved more than any other man, and Ana, whom he loved above any other. He wished he could talk to Iridor. It was eating away at him that the dwarf, with whom he shared his most intimate thoughts, would desert him at such a critical time, especially after years of being his most trusted confidant. He suddenly wasn't sure he could forgive Iridor the insult either. He asked nothing of these three people but their loyalty and now each had betrayed him. Perhaps the only person he could trust was the one who professed the greatest love; for all her deceits and cunning manipulations of those around her, Herezah was the only one who had been true to him.

"We need go no further," Tariq said, breaking gently into his bitter thoughts. "What has occurred?"

Boaz knew the Grand Vizier could not see the glare of his expression, but his hesitation was telling and the fury emanating from him was probably all too obvious.

"Ah, my Zar, you have tested the Spur, haven't you? What did you discover?"

"Lazar answered my questions plainly and I suspect truthfully. His loyalty is to Percheron."

"I see. So why are we skulking about in the darkness, avoiding the Spur's hearing?"

"Because I want to know what you meant earlier," Boaz demanded. "Don't play games with me, don't speak to me in a cryptic manner. If you've got something to say, say it plainly, or so help me, Tariq—or whatever your name is—I'll have Lazar run you through with a sword and I'll leave your body for the vultures we saw circling earlier."

"There is no need to threaten me," the Grand Vizier replied mildly but in that eerily deep voice he had adopted earlier.

"Why do you speak like this all of a sudden? What has happened to your voice?"

"I am being honest with you. I am revealing the true self that you demand to know. Now tell me, what have you discovered?"

Boaz paused. Nothing about this felt right, but then nothing about his life felt right all of a sudden. He had been treated with the ultimate disrespect by his wife and his most trusted friend. Both swore absolute loyalty to him, whilst behind his back had loyalty only for each other, it seemed. No matter what anyone else said, Boaz knew the deception was true, certainly on Ana's part. No one could ever know how he could be aware of it or why, but he was. And so he would do the only thing that he could do as Zar, take the only course his father would have demanded. He would kill Ana, cut her throat himself. He would watch the light die in those beautiful sea-green eyes and he would know in his soul that with her death and that of the baby she carried, went his heart. Although he would sire more heirs, beginning immediately, he would never love again, he would never open his hardened heart again, and he would never trust a woman again.

24

Maliz didn't need to see Boaz's face to know that the young Zar was struggling with his emotions and that something had happened to force his hand. His suggestion to the Zar had been nothing but a ruse—a stab in the dark to see what such wickedness could yield. He had no idea whether the Spur and the Zaradine had sneaked any time alone; he suspected not, given the close scrutiny under which they all lived during that time in the desert. But he had no doubt at all that the pair of them harbored unspoken desires for each other, perhaps even a forbidden love pact. Maliz believed the Zar would not find any possible forgiveness for a cuckolding. "You've brought me here, ready to talk. So tell me."

"The Khalid man unwittingly betrayed Lazar to the stupid youngster Fayid, who dreams of following in his hero's footsteps and being a soldier in the Protectorate."

"Really?" Maliz could barely keep it from his voice. "What have you discovered?"

"I shall tell you nothing until you tell me what it is that you are offering and what it is that you were alluding to earlier about your powers. I want to know who you are."

"I told you, who I am is irrelevant."

"Not to me."

"I matter not, trust me. What is relevant is what I can do for you."

"Which is?"

"I hear anger and bitterness in your voice. I presume you want someone to pay for whatever is prompting it. You would not be a Zar if you didn't believe you have right on your side to take revenge against any offense to the Crown or to you personally."

"Go on."

Maliz shrugged. "I offer you the ability to take whatever revenge you seek."

"How?"

"I can make you more powerful than you ever dreamed possible."

"What makes you think I dream of power?"

"Surely all rulers enjoy power."

"In all likelihood, yes, but not necessarily do they dream of wanting more power than they already have. And I am already the most powerful person in Percheron. I have no design on empire."

"Oh, nicely said, Zar Boaz, but either you are not worthy of your title or you're simply too insular and immature to understand your role."

The silence that met his cutting sarcasm was frigid and Maliz half expected Boaz to start howling for Lazar and his trusted blade. But he had to risk it. Had to take the chance that he could blind Boaz with so much anger that he could no longer think in that straight, rational way of his.

"It seems you wish yourself an early death, Tariq," Boaz said, and Maliz could hear the control being exerted to keep his voice steady.

"Not at all. But the time is here for honesty—bluntness even—and you must understand that your very throne is at stake if you continue to allow people to treat you like a child. Your mother probably wishes you were still a baby so that she could run the realm without you; the harem girls probably continue to hope that you are not ready to take much interest in them yet; Ana thinks of you as a boy but lusts for the touch of a real man—a foribidden one; whilst Lazar has clearly always carried a torch for the young woman you have made your wife, marking her with his own scent at the first opportunity. Pez has spent years keeping you young and giggling at his silly antics—you're the only one who finds him even vaguely amusing. And now the Galinseans are here to overthrow the boy Zar. Think about it. It's time for you to show that you are a man, that you alone will make decisions for Percheron. What you're doing here in the desert is part of that. Don't be fooled, this will be the making of your reign, but you need to cut yourself away from those who do not serve you as honestly or loyally as I do."

"And what do you want? Please don't insult me by saying you just wish to serve, I no longer believe that."

"I serve Zarab."

"Zarab? What has our god to do with this?"

"Everything!" Maliz laughed softly. It was the most honest word he'd spoken to the Zar since he'd taken over Tariq's body.

"I don't understand. You are my Grand Vizier but you talk as though you wish to be a priest."

"You don't have to understand. You just have to know that what motivates me is embedded in the notion of serving my god."

He watched Boaz step away, hands on hips under the moonlight. "I'm lost, totally lost."

"Do you recall the name Maliz?"

"The warlock-turned-demon from myth who supposedly turned Beloch and Ezram to stone?"

"The very one. Well, I support his notion to keep Percheron's faith clean, untainted by those who work to see the Goddess Lyana returned to her pedestal."

"You jest!"

"No. I speak only the truth. I am not interested in riches or the sort of power that other men crave, although I do enjoy them. But my life is committed to preserving the faith of our region. I am a mystic; I can tap into powers that are way beyond anything you can imagine."

"Lazar just accused me of behaving obliquely. I think it's time for you to stop speaking so obliquely as well, Tariq. Tell me what you want from me," Boaz ordered, and Maliz could hear that he had pushed the young Zar far enough.

"Do you believe that Lazar and Ana have made a mockery of you?"

"Yes."

"You have proof, not just my hearsay?"

"That is my business. Continue with your own."

Maliz had to stifle a laugh. He could barely believe how easily the Zar was falling prey to his own insecurities. "If you believe you have been cuckolded, Highness, it is irrelevant who knows. You do. That in itself demands the gravest punishment."

"That is my decision, Tariq. You have yet to say anything I don't already know."

"What if I could allow you to see Ana?"

The silence was long. "How is that possible?" Boaz finally asked.

"Magic, of course," Maliz answered mildly. "And what if I could allow you to listen in on Ana, watch her when she sees Lazar again? That way you can know for yourself how they feel about each other before you do anything rash." He was impressed with himself; he sounded so extraordinarily caring.

"Lazar and Salim are leaving us tomorrow. We are apparently within one hour's striking distance of the fortress."

This was news to Maliz. "I see. That close, eh? Then we must make a decision this night, my Zar. Time is surely against us."

"We can see her tonight?"

"We can see her immediately, my Zar—it's up to you to simply say yes."

"To what?"

"To allowing me to enter your life," Maliz said, feeling himself hold his breath in anticipation.

"I don't understand."

"For me to show you Ana, to eavesdrop on her conversation . . . for me to be able to show you Lazar's attack on the fortress and his rescue of your wife; for me, Zar Boaz, to give you unequivocal proof of her infidelity—which she will surely reveal upon seeing Lazar—I must enter you magically."

"Enter me?" Boaz whispered, the anger evident in the

way his words came out as a growl, but Maliz heard his confusion, too.

"It's painless, Highness. We share a body but momentarily."

"Share my body," Boaz repeated, and Maliz could hear the rising confusion laced with disgust in his voice. "How so?"

"I have the power to join you, to transport you magically to wherever Ana is," Maliz lied.

Again a long silence ensued. The shock emanating from the Zar was palpable. He began to pace. "I can barely believe what I'm hearing and yet I can't imagine that you are teasing."

"Let me assure you I do not jest, Highness."

"And can we also find Pez? He was supposed to be here."

"Er, yes, I don't see why not." Maliz would agree to anything Boaz wanted in return for access to his body. He was already imagining how wonderful it was going to feel to be in charge of that young, fit, healthy physique.

"How does this occur?"

"Well, you need to give me permission. Then, with the use of the magic, I can lift your spirit and together we can travel anywhere you wish us to go. You can roam to Percheron and peek at the Galinsean warships, you can look in on your mother, you can eavesdrop on Salmeo, you could even—"

"And Lazar?"

"Well, Majesty, if you wish, you can travel alongside him tomorrow. He would be none the wiser, for you would be invisible," Maliz lied, impressed by how convincing he sounded.

"And then what?"

"And then when you're satisfied, we return to your body. Simple."

"My body is safe?"

"We would hide it."

"And what happens when 'we' return?"

"I leave you, Highness."

"What's in this for you, Tariq?"

"A clear conscience. I cannot imagine you would take my word against Lazar without proof. I wish to give you conclusive proof that he has been alone with your wife against your wishes. You obviously have your own suspicions. My considered counsel is that you don't take any action without proof."

"Always being helpful, Tariq," Boaz said with condescension, "but I still don't know who you are or how helping to ease my conscience helps you serve Zarab."

And here was where Maliz knew he had to be convincing. "My Zar, I know this is going to come as a shock, but I believe Ana and Lazar to be followers of Lyana."

"So? We do not persecute anyone in Percheron for their beliefs, Tariq, you should know that. And I have seen no outward signs that either of them holds any unhealthy interest in the Goddess."

"No, my Zar. That's because I believe they are plotting against you."

"What?"

"Hush, Majesty. We shall be found out."

"This is treacherous talk, Tariq. You should consider carefully before you say any more," Boaz warned, anger and more shock evident in his voice.

"I already have, Highness, and it grieves me to tell you this but I believe Ana and Lazar would like to return Percheron to a realm that prays to Lyana rather than to Zarab."

Boaz frowned. "We do not punish people based on their religious beliefs but I will not tolerate any sort of schism. That would require repercussions from the Crown; Percheron follows Zarab."

"But a schism is precisely what they're aiming to fuel, Highness."

"Well, have you confronted either of them about this?"

"I dare not. Lazar is a man of violence. And we have witnessed what he can endure when he feels Ana is threatened. And speaking of that, where did he ask for his body to be taken when he was so injured? Lyana's Sea Temple. Who cared for him, nursed him back to health? The priestess Zafira. He is linked to Lyana, whether he cares to admit it or not. I'm told they found Ana in the Sea Temple with the priestess when she ran away from the harem. She could have run anywhere, Highness, and I think we'd both agree that she stood a better chance if she'd melted into the crowds at the bazaar or joined one of the caravans leaving the city. But she chose the lonely temple. She, too, is linked to Lyana through that curious choice."

"I shall ask Lazar," Boaz said angrily.

"No, wait, Highness," Maliz said, grabbing the Zar's arm, apologizing immediately with a small bow for the indiscretion. "That is not the way to approach this. If there is a conspiracy afoot, Lazar will have all of his excuses and cunning rationale in place. A direct approach will not work. The only way to discover the truth is to use guile, Highness. We must watch, eavesdrop. We must use the magic I offer."

"I can't believe this, Tariq. It's one thing to accuse Lazar of coveting a beautiful woman who is not his to look upon. It is another to accuse that same man of treachery when he has been exemplary in his loyalty to our Crown."

"They are one and the same, my Zar. Both acts—carnal or spiritual—betray you."

Boaz shook his head, but before he could speak, Maliz pushed him further still.

"Do not risk further humiliation, my Zar. If I am wrong, have me killed. That's how strongly I feel about this. I have no reason to lie to you. I have powers at my fingertips that I can make yours—just invite me in. All you have to do is—"

"Maliz!" the Zar finally said as some understanding that the demon could not see must have broken across his expression. "You are the one they call the demon?" he accused uncontrollably.

And now, finally, Maliz revealed himself fully. He permitted his true, deep voice to emerge. "Do I frighten you?" He heard Boaz's hesitation. "You have nothing to fear from me. I will not interfere with your Crown, your realm, or your people. I want only that Percheron remain true to Zarab."

"I don't believe this is happening," Boaz admitted, his voice fearful. "You have been hiding as Tariq all along?"

Maliz shrugged the Grand Vizier's shoulders. "Quite a short while, to be honest. Percheron is under threat, my Zar—I am here to help you."

"Why couldn't you declare yourself? Why the secrecy?"

"People fear what they do not understand. It is easier to work invisibly when you are on a mission such as mine."

"Where is the real Tariq?"

"He died of natural causes, Majesty. I had hoped to persuade him to join me, to be my eyes around the palace. He was ready to help but he wanted power and riches. I could give him anything he wanted and he was greedy. He sampled the fruits and died one night in a lascivious combination of women and wine. He was old, Highness; his body could not take that sort of excitement."

"And then what happened?"

Maliz sighed. "I took my opportunity. He no longer needed

his body. You could say I borrowed it. I have treated it with deference and I have made Tariq into a man that everyone—including Lazar—can grudgingly respect."

"I cannot fault you there," Boaz admitted, wonderment in his voice. "And so now it all makes sense—the stoop is gone, the adornments disappear, the more likable Tariq emerged."

"Thank you, Highness. May I say you seem to be taking this news rather well—is it because you hated the old Tariq so much?" Before Boaz could answer, Maliz added, "Or has someone given you a clue to my presence?"

Boaz hesitated. "Don't be ridiculous. How could anyone know?"

But Maliz heard the discomfited pause and he stored it away. Lazar was definitely onto him. He wished he could kill him right now but he needed him as a guide and protector for the desert. He would bide his time and deal with the arrogant Spur in due course.

"I just wondered," he said, turning suddenly, unsure of why. He frowned into the distance.

"What's wrong?" Boaz hissed.

Maliz listened carefully. "I'm not sure."

"I can't hear anything."

"No, neither did I. But I sense something."

"What?"

Maliz felt distracted and irritated. He didn't have any more time and knew this was the moment to strike. Even though his mind felt a presence nearby, he needed to push Boaz into saying yes—there might never be a better opportunity. He whispered now. "My Zar, you must make a decision. We have little time if Lazar leaves in a few hours."

"What must I do?"

"You simply give me pemission to join you. The words are ancient. You must not be frightened by them. And then you must kill me."

"What?" The Zar instinctively stepped away.

Maliz had expected as much. "Don't be scared. By killing me, you release me. It is nothing. I feel nothing."

"But . . ."

Maliz smiled, crafting his whispered lies with care. "And when we return, I will claim back the Grand Vizier's body, heal his wounds, and reignite his life."

"You can do that?"

"I did precisely that before when his heart gave up during his sexual orgy. It is easy with my powers. I know it is distasteful to plunge a blade into me but I promise you I feel nothing." He handed Boaz a vicious-looking knife he took from his robe.

"I . . . I'm not sure I can do—"

"You can and you will. Now utter these words and all will be well. I can show you Ana in the next moment or two. You must say this: 'Maliz, come into me. Take my soul.'"

Boaz stared at him uncomprehendingly. "I will not say that."

Maliz gave a soft sound of admonishment. "Zar Boaz, these are ancient words that have no meaning today. The language is quaint. *Take my soul* may sound daunting but the dramatic phrasing relates only to the fact that I will claim your body, guide your spirit. In centuries gone by, soul meant body. Just ignore how theatrical it sounds."

"Fayiz?" Lazar's voice suddenly drifted from the other side of the dune.

Maliz gave a new hissing sound. The sensation he had felt must have been the Spur creeping up on them. "It's now or never, my Zar. We shall hide both our bodies and go. Call out, tell him all is well."

Boaz nodded. "Lazar, we're fine. Tariq is suffering a bad bout of the Haste." He feigned a laugh. "He doesn't know which end to let fly from."

Lazar's reply was cautioning. "Just a minute more then and I'll take over. You need some sleep this night."

Boaz hated lying to Lazar but he was shaken to his core from the revelations he had heard this night.

"Answer Lazar, Highness," the Grand Vizier urged.

"One minute, I promise," Boaz called. He heard Lazar grumble as he walked away.

Maliz nodded. "Good. Are you ready?"

Boaz was frightened by the magic. The demon's offer seemed to offer a solution for his most bitter suspicions and yet it went against everything he trusted or believed in. "I'm not comfortable with—"

"My Zar, there is nothing comfortable about your life right now. The Galinseans are threatening to raze your city; a madman rebel has stolen your wife and child, and as there's no ransom, presumably he's after something far more sinister. You've got your mother acting regent in a palace under threat whilst you're not sure whether the wife you risk your own life for has a lover who happens to be your own head of security, and, even more tangled, he's your mother's new consort! Your life is certainly not comfortable but I alone have the power to bring some sanity back to it. And it begins here by either dispelling the notion that you have been cuckolded or proving it and taking appropriate action to set your house in order, Majesty. Take what I'm offering. I am more faithful to you than any of those you have previously trusted. I know you sense their betrayal—I can hear it in your tone, I can see it in how your body reacts. I know nothing angers you more than treachery. Seek the truth—and set things straight."

It was as though the demon could listen in on his thoughts. Everything he said was right.

Boaz opened his mouth to voice some conditions, but before he could speak, men in dark robes melted out of the darkness, surrounding him and Maliz.

"Boaz!" he screamed. "Do it! Say the words. I can save us."

"I—" The Zar felt out of his depth suddenly and utterly confused, certainly overawed by the men with curved blades advancing upon them. He heard a pain-filled roar go up at the camp, knew it was Lazar. There was no hope for them if Lazar and his blade were captured.

"Now, now!" Maliz growled in a deep voice, chilling Boaz's blood. "You stupid, imbecilic boy. If you are ever going to—"

And that voice, bullying him, ordering him, forgetting who he was and what sort of respect he was due, tipped all the anger he had been doing his best to control over the limit of his tolerance. Boaz yelled words in such wrathful tones that even the men stalking him froze momentarily. And then he lunged.

25

They had come upon them with such terrible silence that Lazar had not even had time to reach for a sword—the best he could do had been to shout and warn Boaz. He had not even been asleep, simply standing over the embers of their small fire and giving the Grand Vizier the one final minute of agony. He had been happy to hear of the discomfort—the demon deserved all and more. But that distraction had been his undoing. Now men in black robes he recognized from many moons before surrounded them, others manhandled him to his feet, and he could hear Ganya shrieking.

"Get away from her, leave her alone," he yelled, straining to see the Khalid, knowing how helpless they all were.

"My men do not understand, Spur," said an all-too-familiar voice. "They do not speak your language. Frankly, I'm surprised that you risk yet another excursion into my land. I warned you once before—I am shocked after what you saw me do, you did not believe or heed that warning."

Lazar had been making guttural sounds as the men tied his hands tightly behind him. Now he addressed his attacker. "Arafanz, you—"

"But then, I shouldn't be too surprised," Arafanz continued conversationally as if Lazar had not spoken, "because Ana told me you would come after her, and she knows you best of all, doesn't she, Spur Lazar?" Ganya and Salim were brought before the rebel as he continued: "And who have we here?"

"These people have nothing to do with—"

"Quiet, Lazar, or I'll have your tongue cut out. Don't test me." He switched to Khalid. "And what is your name, my beauty?"

"I am Ganya, lajka of the Khalid Doraz tribe," she said proudly, lifting her chin. If she was fearful, she was not showing it.

"And this old man?"

"He is my father."

"Why are you here?" Arafanz held a finger in the air to the Spur. "Er, careful, Lazar, no speaking. You want to hang on to that tongue of yours, don't you?" He smiled in the firelight. "Ganya—pretty name—answer my question, please."

Her eyes glittered defiantly as torches were lit by some of the men from the embers. "My father sold camels to the Percherese to make this trip."

"I see. And you are a camel?"

No one laughed, least of all Arafanz.

She ignored his sarcastic gibe. "Our women danced for the Percherese and our men played music to entertain them, in honor of the Spur."

"And you were one of the dancers?"

"That's right."

"And are you still dancing for the Spur? Is that why you're here?" His words, spoken evenly and with no change of expression, nevertheless carried a tone of innuendo that neither Ganya nor Lazar missed.

"That is my business."

"You've answered my question, thank you." The rebel turned to Salim. "So, old man. What is your story? I have no quarrel with the Khalid, until they start to work with my enemy and against me. Then they become my enemy. Are you my enemy?"

Salim stared at Arafanz. "I am here because I believe you stole my son from me. I want to find him, find out if he is still alive."

Arafanz shrugged. "I could not tell you. I never ask their names. I simply give them new ones."

Salim nodded. "I hoped he might recognize me."

"If he is among us, he chooses not to. If he is at my fortress, you will never know." Arafanz moved as fast as a snake striking as he swiped a blade across the Khalid's neck in a fluid movement.

Ganya screamed and Lazar lunged forward, howling threats of revenge, but his captors pulled back savagely on the rope he was attached to and the Spur was dragged to his knees as Salim fell, his eyes wide with disbelief.

The Khalid clutched at his throat, his daughter shrieking beside him as blood gushed between his fingers. He had eyes only for Lazar and he choked out two words only—*"Find him!"*—before he toppled to the sand, gasping one final time as the liquid of life slowed to a trickle and death claimed him.

"Kill me now while you can because I intend to see that you

die at the end of my blade for that act alone," Lazar growled, his voice shaking with rage.

Above Ganya's wails, Arafanz spoke mildly. "Not yet, Lazar. I owe this much to Ana—she should see her brave Spur one more time, know that he betrayed her with a desert dancer, before I end your life." He looked across as his men arrived from the darkness beyond the camp, dragging a haunted-looking young man. "And who is this?"

"He is no one," Lazar said, stunned by the expression on Boaz's face. The Zar looked more than shocked; he looked dazed. "He is nothing but a lowly servant. Are you going to kill him, too?"

The rebel made the soft tutting sound that a parent uses with a wayward infant. "Let him answer for himself, Lazar. Your quick defense makes me instantly suspicious." He turned to Boaz. "Who are you?"

The Zar did not speak. His lips moved but no sound came out. "I killed," he stammered unable to finish his sentence. Looking up at Lazar, terrified, he managed, "I'm so sorry. I don't know what came over me."

Lazar frowned. "What's happened? What have your men done?" It was only then that he noticed the blood on Boaz. And his sense of helplessness doubled. "Are you hurt?"

The rebel's eyebrows arched in surprise. "Quiet, Lazar. Who are you, boy?"

"I am Fayid. I work for the Spur," Boaz answered. He looked again at Lazar, still terrified. "Spur, the Grand Vizier is dead. I killed him." He looked down at the blood spattered all over his white garments. "This is his blood, not mine."

Arafanz laughed, but Lazar barely heard him; he was still reeling from Boaz's news. He was sure Iridor had warned that the demon could not be killed by conventional means. What did this mean? Had they been wrong all along?

He heard Arafanz address him. "You're to be strapped to your camels, the woman as well."

"What about the Grand Vizier? I want to see him, make sure he is truly dead."

"Here he comes now, it looks like. Bring him here," Arafanz called.

The Grand Vizier's body was thrown down at Arafanz's feet. The rebel rolled him onto his back using the toe of his boot. "It is him indeed. I'm amazed, Lazar, that both you and the Grand Vizier would return for a second helping of my wrath. I can understand your motivation, perhaps, but his? Why would he come here with you and a boy?"

It took all of Lazar's focus to pull his gaze from the dead Tariq. He knew he had to concentrate or Boaz's life was surely forfeit. "I cannot say. It was the Zar's wish that he return."

"How strange. The old Vizier seems more of a liability than an asset."

"Perhaps he preferred to risk your sort of desert justice to that of the Galinseans. I'm sure your spy network has kept you informed of what is happening in the city," Lazar replied non-committally.

"Indeed. But all seems quiet just now. The Galinseans are seemingly biding their time. For what, I cannot guess. Do you know?"

"If I did, I wouldn't tell you."

"Even under torture?" Arafanz smiled.

"Even under torture. But I don't think the Galinsean war threat interests you in the slightest, Arafanz."

"You're right, it doesn't. It only makes my task easier. While the Percherese panic over their warlike neighbors, no one is noticing me or my men."

"As you do what?"

"Ah, that's our business."

"I thought you simply wanted Ana. But it's beyond that, isn't it, Arafanz? Why don't you tell me? I'm hardly in a position to do anything about it, and as you say, there will be no amnesty granted me this time. I'm not even sure I understand why it was given the last time we met."

"Again you're right. There will be no escape this time, Lazar. All right, I shall share my plans with you. I intend to kill the young Zar and all who support his right to the throne."

It explained everything and nothing. The shock of the truth was tempered by total confusion. "Why? What can you possibly have against Zar Boaz?"

"You have no idea. But let's not do this just now, Lazar." Arafanz returned his attention to Boaz. "How old are you, Fayid?"

Lazar was desperate to answer but it seemed Boaz was up to the task of protecting his identity.

"I am nineteen," the Zar lied.

"And loyal to your young doomed Zar?"

"Of course."

"You would die for him?"

This sounded dangerous to Lazar. "Listen, Arafanz, if—"

"Quiet, Lazar, I'm talking solely to this youngster. Answer me, Fayid."

"I would die for him, yes. I am a loyal servant of the Zar."

"Can you prove that? Would you slit your own throat if he asked you to?"

"He would never ask me to. From what I know of him, he is above those sorts of games."

"Proving one's loyalty is not a game."

"Making someone kill himself for no other reason but to prove it, is. But to answer your question: no, I would not slit my own throat to prove a point. I would, however, step in front of a blade for him."

"Does he impress you?"

"I do not know him well enough. He is my Zar. I can think of no greater honor than to serve him."

"How can you care about this young man if you have not met him?"

"I have been raised to do so. I gather from those who do know him that he is worthy of loyalty. I also hear that he is something of a scholar, that he plans to lead his people into an era of prosperity. He cherishes peace. Prefers art to weapons . . . I want to be a soldier but still I respect his ways."

"And who has told you this about your Zar?"

"People like Spur Lazar who know him well."

"I see. And what is your role in this expedition, Fayiz?"

"I am training to join the Protectorate. I am along on this journey to help Spur Lazar."

Arafanz nodded. "You must be of an age with your Zar. How old is your Zar?"

Boaz shrugged. "I don't know for sure. He was born after me but not by much, I don't think."

"So you don't know what he looks like?"

Boaz shook his head. "Not really."

Arafanz nodded. "Neither do I," he said regretfully. "He is elusive. But I intend to know. I plan to look into his eyes before I kill him, snuffing out the last of the Percherese Crown bearers who worship Zarab."

"Is this what it's all about?" Lazar asked, aghast. "About faith?"

Arafanz ignored him. "One last thing, Fayid, before I make up my mind whether to let you live awhile longer. Why did you kill the Grand Vizier?"

"He . . . he made a lewd suggestion."

The rebel frowned. "What sort of suggestion?"

Lazar watched Boaz struggle, then lift his chin with defiance. "He said he wanted to enter me."

Arafanz actually laughed. "I hadn't realized that the Grand Vizier's tastes swung that way. But I'm not surprised. And you killed him for that?"

"He laughed at me. Mocked me for my admiration of Spur Lazar. Said he was not as honorable as I thought, that the Spur would allow any number of the soldiers to have their way with me. He said he could teach me how, so that it wouldn't hurt."

Lazar felt his bile rise, even though he couldn't imagine that Maliz would have risked Boaz's temper in any shape or form. Clearly the Zar was crafting a story for Arafanz's benefit. But that didn't negate the fact that the Grand Vizier was now dead by Boaz's hand. He stared uncomprehendingly at the corpse. He was certain that Boaz would not have resorted to such violence unless he really had felt threatened. What had scared Boaz so much? He didn't have to wait long for an answer.

"Tell me what he told you about the Spur's honor and why it was not true."

"I don't wish to repeat it."

"Oh, but I insist, Fayid. It's either that or your throat is slit. You can see we now have two corpses rotting in the sand. I have no problem with making it three."

Boaz's eyes widened. He glanced at Lazar, who nodded. He couldn't risk Arafanz taking the Zar's life as casually as he had taken Salim's.

"Don't make me ask again," Arafanz urged, throwing a pointed look toward Lazar.

"He told me that Spur Lazar had cuckolded the Zar, that he is in love with his wife, the Zaradine Ana."

"Ah, indeed. And do you believe him, Fayid?"

"No! I believe the Spur is too principled for such behavior. He would never, never dishonor his Zar in this manner."

Lazar swallowed hard and resisted the urge to stare at the sand in shame. Instead he fixed Boaz with a hard gaze, relieved that his flushed cheeks would not be noticed in this low light.

Arafanz chuckled. "I think you killed the wrong man, Fayid. You may find that the Grand Vizier—despite his persuasion and obvious interest in you—was telling you the truth about your precious Spur."

Lazar forced himself not to react, though he felt his jaw grind with fury. This was exquisitely dangerous ground he trod now. He desperately needed Iridor's counsel, and with Maliz dead, perhaps they could risk opening a mindlink.

Surprisingly it was Ganya who broke the frigid silence. "Do not listen to him, Fayid. He deliberately creates problems between you and your Spur."

Arafanz looked unfazed by her warning. "Believe what you want, soldier boy. But I've heard from the Zaradine herself that she and your precious Spur Lazar are lovers."

It was too much for Lazar to bear. "Unless you can back up that claim, Arafanz, then, Fayid, you have to ask yourself who you trust more. This madman—his brains baked by the desert sun—or this man," he said, pointing to his chest with private self-loathing.

Boaz turned to Arafanz. "I killed the Grand Vizier for his

lecherous behavior toward me, and if I could kill him twice, I would, for his lies against the Spur."

Arafanz shrugged. "You speak very defiantly and with great composure for a mere servant and for one so young in years. You intrigue me, Fayid. You should have left the Grand Vizier to us—we would have killed him for you and then you would have no blood on your hands. But then soldiers need to be blooded early. I congratulate you. He was not a good person, from what I know of him." Then he smiled and quipped, "And you keep thinking good things about your Spur."

Lazar felt relief flood him. The immediate threat to Boaz was past. He wished that Iridor was near. Did this mean they no longer had to be careful? And if this interference by Arafanz was also connected with faith, did it mean they were all fighting on the same side, killing one another over the same cause?

Arafanz interrupted his confused thoughts. "Strap them to camels, tie their hands using rope beneath the beasts' bellies. We ride for the fortress. And free that hawk. I don't want the Spur laying claim to anything from my desert."

Herezah's face was still ashen. She was curled up tightly on a divan, hands around her knees, trembling. She had not slept, she had not eaten, she had not so much as bathed her face or changed her clothes. Her robes were disheveled and her hair fell in straggled clumps around her tearstained face. Pots of tea cooled around her, untouched. All servants had been banished and she refused all messages. She had cut herself off to think but she had done no thinking; instead she had cocooned herself in the silence, and her mind had gone blank with shock. She knew the Elim guarded her outside but they would not be able to protect her against the might of the Galinseans. King Falza was coming, and from the terrible stories she'd heard of Percheron's barbaric enemy, he would look forward to seeing her head presented to him on one of the Zar's solid silver plates. She began to imagine how it would feel to be beheaded . . . how long did one's senses last? Long enough to register that the body was no longer attached? Would she be able to see for a few moments? Hear the glee of her executors, perhaps? She gave a low moan of despair as the door opened.

"Crown Valide, it is Bin," her servant whispered. He was the only one brave enough to risk her wrath. "Make I come in, please?"

"Have you found him?" she croaked.

The servant hurried to bow before her.

"Well?" she asked, not even bothering to raise her head. She knew what the answer was going to be.

"He is nowhere in the palace, Highness. I have Elim combing the city now."

"I know Salmeo too well," she groaned. "He would have worked out his escape route and method long before he executed his plan. I just don't understand his behavior. Why did he do this?"

Bin surprised her by sitting on the floor near her feet so he could look into her face. She flinched but didn't pull away.

"Crown Valide, may I be candid with you?"

"Were you with my son?"

"Always."

"Then speak your mind, Bin, for I have no one else to offer me advice, no one else to seek counsel from. You are young but you are all there is."

He nodded gently. "May I suggest that the Eunuch Salmeo

was likely scared of you, Crown Valide. Until recently you were equals—if anything, he held the balance of power in the harem, I suspect, while you held the balance of power outside of its walls because of your connection to the Zar. You were, in effect, each other's counterbalance."

"That would be fair to say."

"But when you were made Crown Valide, the balance was upset. Suddenly you had genuine power. I imagine he felt nervous. I have no doubt there are secrets within the harem that we, on the outside, will never be privy to. Perhaps Salmeo was anxious they remain that way."

She was intrigued and surprised by how helpful this smart servant was. She could imagine that his bright, quick mind put him in a position to do plenty to harm her cause if he chose to . . . but he didn't.

"Bin, why are you so loyal?"

"Pardon, Crown Valide?"

"You heard me. I was just thinking how odd it is that you have so easily transferred your loyalties from my son to me when I am likely not someone you would normally feel beholden to in any way."

As she expected, he understood completely her message, both what she said and what she didn't say. He sighed.

"Be honest, Bin. We could all be dead tomorrow." She laughed mirthlessly.

He did not so much as twitch at her dark humor. "I am loyal to the Crown. Since I began working directly with Zar Boaz, I have seen that, despite some of your more questionable decisions, you, too, care about the Crown, about the realm and its longevity."

"And I have strange way of showing it—is that what you're not saying, Bin?"

"All that matters, Crown Valide, is that I will do whatever is required to protect the throne. Right now you sit that throne, so everything I can do is at your disposal. I will serve you with due respect and with honor."

"And you will do whatever I say?"

"No, Crown Valide, I will do whatever I believe Zar Boaz would wish me to do. I hope that doesn't mean you will now have my throat slit—you did ask for me to be honest."

She smiled genuinely. "I did indeed. So what are we going to do? Tomorrow the Galinseans will arrive in our harbor. And the day after tomorrow they begin their killing."

"You cannot be here, Valide. We must secure your safety in the morning."

"No, I refuse to run. Get the girls out of the harem. Make arrangements for them to be farmed out to families. They must blend into the population, not be noticed by the Galinseans. Their fate, if they are discovered as the Zar's women, will be hideous."

"I think we have to accept that the fate of every Percherese is hideous to contemplate under Galinsean rule."

"No! King Falza made it clear. He will spare the people, who he believes are innocents forced to follow their Zar's ways. His targets are the palace people closer to the Zar, his relatives, his confidants. You, for instance."

"I also refuse to run," Bin said calmly. "I took an oath for my Zar. I shall keep it, whatever the cost."

Herezah could have kissed him for his loyalty. She didn't expect many others beyond the Elim to show such fortitude. "Thank you, Bin." She hadn't expected such genuine appreciation to feel so good, or to prompt her aide's soft smile. "Let everyone know. I don't care who flees. But we can offer no protection if people choose to leave the city boundaries. I shall need to speak with the head of the Protectorate. Without Spur Lazar, I fear we are lost, but we must go through the motions—although, between you and me, I don't anticipate allowing all our soldiers to die. It's pointless. We are no match for the Galinseans."

"We could, of course, fight back. We outnumber them significantly. Weight of numbers could prevail if we can protect our harbor."

"You really are a surprise, Bin, aren't you? Fight back? I don't know anything about our military other than its loyalty to the Zar, and especially to the Spur. Well, I shall ask Captain Ghassal, for I won't be held responsible for carnage. I do feel this war is lost before it even begins. I'm sorry to sound so defeated but I . . ." Her voice trailed off and she looked at Bin, embarrassed.

Bin nodded. "I know." It didn't take a seer to see that all the fight had gone out of the Crown Valide after today's atrocity. "I shall fetch Captain Ghassal personally and immediately. And the Grand Master Eunuch?"

She shook her head dejectedly. "Unfortunately, it seems he has been too cunning this time. We have no resources to use against him."

"He should be made answerable for this. He alone provoked war. You thought you were brokering a peace."

"Falza saw only his dead wife on a royal barge of Percheron. The fact that the poison was meant for me seems somehow lost on him." Herezah's hand shook as she reached for a cup of cold tea to sip. "Where Salmeo would escape to is anyone's guess. Do we even know where he is from? My understanding is that he came to the palace as a very young child."

Bin gave a disappointed shake of his head. "I'm afraid not, Crown Valide. It was so long ago that no one remembers. I checked our library records, though, and it seems the eunuch is ahead of us. The particular book that recorded the purchase of slaves for the year of his arrival at the palace is gone."

"Stolen?" She gave a small gasp of despair.

Bin shrugged. "We have to assume so. He has thought of everything."

"But that means he must be returning to his birthplace. Why else would he bother stealing the records?"

"You are probably right, Crown Valide, but we shall never know where that birthplace is. Unless we can find the slaver who bought Salmeo as a child."

Herezah nodded miserably. "Salmeo has to be sixty summers, possibly more. That means his slaver is likely dead."

"Let me try, though," Bin offered.

"Go ahead. It could, of course, be his way of sending us on a donkey chase. He is cunning enough to steal those records purely to make us think one way whilst he goes another."

"I shall send the captain up immediately."

"And then we must get the girls out. I would give anything for the benefit of the Spur's wisdom right now," Herezah said, standing. "But we must do this alone, Bin—you and I."

"I shall gladly stand by your side and face whatever we must, Crown Valide," Bin said, bowing.

How death felt suddenly so honorable was beyond her but Herezah felt inspired by his words. She wished her son and Lazar could see her now. It was a pity she would likely be dead before either of them returned.

26

Lazar, Boaz, and Ganya had ridden uncomfortably strapped to the camels. Finally the beasts stopped and lowered themselves, knees bending neatly into the sand. Warm golden grit was stirring in small angry eddies around the imposing fortress walls and Lazar was glad of the shield of his headdress. The sky had already begun to lighten, and despite the precariousness of his situation, he felt his hopes surge that he would at last see Ana again.

Arafanz walked up to him and Lazar refused to show how stiff he felt from the hours of ungainly travel. "Welcome to my home," the rebel said. Although the words were gracious, his tone was anything but sociable. "You'd never have found me. You must admit, we blend too well."

"It's certainly impressive . . . from a distance, yes, you're right, the structure is easily missed. But don't fool yourself, Arafanz, I knew precisely where we were going."

"I can't imagine how."

"Nor will you ever know."

"You must be desperate to see her," Arafanz baited.

"I am desperate to return her to her husband, the Zar."

"I know you lie, Lazar. I can see in your eyes how you feel about Ana—and I understand. She is not a young woman any man could easily forget."

If Lazar's hands had not been tied, he was sure he would have attacked the arrogant man standing before him. "I will die before I let you keep her."

"Excellent. Your death is desired."

"Be assured, Ana belongs in Percheron. That is where she will be returned to."

The rebel sighed. "It will have to be over my corpse, then," he said, and smiled, genuinely this time. Lazar understood how rare that expression must be on his otherwise grave countenance.

"That would be my intention," Lazar replied.

Arafanz barked a small laugh. "You're amusing, Spur. No weapon, no camels, no sense of where you are or which direction to head in, no food, no water, but you're still going to rescue Ana, kill me, somehow navigate your way around my dozens of men, and escape, *plus* get yourselves back safely to Percheron?" He began to clap, a new look of irony on his face.

"Something like that," Lazar said.

"I should just kill Ana now in front of you and release you from your pathetic delusions."

"You could, but you won't," Lazar said.

"And why not?"

"Because you've already revealed yourself to me, Arafanz. You've told me so much more about yourself than you intended. I know what motivates you now; I know how you feel about Ana and about her husband. Whatever happens, you are not going to kill Ana. She is your whole reason right now for breathing and it has nothing to do with how your heart reacts to her."

Lazar watched the rebel's eyes narrow and knew his words had struck home. So Iridor was right—the rebel was not as ruthless as he liked to think he was. Ana had possibly stolen his heart. Lazar had to bite back the groan of anger that rose in his throat at the notion that this man had touched Ana, had probably won some affection from her in return.

Arafanz sneered at Lazar before motioning one of his men forward. The leader spoke to the man in a language the Spur did not understand. "Take the woman, put her in a holding cell." He turned to another. "Put the young one behind the camels until I call for him." Boaz was manhandled away from Lazar, who tried to reassure him with an encouraging glance whilst Arafanz signaled to a third minion. "Bring Ana out."

Lazar heard Ana's name and felt his insides clench with fear. If Ana showed recognition of Boaz, all was lost; the Zar's blood would be spilled in moments amid the sands of the fortress. He glanced at Ganya being led away and was proud of the way she threw him a look of courage. Her expression begged him to stay strong. He didn't really understand her defiance. To him the situation felt lost.

Iridor hid behind one of the many boulders that made up the rooftop of the fortress and watched keenly in the dim predawn light as Arafanz's men led Ganya away. He felt sick to his wing tips. Something had gone badly wrong. One of Arafanz's many lone riders must have stumbled upon the group. He wondered how much Arafanz knew of Boaz; he suspected not as much as he needed to know or the young man would already be dead. So perhaps the Fayid ruse was still working for them? Where was Maliz? And Salim? He felt the chill of fear grip him. Were they dead? Maliz could not be killed! But where was he? Lazar would hardly have left him to perish in the desert—as much as the demon meant harm to them, the Spur was wise enough to keep enemies close. Had the impostor escaped? He couldn't risk a link to Lazar, not yet. He looked at Boaz, and was surprised by the young man's calm, and it was only then that he noticed that the Zar's clothes were bloodstained. Fresh fear coursed through him. He saw Ganya swing around and throw a look back to Lazar. Ganya was now his only chance. He had to hope they took her to the cells in the bowels of the fortress that had first held Ana. It was still dark enough for him to move relatively unnoticed, but once the sky lightened fully, he would have to disappear and hide. It wasn't the humans so much as the hawks who were the greatest danger to him.

He moved with stealth, hopping down from level to level as best he could using the cover of the relative darkness of the morning. He waited, and as he had guessed, Ganya was pushed into one of the dark holes that passed for holding cells. He tapped at the bars of her cell until she turned and saw him. She ran at the tiny window and grabbed his foot. He knew to wait whilst she found her inner peace.

Soon enough Ganya's voice entered his head. *We were set upon by his men. My father was slain.*

Oh, Ganya, forgive us his death.

I refuse to think about his murder right now. We must survive before we mourn him.

Where is the Grand Vizier?

Dead.

He can't be!

I saw his corpse.

Arafanz killed him?

No. Fayid, the boy. Stabbed him because the Grand Vizier apparently made an improper advance on him.

What? he stammered. *What sort of advance?*

I don't know. The youngster was in shock. All he would say is that the Grand Vizier wanted to enter him. Fayid reacted angrily at his manhood being threatened. He stabbed him just moments before they were grabbed by Arafanz's men.

No, no, no! This is not right. It can't be.

There's more. I think they're bringing the Zaradine out. The leader, Arafanz, obviously wants to humiliate Lazar as much as possible. He might kill him while she watches or slay her before him. But he is suspicious of Fayid. He may just want to kill the lad in front of all of them. He's certainly ruthless enough; he killed my father in front of me.

Ana's going out there?

I'm guessing; I don't know for certain.

Hold this link. I can't risk that we are heard.

She frowned. *By whom?*

I'll explain all soon. For now, keep me safe. I have to speak with Ana.

How?

In the same way, through you. Ana! he called. *Ana, it's Iridor.*

Iridor! Her voice suddenly called into both of their minds. *Where are you?*

There's no time. Ana, listen, you're being taken outside, am I right?

Yes, I'm just being led out of the doorway.

Don't recognize Boaz, whatever you do.

Boaz! The Zar is here? She sounded terrified.

He is posing as an aspiring soldier. A servant to Lazar. Whatever you do, don't bow to him, don't give him eye contact, don't recognize him as your husband. If you do that, he is as good as dead. His name is Fayid. Can you remember that?

Yes, but I'm confused.

Remain that way. It will protect you.

What about Laz— And then her words stopped dead.

She's seen him, Ganya said, across the link. *Go watch. Be our eyes.*

Iridor hopped away and launched himself quietly, flying effortlessly and silently behind the cover of the fortress to reach the rooftop again.

The wind was gaining strength around them. The eddies of sand had turned into much larger swirling cones. They could hear the sands shifting and blowing in the distance, though it was still rocky enough to feel protected.

"Do you know what this is, Spur?" Arafanz asked.

"I can guess."

"It is early. It should not be here yet."

Lazar decided if the man was so motivated by his faith, then it wouldn't go astray to try to unnerve him by seeking out his spiritual weakness. "I'm told the Samazen answers to Lyana."

"What would you know about Lyana, Lazar?"

"More than you, obviously—the great desert wind is her weapon. Does it not occur to you that you have angered your Goddess for the Samazen to be blowing so early?" Again Arafanz stared at Lazar hard, unblinking, weighing him up. Lazar refused to cower beneath the penetrating gaze. "Perhaps you should be thinking about how you've offended her. The wind sounds very angry indeed and this has only happened during the short while since our arrival. In fact, in just the time we've stood here discussing it, it's gotten worse."

Arafanz turned away. "Here comes Ana," he said coldly. He had to raise his normally quiet voice to be heard above the wind's noise, which had elevated itself from a wheeze to a constant groan.

If Lazar had hit upon Arafanz's weakness, the rebel had hit upon Lazar's. At the mention of Ana everything went out of his mind—even the death that seemed so close became meaningless. His attention snapped away from his captor to the woman who had just appeared from a doorway, flanked by several dark-robed adversaries. She was huge with child; her normally svelte frame was bloated and round; her normally graceful movement had assumed a slightly rolling gait. Her hands moved to her belly in support, and even those hands looked swollen. But her face—her beautiful, achingly sweet face—had not changed. It was slightly plumper perhaps but somehow it suited her, and despite her incarceration these last eight moons, her complexion reflected a healthy glow from the torch flames and her golden hair glinted softly in the dewy early light.

Lazar's heart felt as though it lurched in his chest, as though straining to meet her. He would give anything—anything!—to hold her; to hell with the consequences. But this situation was so fraught with danger, to move would be risking her life as much as Boaz's. He remained as still as a statue, simply drinking in her beauty as he thanked Lyana privately that his Ana was still alive, still safe.

"Not quite how you remember her, Lazar, eh?"

"I suppose I should be grateful to you for keeping her well. She certainly looks hale."

"I did more than that. I kept her safe, which is more than any of you could do," Arafanz replied.

It was as he listened to the rebel's caustic response that Lazar noticed how the sand swirled up and around but never touched Ana. The cones and eddies of sand raced over the boots of her guards and sometimes blew high enough to make the men blink, but Ana walked untouched through the tiny maelstrom. And now, as he watched this strange phenomenon, he realized the sand was stirring more angrily around them all. He could feel his face beginning to sting, his fingers being whipped by the grains as they whisked by. Even his normally loose trousers were beginning to flatten against his legs as the wind picked up its tempo.

"She looks every bit the Zaradine," was all Lazar could say as Ana finally drew close enough for him to see the soft green of her eyes. They were filled with tears but she blinked them away, hurriedly.

"Ana, I'm sure these people need no introductions," Arafanz said.

"Hello, Lazar," she said, her gaze riveted upon him, her voice trembling slightly. "I knew you would come."

He bowed formally. "Zaradine Ana, it is very good to see you safe."

She put both hands on either side of her belly. "We are both well." A smile ghosted across her lovely face. "I'm sorry that you are here. It does not bode well for you."

"That is as it may be, Zaradine. But this is my duty."

"How touching," Arafanz interrupted, sneering at their

forced politeness. "Why don't you tell her how you truly feel Lazar—this may be your last chance," he goaded.

Lazar refused to be drawn in, kept a grim silence, his gaze unwavering on Ana and the belly that held the new Prince of Percheron. He prayed the baby would stay cocooned in her womb for now. With the arrival of the Samazen, he had no idea how he would protect the three of them—four, including Boaz. Guilt stabbed in his chest that he hadn't included Ganya in his plan. She deserved more.

"Ana, I have someone else I want you to meet." Arafanz called across to his men, "Bring the young one," before he returned his attention to her. "I'd like you to tell me who this is."

She looked at him dubiously, then back to Lazar.

"Say nothing, Lazar, or I will kill the youngster right before you."

Lazar's lips pursed. He was trapped. All he could do was stare at Ana and hope her normal perceptiveness picked up the peril they faced. He felt sickened when Arafanz put an arm about her and tenderly kissed the top of her head. "Who is this that you see coming out from behind the camels? Don't be scared, just tell me the truth."

"Is this one of your trick questions?" she asked hesitantly. "You're not going to ask him to prove his loyalty or—"

"Nothing like that, but this is important. Ah, here he is. Do you know this person?"

Boaz was brought close and Lazar looked down, his insides twisting with fear and helplessness, his wrists tightly bound. Lazar decided he could kick, perhaps bring down one or two men before he was felled, but that would not save Zar Boaz the evil blade of Arafanz. To his surprise and small relief, the young ruler knelt before Ana. No one could ever accuse Boaz of too much pride, nor could they say that if he perished here, it was because of his own stupidity or pride. Boaz had done everything he could to maintain the ruse.

"Zaradine Ana," he said, bowing his head.

"Say no more, boy," Arafanz warned. He looked back at Ana. "Tell me, my dear, who is this?"

Lazar held his breath. She couldn't be blamed.

"Why, this is Fayid, if I'm not mistaken. He is a servant of Spur Lazar's, training to be a soldier in the Protectorate. I'm right, aren't I? You are Fayid?" She gently leaned down toward Boaz.

Lazar couldn't believe it. His head snapped up and he had to temper the delight that he was sure was flashing across his face. How could she have known? Unless Iridor—yes, that was it. Iridor had told her. He'd risked using magic. Was that because Maliz was gone. That whole notion of the seemingly indestructible demon being dead still didn't sit right with him but there was no time to dwell on it. Deliberately controlling his features, he stared steadily at the rebel, who was also eyeing him but talking to Ana.

"And how is it that a woman of the harem—now a lofty Zaradine—would know such a lowly person as Fayid?" he asked.

"Fayid was kind to me. Before I was Zaradine, I tried to escape the palace. He was one of the guards who marched me back to the palace gate," Ana lied. "We are of an age, I suspect, and no doubt he felt sorry for me. He told me his name. He was the only one of the guard who spoke to me. His gentleness is not something I choose to forget from a time when everyone treated me with disdain . . . everyone, that is, except Spur Lazar, of course."

"Oh, of course," Arafanz echoed, irony heavy in his response.

"Arafanz, I feel quite weak if you don't mind."

"Tsk tsk, Ana. Desert women can ride a camel all day, deliver through the night, and be back on their camels the next, suckling their babes." He smiled gently at her.

"She is not a desert woman!" Lazar growled. "This woman is royal. Have some respect."

"Don't talk to me about respect, Lazar, not when you have lain down with this same woman. She was a Zaradine then, too, but that didn't seem to stop you. I don't recall your worrying too much about respect or being overly intimate with a royal when she was dangling on the end of your—"

"Enough!" Lazar roared above Arafanz's words and the increasing noise of the wind, not daring to look at Boaz, who to his surprise had not lurched to his feet or leaped for his or Ana's throat. "You have no proof!"

"Don't I?" Arafanz asked, his hand gesturing toward Ana's belly.

Lazar looked uncomprehendingly at the rebel. He knew his mouth was open and he wanted to say something but nothing was coming. His mind had gone blank with the shock of Arafanz's claim. All he could hear was the sound of the sands. He raised his eyes to Ana, who refused to look at him, which in itself was unnerving—looked like an admission. He looked around him at the men, glancing Boaz's way but not lingering. Boaz looked surprised but there was no rage gathering in his eyes, but then again, Boaz would be working very hard to conceal himself. He wished he could explain to his Zar but the situation was hopeless. All he could do was continue to protect the royal's identity.

He finally found his voice. "It is easy to cast aspersions, but no one here is impressed with your lies and half-truths, your innuendo and your base claims. The child is the heir of the Zar. If the Grand Vizier were alive, he would tell you about the wedding and the bedding ceremony."

"Is that so? You think I lie? Let me paint a clearer picture for you, then, Lazar, and let me prove how much I do know. Razeen."

"Master?" said one of the black-robed men, stepping forward.

"Show yourself."

Lazar watched with shock and increasing despair as the man he had known as Salazin but more recently as Razeen, Iridor's spy in the Mute Guard, unraveled the linens from his face.

"You were his man all along?" Lazar croaked.

Razeen nodded somberly. "I saw her steal out and away from the camp. I followed the Zaradine, although no one knew. I saw you both together. Naked." He looked down, suitably ashamed.

"I'm sure you don't wish Razeen to paint the picture any more clearly, do you, Lazar?"

Lazar's throat was so dry he wasn't sure he could speak. *Razeen!* "But you fought alongside me. I watched you die!"

"You thought you saw him die, Spur. It was a ruse and his only way to return to the fortress."

Lazar ignored Arafanz. "How could you do this to us? We trusted you."

Razeen stared back silently as Arafanz continued to speak. "You were trusting the wrong person. Razeen is my son. We have been planning for this for a long time. I had to give him up to the Widows' Enclave for much of his life. He has had to pretend to be deaf and dumb for all that time. This is loyalty. This is sacrifice for a cause."

"For what, Arafanz? No one knows what you want."

"I will share it with you before you die, that I promise you, Lazar. But we were talking about the Zaradine's infidelity. And I notice you do not deny it."

Lazar grasped at the last straw he had. "Zaradine Ana was pregnant before her trip into the desert. I refuse to accept your lies. And I don't even know why we are having this conversation—whose benefit is it for, anyway?"

Arafanz laughed, actually threw back his head and showed his even white teeth. "For the Zar, of course," he said, finally turning to the kneeling Boaz. "Rise, Mightiest of Mighties—there is no need for you to keep up your pretense any longer, although I congratulate you. In fact, I congratulate all three of you for a marvelous display of loyalty and faith in each other."

Ana looked as distraught as Lazar felt and he watched her crumple, reflecting his pain and his despair. Arafanz had been toying with them all along. Falling to her knees, she reached for Boaz. "Forgive me. We never meant to hurt you."

"So it's true?" Boaz said, not moving, eyeing her directly. "Even though we discussed it before you left. Even though I gave you a promise and you swore an oath. Even though I warned you what would occur if you or he laid a finger on each other?"

Lazar saw Arafanz give an order with his eyes. Not a word needed to be spoken but two men moved closer to the Zar.

To Ana's credit she raised her chin, her voice defiant. "It is true, Your Majesty. I lay down with Lazar in the desert once. I will not deny it. I have loved him since the day he purchased me for your harem. I will love him until my last breath. And I shall die for that love, I'm sure, and not regret it."

"And me?"

"You've always known. Please let us not lie to each other

as death beckons to us both. I tried to be faithful but failed. You should know that Lazar was more faithful than I. He argued, tried to send me away. I went to him. I seduced him. I demanded that he lie down with me."

"I see that he didn't restrain himself too hard, though, Ana, for you are now pregnant. They do say it takes two hands to clap."

"Boaz," Lazar interrupted. "Ana was pregnant before we—"

The Zar turned to the Spur and Lazar felt as though, despite the heat of summer blazing around him, only winter existed between himself and Boaz. "That is strange indeed, Spur, for Ana was sent into the desert with you a virgin," Boaz answered coldly, his gaze not leaving Ana's. "We made a pact. She was not ready to become my wife fully. And I did not force her because she was young and much had happened that day of our wedding. How curious that it was arguably the happiest day of my life—because her life had been spared, because the woman I loved had become my wife—but I now realize it was the saddest of hers . . . because she has always loved you."

"But . . ." Lazar couldn't finish whatever he was going to say, his eyes turning to Ana. "You were sickening. The Valide, even the Grand Vizier, believed you to be pregnant."

A small vial landed in the sand at Lazar's feet. "Razeen brought this back. Do you recognize it?" Arafanz asked.

Lazar shook his head.

"Either you're lying, Spur, or you, too, have been part of an elaborate ruse that is none of your own doing. This is called Perelin. It comes from a rare plant found only in the desert. Its petals are curiously opaque, very bitter to the tongue. I tasted it once out of curiosity. Can you imagine what it prompted?"

Lazar shook his head miserably.

"I was sick for many days afterward. I lost my appetite and what I could eat I couldn't keep down, vomiting it up soon after. It was easier not to eat until the poison worked itself out of my body. Does this remind you of anyone you know?"

Lazar looked at Ana, aghast. Ana stared back at him, the face of the glowing mother who had come out of the fortress just minutes earlier now an ashen mask. Her head was moving from side to side in denial.

"Your dwarf friend was poisoning the Zaradine. You may recall he was allowed to wait on her when she was eating. But what the crafty dwarf was actually doing was deliberately ensuring that she appeared pregnant to everyone in the company. And it worked. My son knew the truth—he was an artful spy and had watched the dwarf in his poisonous deeds. Ah, poor Lazar, I think I can see from your expression that you knew none of this . . . although you did, of course, know that Pez was not mad, but simply feigning his insanity. I thought my son was clever but Pez is a master at guile. I'm right that no one in the palace save the three of you probably knew. How sad for you, Lazar. Such treachery all about you."

"The baby," Lazar stammered, finally piecing together his shattered thoughts.

"Is yours!" Arafanz exclaimed. "We are about to have a Galinsean prince on the Percherese throne." And the wind began to howl around them as if echoing the rebel's glee. He looked at Ana. "That is the one lie I uttered between us, Ana. I care not that the blood is not of the Zar's line. I care only that the child follows Lyana."

Ana groaned and looked down. They all followed her gaze and saw that her waters had broken, running in a torrent down her legs, puddling in the sand momentarily before being sucked down by the parched earth. "My baby," she murmured. "He comes."

"Take them to the cells," Arafanz ordered, "and await my instructions. Come, Ana," he urged. She all but collapsed into his arms as he picked her up. He turned back to Lazar, who stared at the dissipating pool of life-giving liquid that had kept his son safe thus far. "If it's any consolation, Lazar, blame the dwarf. He has worked against you and your precious Zar and even Ana all along."

27

Iridor had not been able to hear most of the confrontation, but from the way Lazar hung his head and Ana's body sagged into Arafanz's, he had to assume their situation was hopeless. He had not understood the man unwrapping his headdress or the subsequent shock written across Lazar's face but he could only see the back of the man's head, so he could not even guess what Lazar was looking at. Boaz kneeling was also a mystery. Iridor felt helpless, trapped in the body of a bird, unable to communicate without magic he still dared not risk using.

Why won't you draw on your powers? Ganya demanded when he returned to tell her all that he'd seen. He had to trust her; she was his only protection now.

I don't trust that we are safe.

This is connected with the Grand Vizier; I can feel his presence in your mind and yet I have assured you of his death. I saw his

*body, bloodied and lifeless and left to rot in the desert beneath the
sun, fed upon by the hawks and buzzards and vultures.*

The vultures. Of course! That's how he found us.

What?

*Arafanz's lookouts would have seen the vultures circling. They
would have followed the small caravan. That is how he was able to
surprise you.*

Birds have no loyalty.

What's that supposed to mean?

She sneered but said nothing.

*Listen to me, Ganya. I am in Lyana's cause. That's all that
matters.*

So the rest of us can die and you don't care?

*I do care. Those are my friends who are in trouble. Your father
was my friend, too. I am trying to find out what's best for all of us.*

*You have magic inside you. Use it. Why does the Grand Vizier
frighten you? He is dead and still you fear him,* she urged through
the bars of her cell.

I do not think he's dead, Iridor replied with similar forceful-
ness.

She laughed. *I just told you—*

You saw a corpse. It is meaningless.

She stared at the owl. *Meaningless?*

It is merely a shell. No use to him anymore.

Him?

The demon Maliz.

She shrank back in horror at the mention of this name. Iridor felt their magical shield waver.

*Be careful, Ganya—now you know why I need your ring of
protection.*

It strengthened again.

You know this for certain? she asked, eyes wide with alarm.

That he has risen, yes. That he had possessed the Grand Vizier, yes.

And now?

Iridor couldn't say it. It was hard enough to think it.

She said it for him. *You think he has taken over Fayid?*

Fayid doesn't exist, Ganya. Fayid is a cover for who the young man really is.

And who is he? He could see he was giving her too much disturbing information at once but there was nothing he could do about it. She needed to know everything.

The youngster is Zar Boaz.

She said nothing for several interminable seconds as the day lightened around Iridor and the strange wind that had been gathering since dawn began to test its powers. He would need to find shelter very soon.

I'm sure you can piece together the puzzle, he said distractedly. His thoughts were already racing to what Arafanz now had in mind.

You believe that the Zar of Percheron—the real one—is dead but that his body is inhabited by the demon Maliz.

The owl swung its neck around in the disconcerting way owls can. *Precisely. But I cannot be sure, not until I look into Boaz's eyes or he gives me a clue. Until then I have to be suspicious. The demon Maliz cannot die through mortal means!*

I'm sorry, was all she could whisper, which served only to make Iridor feel even more distraught. Ganya, trapped in a desert prison, having just witnessed her father's murder, was trying to comfort him.

Don't be, he murmured back, forcing back his grief. Only Lyana's success mattered now. *If Boaz is dead, then he is gone.*

As with your father, we have no time to mourn those lost. We must concentrate on the living. I must leave and get to safety. This wind is going to blow me away otherwise.

This is no wind, she warned.

Pardon?

This is the Samazen. It will kill you. Get to safety. I will try and warn Lazar if I can.

Good luck, he said, and broke the mindlink, turning himself invisible for the short while he needed to fly into open space before he disappeared into the haze of swirling sand.

Arafanz laid a weeping Ana onto his bed. "I'm sorry you had to find out like that."

"Are you?" she hurled at him. "It didn't sound like it when you baited Lazar, with my husband kneeling in the sand before me as you did it."

"It's where he belongs, Ana. Kneeling at your feet."

"He is going to kil—"

"The young Zar is going to do nothing except die at my command."

"Don't, Arafanz, I beg you." She grabbed for his hand. "I am pleading with you to spare Boaz's life. He is a good Zar. I have never heard him speak ill of Lyana. He was born into Zarab's world. He didn't choose it."

"He knows no better—is that what you're saying?"

"Teach him! Tell him about Lyana and all that you believe in. Boaz is a scholar at heart. He loves knowledge, he loves to learn new things. He can be convinced if you're persuasive enough."

"To change faith?"

"Yes," she said, her eyes searching his face.

"To change a whole nation's faith?"

Her eager expression faltered. "He can try. At least with him it's got to be easier than how you plan to do it."

Arafanz shook his head. "He is too much part of the old traditions, Ana. He will cling to them."

"No, no—that's just it. Boaz likes change. He has been trying to introduce new ways into the harem and the palace since he was crowned."

"It's not fast enough. I'm talking about a change that will shake the world of most Percherese. He can't do that."

"What makes you think my baby can?"

"Your baby will herald a new era. And the Galinsean war only aids my plans. War always brings change—a sweep of the broom, you could say. King Falza's timing couldn't be better."

"What do you plan to do?" she wept.

"I await your son. Give him to the world soon, Ana."

"He'll come when he's ready and not for me and not for you. I have no say in it."

"Well, until I hear the cry of a prince, I shall have to find some way to pass the time whilst the Samazen keeps us imprisoned in our own fortress."

His intention was obvious. "What are you going to do to Lazar?" she demanded.

"Whatever I choose. He is my prisoner. He is also my enemy. I normally kill my enemies."

"If you kill him, then I become your enemy!" she hurled at him.

"Do you remember our time together at Lyana's cave, when her Crystal Pillars sang for you? That was a good day. We became friends that day. We have hardly been out of each other's sight since. I don't think you hate me."

"But I am your enemy, Arafanz. If you hurt him, I will hate you in a way I know I haven't been capable of yet. And so help me, if I can call down the wrath of Lyana, I will beg her to use it against you and to tear you limb from limb."

He faltered at the ferocity of her tone. "And I love you in a way I know I haven't been capable of before, no matter what you choose to do. But I cannot save your precious Lazar. I told him not to come back. I allowed him to escape the last time he trespassed. He can live on through his son. He knew it would mean death for one of us if he returned."

"Then I hope it is you," she said, and turned her back on him before groaning as the first genuine pain of labor began to take its relentless toll on her body.

Lazar and Boaz sat bound and chained to the wall on opposite sides of their windowless cell. A single tallow candle sputtered on the floor and dimly illuminated the gloom of their prison. Lazar had shouted for Ganya but either she couldn't hear him or was located nowhere near them.

Boaz had spoken not a word. His head hung between his legs in the silence.

It was hard to find any words of comfort but Lazar tried at least for some sort of conversation. If he could keep Boaz talking, no matter how angry the Zar was, it meant he wasn't giving in as he appeared to be; talk, rage even, meant he could get Boaz to fight back, perhaps work with Lazar to save themselves . . . or at least, the Zar.

Lazar turned to face his Zar. "If you knew, why didn't you just have me killed?"

Boaz took his time formulating a reply. "Because I'm a pragmatist, Lazar. The announcement of an heir at the time it came was helpful for the Crown. And I needed to be sure. No one had confirmed Ana's pregnancy, so I didn't want to make accusations without having the correct information. Now I do."

"Pez had—"

"Pez? Do you believe that story from the desert, that he could survive that time alone, lost, and still somehow find his way back to us? I didn't know what to think about Pez's return. I was incredibly happy to see him alive, safe, but I didn't know whether to trust him."

"You mean after all these years you don't?"

Boaz looked up. His face showed none of its usual serenity. His peace and his good looks had transformed themselves into a mask of hatred and bitterness, fueled by anger. "Do you still trust Pez? Now that you know how he hoodwinked you?"

"There had to be reason for it. We have to—"

"We? There is no *we* anymore, Lazar. There is the treacherous Spur and his trusting Zar. We are enemies, you and I. From now on, don't even mention us in the same breath. *We* no longer exist."

"Boaz—"

"I am Majesty to you, Spur. If you're going to address me, use my title." He stood, shocking Lazar by beginning to yell and shout for the guards. Predictably the door was opened and three men came in, checked their prisoners were still secured. "Get me Arafanz!" Boaz began to demand. His demands escalated to screams, repeating the rebel's name over and over to make himself understood. Language barrier or not, they understood. Several minutes later, after one of the captors had disappeared and Boaz had kept up his howling demand, the rebel himself appeared.

"Zar Boaz?"

Boaz slumped against the wall; his wailing stopped as Arafanz continued: "I'm attending to your wife at present, who seems to be in labor. Perhaps it was the shock of seeing her lover again, or maybe it was seeing you both, or, most likely, having her secret shared. It matters not, for the next Zar of Percheron is soon to be born—shall we call him Lucien, out of respect for his soon-to-be-dead father?" He threw a sly glance toward Lazar. "What seems to be the problem, Your Highness?" he asked, his last two words, though polite, loaded with irony.

"Get me away from him. I don't wish to be near him, to lay eyes on him. Or give me a blade and I'll kill him for you."

Lazar stood, knowing that he was in no position to defend himself.

"How interesting, Majesty. Now, that might be amusing to witness. But I have a better idea. Take him from here," he ordered one of the men, who did as asked, pulling Boaz from the chamber.

Lazar saw the look of hate thrown at him by the Zar. His sorrow deepened at knowing he had lost Boaz through his own weakness for Ana.

"We shall be back soon, Spur. I would take the opportunity during this quiet period to say your final prayers. Your time has arrived," Arafanz suggested.

Lazar ignored the warning. "What about Ana?"

"She is laboring. First child? Who knows how long—you may be dead before you see your son, Lazar. Now, wouldn't that be cruel?" He turned to leave, looked back. "Don't waste the precious little time you have left. Make peace with yourself and your god. I make you this promise. I will put your son on the throne of Percheron—he will be safe and protected for all his life. He will never know that his father was not Zar Boaz, nor will any of his people."

"Do you expect me to thank you?"

"The only thing I expect is that you will try and upset my plans."

"You can count on it, Arafanz. I and only I will decide the fate of my son . . . if that is my son. He could be yours!"

Arafanz left, smirking. "No such luck, Spur. The boy has Galinsean blood running through his veins. But forget escape, Lazar, none of us are going anywhere right now. You can't hear it but the Samazen began howling this last hour. No one can survive it."

Ana was restless, unable to sit or to lie. She found it easier to pace through the waves of pain.

"I cannot eat, Ashar," she warned as the young man sidled up to her.

"I brought you some juice of the fresh relicca."

"How?" she wondered aloud, despite the sharp ache.

"Some of our members are in the city regularly. Fruit is a rare delicacy in our life but I stole this for you. He won't mind. Everything's for you anyway."

"They say relicca can stimulate," she said, hesitating to take the cup of pale green juice.

"It will aid your stamina for the day ahead. Please, take it."

"Thank you," she replied, sipping. It tasted wonderful as it slipped down her suddenly parched throat. "Ashar, I don't know how to do this."

"Don't be frightened, Miss Ana. Your baby will find his way out."

She smiled sadly. "Where do you come from, Ashar?"

"He has told me I was taken from my tribe at a young age, though I have no recollection. This is my home."

"Wouldn't you like to know your real home? Know if you have family?"

"I don't permit myself to think on such things."

"I was taken from my home—a father I loved, brothers and sisters who were my playmates. I think of them often. I refuse to forget them."

He shook his head. "I have no memory of family."

"I can see that you lie. You do remember. Oh, Ashar, stop this—this is not your crusade, it is his! His vision, his dream, his madness! Run away while you can."

"He will hunt me down."

"No. Once, maybe. But not now. This is the end of it. This is what Arafanz has worked toward. Whatever happens over the next few days will be all that consumes him. He will not care about a runaway."

"Loyalty is my life."

"Not to him and his madness. Be loyal to your family. He stole you. He admits that. They did not sell you as my family did me. You were taken without their consent. They must love and miss and no doubt mourn you to this day."

He looked uncertain. Ana had worked hard on Ashar since that first day they spoke and found that fragile connection that often springs up between two lonely people of like age. In a strange way they had become friends. Perhaps now she could use that friendship—not for her own safety, for her future was here, certainly for the next day while her son arrived. But for Lazar. Lazar could be dead within that same time frame and she had to find some way to help him flee . . . she was sure he would rather die consumed by the desert, trying to escape, than help-less on the end of Arafanz's blade.

She pushed Ashar further. "Find the woman. She was of the desert tribes, wasn't she? I only glimpsed her but perhaps she can tell you which direction to head in—she may even know something of your family. Try, Ashar, try. This is no life for a young man. This is for clerics, mystics, and—"

"Madmen?"

She sighed softly. "Yes."

"I thought you liked him."

"I do. When he's not being cruel, he's such a sad, vulner-able, beautiful man. He could have been so much more than this."

"He told me he was chosen. As I was chosen."

"Yes, and I believe him. But whilst he was chosen by some-one he considers his god, you were chosen by him—a mortal. If anything, he has been a destructive influence. Surely you want more than to die in the service of a god who has yet to ask anything of you? If Lyana calls to you, that's different. But I suspect she calls only to him. The rest of you have been co-erced, your minds stripped of everything you once knew and loved and trusted. He has replaced that with himself and his crusade. It is wrong, Ashar. I promise you, it is wrong."

He looked at her and for the first time she saw the usual zeal blur and a new, fresher clarity shine in his eyes. "Go and see the tribe woman if you can . . . and, Ashar, if you can think of any-thing to help the tall, golden-haired man, I beg you to share it with me or do what you can. He is a good man. He is of Lyana, he is not your enemy. He is in tune with the desert, respects your people. He is the man I truly love, the father of the child I carry. He is the Crown Prince of Galinsea. You have a future king preparing to die in your prison. Help me find a way to save him, I beg you."

Ashar backed away, fearful. She had said too much, frightened him.

Another wave of pain grabbed her, took her on a long ride of agony, leaving her gasping. When she had recovered her wits, Ashar was gone and she was alone with her fears and the laboring child who would be soon pulled from her womb and taken from her.

Ana wept.

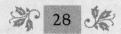

28

Herezah could feel the tension in the city escalating. It unfurled from the crowded lanes of the bazaar and moved like a blanketing but invisible mist throughout the streets of Percheron, reaching up the hillside to the palace and the balcony where she now stood. Panic!

It was nearing fifth bell, not even noon, but the day was already unbearably hot. She had insisted that the messengers spread word that the general population was not under any threat from the Galinseans, that although there was no need to flee, those who wished to leave the city should do so immediately. Even to her ears it sounded hollow. If she were an everyday Percherese, living beneath the Stone Palace, she would grab her family and head for the foothills as fast as she could.

And whilst the city looked to be a roiling cauldron of activity, the palace seemed unnaturally calm. An hour ago all dignataries and senior members of the staff had gathered in the throne room as she had delivered them the news she had hoped to avoid. Herezah had deliberately gone nowhere near the throne itself, but had kept herself a step down on the lower plinth to make her announcement. She was sure her humility had not gone unnoticed—not that it mattered right now. No one was thinking about her dignity or her succinct speech. They were thinking about their loved ones, deciding whether to stay put and take their chances or leave everything behind and flee.

It wasn't an easy decision. Most of the people in that chamber were certainly under threat. Bin had stood stoically below her, glanced once or twice with approval at her calm, precise delivery, and then had escorted her briskly from the room full of stunned people to the balcony, where she now awaited the captain of the guard.

As she stared out across the harbor toward Star Island she was reminded of Lazar. She badly needed his counsel right now. She had since realized that it was only because of the letter he had left that the Galinseans had agreed to the private parley on the Daramo. What trust they had given her, and what fatal treachery the Percherese had shown in return. The nausea rose again, as it had so many times since the previous day, and threatened to overwhelm her. The temptation to simply curl into a ball, locking herself into her old room at the harem and awaiting whatever fate came, was seductive. But as irresistibly as cowardice beckoned, this was not Herezah's way.

Fighting wasn't her way either, and though deviousness and cunning were her weapons, she didn't know how to wield those for this situation, which had long spun out of her control. So fight she'd have to, and she would pray to Zarab that she could achieve a stalemate for long enough to allow Boaz and Lazar to return. Hopefully the Spur would have the ability to persuade his estranged father against the savage reprisals. In her heart the hopes felt hollow, but for the sake of the pride in the Crown she represented, she knew she must not lose hope.

Bin interrupted her thoughts. "Captain Ghassal is here, Crown Valide."

"Bring him in," she said, not turning yet. "Does he look frightened?"

"No, Majesty. Resolute."

"Good. I need his courage and reassurance."

Bin bowed and disappeared. Herezah took one last look at the uncharacteristically quiet harbor and imagined it filling with war galleys. She turned away to greet Ghassal of the Protectorate and wondered if she'd be dead by this time tomorrow.

Ashar brought a clay flask of water and a goblet into the prison area of the fortress. "I've been told to give the female prisoner fresh water," he answered the guard at the top of the stairs, a man Ashar knew well. The prisoners needed no more than this single person, for Arafanz felt safe in the knowledge that his prison was impregnable.

As the man checked the contents of the flask, Ashar asked, "Is everything all right?" He jutted his chin in the direction of the cells downstairs.

"Quiet," the man replied. "Why do I get this boring task? You get to look after the beautiful woman."

Ashar grinned. "I'm no more than nursemaid right now. She is in labor."

His companion's mouth widened. "It's happening?"

Ashar nodded. "It's almost time," he confirmed, his voice quiet.

"Hard to believe we're here at last. It's been years. We'll be riding for Percheron imminently."

"Seems so. We have to pray that Lyana keeps that baby safe and he arrives without problem."

"Have faith. He is Lyana's future. She will protect him."

Ashar nodded. "I'd better get this delivered. What about the others?"

"They took the young one away—he began to scream to be removed from the tall one's presence."

"Were they fighting?"

"No. I think the tall one frightened the younger one. Here are the keys. She's in the one at the end, with the window. As you're here, I need to relieve myself. I won't be long."

"Don't be. I have to get back to my post."

His friend grinned as Ashar disappeared down the stairs and into the dimly lit corridor. He hurried along to the last cell and put the key in the lock. What he was doing was wrong but he was too far down this path to turn back now. He had to satisfy his increasing hunger for the world outside the sheltered existence at the fortress. All the other young men seemed to be happy and dedicated to their cause, but their leader's influence had never fully claimed Ashar as it had his peers. He'd worked hard to be like all the other Razaqin but something inside refused to allow him to give up all of himself; he had kept back a tiny portion, locked it away. Ana's arrival and his closeness to her had opened the vault where he'd stored his few memories. He was a chief's son. He had older brothers and sisters. He had worshipped his father, a wise, gentle man, and he could still remember his sweet-natured mother, who had died in childbirth trying to push out a baby brother, who had also perished. Ana's painful labor was calling up these old memories. He desperately wanted her to survive and for the boy to survive. Ashar covered his face as he entered, in accordance with Arafanz's rules.

"Who is it?" said a woman's voice from the darkest recesses of her cell. Morning light would normally be flooding sharply through this cell's windows but the Samazen's wrath had turned the day dark. Sand whipped around the chamber and Ashar could feel its grittiness beneath his sandals. He could just make out the woman in the corner, her robes pulled over her head to shield her.

"I have brought you water," he said, unsure of what to say, "but perhaps you need shelter more than anything."

"The wind can't hurt me and I like to feel the sand in here," she admitted. He could hear the puzzlement in her tone. "I didn't expect any kindnesses."

"I brought it of my own accord, not at his behest," he said, feeling awkward but preferring to be truthful.

"Why?"

"Miss Ana said I should meet you."

"How is she?"

"In labor and very sad, although I could be killed for telling you this."

"Then why do you share anything with me?"

"I don't know, I . . . I really shouldn't be here. Let me give you this water and then I shall leave." He bent to place the flask on the ground.

"No, wait!" she cried, pulling back the linens that hid her face. In the eerie half-light he froze, his face blanching.

"Ganya?" he whispered, barely able to form the word.

She stared at him. "How do you know me?"

Ashar hesitantly raised his hand to pull free the black fabric that covered his face. "I am your brother, Ashar," he prompted, realizing she probably couldn't recognize him; he had been secreted away from their tribe as a child and now he was a man.

"Ashar?" she croaked, her expression telling him that she barely dared to believe what he said. He understood that in growing up, he had obviously changed enough not to be immediately recognizable to her.

"What are you doing here?" he breathed. Before he could say anything else, though, recognition swept across her face as she did make out the beloved features of a brother and he was swept into her arms, was hugging and kissing through tears and smiles.

"Our father came to find you," she explained finally. "He never stopped searching, never gave up hope."

"I think he's the reason that I took this risk. This place has become my home and the other Razaqin have become my family but I have not forgotten my real home, my real family. I want to see my father again."

Ganya began to weep once more. "Oh, Ashar. My poor little brother. Our father is dead. His body still likely warm, his murder is so fresh."

"Murder?"

"Your precious Arafanz. I had to stand by and watch the madman slit our father's throat as he tried to explain why he was in this part of the desert, that he was searching for his son."

Ashar felt as though his lips had gone numb. He had trouble forming a response. The shock that his beloved father had come so close, only to be denied so much as a sighting of him, broke his already bleeding heart. "You saw this? You know Arafanz wielded the knife?"

"It was his own blade, I tell you. I witnessed our father gasping about finding you as his blood spilled into the sands and the man who sees himself as Zar maker talked over him as though he were a mere dog being put out of its misery. His body was left for the vultures circling overhead."

Ashar violently pulled away from her, hammering the walls with his fists until the skin of the knuckles broke and bled. He groaned his despair, his head swiveling in denial. Ganya let his pain pour out before she put her arms around him and hugged him tightly.

"We must get you away from here," she whispered.

"He killed my father," Ashar said. "He must pay for that."

"No! Ashar, listen to me. You know he has a small army behind him. They are fanatical; they will cut you down if you so much as threaten a hair on his head. Let them do whatever it is they need to do. You escape. You get yourself far away from here so that our father's death will have achieved something."

"And you?"

"They will miss me—not that I'm important—but they won't miss you. What's one less black-robed killer amongst so many?"

"He has given me a specific task. He expects me to be at my post."

"Then feign illness. Think of something, Ashar—anything that allows you to get away."

"There is nowhere to go. It is Samazen season and this is an angry one. Look at your chamber—this is just the beginning. We have days to go yet; its strength and ferocity are only going to increase."

"Promise me you will do nothing rash," she begged.

"Nothing rash, I promise you," he replied. He knew Ganya heard the message behind his words.

"Talk to Lazar. He's incarcerated here somewhere. He will

know what to do. I beg you, Ashar. Take him into your confidence—he is . . . was . . . your father's friend. He has sworn to avenge his death."

"Then he is my friend, too."

"Find him. Tell him all that you know. Help him to escape if you must."

"That's what Miss Ana asked me to do."

"Then listen to her. Don't bother about the young one. He is not to be saved. Go. Lock me back up and go. Here, take the flask, and give it to Lazar. Use that as your excuse. If anyone asks, tell them that Miss Ana instructed you to do this. It will leave you blameless. Your leader clearly has no intention of harming her."

Ashar obediently took the flask that she anxiously pressed into his hands.

"Go, Ashar. Be safe."

"You, too, be safe," he said, his eyes trusting.

Ganya pushed him back out of her cell door. He carefully locked the door behind him. There were five cells. He tried two that were empty before the third opened to a sigh from the darkness. With the soft light that spilled from the small lamps in the corridor, he could just make out the figure on the floor, his knees pulled up to his chest.

"Lazar?" he whispered.

"What?" The man spoke in Percherese. His meaning was clear, though Ashar didn't understand the word.

Ashar spoke in the desert language rather than Sharaic of the fortress. "I'm here to help," he tried.

"And who might you be?" came the reply in Khalid.

The youngster felt a spike of relief. They could comprehend each other. "I am called Ashar, I—"

"Salim's boy!"

"That's right."

"Your sister is—"

"I know. I also know about my father. I will avenge his death."

"With your own?"

"With your help, perhaps." Ashar slipped farther into the dark chamber.

"I am not in a position to do much right now."

"Miss Ana sent me to find you," Ashar whispered.

"Is she . . . ?"

"She is managing. The pains are more frequent now."

"Where have they taken Boaz?"

"He is accommodated on a floor below Miss Ana."

"What are they going to do with him?"

Ashar shrugged. "I have not seen him. I know nothing about him, although our leader has specifically given me orders to take care of his needs."

"Arafanz obviously trusts you."

"Yes."

"All right, Ashar, listen to me. If you want to avenge your father's murder but you also want your sister and yourself safe, you will have to think with your head and not your heart. Right now nothing you do can bring Salim back. So do what he would want you to do: find a way to save Ganya and yourself. And I need you to help me get Miss Ana away from here, too."

"She asked me to help *you* get away. She is going nowhere, Spur Lazar. She is too frail, too heavy with child. She could move into the next stage of her birthing process anytime, or so I believe. I have watched camels give birth. It can't be much different."

Lazar smiled grimly in the dimness. "Not much," he said, a tone of irony in his voice. "Do you have access to the camels?"

"I know where they are kept. They will all be under cover now."

"I want you to get one readied for Miss Ana and one for yourself and sister. Two only."

"You're going to risk the Samazen?"

"Our chances are better out there than in here."

"What about you??"

"I will find a way, I promise you. Take your sister with you. Dress her as one of the hooded Razaqin. But have that camel for Miss Ana ready. Does she know her way to where they're kept?" The boy nodded. "Good. No one will be checking. Only a fool would be out in this storm."

"What about the Zar?"

Lazar shook his head. "I'm not sure how to help him. I fear he will kill Ana. I'm beginning to believe that's why he came with us into the desert in the first place. He is seeking revenge. I cannot permit him to harm her or the child."

Ashar nodded again. "Will you allow Arafanz to kill your Zar, then?"

Lazar looked lost. "No. He is the Zar and I must still consider his protection. Although the child now takes precedence." He sighed. "I swore an oath to protect the Zar. I cannot break that oath, will not break it."

Ashar didn't envy the Spur his choices. "I shall go," he said, moving toward the door. But before he could leave, they heard footsteps. Lazar just had time to raise his fingers to his lips before suddenly men blocked the doorway. As Ashar stood rooted in place, unsure of what to do, Lazar picked up the clay flagon, smashing it against the wall with a howl of rage.

"Tell him to go to hell. I'll drink not a drop unless it's his blood," he raged at Ashar.

"What's going on?' one of the men asked Ashar in Sharaic.

Lazar continued in the desert language. "I don't want Arafanz's pity or his water. Tell the boy to clear off," he yelled.

Ashar shrugged at his companions. "I was told to bring him water. Looks like he doesn't want it."

"He won't be needing it where he's going," the Razaqin replied. "He's been summoned to the ring."

Ashar nodded. Glancing toward Lazar, he hoped that the Spur could see that he would keep his end of the bargain although he couldn't imagine how Lazar would be able to do likewise. "I must get back to my post," he said dutifully. As he left, Lazar's cell door was closed behind him. Ashar took his chance and crossed the corridor to his sister's cell and quickly unlocked the door.

"Stay here," he hissed under his breath. "Don't move until I return, and if anyone asks, you know nothing about this unlocked door. They will likely not even notice." Ganya nodded. Closing the door, he ran down the corridor and up the stairs, passing the man returning to his post. "I left the keys on the hook," he said. "They're taking the man away."

"I heard. He's going to the ring. Can't imagine he'll survive it."

Lazar realized that Ashar would need some time to either fetch Ganya or let her know what was going on, as well as to be seen entering Boaz's room and going about his duties, so he distracted the three Razaqin who had been sent to fetch him by shouting obscenities. He knew they likely didn't understand, and frankly didn't care if they did. Finally he feigned exhaustion, collapsing. When one pulled him back to his knees, he put his hands together in supplication and, using gestures, made them accept that he needed to say his prayers.

The Razaqin nodded and Lazar took as long as he possibly could during the period of silence that they granted him to genuinely send a plea to Lyana to guide him this day and spare his life just long enough for him to save Ana's and that of their son. He also begged Lyana to guide him to do what was needed for Boaz. He wished Iridor would enter his mind; Iridor would help him to sort the confusion he was feeling.

The men manhandled him back to his feet and pushed him out of the cell door, bundled him down the corridor and up the rocky steps he recalled from earlier that day. After that he lost track of their path and had no choice but to follow the leader until he found himself being pushed into what felt like an arena. It felt cool, was presumably deep inside the belly of the fortress, especially as he could no longer hear the roar of the Samazen, and it was lit only by torches flaming around the walls.

The Razaqin had gathered. His quick estimate told him there were at least two hundred men. A small army indeed. The large chamber was eerily quiet as he was led in. Arafanz obviously enjoyed absolute control, for no one spoke, not even a murmur.

He was pushed into the ring, his robes ripped from him to leave him standing in only trousers and boots. The silence was heavy, and meant to humiliate, and he refused to buckle under the searing gazes of the fanatical group of men. Instead he bent his head and closed his eyes. He needed to gather his wits and all of his strength for whatever opportunity might present itself.

He would not go meekly but he would gladly die if in doing so he could find a way to help Ana escape. Lazar did not expect to live beyond this day but he had to be sure that his son did.

Ashar checked on Ana, who was pacing.

"It helps in between the pains," she explained breathlessly. "One has just finished."

"How close are they?"

"Not close enough yet from what I know of childbirth. The baby is still hours away. It is not unbearable but I can't do much except focus on coping with the pain when it comes."

He nodded, moved closer. "Is my leader here?"

"No," she said, dabbing at her forehead. "He was briefly here to check on me but he has left. I don't know where he went."

"I do. He has gone to deal with Spur Lazar."

Her head snapped back. "What do you mean?"

"They came for him when I was there."

"You've seen him?"

"Yes, spoken to him. He insists that I get you out."

She shook her head sadly. "I can't go anywhere. What about him?"

Ashar shrugged. "He made me promise that I would have a camel readied for you and for the other prisoner."

"The woman?"

"Her name is Ganya, Miss Ana. She is my sister."

Ana steadied herself, leaning against Arafanz's bed, her face surprised. "You're sure? You've spoken with her?"

He nodded. "I recognized her immediately. The dead must wait, although I swear I will make Arafanz pay in blood for my father's death. You must come with me now. I have to get you both to the camels."

"Ashar, get your sister and get out of here. I cannot go. It is not only because I will slow you up but because Arafanz is coming back to fetch me. I suspect he wants me to see my lover and my husband being killed."

"He will not hurt you or the baby."

"I know. It doesn't matter. If he kills Spur Lazar, I will die anyway. I shall take my own life. He and the Spur ultimately want the same thing, which is the faith of Lyana returned to Percheron. But Arafanz chooses death and destruction to achieve it. Lazar will not allow him to kill the Zar if he can help it."

"Don't be too sure of that, Miss Ana. Do you remember where the camels are sheltered?"

"Yes. You put them in with the goats when there's a storm."

"Good. Whatever happens, I will have a camel ready there for you. Whether you are with me, with the Spur, or just alone, get there."

"The Samazen—"

"Spur Lazar says we are to take our chances with the sandstorm. I know the story, Miss Ana. You've survived it once before. You can again."

She smiled softly at him. "Your faith is vast, Ashar. I hope Lyana keeps you safe."

"And you, Miss Ana. I must go now. I have instructions to see to the needs of the Zar."

"Will you try and help him get away, too?"

"That is not part of my plan, no."

"You must, Ashar. He is the Zar of Percheron. You must not condemn him to death."

Ashar shrugged. "He is not my king, Miss Ana. And he is ordained by Zarab, whom I don't recognize. Your son is the only Zar to whom I will pledge fealty."

She reached for Ashar. "I am pleased that you are going to save yourself and your sister . . . and I am grateful to you for trying to aid Spur Lazar, but I beg you, Ashar, please do whatever you can for Boaz. He is not a bad person. He does not hate Lyana as Arafanz would have you believe. He doesn't know her; he was not raised in the faith. But I know him. He would like all that she represents, all she can teach him. Give him a chance. Please, I beg you. Take him with you and Ganya—keep him and Lazar apart." They heard footsteps. "They're coming for me," she said, suddenly frightened. "Go, take care of yourself," she added, pushing him away.

"Find your way to the camels, Miss Ana," he begged, before turning and slipping out of the chamber.

He ran as fast as he could to the lower level to do his duty for Zar Boaz, as Arafanz had requested. His leader would take exquisite pleasure in slaying the Zar in front of his followers but for Ana's sake Ashar intended to pay the young ruler appropriate respect, no matter if his life was already forfeit.

As he knocked on the door before entering, he decided he was no longer Razaqin, for he was already betraying Arafanz. No, first and foremost he was Khalid, and to reinforce that decision, he intended to let the Percherese ruler know that the desert people loved Lyana more than they loved any Zar. Ashar suddenly felt himself burning with a new passion. He was the son of a tribal chief, he was no fanatical spiritualist, and suddenly all he wanted was revenge for his family's name and to return to his tribe. He looked at the angry face of the man who was probably around the same age as he was. "Zar Boaz, my name is Ashar of the Khalid. I am here see to your needs."

"I need nothing but vengeance. Can you offer me that, Ashar of the Khalid?"

"I suspect you will not have time for reprisals, Zar Boaz. They will be coming for you next. They have already fetched Spur Lazar and your wife, the Zaradine."

"What do they intend to do?" Boaz asked.

Ashar enjoyed seeing the fear flit across the young ruler's face. "Why, execute you, of course. What else did you think Arafanz and his Razaqin want?"

Boaz's expression changed. He frowned, cocked his head to one side. "But not you, Ashar? Come in, please, and tell me what it is that you want."

29

Lazar had kept his face lowered. He had cocooned himself in his own silence, not meaning to but using some of the time to think over his life, about the death of Shara and how his domineering parents had shaped his life and why he found himself now in this hopeless situation. He thought about Iridor and how helpless Iridor, despite demigod status, was going to be against all these men. He thought about the magic that Beloch and Ezram insisted he possessed, the magic he knew neither how to call nor what having it meant. He wished it could help him now, give him a glimpse toward a means of escape, but he knew this was a useless pathway to follow, and he was relieved when he heard the soft murmur that dragged his mind from his musings. He looked up to see Ana being escorted into the chamber. She looked pale but she walked unaided and with defiance. Always defiance.

Their gazes met and locked and he understood that if his

life amounted to anything, his purpose must be to save his yet unborn child. This boy was already heir to two thrones. He might be the only chance they all had of averting war between Percheron and Galinsea. If Lazar could give his father a new heir, a new beginning, it might resolve the grudge between the two of them. This boy was, by right, the next King of Galinsea, born of a Percherese mother, a royal no less. It mattered not that Ana was a slave. She was Percherese and she had been accorded regal status. And as if they shared one mind, he could sense that Ana felt the same way. She had never cared much for her life but he suspected she cared very much for the boy—the proof of their love. Even if both of them died this day, their son would live for them, a testament of their union.

He wanted the boy to live. He would call him Lucien, for the man Lazar once had been, the man he had turned his back on. His son would live up to his name and claim his rightful place on the Galinsean throne. He would use Arafanz's strategy; if a boy king could be taught to change a nation's faith, then that same boy king could be guided to change the way a nation thought. Young Luc could sweep aside all the acrimony between the two nations and bring peace to the region with the right guidance.

It was a plan that lifted his heavy heart and even made him smile across the sea of staring eyes. And Ana smiled back, both oblivious and uncaring of who watched.

Arafanz broke the spell between them, his voice suddenly cutting across the soft murmurs.

"Come, Ana, my dear, take your seat beside me. We shall not keep you long—I am sympathetic to your predicament."

Lazar watched her hold her belly as she lowered herself into her seat, ignoring Arafanz's helping hand, her eyes refusing to

break their lock on his own. He gave a soft nod of encouragement, ignoring the tear that escaped and rolled down her sweet
face. His attention was caught by a young man who walked
up to stand beside her chair—Ashar. Lazar detected the near-
imperceptible nod of the young man's head. He felt a small
surge of hope—the camels were readied.

"Ah, have you been with our royal?" Arafanz asked him.

"Yes, Master. He wishes to speak with you."

"The time for talk is over. But tell me, why is your hair filled
with sand?" Arafanz quizzed.

Lazar felt his gut twist but Ashar reacted quickly and calmly.
"I have not seen the Samazen ever in such force, Master. I made
the mistake of looking outdoors."

"And paying a price, I see. That must have hurt."

Ashar touched at his cheeks, burned from the whipping
sand. "I learned a lesson."

"Good. That is what makes a mistake worth the pain."

Ashar nodded. "Yes, Master."

Arafanz looked toward a man at the entrance. "Is he here?"

The man bowed an assent.

"Excellent. We are ready, then. Lazar, I suspect you don't
plan to die without a fight, so let's give you one." He gave a
signal and what looked to Lazar to be a score or more of men
leaped into the ring. With a terrifying ringing sound, they
dragged their ferocious curved blades from their hips.

Lazar backed away. He knew there was no escape but he
moved instinctively.

"I plan to make this a little more balanced than it looks,
Lazar. My men will attack in pairs only. For each man you cut
down, another will replace him. There are presently twenty
men in the ring with you. I seem to remember taunting you

with the same number of men the last time we met. Except duty got in the way, then, didn't it? Such a shame—it would have made a spectacle. So let's give you the same scenario. Twenty men against you. Kill them all and I will spare someone you care about."

Lazar whipped around to face the man who taunted him. "You have no intention of killing Ana—so don't toy with me, rebel."

"I do not refer to Ana. I refer to him," he said, pointing. Lazar swirled back to see Zar Boaz being led into the chamber. "We all want the Zar dead, possibly even Ana does, now that she carries your child. The Zar is probably only here because he was looking for revenge. Poor fool. He thought he'd join you and do something heroic and now Percheron will lose its Zar."

"Not if I can help it, Arafanz," Lazar growled.

"Aha," the rebel replied, delight in his tone, "that's the spirit, Lazar. Kill all of these men before you and perhaps I'll spare his life. Or perhaps I'll let you choose. It may be that you prefer to spare the life of Ganya of the Khalid—also one of your women, as I understand it. I gather you took comfort from the loneliness of the quiet nights in the desert inside Ganya's sweet—"

"Shut up, Arafanz," Lazar said, ignoring the look of pain that ghosted across Ana's face. He wasn't sure whether it was her contractions or his desert dalliance. If the latter, he knew he wouldn't be permitted to explain the how or why of it to her.

"Perhaps my treacherous wife should know of his affair with my mother, the Valide," Boaz yelled, joining the fray.

Now Lazar did look at Ana fully. She deserved that much truth from him. He kept his face devoid of emotion but she had always seen through him; he was sure she could tell that not only was Arafanz telling the truth but that Boaz was not lying either.

Arafanz made a show of surprise. "The Valide? Lazar has lain with the Zar's mother? Oh, how daring of you, Spur, you have been busy."

"They are lovers," Boaz confirmed. "They have been for a while, I'm assured by my mother."

"That's a lie! We have nev—"

"Lazar, it seems one woman at a time is not enough. You see, Ana, my dear, this man is not worthy of you. For all we know, the Valide and the desert woman are both carrying his spawn."

Lazar refused to dignify Arafanz's taunts with any further defense. Instead he simply turned his attention to Ana. He could not mistake the injury in her expression but he hoped she trusted him enough to know that the only woman he loved was her. Was it enough, though? Who was to say that Ana was not prey to the same foibles—such as jealousy and envy—as any other woman?

"And so we once again come around to the same question, Lazar. Heart or duty?"

"What do you want from me, Arafanz?" Lazar hurled back, his anger fighting free at last.

"Some entertainment for my men at the very least, Lazar. Will you do your duty and protect the Zar you are sworn to guard at the expense of your own life, or do you follow your heart and try to fight your way free toward Ana and the unborn child of yours she carries? Ana, of course, is under no threat, as you know, so I'll give you a third choice—just to keep it interesting. I will let you go free. You will be followed for the rest of your life—not that you'll be aware of it—and should you ever leave Percheron for the desert again, you will be killed.

Take the third option, Lazar, for your life and that of Ana's and the child's are safe. One way or another, my men will kill the Zar—you might as well let us do it now. But you have a choice to make." He turned to Ashar. "Take her to that chair on the dais."

Lazar watched as Ana was helped to her feet and escorted to a seat not far from the opening they had been brought through. He could see her clearly on the dais if he turned his back on Boaz, who had just been shoved into the ring with him.

"Now you can watch the woman you claim to love whilst you go about your business of killing. Be swift, Lazar, for Ana is in labor and you don't want her suffering her next contraction here, in front of all the men. She is due one quite soon, from my calculations. Or do you choose to walk from here, Spur, a free, uninjured man? I will throw in the desert woman for your ongoing pleasure on the journey home." He laughed softly to himself, seemingly enjoying his own magnanimity.

"Give me a weapon!" Lazar roared, and now Arafanz openly laughed. Lazar ignored him, turned to Boaz. "I can't promise you anything, Highness, but stay behind me for as long as you can."

"You're still going to try and save me?" Boaz asked.

"I gave a sworn oath. My life before yours."

"You are a constant surprise, Spur," Boaz said curiously.

Lazar walked over to where a Razaqin had laid out the two swords they'd taken from him.

He picked them up and weighed them. He had fought twelve men at once for Zar Joreb's entertainment many years previous and he was a better swordsman now. With Lyana's guiding hand, he would slay the twenty and win the Zar's freedom.

"Ready?" Arafanz asked politely.

"I hope they've said their farewells," said Lazar.

The rebel laughed delightedly and signaled the first pair of Razaqin to take their chances against Percheron's famed Spur.

Ashar was feeling light-headed. He had taken Ganya fresh water after his strange visit with Zar Boaz. The words of the young ruler had piqued his interest. He had been offered power and riches to help Zar Boaz escape, and although he had fled the room, he had heard the prisoner out, heard his promises and pledges. If he accepted the royal's offer, he could take Ganya back to their people. Safety was guaranteed, as was wealth. They would never want for camels or food, or blankets again. The Zar had even mentioned trading. Ashar remembered how that had always been his father's dream, to work as a merchant between Percheron and its western neighbors. They had never had enough money at one time to buy the goods to sell, though; instead, they had been forced to live hand to mouth. With the Zar's support, Ashar could fulfill his father's dream and set up a Khalid trading route.

No one had noticed the two pails he had brought into the arena as the other Razaqin were filing in. He wondered if this whole plan of his and the Zar's could work. He hadn't been able to discuss it with the Spur, or even Ganya. He'd just had time to throw some black robes on her and smuggle her out of the fortress, leaving her with the camels, where she was waiting for him now. No one would miss her, he hoped; everyone was in the arena and her guard would rightly assume she was still secure in her prison. He wished he could somehow get a message to Lazar but it was too late. Arafanz had just signaled the first pair of Razaqin warriors to engage the Spur.

He held his breath as Lazar murmured something to the Zar,

then raised both swords, initiating an explosion of jeering and cheering as the formerly silent audience suddenly started baying for blood.

"Be brave, my Zar. As long as I'm breathing I won't let them touch you."

"Don't let me die, Spur!" Boaz screeched.

It briefly occurred to Lazar that Boaz, although squeamish, had never lacked courage. His near-hysterical response was surprising, as was his recent use of Lazar's title, which he normally reserved for formal situations. But Lazar didn't have time to dwell on trivialities. All he could do now was take a deep breath and raise his swords.

The audience, clearly thirsty for bloodletting, especially the blood of Lazar, roared its approval as the first of the Razaqin approached.

Lazar didn't move initially; he just watched. The footwork of the one on the left was heavy. He would be slower, so he must focus first on the man on his right, who was now moving around in a wider arc. Arafanz had watched him fight before and had probably instructed his men accordingly. Still, he could take these two, he decided, faking a lunge to his right before spinning low and slashing at the fellow's knees, allowing his movement to twist him all the way around to hack into the neck of his attacker to his left. He finished off the man on the right with a slash across his neck as well. There was no time to breathe. The next pair entered the arena. They were more cunning, took their time sizing him up. Others rushed to pull the dead away.

"We're all going to die," Boaz said from behind him. "How can you hold them off?"

"It's what I do," Lazar growled back, waiting, watching.

"You're doing this for Ana, not for me! It all makes sense now. Feigning loyalty to me and yet both of you traitors."

"This is not the time—"

"She'll never have her 'red blanket time' with you again," Boaz spat.

And Lazar couldn't respond; he instinctively took the hammering blow, crossing both swords above his head. He kicked the man at his left, heard the knee break. Good. Down but not out, so he skipped forward, out of the felled man's reach, whilst he dealt with his partner, dispatching him in a whirl of glinting sword moves. He didn't have time to return to the first man before a replacement had arrived, fast and accurate. The men were unmasked, so he could look into their eyes. This one's eyes were dead, grimly determined with the desire to be the one to kill the Spur. Lazar realized that Arafanz had destroyed his soldiers' ability to think for themselves and he began to wonder, now that he focused on the slightly glazed expression of his opponent, whether these men were drugged. It made sense. To make any rational person walk into unnecessary peril, one would need to trick him or remove his inhibitions. Their beloved leader must encourage them to drink before they fought and in that drink would be a potion capable of dulling their sense of fear. Lazar stabbed the man, knew the blow was fatal, ran quickly over to the man with the broken knee, and with a vicious blow cut off the arm that was reaching for his blade. Lazar had barely a second to register the Razaqin's incredulous look at his arm in the sand before Boaz was screaming at him to look behind him. Squatting instantly, Lazar spun in a fast, killing arc, taking out both men at once, waist-high, their abdomens splitting open like ripe fruit, spilling their contents.

The smell of blood was strong in his nostrils and now the odor of punctured bowel joined to form a familiar battleground stench.

The next pair was already arriving. Just before Lazar gave himself over entirely to the business of killing, Boaz's mention of his red blanket forced him to pause, just for a second. Something was wrong. But his arms had already begun their controlled but whirlwind killing maneuvers and Lazar's mind turned blank as he became one with the weapons, no longer registering death or pain. He was being injured, and he felt each bite of the blade that opened his skin, the superficial wounds neither slowing him nor being permitted to enter his thoughts.

Behind him Boaz continued to yell, but although Lazar heard the noise, he could no longer comprehend the words. The only element he was aware of in the whole chamber, in fact, was Ana's presence. She was his anchor, holding him steady, giving him a reason for this terrible choice of murder that he was making over and over again.

As though awakening from a dream, he found himself on his knees, bleeding profusely. The skin of his chest and belly was a profusion of wounds and blood. He was breathing hard, feeling slightly dizzy and suddenly weakened. There were only two Razaqin standing in the ring. Eighteen bodies had been carted off; the chamber stank of sweat and blood, of urine and feces, of undigested food spilling from intestines and of leaking wounds from already rotting corpses. He tasted salty tears—was he crying? He could not tell. He sensed one of the men moving around him, obviously determined to reach Boaz, leaving his partner to finish him off. He wasn't sure he had the strength to be fast enough. Boaz began to moan.

Red blanket? It echoed through his mind again. His old sword teacher had warned him of this—he had taught Lazar to empty his mind of all thoughts, but cautioned that when rationality returned to the fighter's mind, the distraction could threaten death. It was the body's way, his tutor had said, of giving you some final moments to yourself to pray, to think of your loved ones, to hate the man who was about to kill you.

He had no intention of dying. Why was he thinking of the red blanket he had given Ana to sleep on during their original journey from the foothills? The same blanket she had mentioned in the desert during the second doomed journey in an innocent-sounding, couched message of love spoken in front of the Valide and Grand Vizier . . .

"Spur!" Boaz howled, and instinctively Lazar stabbed upward and behind him, sticking his attacker through the throat. He twisted the blade out, felt the gush of blood hit his bare back, but understood there was no time to haul himself to his feet as the last of the twenty gave a warrior's cry. As he ferociously twisted the sword out of the man's throat, he brought his other arm down in a swinging motion, hurling the blade directly at his companion, who was running toward Lazar. As if he saw it happening at one quarter of life's normal speed, Lazar watched his sword arc, tip over hilt, before slamming into the man's chest. The Razaqin barely had time to register the spume of blood before he dropped dead, hitting the sand like a stone dropped from a height, barely a step from where Lazar was breathing in heavy rasps, only the whites of his eyes visible through the blood that seemed to cover him from head to toe.

Silence greeted the last man's death. Although the cheering had long since dissipated, a lone person clapped. Lazar knew it would be Arafanz. He painfully hauled himself from his knees, swaying dangerously on his feet. He ignored the rebel,

looked instead through the blood that dripped from his hair—
he wasn't sure if it was his own or some other poor fool's—to
search out Ana.

And it suddenly fell into place for him. He had been fighting
for the wrong life. As the ironic clapping continued, he struggled over to one of the dead Razaqin and retrieved his sword.
As he did so, he heard the Zar yell at Arafanz.

"I am free, rebel! You have witnesses!"

Suddenly nothing sounded right to Lazar's ears. Not the
eerie silence of the audience around him, not the voice inside
him that was desperately trying to persuade him against the terrifying notion that was suddenly consuming him, forcing him
to think about doing something he had never thought possible.
Not even the insincere praise from his captor sounded right.

"My compliments, Spur Lazar. You truly are a one-man
war all of your own. You have won your Zar a pardon from
death . . . for the time being."

Boaz clapped once in victory, turning to Lazar and giving
him a grin so malevolent that it made the Spur stop in his tracks,
the sword held loosely at his side.

"I hear you fought a dozen men for your own freedom
once," Arafanz commented, "and now you fight almost twice
as many for your Zar. He should be proud of your courage,
even if it is not rooted in loyalty. You are still a cuckold, Your
Majesty," Arafanz taunted.

"Wait!" Lazar roared.

"Is something wrong, Spur?" Arafanz replied. "Fret not, I
am a man of my word. I said twenty men only and you have
bested them all. What I plan to do with you is—"

"This is not the Zar," Lazar said, hardly daring to believe his
own words as he stared uncomprehendingly at Boaz.

Arafanz laughed but Lazar saw Boaz blanch.

"What?" the Zar yelled. "What are you talking about?"

Lazar shook his head, began advancing on Boaz, squeezing away helpless tears. "Boaz, I am sorry," he said, raising his sword. He heard the Zar scream a name and then pandemonium broke out as his blade crashed down into the skull of the Zar of Percheron, Mightiest of the Mighties, and Lazar watched the face of the young man he had loved since he had been a sweet-natured infant, and to whom he had pledged eternal loyalty, cleave into neat halves, falling away in a mass of gore as Boaz's body crumpled beneath it.

He heard a woman's scream above the roar of the Razaqin—knew it was Ana calling him—before he took in the frightening scene of Ashar throwing pails of liquid over the gathered men. It was lamp oil by the smell of it and this was confirmed when Ashar ignited the men with a burning torch he grabbed from the wall. Through the erupting flames and the subsequent panic, Lazar saw Arafanz roar his despair, and then Lazar, unsure of where he found the strength, was running.

30

Ganya remained hidden behind the camels. She still wore her black robes and she was helplessly trembling. To be found now would mean instant death but she worried more for Ashar. He was taking such a risk and he had been babbling about getting the Zar out as well as Ana and Lazar. Could they all make it? The Samazen was in full roar outside. She knew from experience that it was impossible to see so much as a your own fingers in front of you. How were they to escape in this?

She had no idea where Iridor was, or how he fared. She had even tried to discover the special magic pathway that was so easy to open up when she was touching him, but it eluded her and she had now lost track of time. She wondered if Ashar would ever come for her and what she would do if he didn't. She had just decided she would wander into the Samazen and let its wrath kill her before she permitted Arafanz or his Razaqin to do so. She was of the desert; she would commit her body to it.

As she was making this decision the doors of the shelter burst open, bringing with it a swirl of angry sands and three hooded figures. She recognized Lazar's body immediately, despite its bloodstained state. In his arms was Ana, who, despite her pregnancy, was petite. Ganya had seen women nearly double their size in pregnancy but this girl carried her weight well, although she was certainly heavy with child and looked ready to birth, what with the stains on her garments and the grimace on her face. Ganya took all this in with one cursory glance before she threw her arms around Ashar.

"Where's the Zar?" she asked, realizing already he wasn't coming.

"Lazar killed him."

"You killed the Zar?"

Ana moaned. "Lazar, what possessed you?"

"He was going to kill you," came the stony reply.

As Ganya began to protest, Lazar cut her off. "No time, Ganya." He looked at Ashar. "Which one?"

"Her usual—Farim," Ashar said. "This one, already saddled."

"All right. You know the beast, get it up."

"Lazar, how do we go out in this?" Ganya demanded as she watched her lover place the young woman gently in the saddle, whispering softly to her.

"We take our chances," he growled. "No, go! . . . Hup, hup!" he called to the camel, swinging up behind Ana. "Stay strong for me," Ganya heard him say to her. "Ashar?"

"Yes."

"You're responsible for your sister. You head east now. You know the way. I know you can't see anything, but force the animal in an easterly direction. Your head, your heart, know the direction. Trust them. We cannot help each other. We are going to lose sight of ourselves the second we move out. So we travel alone. If you can travel east for one hour and survive it, there's shelter at our old camp, remember? There's some rocky outcrops there. Get below them and hole up for however long it takes. Did you pack water?"

Ashar nodded, looking frightened.

"That's all you need. Your camel will give you eighteen days so long as you can survive these first few hours. The Samazen will only last four days. We can do this."

"We don't have much choice," Ashar admitted.

"Lyana guide you," Lazar said to Ganya, and she knew he was saying good-bye.

She had no time to say anything. Her beast was moving, her arms around the waist of her little brother, and the Samazen was howling. They were heading into night and the fiercest sandstorm she had encountered in her nearly four decades.

As he suspected they would, Lazar lost Ganya and Ashar within moments of their two beasts reluctantly stepping outside their shelter. The other beast blundered, spooked by the Samazen, and Lazar cast a prayer that Ashar would wrest back control. The camel he and Ana rode refused to leave the walls that cocooned her, but begging Ana to hold her seat somehow, Lazar jumped down and with strength he didn't know he possessed, dragged, pushed, and pulled the animal into the angry maelstrom.

What he had only prayed might happen nevertheless took his breath away when it did.

The sands miraculously went still around them and then, as

if on some signal, danced back. As the camel and its cargo fully emerged, they found themselves moving in a strange void. It was late afternoon; Lazar could see the fiery ball of the sun dipping to the west. He could clearly see the rough hair of their beast. The noise had dulled to a soft roar around them. They moved in gentle warmth, rather than fierce heat, and what seemed to be an impossible safety. Around them he knew the Samazen raged. Ahead he saw the first camel; Ashar and Ganya had their heads bent against the storm; though they looked beaten, Lazar was relieved to see that Ashar was guiding them east.

"Hang on," he whispered toward them. "One hour, that's all."

And then, curiously, Lazar and Ana's camel swung in a new direction.

"Hey," he called, pulling on the reins, but she ignored him.

"She knows only one way," Ana murmured.

"What did you say?"

"Her name is Farim. She knows only one path. She will take us there safely."

"Where are we going?"

"You will see."

"Look, Ana," he said, pointing.

She raised weary eyes.

"It's Arafanz. Look at him squinting. He can't even see through the sands this far, but I swear I could reach and touch him. I know he can't hear us either."

"What is happening?" she asked softly.

"This is Lyana at work. The Samazen is your friend, Ana. It protected you once and it is doing so again. I'd hoped it would."

"How did you know?"

"I didn't. I took a terrible risk."

It had to be the magic surrounding them but Lazar suddenly felt young and uninhibited again, the way he'd felt before he'd even met Shara; a boy on his way to greatness, without any need to be shy or to shield his feelings. "When I saw you walk out of that fortress, my heart felt as though it stopped. In that moment I have never known such terrible pain and yet such a sense of elation. And I didn't even know you carried my son," he said, reaching around to stroke her taut belly, swollen with life. "All I knew was that if Arafanz had killed me then and there, I would have led an enviable life because you were in it and you had loved me."

"I still do," she sighed.

"Are you sure?"

"Why do you doubt me? I carry your child."

"Arafanz—"

"How he feels about me is his business. I have been his prisoner for many moons. I had to survive for our baby's sake."

"Did he ever . . ."

"No. He never pushed himself upon me. In truth, Lazar, he was tender and sweet. He is a different man when he is separated from his crusade."

"You like him," he said, keeping his tone even.

"Helplessly, yes, I do. He has a warped way of viewing loyalty and commitment to his faith, but when he's just being a man, on no mission, he is intelligent, gentle, amusing."

"As I said, I should be grateful that he kept you safe."

"I would be lying if I said I was unhappy here."

Such a notion had not occurred to Lazar. He felt his shoulders sag. "Do you regret me coming?"

Ana turned as best she could in the saddle. "No, Lazar, no."

She leaned back against his bloodstained chest. "How could I? My son's father is here. The man I love, the only man I have ever loved, is here."

"Are you angry, Ana?"

"About Ganya? No. You are a man; I imagine—"

"I want to explain. There is so much to tell you, it's hard to know where to begin."

"Tell me from the day you rode away. Tell me all of it."

And so on the journey to the cave, above Farim's steady plod through the Samazen that howled around them but left beast and its cargo untouched, Lazar told Ana everything he could remember from the moment he slew the last of the Razaqin and picked up Herezah, to the moment Arafanz recaptured them.

"So Boaz was lying about Herezah?"

"He didn't know any different. She would have told him we were lovers. How was he to know it wasn't true?"

"You could have denied it."

"It was a delicate moment, Ana. We are facing war with my realm—there were more important things to worry about than Herezah's lies. And anyway, I looked guilty because Salmeo did interrupt us—"

"Oh, please don't tell me. It's not important. Nothing's important anymore other than the safe delivery of our son and the fact that we are together."

He hugged her, kissed the top of her damp hair, loving her all the more. "How are you feeling?"

"Weak. I'm sure I'm meant to be feeling stronger, Lazar. I have a long way to go in the birthing process yet, but I feel frail."

"You've been through a lot, had too many shocks, your waters broke early, and your baby is coming before it really wants to. This place we're heading for, is it proper shelter?"

"Yes. It is warm and dry, silent and calm. It is where I'm meant to be—I sense it is the place I've always been meant to be."

"Don't make it sound so final. I will keep us safe."

"Tell me about Iridor."

"Well, as I explained, he is now fully Iridor."

"But he continues to elude Maliz?"

"Yes, it's why he refuses to use his magics."

"I can't believe Boaz is gone," she said miserably.

"I realize now that I lost Boaz in the desert. I wasn't there. He died alone, no doubt fighting for his existence against a demon." A soft sob escaped Lazar. He hadn't meant to break, thought he was in control of himself, but this day had been like none other. Fighting was easy in comparison to the emotional turmoil he was struggling with. And worse, he felt nauseous and dizzy. He didn't want to admit what was nagging at his thoughts, refused to allow it to take hold in his mind.

Ana heard his choked breath. "Lazar, don't. I need you to be strong. You've always been so strong."

"I let him down. My Zar is dead and I could have prevented it." Was it a trick of the cocoon or was his eyesight narrowing.

"No, you're wrong," she said, reaching back to touch his unshaven face. "How could you know that this is what Maliz planned? He is a demon. He is relentless. He would have seen Boaz's weaknesses and preyed on them."

"You were his weakness, Ana. Only you made him vulnerable."

"So you see, I am to blame, not you."

"I didn't mean it like that, I—"

"No, I know you didn't. I'm simply stating a fact, Lazar. Boaz was vulnerable to any negativity about me. The demon would have sensed that from the earliest moment of his arrival into Tariq's body. Which meant he's had almost two years to prey on Boaz's weakness, especially if he's suspected me of being Lyana. And unfortunately Boaz paid for his vulnerability with his life."

"I had to do it, Ana."

"I know. Do you think Maliz is dead, then?"

"Iridor said he cannot be killed by mortal means. Only Lyana can destroy him."

"And we are no closer to her."

Lazar kept his own counsel on what Iridor and Ganya believed. This was not the time to share with Ana their suspicions. She was too emotionally fragile and Ana had enough to think about and cope with right now. "Don't worry about Lyana just now. Think only of our child."

"Lazar!" she moaned. "Here comes a contraction. I need to stop."

Obediently Farim halted at his call, and in their desert womb, Lazar laid Ana down and held her hand as she groaned her way through the pain he could not hope to save her from. When it was over, she was left panting, perspiration beading on her face.

"That was a big one. He's closer. Our boy is nearly ready to enter this cruel world," she said, then she screamed as Lazar toppled forward on top of her, his skin burning with fever.

Somehow—Ganya would never know how—they had stumbled through the storm. Their camel had walked into dunes and at one point refused to move any farther, so they had taken turns hauling at her, unable to see beyond their noses but moving forward inch by painful inch.

Now night was falling and it was certainly cooler. The Samazen's might had lessened slightly, she was sure of it, but not enough to feel in any way safe. Despite the fury of the storm, she was grateful for it. Without the Samazen they would have been pursued and killed, and although it would probably kill them itself, it made them invisible and allowed them to die more nobly in the desert.

She wished that they could have stayed with Lazar somehow, and was surprised to find herself envious of Ana. Envy was not an emotion she normally suffered. Even when she had unintentionally glimpsed some of the turmoil within the Spur, had felt the power of the bond between him and the Zaradine, the helpless love that drove him toward her, she had not felt anything other than sorrow on their behalf. But now, having shared his body and felt so close to his problems, she wanted him.

"We have to stop," she begged Ashar, who had chosen to trudge beside her.

"I think we're almost there," he shouted.

"How can you know?"

"Oh, I have a great sense of direction—it's like magic," he said, surprising her by chuckling.

"You know, I hardly know you, Ashar."

"Yes, I really am very different from the boy you remember," he replied, irritating her already vexed mood further by laughing. "Just a few more minutes."

"I don't understand how you can know that. I can't see anything, can't recognize anything. We are blind."

"You, perhaps, but not me," he said cryptically, urging the camel harder. "No more talking," he ordered, and she pursed her lips at his abrupt manner, doggedly pressing on in silence, telling herself to be comforted that they were still alive.

The light was fading and Herezah felt like a hapless moth, drawn to the harbor as to a flame. So many Galinsean warships were gathering. The city was silent. Only ghosts walked through the bazaar now. Percheron was empty of the usual smells of spices and cooking; even the fragrance of jasmine and the exotic scents from the palace gardens seemed to have faded.

The ships were not elegant like the Perchereste craft. They seemed crude in structure but they were far more intimidating for that rough dark timber and the brightly painted creatures that were carved proudly at the helm. She saw dragons, winged lions, all manner of mythical beasts. They were close enough now that she could make out the tiny figures of men scampering up and down the masts, pulling down sails, going about the business of preparing for war.

Percheron, by comparison, was frozen in fear. Captain Ghassal had come to her once again for instructions but she had refused to give the go-ahead to engage their enemy.

"But, Crown Valide, perhaps if we strike first before they can amass—"

"No, Captain Ghassal. I will not give the Galinseans the satisfaction of saying we loosed the first burning arrow. I don't want war. If it is to find us, at least we will not provoke it."

"Crown Valide, with all due respect," he had pleaded, "war is here. There is no more waiting. The Spur would demand that we defend ourselves."

"Defend. Absolutely we defend. Do you know the meaning of the word *defend*, Captain Ghassal?"

He had stammered, looked toward Bin for help, but the secretary had looked away. "I—"

"Let me define it for you, Captain. *Defense* is about resisting attack. It is not about attacking. *Defense* is about protection from attack. And I intend to take the literal meaning of *defense* and live by that creed. In your book, *defense* might mean taking a more aggressive position, but, Captain Ghassal, we will lose hundreds of our innocent men in such a move. I feel utterly sure that, as proud as Spur Lazar is, he would see the hopelessness of our situation and he would move toward diplomacy."

"But, Crown Valide, diplomacy was finished when Queen Angeline died on the barge."

"You don't have to remind me of the facts, Captain Ghassal. I am a woman, which I know you're not used to dealing with. Please be assured that I am not stupid and I can see that the Galinseans want us to fight. They are hoping for any excuse to take out their grief, their anger, and their long-held bitterness about beautiful, naturally endowed Percheron on this city. I will not give them any further excuse. Falza is shrewd—we know this much—and he would be seen as less than a warrior if he launches an attack against a helpless woman, a regent at that." Herezah had loaded her words with sarcasm. "As long as I appear pathetic and terrified, it buys us a little time." She had held up her hand when he'd tried to speak. "No, Captain. I am not naive enough to believe it will stay his anger entirely but time is all we can count on. We are no match for their might or fighting prowess, and with all respect to your own talent, I think our inexperienced army needs its Spur if it is going to have any chance of standing up to the bullying Galinseans. And we wait. Those who wanted to have already left the city. Those who wished to stay are now behind the city walls, and indeed most are behind the palace walls." She had looked at Bin, who had nodded. "I have no issue if you offer your men the option to put down their weapons. This is not a lack of courage. This is sensible."

"I'm afraid I can't do that, Crown Valide."

She had smiled behind her veil. "I had expected you to feel this way. They understand that any resistance will be met with stern repercussions?"

"They understand that to be part of the Protectorate is to be prepared to die for Percheron."

She nodded. "Then I suggest you call in the priests to say final prayers. No soldier who resists will be spared. I will not think less of you, Captain, if you take your family and head for the foothills."

"But I would think less of me, Crown Valide. I am Spur Lazar's chosen deputy. My family has been sent away. They understand it is likely I will not join them or see them again."

"I applaud your bravery."

"As I do yours, Crown Valide. We will not resist until the Galinseans strike the first blow, as you wish."

"Thank you, Captain. Zarab bless you and all your men."

He had nodded once, bowed, and strode away from her rooms.

"I hope I'm doing the right thing," she said quietly now as Bin returned to her salon.

"We will know tomorrow morning, Crown Valide. Either way, I am proud to have served you."

She turned to him. "No one has ever said that to me before."

"Your courage—although it could be misinterpreted as inaction—is daunting, Crown Valide. If I survive this, I will tell everyone I know of your strength and composure."

"You'd better not mention the tears and histrionics, the fear and anxiety, then," she said in a rare show of self-mockery.

"What happens behind closed doors is between us, Crown Valide. All that matters is how you're perceived beyond them, and your people, Captain Ghassal, all the palace staff, will see only that you carried yourself with stoicism."

Herezah laid a hand on Bin's arm. "Thank you."

"I shall send Elza in, Crown Valide. I know you probably can't sleep but perhaps she can prepare some tea or see to your needs better than I."

"No, Bin. Stay with me. This could be our last night of life and I would rather share it with someone than be alone. If you have nothing more pressing to do, I would be honored if you would be that someone. We'll take tea together on the balcony and admire the stars over Percheron. Let us drink to our city's beauty."

"And our enemy's downfall," he said. Surprisingly, they both laughed.

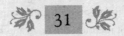

31

He heard her cries, roused himself from the stupor, and realized with a fright that he was on top of Ana.

"I'm sorry," he slurred. "What happened?"

"You collapsed," she panted. "Are you sick?"

"Yes," he replied bitterly. "It returns."

"You were never really well, were you?"

He shook his head. "Ellyana said the drezden sickness would never leave, would strike whenever I was vulnerable or my health low."

"Can you ride? It's not much further."

"How can you tell? We've been following this rock face for a while."

"I learned to read the markings in the rock. Farim can have us there soon if you can stay upright on her."

"I can."

"I'll ride behind you. That way I can see what's happening to you."

"Some savior, I am."

She smiled, breaking his heart. He'd lost Jumo, Boaz, Pez even, if he looked at it a certain way, and he'd lost Salim. He would not lose Ana, not now. He struggled to his feet and clambered aboard the patient camel, turning to help Ana. She struggled up behind him, and without being asked, Farim lumbered to her feet and plodded forward.

After a few minutes he said, "This camel of yours should be given a special reward."

"An endless supply of grain and dates?"

"Or male camels. Perhaps a crown as well—a queen amongst her own."

He could feel Ana's cheek against his back as she laughed softly. "Your sickness goes to your head," she warned. Then she jerked away from him. "Lazar, this is it!"

"She is slowing, you're right."

"Clever Farim," Ana cooed as the beast lowered herself.

Lazar helped her down. "Where are we? I see no cave."

"You will. Lazar, your body is burning."

He managed a nod through the increasing dizziness. "Your voice sounds as though it's being spoken through a tunnel. I don't know how long I've got."

"I know I have a while before my next pain. We can make it. What about the camel?"

"Where is the opening to this cave?"

"It's very narrow. You can't see it from here."

"Narrow? Once you leave Farim, so does the protection you offer, I assume. I had hoped she could come into the cave."

"No, it's too small. Oh no!" She looked grief-stricken.

"There is nothing we can do. She must take her chances."

"We can get her head through the opening. She can have that much protection."

Lazar didn't want to tell Ana that the camel would likely wander off. "Good idea," he said, "but hurry, Ana, I'm fading."

She took his hand and dragged him toward what looked like flat rock.

"Intriguing," he murmured, despite the fact that he could no longer see terribly well. He was staying upright through grim determination alone.

She must have sensed as much because, without speaking, Ana hurriedly bundled him in through the narrow opening, making sure that Farim's muzzle was poking through that same opening and well protected from the storm. She kissed the beast in thanks and farewell. Inside it was quiet and he could hear water but he was feeling too weak and disoriented to mention it and soon convinced himself he was imagining it. Almost blindly he followed Ana's guiding hands.

"We have to make a jump. It sounds worse than it is and there are rock steps to help. Stay calm in the tunnel. It's narrow but short and there's safety at its end, I promise."

In the blinding darkness, he had already lost any sense of where they were and what they were doing. He trusted her completely and followed her directions, soon enough finding himself on a ledge at the other end of the very short tunnel she spoke of.

"Hold on, Lazar," she begged from behind him. "I don't have any means of giving us light but—" and as Ana emerged, Lazar was stunned to see the cavernous chamber he had sensed himself in erupt into a soft glow.

"What is this place?" he asked, shivering uncontrollably.

"Arafanz called it a temple of Lyana. Over there are the Crystal Pillars."

He looked toward the dulled columns he could see in the distance. "What are they?"

She shrugged. "I don't really know. They communicate with me."

"What?"

She smiled wanly. "We don't have much time. I can feel another contraction building. That means they're getting closer. I must find a spot to have our son. No, wait," she said, pushing him lightly. "You are sick, weak, feverish. You are no help to our boy right now. Just rest."

"Here?"

"Actually, I have an idea. Do you think you can move?"

"If I must."

"Come to the pillars. I'm interested to hear what they say to you."

"They spoke to you, you said."

She nodded and there was sadness in the gesture. "They welcomed me as Mother. I didn't understand at the time. I think I do now. I think you do, too."

"Ana—"

"It's all right. Our son is the Goddess. This is what it's all been about. You and I were always meant to be."

"To be?"

"Together," she said, helping him to his unsteady feet. "There was so much Lyana couldn't control but that's why mysterious Ellyana worked so hard to save you after the flogging and poisoning, why you and Pez were such close friends. It's probably why you were helplessly guided toward Percheron in the first place. Lazar, it may even go further back to why you were born, how your early life was shaped. Shara, even . . ."

He looked at her through glazed eyes, fighting through the fever to understand. "You think Lyana caused her death?"

"Who knows," she replied softly. "I do believe now that you and I were meant to meet, meant to become lovers, meant to have this child. It's why Arafanz is part of Lyana's plan. You see him as the enemy and yet we are all being helplessly driven toward the same goal of returning Lyana to Percheron—of changing the faith of the people back to that of the Goddess. Our son will banish the priests and tear down the temples of Zarab. And through him and his reign, the faith of Lyana will be restored."

He shook his head to clear it as she gently led him through the cavernous chamber, surprisingly mild in temperature and glowing unnaturally from no light source he could see. The rock face itself seem to have its own illumination.

She read his thoughts. "It has never done this before. But then I have never been here without lamps or at night." She pointed up. "Over there, Arafanz used to loosen that disk at a certain time of the day when the sun would blaze through the circle in the rock and light the pillars."

"I can't get up there," he groaned.

"I don't think you'll have to. I think they will light for us." They had arrived at the stone steps.

"What happens now?"

"You must go up onto the plinth."

"I keep thinking about Boaz."

"He's dead, Lazar. No amount of—"

"No, that's not what I mean," he said, swaying. "Sorry. I'm losing my thoughts as fast as they arrive. I mean I killed the Zar because I was sure Maliz had possessed him. But if Maliz cannot be killed by a mortal, it means he has found a new host. Presumably our son will have to destroy Maliz. Perhaps Boaz need not have died. I feel—"

"Don't," she interrupted. "If what you saw was real and Maliz had taken Boaz, then there was no going back. My understanding, from what Pez had said, is that if he takes a body, he destroys the life that once owned it. If you're right—and it makes sense that you are—then Boaz was already dead in the desert. You simply killed the body, the shell that was disguising Maliz." She sighed. "Only Lyana can destroy him. So, yes, it will be our son who kills him. But how can a newborn do that? What if Maliz finds him before he's old enough to do so. What if we both die here this night?"

Lazar frowned. The fever did not permit him to think clearly. "I . . . I don't know what—"

"Go. You look ready to fall over and I must lie down. A contraction is . . ." Ana's voice trailed off as she reached behind herself, falling against a boulder, slipping to the ground. Her eyes were wide with pain.

"Ana!"

"Just go!" she urged, almost growling, through her groan of agony.

He staggered back, unsure of everything now. He had never delivered a child, had never been present at a human birth. Suddenly he was overwhelmed by the burden of all they still faced: the safe delivery of the baby, surviving in the cave, returning to Percheron.

He lurched up the short flight of stairs, his mind filled with the repetitive image of splitting open Boaz's head and allowing Maliz to escape.

Ashar and Ganya had crawled as far back beneath the rock ledge as possible. It offered minimal yet much appreciated protection, their camel providing a little more at the mouth of the opening. They had been cramped in their shared space for hours.

Sand still swirled in to sting their hands but their linens, now hooded over their faces, saved their eyes from harm.

"How long, do you think?"

Ganya was surprised that he'd ask such a thing. "Probably two more days to be safe."

"Stuck here?"

She frowned beneath her desert veils. "Where else, Ashar? We should be grateful for our lives. I still can't believe we found the camp. Lyana is guiding us."

"Lyana be damned! We found it because we were brave enough to face her Samazen and courageous enough to stick to our easterly path."

"Ashar! Do not take the Goddess's name in vain."

"Or what? She'll strike me down? I'm not scared of her."

Ganya frowned, disturbed by her little brother's bitter tone.

"But it has calmed, don't you think?" he said after several moments of awkward silence.

"Yes, I agree."

"I think we should go, continue east to Percheron."

"Go? Are you mad? If it's calm enough out there for us to ride, it's calm enough for Arafanz's people to hunt us down. East is the direction he'll try."

"He would chase Lazar and Ana first."

"Ashar, it's not that I think he'd forgive the Spur or the Za-radine. He would surely hunt them mercilessly. But I think he would reserve his greatest fury for you. You were Razaqin. You have betrayed him. Ana and Lazar have behaved as expected. But he will want you back and want to make you suffer. We must keep you safe; we will head south. We are two on one camel—we must preserve her strength as well, since neither of us knows how long we may have to ride. She will travel quicker with both of us if we take turns."

"Ganya, my dear, she will travel quicker if we didn't have you along at all."

With dread in her heart and a chill of fear tingling through her spine, Ganya slowly pulled back her linens to look at her brother.

His head covering had already been removed. He was right, the sand had certainly calmed, although she would hardly call it peaceful.

"Ashar, you're frightening me."

"Am I?"

"Why are you behaving like this? You are not yourself."

He burst into laughter, chilling Ganya further. The unholy sound seemed to echo around the rock they hid beneath.

"No, I'm not myself. You're right."

She shook her head. "What's happening, Ashar?"

She saw his hand move, felt something brush past her, and suddenly she was gagging.

"You're dying. Don't fight it, it will be quick. I'm sorry you have to suffer the same fate as your father, but perhaps it's also appropriate to die in the sands as he did. If it helps, Ganya, I'm not really Ashar. He died back in the arena when he whispered the words I wanted to hear. I'd convinced him, you see, that

Boaz possessed special magical powers conferred upon all Zars down the ages. He was naive and seduced by the notion of rescuing his sister and 'Miss Ana,' as he so quaintly called her, not to mention wealth and freedom."

"Maliz!" she choked out as her hot blood pumped through her fingers, as she desperately but in vain tried to close the gaping wound at her throat.

"You must be almost done now. That's it, you lie down, bleed out into the sand, and think of your baby brother. He didn't even fight me, poor fool. He wanted to set up a merchant trade. Good-bye, Ganya. At least you can die knowing you had some pleasant last evenings with the Spur. I shall tell him you went with a smile on your face." He laughed. "And an even wider one at your throat."

She was no longer aware of him, only a darkness, and using the last of her wits before she died, Ganya cast out with her mind voice, searching for anyone who could listen.

Lazar struggled onto the plinth. Instantly he was bathed in shimmering colors as the Crystal Pillars sensed his presence.

We welcome the Amalgama, they chimed.

He twisted around, both frightened and entranced at the same moment.

You are injured . . . and sick.

Lazar realized he could no longer see Ana for the iridescent sparkling all about him, and for all his worries, he suddenly and curiously felt safe, protected, uninhibited . . . perhaps for the first time in his life. He felt lost in the wonder of their light and beauty.

"Ana," he groaned.

The Mother is doing what a mother must, they soothed.

"Who is the Amalgama?"

Lie down. We must heal you.

"I have no drezden. I accept that I'm dying, but my son—"

You will see your son. You will return him to Percheron. We have no need of medicines here. We can heal your fever and soothe your burns, we can mend those wounds on your body. Sleep now. Trust us.

The singsong voices sounded so compelling, and their offer irresistible. Soothed by their chimes and the colors and their warmth, Lazar let go of everything of himself and gave it over to Lyana.

He thought he heard someone cry out from beyond, could have sworn it was Ganya's voice, but carried away on Lyana's warmth and the promise of rest and healing, he ignored it and slept.

Ana could see the pillars sparkling and shifting their iridescence. She knew they were speaking to Lazar. But she could not hear them or him, could not know whether he called to her, for she was on an angry tide of pain. And she had to give herself over to it and be carried along or she would be lost.

She heard herself screaming in agony and knew that very soon her desire to push her baby would become overwhelming. She wept; once again she was alone. She would face this frightening event without help or guidance, without even a hand to squeeze and reassure her.

Always she was alone. She vented her despair now, calling Lyana's name.

Maliz had no intention of leaving just yet but there was only limited water and a few morsels of food left at the bottom of a sack he'd found in the camel shelter, no doubt left from the previous day's riding. There certainly wasn't enough to sustain one person, let alone two. Ganya had been an encumbrance; he was glad to have done away with her. He'd never appreciated the way she had looked at him sideways when he had been Tariq. And now he knew why. Ganya must have been aware of the demon, and probably known whom he'd disguised himself within. How could she know this? The only explanation, he realized, was that Lazar knew.

Rot him! He almost hoped that Lazar had survived the Samazen so that he could ultimately kill him himself. That would have been easy if he were still Boaz, of course; not so easy as Ashar. *Zarab rot him twice over!* If Lazar hadn't worked it out, hadn't attacked Boaz, he could be traveling as a Zar right now . . . women and indulgence at his call, not to mention a healthy, young body in which to move. Nevertheless, Ashar's body was wiry and tough, and no matter how disgusted he felt to have lost the Zar's cover, he was grateful he'd taken the precaution of working on the young Razaqin. What a tragic boy he had been—poor, idealistic, with a head full of delusions. He had been such easy prey.

And Ganya was just as gullible, even sitting in front of him on the camel, still believing she was protecting her baby brother. Stupid woman! Getting to the camp had been easy with his heightened powers of direction; he never doubted that they would reach its cover but he was still relieved that the Samazen's fury had dissipated. Though it could be back with vengeance in the morning, he had every intention of making the most of its quieter time. He lay down; he would sleep against the warmth that Ganya's corpse offered him . . . a few hours, that was all, and then he would leave before dawn. Taking the precaution of wrapping the camel's reins around his fist, Maliz slept soundly and even with a soft smile playing around Ashar's lips.

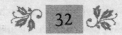

32

Herezah and Bin had spent what was left of the night together, staring out over the Faranel, and she was sure
the servant could sense, as well as she, that dawn was on the rim
of the sky. The killing would begin soon.

"Have you counted?" she asked, as though they were wak-
ing from a long sleep rather than an interminable, sorrowful
silence.

"Forty, I think."

"Probably more," she said. "Not that it matters."

Bin stood and, she noted, stretched surreptitiously, so as not
to give offense. The polite servant to the end; she wondered
again how she had missed not just so much about this young
man but probably about so many faithful people around her.
She regretted it. Regretted it all, in fact.

"I will do one final check around the palace, Crown Valide,

so I can brief you on its status," Bin said, breaking into her thoughts as he bowed in farewell.

"Bin, I can't turn back time, although I would like to. For now let me just say a rather humble thank-you. I realize there have been too many times when I've not bothered to say it and, in truth, not even felt the sentiment."

He nodded and she was pleased that he did not try to protest. She liked him all the more for that moment of absolute honesty.

"If by some miracle we live through this, Crown Valide, it would be my desire to serve you as a royal in your own right, not simply as wife to a former Zar, or mother to our present one. If our own Zar should not return—"

"Do not say it, Bin, I beg you."

"But we must consider the possibility, not just of our own deaths, but of the death of the whole line of Zars as we know it, Crown Valide. Let us imagine, just for this last moment of peace, that Zar Boaz has met his fate in the desert, that he has passed without a known living heir. And let us just say that you somehow survive today and whatever terror awaits Percheron, I would not hesitate to suggest that you, and only you—with the right counsel—are fit to rule Percheron until a solution can be found, a new dynasty begun. I would go so far as to say that you yourself, as the most recent Valide, may even have to consider bearing us a new Zar. It has no precedent, to my knowledge—perhaps Percheron enters a new era."

"A matriarchal one?" she asked, dazzled by his near-blasphemous suggestion.

"Why not? At least until your new son can take his rightful place."

"Let us both survive this day, Bin, and perhaps we'll be discussing your audacious notion with Falza across the treaty table."

He gave a shy smile. "I will go off to my duties, Crown Valide."

"And I shall get dressed in the manner befitting a queen at war," she said archly.

Lazar awoke refreshed; all his previous dizziness and distress had left him. He was no longer feverish or disorientated, could feel no pain or wounds. The weeping burn he had hardly felt during the panicked escape but that had forced him to clench his teeth during the camel journey, had miraculously disappeared. He was healed . . . for now.

"Lyana?" he called.

We are not her. We are her sentinel, you could say, answered the pillars, their colors turning and swirling.

"What do you guard?"

Her, they chimed softly to him. *And you.*

"Where is Ana?"

As you left her.

"But I have been asleep."

Only moments, they reassured him. *She is nearing her time but she is resting.*

"You welcomed me as the Amalgama. What does it mean?"

You are the unification, they chorused. *You are the central pillar, Lucien Lazar. Around you Lyana has built her battle. Everything she has put in place for this cycle has been combined around your role. You are her champion, her protector, her father. She must remain hidden for a few years more until our Goddess is no longer a helpless infant. But you are the blending point for all her believers and supporters.*

"I need you to explain this Amalgama for me. Forgive me for not being able to make whatever leap you need me to."

You have unified with Ana to form the child who will carry Lyana. Furthermore this son of yours must be unified with his throne. That is your role.

"Wait! I thought that was Arafanz's role."

We needed second and third plans, Lucien Lazar. I know it may not feel this way to you but much of how this cycle turned out was left to fate. Lyana is counting on certain people to fulfill their roles but she doesn't have as much control over mortals as perhaps you think she has. She could only set up the plan and hope that you could follow it.

"You mean Arafanz is merely a contingency plan?" he asked, aghast. "People have brutally lost their lives because of him and yet he is only following his mad pathway in the event of unforeseen circumstances?" Lazar's voice had risen and his bitter tone had become demanding.

The pillars appeared to dull momentarily, as if sighing. *Lyana asks your forgiveness but she could not know how all your lives would unfold. As it is, we came perilously close to losing you, Lucien Lazar, to unexpected circumstances.*

"Didn't you have a contingency plan for me?" he asked, pacing aggressively, feeling suddenly trapped by the Crystal Pillars.

It is very important that Luc—as he shall be called—become the next Zar of Percheron. You will be the amalgam that brings Percheron together with Galinsea to forge a partnership so strong— in its politics, its trade, and especially its faith—that the region will never again be under threat. To answer your original question, you are the unifying factor that will pick up the pieces of what is left behind from this cycle and repair them.

You are the common factor between Galinsea and Percheron. You are the common factor between the people and royalty; both sides trust you. You are the mortal—with an ear to the gods.

"And Maliz?"

Lyana will destroy him.

"How?"

That is her burden. It is not yours, Lucien Lazar. You have already fulfilled so much of what she needed from you. Now you must help Ana deliver your son and he must be returned to Percheron immediately. War comes—it begins today. You and he alone can prevent the Galinseans from sacking the city.

"Today!" Lazar cried. "But how am I supposed to return in time to save anything?"

Search yourself. You have the answer and the means. But Ana needs you now.

Suddenly he could hear her wails that had been shut out from him, presumably by the pillars.

"I don't know what to do," he beseeched.

She does. Trust Ana.

Lazar was at her side in moments. Her breath came in shallow pants now.

"He comes, Lazar. Our son arrives. Quickly! Get me onto the plinth."

"Don't move, I can—"

"No," she cried. "I must be over there, where you just were. I need to speak with her. She will help me."

Rather than upset Ana further, he picked her up easily. She moaned as he took her up the stairs again, laying her down softly amid the freshly intense color of Lyana's Crystal Pillars.

"Stay with me, Lazar," she begged.

"I won't leave you, I promise," he said, holding her hand, "but I don't know what to do."

"Sit behind me. Let me feel you against me."

As he moved around Ana so that she could lean her upper body against his chest, she began a deep groaning sound and started to push.

He felt helpless but recalled that while all of his father's bitches, who had delivered litters of pups, had enjoyed the nearness of the people they loved, they had nevertheless gone about the business of birthing by withdrawing into themselves. He sensed Ana was doing just that now as she instinctively began the final sorrowful journey with her baby as it made its way out of her body.

He took her hands, wrapped his arms around her, and held her close as she began to bear down and deliver the next Zar of Percheron and the future King of Galinsea.

Herezah was ready to face her death. She had dressed in a somber charcoal robe and was devoid of all jewelry; her hair was tied in a single simple plait and clasped at the back of her head. The Crown Valide looked at herself in the mirror and smiled wryly. In days gone by, she would almost certainly have opted to look as dazzling as she could. She would have chosen ivory so that, should Falza draw her blood, she would look stark and memorable in death. Even to the end, the old Herezah would have ensured as much theater as possible. But not anymore. She couldn't pinpoint when anything about herself had changed; it had begun in the desert and developed over the time she had spent nursing Lazar. Those months watching Lazar suffer, then slowly bringing him back to good health, had easily been the happiest time of her life. She had smiled a great deal, she had felt an intense glow of pleasure at touching him as she nursed him and watched his body respond to her gentle ministrations. She had felt complete for the first time in her life. It had been short-lived but she couldn't forget how good it had felt to care. And though none of the desire to rule, none of the cunning, had left her, her idea of ruling had changed from the desire for power to a desire to be a memorable Crown Valide whom her people would respect and the history books would remember. The cunning she wanted to use for the good of Percheron now, rather than for herself. Lazar had been right. What a great Valide she could have been if she'd put all her skills to use in supporting Boaz, rather than trying to manipulate him.

"I laid out the cream silks, Crown Valide, if you prefer?" Elza offered, breaking into her thoughts.

Herezah could hear the servant's disapproval. Normally she wouldn't care what a mere handmaiden thought but she surprised herself by explaining. "No, the darker color is best, Elza. Should anything unpleasant occur today, I don't want to make it easy for the Galinseans to show off my bloodied corpse, frightening our people." She could see the surprise and unabashed respect in the woman's reflection. "Let's not fuss any further. This will do. You've hidden the jewels?"

Elza nodded. "As instructed. Everything we could find from your collection is now in a sealed box cunningly submerged in the Daramo."

"Excellent. I don't want them smashing those up to be divided among the Falza's daughters."

"How many does he have?"

"I don't even know if he has one. I don't care. Those belong in Percheron. Her waters can claim them if Boaz never returns to raise them."

Bin suddenly burst through the doors. "Forgive me, Crown Valide. It has begun."

"What's happening?" she asked, rushing toward the windows.

"The Galinseans have begun coming ashore."

"Yes, I can see," she said, her insides twisting as she saw the mass of men in the distance moving out of the horde of rowboats that were arriving at the city's edge. "Captain Ghassal is to offer no resistance. Does he understand my orders?"

"Yes, Crown Valide, but he is not happy about them. He believes Spur Lazar would be ashamed of the Protectorate."

"Spur Lazar is not here to lead our men. Ghassal's bravery is not in question here, nor that of our soldiers. But we cannot win this, Bin, so it is right that I order that we don't fight back. Let Falza come and take the city with as little damage to it or its people as possible. It's the royals he wants and the crushing of the palace hierarchy. Let's make it as easy as possible. No amount of senseless sacrifice will allow us to scare them off."

"I understand your rationale, Crown Valide, but I suspect if the Galinseans start burning the city, Ghassal will act as he sees best."

"That is his choice and his death sentence. Elza, it is time for you to leave. I want you to get into plain clothing and go into the courtyards."

"I am too scared, Crown Valide."

"Listen to me. Whatever they do to you out there, it is safer than what they'll do if they discover you to be one of the royals' personal servants. Do not be found here. Now go!"

Elza's eyes were full of tears. "But Crown Valide—"

"Go!" Herezah ordered. "You, too, Bin."

"No," he said softly as Elza fled the chamber. "They will have to cut me down before they reach you."

"Zarab curse you! I thought we'd agreed," she hurled at him.

"You agreed, Crown Valide. I will make my own decision as to how I conduct myself. This is my choice . . . you can ganche me later if we all survive."

She felt only gratitude. "I shall think of something far more horrible, trust me. Your disobedience is noted."

He nodded and bowed. "Let me escort you to the Grand Salon, Your Majesty."

She looked at him, startled. "I don't think—"

"I do. You are our royalty now, Crown Valide, and we should treat you with the respect you deserve and have lately earned. When they come, we will awe them with the beauty of the palace and its remaining royal."

She smiled bravely "Come, then, Bin. Our executioners await."

Captain Ghassal had no intention of laying down arms to the Galinseans. No matter what the Crown Valide demanded of him, he was answerable to her son, the Zar, but first and foremost to the Spur. And Spur Lazar would never condone this spineless approach. Only a woman would. These were fighting men, trained for war. He could feel their eagerness, their sense of invincibility. They were young, their city was being invaded by the hated Galinseans. No, none of them would be handing over their weapons or their lives without a fight. Captain Ghassal would take whatever punishment for disobedience was levied upon him, should he survive this battle. But he doubted very much that he would survive this day, and he refused to allow Spur Lazar to hear that his trusted second-in-command had behaved meekly.

The Crown Valide's servant Bin had been told that the Protectorate would submit but the captain had already laid ambushes all over the city. Each of his lieutenants knew that from the moment the Galinseans began destroying the city—and he was sure Falza's soldiers would do this—the Percherese must act to protect their treasures. "Death to the barbarians," he muttered under his breath as he watched the first load disembark their rowboats.

"Death to the barbarians!" he now yelled at the top of his lungs. His men began loosing their shafts in a hail of arrows that rained down from the hillsides of Percheron onto the scrambling soldiers.

How could a woman possibly understand? Ghassal sneered to himself. How could she know that the Percherese had the advantage? That's why the city was built this way. No enemy came from the desert. The enemy could only approach by sea and his army had the advantage of height and vision. He would kill every filthy barbarian before he even had a chance to feel Percherese soil beneath his feet.

"Death to the barbarians!" he screamed again, urging his men to use their highly trained shooting skills from long distance.

Falza watched from the crag. He and his second-in-command had squeezed into the basket at the top of the main mast and were looking down upon Percheron.

The King squinted. "So, they're putting up a fight. I wasn't sure she would."

"Did you really believe she would capitulate, sire?"

"If you'd seen her stunned face on that barge and the fear that followed, you would believe me when I say this woman had no intention of fighting us. I fully expected her to meet us at the shore in full royal regalia and beg for her life."

"The men are getting slaughtered, my king. The enemy has the advantage of height."

"Send everyone in at once. At least half should get through. I want the city razed. Burn everything. Kill everyone."

"Everyone?" the soldier echoed, clearly unsure he'd heard his liege lord correctly.

"Everyone, including women and children. If they'd not fought back, I would have spared the Percherese. But the Valide is showing a distinct lack of foresight and care for her people. I'd already given her my terms. If she wants to defend her city, that's her right. But now I shall destroy it before her eyes, and then destroy her. Tell everyone I want the Crown Valide kept alive but everyone else is to be put to the sword. No life but hers is to be left. I will show her the results of her poor decision making before I personally take her life. Is that clear?"

"Yes, my lord. It will be done," his subordinate said, already lowering himself down from the lookout to pass on orders.

Falza squinted again at the palace and hoped the Crown Valide had keen enough eyesight to watch her famed city crumble.

They hadn't departed her chamber when they heard the roar go up. Turning bewildered back to the windows, Herezah and Bin ran onto the balcony. He watched the horror on her face as hundreds of arrows darkened her view, soaring from hidden positions on the hillside as they began their killing path toward the shoreline. Bin held his breath alongside his Crown Valide as dozens of these weapons found their mark. They could hear their enemies' cries, their voices carrying up and over the olive groves where Percherese soldiers had hidden themselves, over the rocky hill upon which she now stood, and past the beautifully tiered gardens of the Stone Palace that seemed to hang from the steep incline on which they were tended.

"Zarab save me!" she hissed.

"Ghassal has disobeyed your orders, Majesty. I was afraid he might."

"He said as much. May his god curse him for this. Falza will kill everyone now," she said, looking wildly at her servant.

He risked taking her hand. "Majesty, perhaps it is for the best. Percheron may be no match for the barbarians, but let history show that our city fought back with courage. Let us leave behind the knowledge that you did not bow to another king, that you bravely held your ground, on behalf of your Zar, in the face of terrible attack."

It was the right thing to say. Bin had never known how to tell the Crown Valide that Ghassal had just stopped short of laughing in his face when he had conveyed Herezah's orders—it had been clear that the captain had no intention of answering to a "mere whore," as he had dared call her. Bin had ignored the insult, realizing it was the result of fear, uncertainty, and bravado. In public the soldiers were respectful of the harem women but Bin was aware that such was not the case behind closed doors. And they reserved their greatest disdain for Herezah. Even in her new role she was still that same slave masquerading as a royal. Ghassal had told him he answered only to the Spur or their Zar. And in the absence of both he would make all the decisions for the Protectorate.

Bin had formulated the ruse of not fully telling the Crown

Valide the truth; it was out of their hands and well beyond their control now anyway. It had seemed best to let her believe her orders were being carried out; what transpired would likely be lost in the panic, especially as Bin did not expect either of them to see another dawn. And in truth he believed Captain Ghassal was doing the right thing. He had tried to reason with the Crown Valide but she had wanted to try to protect every Percherese life at the expense of her own. "Majesty, they are following their own hearts now. They have served the Zar faithfully and they love Percheron. We must allow them to fight for what they believe in."

"Well, I do not flatter myself in believing they fight for my life, Bin," she said, distracted, her voice filled with despair. "I admire them but they are all going to die. Look, already the enemy is winning. See how the Galinseans use their shields as one to protect each other."

He could see it. The enemy moved carefully, slowly, shields interlocked to protect one another. With this strategy they would get numbers through and into the markets, where there was instant cover afforded them. The Percherese archers would become useless from the moment the Galinseans broke through and found protection.

Bin nodded. "Majesty, it's important to the men that they die bravely. Laying down arms is not courageous, no matter how senseless you believe their deaths to be."

She sighed. "Let us continue to the throne room, then. We can watch the carnage from there if we must."

Bin bowed as the first wafts of smoke and the burning of Percheron assaulted him. He blinked back tears and wished Spur Lazar were here to guide the men toward their heroic deaths.

Lazar closed his eyes and rode the tide of Ana's pain through the screams as she worked to expel their son.

"Check him," she begged, exhausted. "He is tearing me in two."

Lazar laid her back gently and moved gingerly around her, lifting her robes to expose the heart-hammering sight of the baby's head. He remembered moments from his childhood during which doctors had rushed out to tell his father of his mother's progress with her deliveries. So this is what they meant. "His head is crowning," he murmured.

"That's appropriate." She laughed bitterly through her agony. "I have to push again. He's going to break me, so expect blood."

Break her? "Let's get him out, Ana. Be brave."

"Be ready," she gasped, "here comes a big one, make sure you catch him," and then she was lost on another huge shriek as she used all her energy to push her son toward his father.

"Push, Ana, push," he called above her groans.

Lazar watched the delicate skin tear as the baby's head fully emerged.

"Twist him slightly," Ana begged through gasps. "Help turn his shoulders to ease him out."

Lazar obeyed. The steaming warmth of the beautiful child and its perfect, soft skin touched his heart, setting off an unexpected wave of emotion. He had thought it was Ana he was worried about and realized now that his heart was also hammering for his son, this tiny bloodied bundle that was twisting gently into his waiting hands.

"Are his shoulders out?" Ana stammered breathlessly.

"Just about. One more push, Ana."

She found the strength and bore down desperately as the baby turned and then almost shot into his hands, an angry rush of bright red blood following.

"He's here, Ana, he's here." Lazar wept, unable to control his emotion. "You've done it."

He held the baby in the air as the pillars chimed their joy and Luc took his first breath, letting it out in a cry of surprise.

Colors of every hue bounced off the rocky walls and chiming music rang out, echoing around the chamber, as Lyana's pillars welcomed their precious child into the world.

Lazar lay the baby onto its mother's breast and wept with her.

"The pillars asked me to call him Luc," he whispered into her ear beneath the cacophony of light and joy.

"Then Luc he shall be," she mouthed back. He noticed that she looked wan and exhausted.

"What now?"

"You must cut him free of me. Over by that rock ledge where

we came in is a small sack. Look for it. Arafanz left it there—it has a blade amongst other practical things, I think."

"But what—"

"Just get the sack. We must cut him free."

Lazar did as she asked, returning with what was little more than a large pouch. Inside he found the blade, as well as a needle, thread, a bandage, and some salve.

"Cut him close. Here," she pointed. "Then tie it off with the thread. Soon I will expel the afterbirth."

Lazar was bewildered by her knowledge. "How do you know all of this?"

The pillars had quietened, were now just throbbing their color and softly chiming, as though listening to them.

"I've watched many a goat give birth in my time," she murmured, almost dreamily. "And Arafanz explained what would need to be done."

"He intended to help you deliver, didn't he?" Lazar couldn't help the tone of jealousy as he took out the blade that was wrapped in a cloth.

"Arafanz intended to help me deliver, yes, but he also planned to steal my son immediately and take him to Percheron. Use the cloth to wipe the blade with what you find in that vial so that the knife is clean before you cut the cord."

Lazar looked at her, suddenly awkward. "I have been given the same instructions by the pillars."

"They asked you to take my child from me?"

"Not from you. They want our son moved to Percheron straightaway, though. They feel he alone can prevent the war."

"I don't see how," she moaned softly. "I feel so weak," she added.

Lazar only now noticed the steady trickle of blood from between her legs. "Let's get the baby separated. I think you can begin healing once you're free of each other."

"You'll need to sew me down there, Lazar. I know I'm broken."

"We'll worry about that soon. Here, I've cleaned the blade."

"Then just follow my instructions. I need to close my eyes for a while." She made an involuntary sound of pleasure. "He suckles. And he's so quiet."

"He is the most beautiful thing ever created. He is his mother all over again."

She closed her eyes as she smiled at Lazar's comment. He hated to disturb the peaceful scene and took another moment or two to etch this picture of Ana and Luc in his mind, both breathing softly, their eyes closed, their oneness intoxicating before he made the cut.

He was alarmed by the amount of blood and watched carefully, waiting for it to be staunched.

"Lazar, don't pull, but keep the cord taut," Ana said softly. "My womb is pulling tight again. It's getting ready for me to help push out the afterbirth."

He nodded, feeling frightened. "All right. Like this?"

"Yes."

As the placenta came free, suddenly mother and baby were rid of the life-giving bond that had joined them and sustained each other during the pregnancy.

"Do I bury this?"

"No. Leave it. The pillars want it."

Lazar felt a wave of revulsion. "Why?"

"I don't know. A part of Lyana's incarnation, perhaps," she said wearily.

"What can I do for you?"

"Nothing. Perhaps some water if you're strong enough now to crawl back through the tunnel. There is a fresh spring at the back of the original cave and a bowl nearby that Arafanz used. Look for it. Come carefully with it, for I have a terrible thirst."

"I'll be back quickly."

"Lazar, wait!"

"What, my love?"

"Will you kiss me once more?"

"There will be plenty of time for that when—"

"Please," she begged.

And he did, kneeling low to touch his lips gently to hers, a hand helplessly reaching toward the softly moaning Luc as he slept at his mother's breast.

"I love you," she whispered. "Never forget that, will you?"

He frowned at her sadly. She must be very tired if she was getting so sentimental. He kissed her again, and then, glad to be useful, he bounded away.

Ellyana had been watching and felt intense relief when she heard the boy's first cry. He was strong. He could survive, and Lazar would, if he unlocked his own secrets, get the child back to Percheron, fulfilling both father's and son's roles.

But Ana's role was over now. She moved swiftly, gracefully across to the plinth, where the pillar murmured a soft welcome.

Ana heard their chimes and her eyes opened. She was not surprised, it seemed, to see the crone.

"Ellyana. It was your presence I felt."

"Yes, dear one. I did not wish to interrupt."

"He is safe."

"Do you mean your son or the man you love?"

Ana smiled sadly. "I think they are now one in my mind."

"The boy is robust."

"You're taking him away from me, aren't you?"

"Lazar must."

"Please, I—"

"Ana, beloved one. It is your time."

Ana stared at her for several long moments before a tear escaped, rolling down the side of her cheek to splash on the rock on which she lay. The rock seemed to absorb the moisture, thanking her with a soft chime through the pillars.

"Must I?"

Ellyana nodded sorrowfully. "I'm afraid so. You are losing a lot of blood. Lazar has noticed."

"But he doesn't understand."

"No. But I don't think we should make this any more traumatic than it already must be. Time is short. I have come to collect you. We need what you have."

"I didn't want to believe it."

"Believe it," Ellyana replied. "The pillars do not lie to you."

"Can I not say good-bye?" she begged.

"You already did. To prolong it would simply be cruel. He will never understand and he still has a long journey and some challenges ahead of him before we can be sure he has fulfilled his role. Best we just do this now. All you have to do is take my hand."

"My son, he—"

"The pillars protect him. They always will. You must let him go. Lazar will find him and Lyana's work will continue."

"Ellyana, why can't Lazar and I be together?"

"Because you are dying, dear one. And we must do what we

must do before you pass away. It was always going to be like this. Did the pillars not tell you?"

"Yes. But they are ambiguous in how they speak to me and I didn't want to believe what I thought they were conveying. I hoped I was wrong."

"Come, sweet Ana. Lyana needs you, but not here."

Ana raised herself and looked at the mess beneath her, clutching her son, who stirred and whimpered. "I will bleed out before we can do this."

"I will not allow that. We have come too far, been too cunning. And now we really must go. Maliz is not dead, and although he is now distracted, he will feel the arrival of his powers once they are triggered. We must be nowhere that he can find us."

Ana began to cry. She carefully took Ellyana's hand and felt a spike of energy pass between all three of them.

"She is amongst us, Ana," Ellyana soothed, tears in her eyes. "We are nearly there. For her sake, you must now let him go."

She watched with a deep sadness as the young woman—still too young to be facing motherhood, let alone death from it—kissed her baby tenderly. "Grow strong, Luc. Love your father and ask him about me. You must know how much we loved each other to understand how much I love you. Forgive me for leaving you." She kissed him again, long and softly, weeping as she did so, her tears touching his soft downy hair, golden and glinting beneath the pillars' colors.

"Place him down, Ana. Lazar comes."

"Where are we going?"

"Back to where you came from. We go into the Samazen that protects the Mother."

"She cannot protect me any longer."

"She will take you gently to your death. You are giving her what she wants and she will always look after those you have loved."

"I never said good-bye to Pez."

"Iridor will feel your passing. He will know you said farewell. Come now, someone awaits us outside."

Ana took one final glance at her gurgling son before, stooped and feeling close to death already, she allowed Ellyana to help her down from the plinth and remove her robes.

"You don't need these anymore," Ellyana whispered, changing into the beautiful young woman Pez had first met in the harem when she had posed as a bundle woman. "Here, I can carry you now, child." And Ana fell into the woman's arms, feeling herself borne away, as if by magic, into the sands.

Lazar struggled down the narrow tunnel, desperately trying to keep the water from overbalancing. Ana would appreciate the cool, refreshing feeling of its sweetness slipping down her throat. And it would help her to feed their boy. He couldn't imagine how they were supposed to travel back to Percheron as swiftly as the pillars had demanded, but at least Farim was still there in the cave opening, much to his surprise and pleasure. He had stolen a moment to stroke her velvet muzzle, thanking her for being so faithful.

He had just emerged from the shaft when the cry of his son grabbed his attention. Startled, he noticed the child was alone on the plinth, crying wretchedly. Where could Ana have gone? And how could she have gone anywhere, bleeding like she was? He felt a surge of happiness at the thought that the bleeding must have stopped. She had probably moved somewhere away from the plinth to relieve herself.

"Ana?" he called. "I'm back with your delicious water. Where are you?"

Apart from the child's fresh cries, he received no answer.

Frowning deeply now, he put the water down and ran to the plinth to pick up their son. It was only then he noticed the robe cast away on the ground. *Ana had undressed? Whatever for?*

He must have muttered this aloud without realizing it, for the pillars answered. *The Mother has gone.*

"Gone?"

Taken.

He stared at their pulsing colors.

Her robe has been left for the child. Wrap him up in it for when you leave.

"Leave? I'm not leaving without Ana. Where has she been taken?"

Away, the pillars chimed, irritating him now. The baby was mewling, determined to win his attention, and he capitulated, bending to gently pick up his son, soothing him with soft words, surprised he could divorce the anger he was suddenly feeling at Ana's disappearance. He strode over to where the robe was carelessly left and wrapped his boy in its soft linen that was stained with Ana's blood.

That was it, that's what was wrong. He whipped around, marched back up to the plinth. "This area was all bloodied just moments ago. Who cleaned it?"

This is an altar. We have absorbed what the Mother left us.

"The afterbirth, it was here, it was—"

We have consumed that also. It is now part of the temple.

Lazar knew there was little point in raging at colorful pillars that speak, but still he did. "This is outrageous. Where is Ana?" The baby began to cry again at his yelling.

Be calm for the child, the pillars cautioned. *It is almost time.*

"For what?"

Ana is about to die.

"What?" he roared. He lost his breath, felt as though he was suddenly seeing double. He looked quickly for something to lean against lest he fall and hurt Luc, and he chose a pillar—it was the least they could do. "You must explain, I beg you."

Ana is dying, Lazar. She was dying from the moment her labors began. You must not blame yourself or anyone. This was Lyana's plan.

"Her plan? Her plan?" he demanded, ignoring the child's squalls now. "She is killing her?"

No, they chimed in their irritatingly soothing way. *She is simply dying. The birth of the Goddess was always going to claim her life. You must not blame the child. Take your son, Lazar. He must go to Percheron and lay claim to the throne immediately. The war has begun and the Percherese are dying, the city is burning. There is nothing more you can do here. Take Luc and go. Ah, the time is here. Watch.*

And at that moment the pillars exploded into iridescent white light, blinding Lazar. They burned so bright they looked to be on fire.

"What is happening?" Lazar called, closing his eyes tightly, holding his son close in Ana's bloodied robe.

The Mother is dead.

"Ana? You mean—"

Ana has died with your name on her lips.

Lazar lost all sense of who he was for the next few moments. All he was aware of was the newborn cradled to his chest and the heartrending sound he knew passed through the child as he let his grief rip forth angrily, throwing back his head, falling helplessly to his knees, and howling his despair. Together, father and son, light blazing all about them, cast their sorrow to the heavens. Lazar felt all the anger that he connected with Ana's ill-treatment well up and overflow like a poison through his body. And through his howls of pain he felt the old scar at his heart tear and finally rip open to loose all the bitterness of his life; everything he had kept private and closed up inside the vault of his heart exploded outward. He saw stars as he hurled his desolation at Lyana, the target of his wrath. And in that desolation he found new words with which to curse her. Ancient words. He threw them at her now, spitting them as if they were daggers to wound. He hardly understood the words, and yet, deep within his heart, he knew he did comprehend them and that they were not words of injury but of an ancient summoning as he shattered a centuries-old curse.

He was answered, but not by anyone he expected.

Lazar! came Beloch's voice. *We hear you. See through our eyes.*

And suddenly Lazar was looking through Beloch's eyes, seeing what the giant could witness from his vantage, and he saw Percheron burning.

The Samazen had died suddenly. One minute the sands had been raging about him, if slightly diminished in their intensity from when he had escaped with Ganya, but now they had quietened to nothing more than soft eddies here and there. No longer was the wind screaming, or his face being lashed by the grit. And in that exact moment as the Samazen died, Maliz felt a pulse of power surge through Ashar's body, so strong that it knocked him off the camel. He laughed from the soft landing that the sand afforded him and the laughter turned to a demonic howl of delight.

Here it was! Lyana had been incarnated. And he understood now. It had been the child. The child that Ana had been carrying was Lyana all along, hiding and biding her time. It all suddenly made sense. Ana had been found, unbelievably surviving a Samazen because she was the mother-to-be of Lyana. He could kick himself for being so dull as to not see this long before the event. He could have killed Ana on so many occasions, and yet, like all those she met, he had been seduced somewhat by her innocence and delicious charm. She had never been Lyana but she had hidden the Goddess and he could not help but marvel at the complexity of this battle.

And so there was now a baby, no doubt being secreted away somewhere. But he would find it. Everyone believed the child to be an heir and hadn't Herezah told him that her crone Yozem had done a blood reading and assured her that Ana's child would be a boy? He staggered to his feet, still laughing. Lyana was going to hide beneath the skin of a male once again. That old trick! He loved it—she'd tried it only once before. Very clever indeed but he would get to that Zar. He would keep changing bodies until he could reach the child somehow. He could feel all the otherworldly power at his fingertips suddenly. Now he could do what he wanted. He no longer needed the camel to travel. He no longer needed to eat, to drink. He was finally fully the demon Maliz.

He fled in the direction of Percheron, using his magics to transport himself and leaving the beast to wander the sands. He would lie in wait for the arrival of Spur Lazar, who he was now absolutely sure would take custody of the Zar now that he knew the boy was his. It was going to be such a pleasure to deal with Lazar and then he would destroy the boy and any hopes of those who believed the Goddess could ever find her way back into the hearts of the people.

Iridor felt it; it was double-edged. First, a strong painful pulse of power that seemed to throb through him. It wasn't his power, though, and it didn't remain with him but instead passed through him. He recognized it from a deep-rooted ancient wisdom, a knowledge etched in his soul somewhere that made him instinctively know that it was Lyana, becoming incarnate. Ana's baby had been born. The second feeling, equally painful, was a deep sense of loss that he didn't understand but realized must coincide with the sudden diminishing of the Samazen.

Iridor had no way of confirming what had occurred but he suspected this was connected with Ana, whose very existence seemed to be in harmony with the Samazen. He felt a flicker of worry. It was time to leave Arafanz's fortress. He would wait and see if he could find out what had happened to his friends—hopefully everyone had remained safe even though they had been incarcerated. As he took his first tentative steps from beneath the rock ledge, he heard a commotion outside and instantly leaped to a vantage from where he could see what was occurring. To his surprise he saw Arafanz, normally so calm and tidy, looking disheveled and stirred up, shouting at his men as they ran toward the place where the camels were stored. And Arafanz's clothes looked to be singed. What could have happened? There was no sign of Ana, Lazar, of Boaz or Ganya . . . and there was certainly no sign of a baby. And yet Iridor could feel it in his very soul that the child had been born. That pulse of power confirmed it. So why were Arafanz and his men now leaping onto camels—whom were they pursuing?

He meant to find out.

Lazar watched, dumbstruck, as his precious Percheron burned. He could hear the screams, he could see his father's war galley proudly flying the royal pennant, and his gut twisted at the sight.

Show me the palace, he groaned. *What do you see?*

Beloch moved his gaze. *People are out on the balconies.*

Lazar could see. *Surely they're not watching the enemy, leaving themselves so open?*

No, I think they're watching my brother and me.

Why?

Beloch switched his view back across the Faranel and suddenly, impossibly, Ezram came into Lazar's sights. Except Ezram was made of flesh, his complexion no longer gray stone but ruddy and real. Lazar could see the individual hairs in his black beard and the dark blue of his eyes. *What . . . what's this?* he stammered, convinced he was seeing something that wasn't there. He shook his head.

This, Spur Lazar, is my brother, Ezram. You made us free with your summoning that revoked the spell of Maliz, may his soul rot in the eternal gloom of Lyana's depths!

Wait, Lazar begged. *You are both real?*

We always were, the deep voice boomed. *We were simply trapped by magic. Ah, here comes Crendel,* and Beloch looked skyward.

The winged lion?

Who else? We are all made whole with the summoning.

I can't . . . I can't—

Spur Lazar. Beloch's voice sounded like a growl. *We have no time for this. Gather your wits. There is a battle unfolding before us. Percherese are dying by the dozens. What do you wish from us?*

All right, just give me a moment. I can hardly take this in. How close are the Galinseans?

From what I can tell, they have breached the bazaar. The spice markets are burning. They will be up to the palace within a very short while.

Can you see the Protectorate?

Some, yes. They are trying to maintain their advantage on the hills but it won't work for them much longer. They have wasted a lot of arrows on the bazaar but the Galinseans have too much cover there. They can wait them out, strike at night, if necessary.

It's Ghassal's inexperience. But even he is not to blame. They should be firing burning torches at their galleys. The Galinseans will not want to be stranded in Percheron, not with their king and queen in tow.

We can smash their boats, he heard Ezram say with glee.

Lazar could hardly believe what he was hearing but it was a good plan. *Do it. But save the royal galley. Destroy the other boats. Then, Ezram, go up to the palace—you can move your legs?*

Of course! came the indignant reply.

Excellent. Protect the palace and all within its courtyards. Presumably the Crown Valide has called as many people behind the walls as possible. Either way, get there after the boats have been dealt with and put out those city fires as best you can.

I'm going, Ezram said, and Lazar marveled to see through Beloch's eyes as the twin giant started wading toward the war galleys, mere toys next to his enormous stature.

And while my brother has all the fun?

Come and get me, Lazar said, his sorrows put aside for the moment whilst his anger came flooding back. And in his anger he found calm, a place to hide his grief. *Can you find me?*

Easily.

How long?

At a run? Minutes.

Amazing, Lazar breathed. *Can Crendel be spared?*

Surely.

I need him to fly over the western section of the Empty. I've a strong feeling that Arafanz will be coming to Percheron.

He is not our enemy.

But he is mine. Tell Crendel this is what I want.

I will tell him.

Can Shakar come, too?

Soon enough.

I presume that he is controllable?

Utterly. He is a disciple of Lyana—as we all are.

Leave word for him to help Ezram. He can torch any of the galleys—or what's left of them. No timber is to be salvaged, but leave my father's ship untouched. He should do a fly over the islands. Sink, burn, destroy any Galinsean ships they've left as spare. And, Beloch?

Yes.

Feel free to frighten any Galinseans before you leave. He heard the deep rumble of the giant's laughter. *He's not dead,* Lazar added, and knew this comment needed no explanation.

I know.

Ana is. He couldn't imagine how he could bring himself to utter those words. But he was looking at Luc, the future of Percheron and Galinsea, who looked so like Ana. Vengeance would drive him now. Grieving must wait.

I felt it. I also felt Lyana. She has risen.

I am bringing her with me. Hurry.

They had been on their way down to the palatial Grand Salon when a massive sound thundered around the bay. Running to a nearby balcony, Bin instinctively taking Herezah's arm, they raced outside to see what new threat confronted them. It was beyond belief as Herezah watched the two enormous giants who had guarded Percheron's harbor for centuries slough away the stone that had formed them. Her hand went to her throat.

"Bin, am I imagining this?" she whispered over the cracking and roaring.

"No, Your Majesty," he replied, his voice equally shaken. "The giants are coming to life."

"How can this be?"

Bin simply shook his head in bafflement. Herezah didn't expect an answer; she just stared, giving herself over to her amazement, unaware that all the soldiers on both sides had also stopped their activities and had turned toward the harbor.

"They're alive," she murmured. "Look, they have skin and hair and they are moving. What are they going to do? Are they planning to kill us, do you think?"

"I can't imagine their purpose, Majesty. I can't actually believe this is happening. I'm waiting to wake from this strange dream."

"They seem to be talking to each other."

"Zarab, save us!"

"What now?"

"The winged lion comes!"

"This is impossible . . . impossible," Herezah moaned.

"Crown Valide, if nothing else, it has stopped the fighting."

"Look, Bin! The giant is moving away now."

"That one's Ezram."

"How do you know?"

"The legend says he was the one with wavy hair."

"You know your history tales. Oh Zarab! Look!"

And together they watched Ezram pick up a war galley as though it were a toy, crushing it into splinters of wood. Herezah clung to Bin, fear mingling with joy that blended with amazement. Another doomed ship met its fate at the giant's hands and his twin began to wade forward, approaching the city.

"Beloch comes," Bin warned. "We're next!"

They watched the Galinsean army scatter in a hundred directions as the giant stepped out onto the foreshore. He was huge, far bigger than he looked from a distance, and his voice boomed across the city.

"People of Percheron," he roared. "You are safe. We will protect you. Galinseans, beware. Lay down your weapons or you will all die. Crendel, the winged lion, is looking for fresh meat," he warned. "And his sister, Darso, is prowling the streets. She will kill anyone who is armed. Heed my warning. Cast aside your weapons. The Galinseans are to gather here on the beach. Any of the enemy who does not arrive quietly, unarmed, will be killed swiftly. Every warship but that flying the royal pennant will be sunk. I suggest you get all of your people off the ships and onto shore quickly. Leave your king on board his galley. He is safe for the time being by order of Prince Lucien of Galinsea, also known as Spur Lazar in Percheron . . ."

"Lazar? Lazar controls them!" Herezah said, excited. "Bin, you heard the giant. We're safe," she added, hardly able to hear herself over the giant's rumbling voice but unable to prevent her relief from spilling over.

". . . will decide your fate upon his return to the city shortly. Crown Valide, do you hear me?"

Herezah felt her throat catch with terror. She didn't know whether to wave, drawing his attention, or to simply prostrate herself on the balcony.

"I know you see and hear me, Crown Valide. Spur Lazar will be among you very soon. Ezram will guard the palace. Do not be afraid of him. He will protect all Percherese, will not permit another drop of their blood to be spilled. Now I must go."

And with that, the giant strode away, back around the peninsula to avoid treading on the city. They watched in silence as he finally stepped up onto land in the foothills, each step covering what Herezah imagined would be the equivalent of a day's ride. A stunned silence blanketed the city for a few moments whilst Percherese and Galinseans alike did their best to absorb what had just occurred.

Ezram's voice broke the eerie quiet. It was an octave lower than his brother's and terrified all who heard it.

"Galinseans! You heard Beloch's orders. Do not test me, I am not as patient as my twin."

And Galinsean soldiers began to stream down the hillside toward the beach, herded by a swooping winged lion who watched their progress from overhead, and by his sister, who sent them screaming from the alleyways of the bazaar.

34

Iridor flew after the riders, his keen night sight a boon. The Razaqin seemed to be filled with a fire in their collective belly with Arafanz leading the charge in the direction of Percheron.

Iridor had never before seen camels driven this hard or fast. The beasts could only gallop for a short burst. The riders would have to slow them down very soon, he guessed. It was easy from this height to keep them in view, however, and he was not worried about losing them. With that security he allowed his mind to wander to what he had felt earlier.

He was now convinced that Lyana had arisen but with that joyous feeling had come a sense of loss, and he believed now that something might have happened to Ana. The longer he flew toward Percheron, the more he worried about it, and the more convinced he became that Ana had died in giving birth to the Goddess.

By the time he reached this conclusion, he had fallen into a deeply maudlin mood, one that resonated deeply, reminding him of something that had gone before . . . many times.

The men below him were slowing and he needed to look for cover among the dunes. They would surely stop to rest the animals and wait for full dawn. Taking cover behind a dune, he decided in his misery that Maliz was nowhere close; he should risk talking to Lazar.

With a hollow feeling of dread he opened up the link.

Lazar?

Iridor! I was just about to try to talk with you.

Were you? How?

It seems I can at will now. If I can talk to the giants, surely I can talk to you.

What are you talking about?

Listen. Time is short. We got away during the Samazen. Ana and I found safety in a cave that is special to Lyana. Don't interrupt; it is all bad news, just let me say it. Iridor wanted to stop Lazar but he remained silent and allowed the misery to wash over him. *Ana is dead. She has also been stolen from me.*

Dead? No, that's not right. That can't be, Lazar! I go first. I always go first!

Lazar ignored him. *The only thing I can think of is that El-lyana took her whilst I was fetching Ana some water. I found her robe discarded. She had been bleeding badly. It seemed unnatural bleeding but what would I know about childbirth? The baby is safe. A boy. He looks like his mother. And for him alone I keep going.*

I didn't say good-bye, I didn't—

Neither did I. She was alive, she asked me to kiss her. Only she knew it was her time. Don't make this harder than it is. I am bringing my son to Percheron.

Iridor had to set aside his grief momentarily. *You will be days, then, I am—*

Not days, minutes, I'm told. That's what I'm trying to tell you. Beloch is coming for me.

Beloch the giant?

One and the same. He has broken free of the spell that cast him in stone. Both he and his brother were, when I last spoke, about to wreak havoc on the Galinseans, who, incidentally, have begun their attack on Percheron.

How is Beloch free?

I freed both giants. I'm still not sure how. All I know is that Beloch is coming to find me and the boy and will take us back to Percheron.

What about Maliz? What happened in the fortress and where is Boaz?

He heard Lazar sigh. *I have little time, so I shall not try to say this with care. Here are the facts. Maliz possessed Boaz.*

What? Iridor nearly overbalanced. *How?*

I don't know. It happened and it's irrelevant now because the Zar is dead.

Dead, Iridor echoed bleakly. *You're sure?*

Yes, because I killed him.

You . . .

I had to. Maliz had already murdered the Boaz you remember and had claimed his body.

And where is Maliz now? Iridor asked, his tone bitter.

I am guessing but I think he moves in the body of Salim's son, Ashar.

And Ganya. Have you left her behind?

Ganya went with Ashar. She thought she was with her brother.

Lazar's sorrowful tone said enough and Iridor remained silent. Lazar pushed the conversation forward. *Where are you?*

Following Arafanz. He's ridden out toward Percheron.

He probably thinks that's where we instinctively headed. Well, I'll be there before him in all likelihood. Fly home, stay safe. I'll see you in Percheron.

Lazar, my friend. I have never been safe.

What do you mean?

Iridor never survives the battle.

But you have! You're alive. All you have to do is get to Percheron. It's two days at most for you.

Iridor said nothing. His mood had slipped deeper into despair.

Iridor?

I'd like to have met your son.

You will. Iridor didn't reply and Lazar, distracted, didn't seem to notice. *I must go out of the cave now and show myself so Beloch can see me.*

Iridor looked up with wonder as he saw Beloch thundering across the desert in the distance. *I see him, Lazar! A wondrous sight. Lyana has indeed risen.*

Get home, Iridor.

Farewell, Lazar. I am proud to call you friend.

Get ahold of yourself! You will meet your Goddess soon.

I don't think so—at least not in the way you think, Iridor murmured as he closed the link and became aware of the terrified sounds of the men who had also seen the giant in the gentle light of the approaching dawn. He could hear them scrambling for their camels, and when he peeked over the dune, he could see Arafanz wearing a triumphant look, his arms raised in the air.

"They walk!" he yelled. "The giants roam the land again. Lyana be praised!"

Iridor wished he could tell Arafanz who was responsible for the giants' reincarnation but he suspected he had not much time left. He wondered how death would find him and he hoped it would be swift.

It was.

He had lifted into the air behind Arafanz's group with every intention of veering away from them, to look for Maliz. He had nothing more to lose; his work was done. Lyana had risen. It was time. He had no idea why he cast the thought: *Take me, Mother, my work is done.*

As he did so, he heard a screech and felt all the air knocked from his lungs. He felt himself tumbling, falling. He didn't struggle; he heard Ellyana's voice in his mind.

Come to us, brave Iridor. Your work is truly done.

He just had time to register that a falcon had attacked him on the wing. Iridor died before he hit the desert ground, clutched in the claws of a falcon that had the distinctive sign of a sword branded on his beak.

Lazar could feel the thunderous steps of Beloch before he saw the daunting figure of the giant lurch into view. He was moving at a slow run and the dunes were trembling the sand from their tops in tandem with his powerful tread.

I'm here. Lazar spoke across a link he had opened.

I know. I am drawn to this place by Lyana's presence. She has a temple here.

She does. It is beautiful.

I shall never see it but I see you down there. You are with a child. Here, let us see if I can pick you both up gently.

As the giant bent, he sighed sadly and went down on one knee, rubbing his eyes.

What's wrong, Beloch?

Did you not feel it?

Feel what?

Iridor. He is dead.

Lazar staggered in his approach to the giant beneath the searing sun. *That can't be. I . . . I was just speaking with him.*

Listen, Beloch said. *With your mind,* he added.

And Lazar heard the voices of Ezram and the animals in his head as they shared their grief.

They all felt it, Beloch confirmed. *He is gone from us.*

How? Why? Lazar moaned.

I do not know. I feel only his loss.

Why don't I sense it?

The giant shrugged. *Protection, perhaps. Of all of us disciples, you have had to cope with constant sorrow. It may be that Lyana does not connect you to all of us at once as a means of saving you the pain of the loss.*

I didn't feel Ana die either. I had to be told by Lyana's sentinels.

Beloch nodded. *Lyana has had to become extremely secretive.*

Pez is gone, Lazar murmured, his tone deeply mournful. *Everyone I love or have called friend is dead.*

You have the baby—I presume it is what we have all fought to protect?

This is my son, Luc, as named by Lyana.

And is he also Lyana?

Ana and I believed so.

The giant's tone softened as he stared intently at the child. *Then Luc is more precious than anything you've ever had to protect. Let us get him away from this desolation. He needs caring.*

He needs a wet nurse.

I shall have you both back in the city in minutes.

Should we look for Maliz, or Arafanz?

They will find you, I'm sure. We must get the infant to safety and nourishment and out of this heat. And you are also needed back there to take command.

Let us go, then, Lazar said, marveling that from this height, cradled in the giant's hand, he could already see the minarets of Percheron and the smoke billowing from the city.

Looks as though Shakar has arrived, Beloch said, *giving a small twitch of a smile. He can be quite excitable, starting fires left and right. It's definitely time for us to get back.*

Herezah had celebrated prematurely. No sooner had she finished helplessly hugging Bin at the extraordinary turn of events than she realized that Lazar's help had come too late.

Secure in the knowledge that Ezram was dealing with the war galleys and would shortly assume guard around the palace, she had made her way quickly to the Grand Salon to prepare for Lazar's arrival only to discover that a small band of Galinseans had fought its way in. She knew they were Galinsean not by their clothes, for each had donned the traditional street wear of the Percherese, but by the man who stood at their front: Falza.

It took all of her years of training in composure and every ounce of her courage to remain calm. "King Falza," she said evenly, dipping her head. Beside her, she felt Bin freeze.

Herezah regretted asking the Elim to offer special assistance to the Protectorate for the people's protection around the palace. Although none had been happy to leave their posts, there were no longer harem members to keep safe, Herezah had argued, as the girls were among the people, posing as ordinary citizens. The four Elim left behind to guard her had obviously been killed, for they were nowhere to be seen. She was not going to escape death on the end of Falza's sword, she realized.

She had nothing to lose other than pride and she was certainly not giving that to the barbarian. She sneered instead. "I'm sorry I couldn't find it within myself to give in meekly to your threats."

"But I'm not sorry that I no longer consider it inappropriate to make war on a woman. You have brought this upon yourself."

"You are aware of what is going on outside, aren't you, King Falza? Or have you been too long fighting within the palace to know that your war is already lost? Your son takes command as we speak." She noticed his frown of query. And laughed at him. "Oh my, you don't know? Send your men to look outside. The Grand Salon has no lower windows, they'll have to go to one of the many balconies that face out to the Faranel. Check your ships, check your so-called war."

Falza's eyes narrowed as he regarded her.

"This is no trick," she said. "My aide, Bin, will show them. He is unarmed, as you can see."

Falza gestured to two of his men to secure the doors and one to go with Bin. They waited in silence until the Galinsean soldier returned, babbling about strange creatures roaming the city.

Herezah laughed. "If you can make any sense from him, do so; otherwise, we'll be happy to tell you."

The King slapped his man, berating him in his own guttural language. The man slipped to his knees, contrite, tried to tell his monarch. But he seemed to fail as Falza kicked him aside. "What is going on?"

"He's too shocked to explain. I can understand that. Frankly,

I'm baffled, too. You may recall, King Falza, that Percheron's bay is guarded by two famed twin stone giants, Beloch and Ezram."

"So?"

"Well, it seems they are no longer formed of stone but are flesh and blood, and the new protectors of Percheron. They answer to your son alone."

Falza stared at her for several long seconds before barking a command to his men. He strode from the room, returning soon enough, and Herezah could see how hard the King of Galinsea fought to tamp down his fright.

"Surprised? We were. But they're on our side. Let me acquaint you with their demands." She told him quickly what the giants had ordered. "That's why you see none of your men on the hillside or streaming into the palace. They're not cowards, Falza, they're sensible. Beloch told them that every last person found armed would be killed, Percherese or Galinsean, it mattered not. No man with any weapon is a match for these two. And I'm not sure if you had time to notice but they are not alone. They have friends. Do you need me to list them? There's Crendel and Darso, as well as—"

"I know who will be with them," he cut across her words, regaining his composure. "And I don't care."

"Oh?" She felt a fresh wave of fear tingle through her. He had nothing to lose, it was true. The war with Percheron was lost but his grief and need for revenge throbbed on. "How do you see this ending, Falza?"

"It ends with your death. Queen for queen."

"But I am not a queen."

"Oh, but I can see it in your eyes, Crown Valide. Slave, whore, whatever others see you as, you see yourself only as royalty."

"And what does my death solve under these circumstances?"

she asked, begging inwardly that the giants' promise to deliver Lazar swiftly would be honored. He was her only hope now.

"It will give me the satisfaction of avenging my wife's murder."

"And then what? Do you think you'll be permitted to sail back to Romea?"

"I expect to die here. In this room, probably."

"Then don't, Falza. Killing me seals your death, and your wife is not alive to thank you for it. I did not kill her. You know that poison was meant for me."

"Then perhaps I fulfill the wishes of your Grand Master Eunuch."

"In which case you would certainly be considered mad."

"So be it," he said, swapping to Galinsean and barking a harsh command.

Bin stepped in front of Herezah as the men suddenly moved. "Wait!" he yelled helplessly.

Falza snapped another order and Bin's throat was slashed a second later. The young man who had guided Herezah in many more ways than as a mere secretary gasped and died in her arms, his blood soaking her charcoal gown. She knew hers would be mingling with it shortly. Herezah wept for him.

Falza no longer waited for his men. He strode to her, kicked Bin's body aside, and grabbed her by her hair, dragging her through her servant's blood. She did not struggle. Nor did she give him the satisfaction of hearing her ask for mercy.

Set me down as close to the palace as you can, Lazar told Beloch. *I'll leave you to control what's happening out here. I must speak with the Crown Valide.*

Beloch nodded. *I will go around and approach the city from the sea.* He leaned down and gently placed his hand on the ground, allowing Lazar to slip down from the height, his son now angrily demanding nourishment. *You'd better see to that wet nurse first,* he suggested.

Beloch.

Yes?

Look to the west. I want to know where Arafanz's people are. I want him alive. Use Crendel and Darso. If the black-robed Razaqin must die, so be it. But keep Arafanz for me.

And then he was running. He knew precisely where he must go. Close to the palace was a home for mothers who lost their babies at birth. It had been set up by the previous Valide, who understood the pain of losing a child, having lost her first two sons. The home gave the mothers a place to convalesce and grieve in quiet. Food and accommodation were provided by the Crown and a small amount of money was sent to each woman's family so that they could manage without her for the days it took for her to feel strong enough to return home. Although it was a place of interminable sorrow, it was also a place of peace. It was where young new mothers who had trouble feeding their newborns often came; here they would find a plentiful contingent of wet nurses, eager to have babies at their breasts.

An older woman greeted him at the door, recognizing him immediately, surprise in her voice. "Spur Lazar? How can I help you?" she asked, frowning at his obvious hurry. "Oh, my stars, you have a baby there?"

"Yes. He's hungry, desperately in need of a feed."

"His mother?" she asked, reaching for Luc.

"She died."

The woman made a sound of sympathy. "Poor mite. And what are you doing with her?"

"Him," he corrected. "His name is Luc. I am his father."

She glanced up at him in fresh surprise, then pursed her lips, stopping whatever comment was about to rush from them. "I see. You need a wet nurse."

"I do. Er, I'm sorry, I don't know your name."

"It's Falip. Wait, let me find someone. Harras, where is that new girl who came in this morning?"

"She is resting."

"Fetch her, would you? Hurry now." On cue Luc began to squall. "You seem in a rush, Spur Lazar. I presume you are needed at the palace, considering what has gone on today."

"And you seem terribly calm, Falip, considering what has gone on today."

She smiled gently and shrugged. "Where could we flee to? Most of the women I care for are grieving. We took our chance, kept faith that all would be well."

His eyes narrowed. She reminded him of Zafira. "You follow Lyana?"

"Not openly," she admonished. "We respect the religion of the god. I simply choose to keep my faith with the Mother. She is, after all, what my vocation is about."

"I, too, Falip. I love Lyana with all my heart," he said, handing over his precious son with great relief into the old woman's arms.

She beamed at him. "That pleases me, Spur. Ah, here she comes. Alzaria, this is Spur Lazar. He could use your help with this infant. Are you happy to feed the child? I know you're tired but you are also heavy with milk. Perhaps—"

"Yes, I would like to," the young woman replied. She looked at Lazar, her dark eyes wide and curious, but he could see how haggard she was.

"Are you sure you're well enough?" He glanced at Falip to be sure.

"Alzaria delivered a stillborn son during the night. If you don't mind, I think it would be very good for her state of mind if you would permit her to nurse Luc."

"Of course." Lazar shrugged, feeling the emptiness of Ana's passing uncoil through him again.

Falip handed Luc to the young woman. "I shall be with you shortly." She patted the woman, gave a glance to Harras. "Go with her. Don't leave her alone with the baby for too long. She mustn't get attached." The aide nodded, bowed silently to Lazar, and left with Alzaria. "Can I offer you something to drink, Spur? You look rather disheveled."

"No, but thank you. I see the immediate panic is passing here—now that we have our giants." He smiled briefly, awkwardly. His frown returned to straighten it.

"How extraordinary it all is. I'm waiting for someone to explain it all to me."

"I don't think there is an explanation, Falip. Now I must go to the palace. I shall send for Luc very shortly, if that's all right?"

"Of course. Alzaria will need a half bell, that's all. He's hungry, I imagine he'll feed greedily and then sleep for many hours."

He took both her hands. "Thank you," he said, never meaning gratitude as deeply as he did at this moment.

"I won't slit your throat, Your Majesty," Falza said, loading the royal title with derision. "You deserve beheading. I shall sit that beautiful head of yours on the throne you so crave for your cowardly son to find when he deigns to return to the realm he is meant to be ruling."

Beheading scared Herezah more than anything. But even so, the fear of the blade crystallized to anger as she glanced again at Bin's corpse. "Do your worst, Falza, and let the history books show that whilst your armies were fleeing from their Percherese pursuers, you brought—what is it, twelve men?—to murder an unarmed woman. How pathetic you are. A greater man would rise above his grief to lead his nation by example. That is why it is such a pity that your son, Lucien, who is more than twice the man you are, has walked away from his realm. As ruler, he would lead Galinsea into a proud era, not a prideful one. Like my son, he is neither coward nor aggressor. Hack my head off, kick it around the room if you will. I will not know and I do not care. I die knowing that Percheron never bowed down to the Galinsean barbarians, that we prevailed against all odds with a prince of Galinsea at our helm and a whore, as you put it, doing her best to hold her people strong."

Falza had sheathed his sword but now he drew it. Its ring chilled Herezah. She begged herself to stay courageous to the last. She prayed that she would live up to her son's hopes, and that somehow Lazar might hear of this, might know that at the end she had not disappointed him.

"I hope you're muttering your prayers, whore," Falza said, raising the sword behind Herezah.

"Move another muscle, Father, and I won't be held responsible to my siblings for the number of pieces I shall cut you into after you're dead."

Everyone looked up to see Lazar and a line of archers with arrows trained on the King standing in the high balustrade windows. Taking advantage of the shocked silence, Lazar swung to the pale marble floor of the Grand Salon on a rope that the archers lowered. "It's so very convenient to have giants on one's side in wartime, don't you think, Father? That's how we all got up there, in case you're wondering. And right now it will take just one word from me to have every one in your army squashed to a pulp. I'm sure you know I'm not lying, if your wrecked and torched fleet is anything to go by." Lazar smiled and Herezah saw nothing but menace in it. She had never seen that expression on the Spur's face before; clearly there was no love lost between the Galinsean King and his heir.

"May I?" Lazar said to his father, the politeness embarrassing suddenly. The King didn't flinch as Lazar bent down to help Herezah to her feet. "Crown Valide, are you hurt?"

She looked into the face she loved, saw a terrible underlying sadness reflected there, but also fury. She had never loved him more than when he was being heroic for her benefit. She felt as though she'd lived a lifetime in the space of the days since he'd left. One of the archers who had scampered down the same rope had opened the main doors, allowing several Elim in. The Galinseans were being helped free of all their weapons.

Everyone waited for her response. She took her time, enjoying the extra moments of holding Lazar's hand.

"A little bruised perhaps," she said, touching a patch on her scalp that had been ripped clean of hair. "Nothing a Percherese slave can't handle. Please, Lazar, ask the Elim to cover Bin's body for me. He died horribly and unnecessarily trying to protect me from your father's men." Lazar nodded, sending a runner to fetch sheets. "He called me Majesty whilst your father calls me whore," Herezah murmured as if to herself. "Thank you," she added, lightly touching his chest but not lingering. "Once again you've saved my life."

Lazar looked toward Falza. "Father, it would be appropriate now for you to apologize for the offense you have given to the

Crown Valide. She was regent for Zar Boaz, was endowed with royal status, and must be treated accordingly. Even a Galinsean barbarian should know that much." His tone was acid.

"I don't apologize to murderers," Falza spat.

"I'm sure you took the first aggressive action."

"I don't refer to our battle, Lucien. I refer to the person responsible for the murder of your mother."

The chamber was suddenly deathly silent. Herezah forced herself to take a deep breath in order to prevent herself from babbling at Lazar as she denied the accusation. "King Falza, you know that is untrue. You were present when the Queen was assassinated." She turned to Lazar, saw how his complexion had blanched at the news. "Forgive us that you hear such sorrowful tidings in this manner, Spur Lazar. Your mother and I met to parley on the Daramo. I made the mistake of taking Grand Master Salmeo. I needed someone I could trust—I realize my folly now but I had no one of status to rely on. Don't look at me like that, Lazar, I give you my word, on the life of my son, that this is the truth. Salmeo tried to poison me. He was serving refreshment; he placed the goblets before us. I offered your mother to have hers tasted. She declined my offer but instead took my goblet and drank from it. She drank the poison Salmeo had intended for me. Your father can deny none of this, for he was present alongside Queen Angeline."

She watched Lazar grind his jaw. "And Salmeo is incarcerated? Or is the worst part of this story yet to be told?"

Herezah nodded, glanced at Falza. "Salmeo escaped. I couldn't send anyone to give chase because your father had declared war. He gave us days to prepare—at least he did that much. Lazar, I am sorry for your mother's death, I truly am. I have already conveyed my deepest regrets to your father. I can't imagine why he'd think I would provoke war when our parley to prevent that very event was under way."

"And with that few days' grace you still chose to stay."

She nodded.

"You knew he would kill you."

"I couldn't run, Lazar."

Lazar turned to the King. "An eye for an eye, Father?"

"Precisely," Falza replied.

"Except you are the first to call our Crown Valide a slave, a whore, not a queen."

"It's what she masquerades as."

"No, I must correct you there. She masquerades as nothing. The Valide knows her place. Until recently she was the mother of the Zar, that is all. The position of Crown Valide was bestowed upon her by her son while he hunted down the man who had stolen his wife and Absolute Favorite. And now, my lord, she is nothing but former Absolute Favorite of Zar Joreb."

Falza frowned. Herezah kept her peace, although a question leaped to her lips. It seemed Falza had the same question, however, and asked it for her.

"She is Crown Valide still, if I'm not mistaken, Lucien?"

Lazar ignored him, turning instead to Herezah. The Crown Valide suddenly no longer wished that question had been posed. "Herezah, forgive me for bringing this harsh news so fast on the heels of everything else you've endured these past days, but Boaz didn't survive."

She stared at Lazar, waiting for him to finish that sentence. "What do you mean?"

"Boaz is dead."

Murmuring erupted among the Elim and the intently listening archers. Even Falza looked stunned.

"He was killed trying to save Ana. I am deeply sorry."

She understood the words but her mind kept rejecting them. "No. No, this can't be right. He was simply going along for the journey. You were meant to keep him from danger. You were—"

"Boaz was a man possessed, Herezah. It is a long story but we were all taken prisoner. The Zar died with courage—as you would imagine—against impossible odds."

"And Ana?" she asked, her voice taut with the despair she was barely controlling.

"She is dead, also."

His tone was flat but she had already seen the sadness in his eyes.

"The child?"

"Alive. A son."

"Where is he?"

"Safe. I shall send for him now. There is something I need to explain to both of you, but especially to my father." Lazar called over one of the Elim, gave instructions to bring the woman Alzaria from the hospice. "Let us all wait until she arrives. I will explain then."

35

Alzaria cradled the infant under Harras's watchful gaze. "He is beautiful," she said, stroking the boy's downy, golden hair.

"Doesn't look like he could be the son of our Zar with that coloring," Harras admitted.

"He's not. It's my understanding this is the Spur's son with the Zar's new wife and Absolute Favorite."

Harras's eyes widened. "What blasphemy is this? Hush your mouth, woman."

"It is true. You can see it yourself. You know this child is no product of the Zar."

Harras flounced to her feet as someone called to her through the open door. "Hurry, clothe yourself. He is done." She left to talk with the person just outside in the hall.

Maliz looked down upon the baby, knowing it was time to leave. Alzaria's role was finished with here. "You are not Lyana after all, are you, Luc? You are merely mortal. An illegitimate spawn of the lusty Spur. I could kill you now, snap your neck, throttle you, and they would be none the wiser. But I rather like that you are a delicious thorn amongst the flowers, proof of the Spur's betrayal. So you are very lucky. I'm going to let you go back to your rightful father and I will now disappear. I have a Goddess to hunt."

"You are wanted up at the palace by the Spur," Harras said, returning to the small chamber.

Maliz shook Alzaria's head. "No. I am not strong enough. You take him. Here," he said, handing her the sleeping bundle. "I might rest a little."

"If you're sure?"

He could see the delight in the helper's eyes. She was going to enjoy the responsibility not only of taking the child up to the palace, but of delivering him into the arms of the handsome, eligible Spur. Maliz smiled inwardly. Lazar would never be any the wiser that the demon had laid hands on his precious son . . . or should he leave a clue? It would be so much fun to leave the Spur with the thought that Maliz had been close enough to cradle the child. "I'm sure. I hope the baby thrives. Please tell the Spur."

"He'll want to compensate you, of course."

"Yes. My real name is Garjan. Will you tell him that?" Maliz shrugged. "I used a different one because I was embarrassed. I'm not married."

"I understand. Where will we find you?"

"I can collect anything from here if you leave it in my name. Garjan . . . you won't forget, will you?"

"No. I must go. You rest," Harras said, hardly able to contain her excitement.

As soon as the woman had left, Maliz climbed through the shutters and disappeared into the bazaar. They would never see Alzaria again. He'd found the stupid slut wandering the spice markets, begging for money, her newborn illegitimate son suckling beneath her worn robes. How could she resist the promise he'd given her, the pouch of money from the young Ashar, as long as she repeated the words he gave her and stuck a blade in him? He had drowned the squealing infant the moment he had become the woman and had made his way to the hospice to lie in wait. He had suspected Lazar would bring the child. Had taken the gamble that a wet nurse would be required. Except Lyana was not here.

She existed. His powers and the giants coming to life were testimony of that. The sight of Ezram standing guard had filled Maliz with dread and his fear had intensified when the giant had only briefly paused as he had cast his formerly potent spell. No turning to stone. Not even a flicker of pain.

Maliz couldn't understand how the giants had been released or how they were resisting his spell-making but their protection was at once ancient and unfamiliar.

How could Lyana be incarnated and not visible? He had not imagined the rush of power; it had filled him with the usual thrill and anticipation of the battle ahead but now it was dwindling. He didn't understand. This was not meant to happen.

Maliz was painfully aware of the heaviness of Alzaria's breasts. The boy had taken little—he had so much more milk to give. It was time to get rid of Alzaria. He needed a new body. He needed to think. He found himself walking the lanes that would lead him to the spice markets and, ultimately, the realm of Percheron's undesirables. The ones Tariq had so long wanted to eradicate, the ones that Zar Boaz wanted to help. This was where he would find weak-willed bodies, eager to take up any offer he gave in exchange for money or food. He had plenty of money that he had stolen from the Grand Vizier's house before he'd gone to the hospice, but it infuriated him that he was back among the slums. He had envisaged himself roaming the palace halls as a Zar by now, planning endless nights of orgy with his young concubines.

But now he would have to resign himself to moving in the body of someone infirm, someone who needed very little of himself. He needed to preserve his power, to return to that state of not being fully committed to a body. The more he walked, the weaker he felt. And it was not the woman's body that was weakening. It was him. His powers were leaking out of him. He knew this feeling. This was the sensation he normally lived through after a battle, when he had defeated Lyana and was required to return to his dormant state.

That was it. He was becoming dormant. What was happening?

Maliz forced Alzaria's legs to run. He did not want to go dormant in her guise, with milk running from her nipples and the likelihood that she would be raped each night when the lowlifes came looking for cheap sexual favors. Running breathlessly now past the eating house, Beloch's Table, he burst through the red door that led into the backstreet slums of the bazaar and looked frantically for a potential donor.

There he was. Covered in sores. Starving, probably younger than he looked, but certainly not as strong as a man of his age should be. He would accept money. He would whimper joyously as he uttered the words Maliz gave him. He would stick a blade in his mother right now for a glass of the amber-colored vinco and a plate of stuffed vine leaves. Maliz did not want to be this man. But he had no choice. He realized with deep dismay and confusion as he regarded his next body that his powers had leached from him as though Lyana no longer existed on the land.

Razeen sat on the plinth, the Crystal Pillars pulsing their colors around him, bathing him in light and warmth.

"My father never knew I knew of this place."

We are sorry that you were forced to keep this secret from him.

All Lyana's disciples have keenly felt the strain of not knowing who is friend or foe, of not having access to information. It was the only way to protect her this time.

"My father worships her. He committed his life to her."

Without him, she would not have prevailed.

"He kept Ana safe."

As no other mortal could. He chose the man who would raise her. He chose the man who would ultimately find her and buy her—without his whisperings in the right ears, Lazar would never have learned about the girl in the foothills. And when Ana was under most threat, it was your father who stepped in and removed her from those who might ultimately design her downfall. We needed the child. You know that. And now you know who needed to father that child. Everything was a risk.

Lyana could not always foresee how events would unfold. She can only choose her disciples with care. Their free will is always the unknown.

"My father would have succeeded in putting the child on the throne."

Yes, that is likely true. But now someone else has.

"And I must do this? There is no other way?" he asked, head bowed.

You alone.

"You believe he is a danger now?"

He is. A new urge drives him. We cannot permit his threat to those who continue her work.

"And when it is done, what then?"

You must speak with Lazar. Tell him the truth and then return here. There are years to wait in solitude. And then you must fulfill your final task, the one you were born to accomplish.

"That one I most look forward to."

We know.

"I shall go now. Farim waits patiently."

The pillars glowed, hummed softly in farewell to the young man who left the cave with a heavy heart.

Maliz coughed out the old man's spirit in a spume of blood and slumped to the stone floor, glad to be rid of Alzaria's body, which lay in a crumpled heap nearby. Now his powers were almost non-existent again and he felt that familiar sense of dislocation from the body he inhabited, when he was simply a presence within it, able to guide it but without much strength or magic. He was definitely in his dormant phase again but it made no sense and it was distressing him as nothing had before. He had felt Lyana's rising, felt her very presence in the land, felt it by the powers that claimed him. And then they were gone, draining from him fast, leaving him just enough time to return to this Zarab-forsaken place where he must live as mortal in filth and squalor.

With Iridor at the bottom of the Faranel and Lyana no longer apparently of this earth, his time as the demon was done with for another cycle. He didn't understand but he had held that child and there was nothing within it, not an ounce of power, not an iota of magic. A babbling, hungry, squalling infant was all that he had held in his arms. He had not killed Lyana. He had not even sighted her yet.

He leaned his wizened head back against the walls of the tiny alley in which he found himself and accepted his exhaustion. He needed to find food again. He needed to take care of this body as best he could. And he needed to lie low and wait, presumably for the next cycle. He twitched at the thought. Where had Lyana gone?

The awkward and false calm got the better of Falza. He had tried to wait it out but realized his broody son had only become better at maintaining difficult silences over the years.

He spoke in Galinsean to cut out the Percherese whore from the conversation. "Your mother had hoped to see you."

Lazar lifted his stony gaze to the King. "I am sorry for your loss, Father. I know how much you loved her."

"She died on enemy soil, blue of lip and gasping for breath in my arms, Lucien. That is no way for a queen of Galinsea to leave this earth."

Lazar nodded. "No way indeed. The perpetrator will pay, that I promise you, but the Crown Valide is not the one who should take the punishment."

"The Zar is ultimately responsible for his people's actions. She was his regent and is answerable for the murderer."

"And she will see to it that he is punished in a manner befitting his deed. But I will not permit you to take your vengeance out on her, or this city. You used me as the excuse to wage war and now you are using my mother as an excuse to commit regicide."

"I came to avenge my son's death."

"I am, as you see, alive. There is nothing to avenge."

"My wife—"

"Your wife died in battle, King Falza. If you had not wished to risk her life, you should never have brought her with you to Percheron amongst war galleys."

"She came to see her son."

"No, Father, she came to watch the Percherese humbled, to walk this palace and claim it as her own—a summer retreat, perhaps? I can hear her saying it. My mother was every bit the aggressor, alongside you. You both took the risk. She paid a heavy price for it."

"You don't even mourn her, do you?"

"Father, if you knew the number of people I have loved and lost these last moons, you would know that my mother's passing is one among too many and I haven't even begun my private grieving for any of them."

Falza pointed at Herezah. "You put a Percherese slave above your mother, the Queen?"

"I put innocence above simple vengeance. This woman is innocent of what you claim. She is guilty of many things but I know she would not have knowingly threatened the stability or safety of Percheron."

Falza lost patience with the words. "Despite all that has happened between us, we admired you, son. You are the heir of Galinsea! Can't you—"

"I renounced my claim on the throne the last time we spoke to each other. I have not changed my position on it. I do not wish to rule Galinsea—I never have."

"Then who, Lucien? Your brother, Aeron, is—"

Lazar lifted a hand to still his father's words. "I have something to show you. Show her in," he said to the Elim who had silently arrived at the doorway.

Everyone watched Harras enter, carrying a bundle that whimpered briefly before settling to sleep.

Lazar saw Herezah's eyes flare with joy and his father's brow crease with puzzlement. Lazar took the baby, flooded by an inexplicable wave of love for the child. First in Percherese he gave an order. "Everyone is to clear the room including archers and guards. Elim, you can remain outside the doors but everyone is to leave. Fret not, I can handle the King. You, also outside, please," he said to Harras. He gave similar orders in Galinsean and the eleven or so enemy men were escorted from the chamber by Elim.

"What is this?" his father demanded.

"You will see," Lazar said, waiting patiently for the last of the people to leave. "Wait until we're alone," he added, handing the child to Herezah, who gladly accepted the baby.

When they were finally alone, he switched to Percherese for Herezah's benefit. "Father, this is Luc. He was born to Zaradine Ana, wife and Absolute Favorite of Zar Boaz."

"He is an heir, so what?" his father grumbled.

"He is the only heir. The only potential next Zar of Percheron."

"And why is this supposed to impress me?" Falza demanded.

"Because he is also your heir."

"What?" Falza and Herezah asked together.

"This is my son. Ana was not pregnant by Boaz."

"But—" The Crown Valide began to stutter.

Lazar gave her a sympathetic glance. "I'm sorry, Herezah. It seems the royal marriage was never consummated. But I can assure you that Ana and I certainly did consummate our love for each other in the desert. She became pregnant by me. Both Boaz and Ana confirmed it, and one look at this child will tell you he is not your son's."

Herezah looked distraught.

"Wait, let me finish," he told her, stemming whatever tide of insults and recriminations he was sure she was preparing. "Father, I renounced my claim to the throne of Galinsea but I do not renounce Luc's. He is your grandson and his veins run with the royal blood of Galinsea. From what I recall, my brothers, much as you love them, were never good material in your eyes for monarchs. And, sadly, as much as you detested me, I was always your firstborn and indeed first choice."

"You were born to lead, Lucien, no matter our differences. Your mother always loved you, you know that."

Lazar nodded. "Then here is my proposal. I am providing you with a way to withdraw peacefully from Percheron and save face. There need be no further bloodshed."

"What is this proposal?" Falza said testily.

"Luc becomes Zar. He is also named your heir."

"Preposterous!" Herezah exclaimed. "He is not a Zar! He is no—"

"And you are not a queen, Herezah. You are relegated now to slave. I could have the harem disbanded and you turned out later today and no one would argue and no one would mourn your departure. I offer you a proposal as well. Be Luc's guide. No one knows Percherese politics better than you. He has no mother. Be the grandmother you would have been had you never known the truth of his parentage. You have an opportunity now to be the leader you've always wanted to be."

"You mean rule until he is of an age?" she asked, aghast.

"I mean help to run the realm, yes. Be the regent that Percheron needs. The people know how courageous you've been these last few days. Build upon it. Win their favor, win their trust. But win it for him. He is Zar, not you. Raise him to be the ruler you would be if you were a man. Raise him to know that cunning you possess but to put it to better use. Raise him with all that knowledge of politics you possess. He could have no finer tutor if you accept this role properly."

"I," she stammered, clearly stunned. "You trust me?"

"I want to. Can I?"

"Yes! But what about you?"

"Oh, I shall be around. I have something I must do first. And then I have some journeys to make that concern neither Percheron nor Galinsea but must be done."

"So the boy stays here?" Falza asked.

"Yes, he is Zar Luc now. And when you pass away, Father, he will be Zar Luc of Percheron and named as your successor, King of Galinsea. If you have a senior Galinsean noble's daughter of an age, we can discuss a formal marriage to seal the realms in more than just word. I was thinking one of mother's nieces' children?"

Falza nodded thoughtfully. "I can think of two now who may suit and she seems to have all girls on her side; I am sure they will produce more females for us to choose from."

"That is settled, then. You will send the Crown Valide a list of suitable names in due course and she will make that final decision." He didn't need to look at Herezah to know how much that pleased her. "She will see to all the necessary formal arrangements. Perhaps Marius could act as emissary between the two realms. Base him and Lorto here. They could learn the language and begin a new era of our two nations working closely."

"I am impressed, Lucien."

"That must be the first time, then, Father." The two men shared a wry smile and Lazar continued: "I'm also suggesting that any of your soldiers, with no family ties to Galinsea, who wish to stay will be made welcome in Percheron. And perhaps you can offer the same courtesy? I can't say how many Percherese might take up the offer to move to Galinsea but we can begin by relaxing all rules and indeed problems associated with trading. The sea routes and the desert route can be developed for a more open trading policy. Merchants will become the lifeblood between the two regions—they will lead the changes."

"Lazar, how do we explain this to the people of Percheron, though? Luc may be of Galinsean royal blood, but he is not of the Zars'," Herezah interjected.

"We don't tell them."

"You jest!"

"As far as the people of Percheron are concerned, Luc is the son of Boaz, the reason he courageously went into the desert to rescue his pregnant wife. And he becomes King of Galinsea because it is what we demanded in our peace treaty. No one but the three of us is ever to know the truth."

"But you yourself said Luc couldn't be my son's child."

"But he is clearly Ana's. They may have their doubts but the truth is the people just want life to go back to normal with a Zar in the palace. In years to come they will have accepted him, no matter what the gossipmongers say."

"I understand. Leave it to me. I will start promoting the story that Yozem did a blood telling and that Luc took none of his father's looks, only qualities from his character."

Lazar smiled briefly. "That's right. Put that cunning to good use for the benefit of your people. Sometimes the truth need not to be told if it's in the greater interest. The people may have their suspicions but it won't matter in years to come when they have a royal marriage to celebrate across dynasties."

"So the harem and the life of the Zar as we have known them will change, I see."

"Yes. There will be no harem. Luc will marry a Galinsean bride and bind our realms. When he takes the Galinsean throne—pardon me, Father—he will be known as Emperor."

"It will take time, Lazar."

"We have time. There is one more important point that is part of this proposal." Both Herezah and the King eyed him expectantly. "Both nations will formally accept the Goddess as their faith."

Herezah looked at him quizzically. "It matters not to me but why would you ask this?"

"It will bind us closer still through faith. Father, Galinseans are closer to the Goddess's way than Percheron but it still has a number of gods it pays homage to. Be the first King in a long time to unify your people in one faith. Herezah, Luc can do the same. His mother followed the Goddess and it was her disciples—the giants, the creatures once bound in stone—who came to our rescue. The Goddess heard our prayers and she answered them. Zarab does nothing for the people and this is about a fresh beginning. To embrace a new faith cannot happen quickly, I understand this, but it is new and can be a part of Luc's legacy and indeed Boaz's."

"Boaz loved the Mother?" Herezah queried.

"Indeed he did," Lazar answered truthfully. "Loved her since the moment he was first introduced to her," and again Ana was reflected to him from the peaceful expression on her son's sleeping face.

"That's news to me."

"I told you, you spent far more time plotting against his desires than listening to them. Learn about Lyana, Herezah.

She was once the only faith of our region. Start the revolution today."

There was silence as the three looked at one another, each waiting for the others to speak.

"That's all," Lazar concluded. "We can keep this simple. King Falza?"

The King of Galinsea nodded. "I am in agreement with your terms, Lucien. Marius will sit down with whoever you need to draw up the terms of this treaty."

"Thank you. Herezah? Can you keep this secret and agree to its terms?"

"Yes. I wish no further war or even threat of it between ourselves and Galinsea."

"Good. Then have the treaty drawn up, Herezah, for Falza and yourself to sign. It will declare you simply 'Crown' from hereon. You will act as regent for Zar Luc until he is of an age to fulfill his formal role."

He saw Herezah barely control the shiver of delight at his words.

"What's to stop her from simply saying yes now and ignoring your terms, Lucien?" his father demanded. "You intimate that she could not be trusted previously."

"Father, Herezah will rise to this office. She will make us all proud. I'm sure of it." He gave her a sideways glance and realized with a certain amount of sadness how much of her life had been wasted in the harem. She should always have been a queen. "Besides, I remain Spur and the army is loyal to my command."

"You should come home sometime, Lucien."

"I am home, Father."

"All right. Let me invite you back to your homeland sometime. Bring your son. I'm sure our people would be thrilled to meet you both."

"I'll bring Herezah. The Galinseans should meet the person grooming their future king."

"As you wish," his father said. "So I presume I can return to my ship?"

"Your galley is untouched. You may return to Romea under your own banner, if you choose, as soon as the treaty is signed. Beloch and Ezram will no doubt agree to transport those who don't wish to remain here back across the desert quickly."

"How quickly?"

Lazar grinned. "Percheron to Romea in the time it might take Herezah to have her hair brushed." His father's complexion blanched. "Another reason not to pick a fight with Percheron again," Lazar added, his smile widening. "And the best reason for us all to join their faith. They are of the Goddess."

"Then she's got my soul," Falza said, irony lacing the King's tone.

"I shall see you before you depart, Father. I need to speak with the giants."

The King gave him a look of disbelief but simply turned to the new head of Percheron and bowed. "Well, you must forgive me my, er, indiscretion of earlier, Crown. Perhaps you would allow me to hold my grandson before I leave."

"Of course, Falza. I'm only devastated that his grandmother could not bear witness to this happy day," Hereza replied diplomatically. She glanced toward Lazar and he gave her what she had so long desired—his approval, with a nod and soft smile.

36

Outside, whilst the proud "grandparents" admired their new royal, Lazar found Captain Ghassal waiting.

"Spur," he said, hand across his heart.

"Captain," Lazar replied, mirroring the gesture. "Get the Galinseans down to the shore. The King is going to speak with his men."

"It's over?"

"With Beloch and Ezram on our side, not to mention the other creatures, they have no choice."

"Spur, I'm still at a loss—"

"I know. I suspect the giants and their companions will be gone from our midst soon enough. For now do not fear them. Calm everyone down, remove the dead, get help to the wounded. Get food passed out to the hungry. Everyone must be very confused and disoriented."

"Fortunately the majority who stayed are not hurt. They took refuge in the palace."

"Get word out amongst the foothills. Send riders in every direction and let people know it is safe to return to the city. Any news on Salmeo?"

"No, sir. But we can return to the search now that a truce has been achieved."

"Someone knows something somewhere. Find that person. I want to know where he is or at least where the eunuch headed."

"Yes, sir."

"And the woman who was here?"

"Er, she's in the sapphire room, Spur. Shall I fetch her?"

"No, I'll go there. Escort King Falza, with full respect, please, to the foreshore." The captain bowed, made to leave. "And, Captain?"

"Yes, Spur?"

"You take your orders from me and only me but don't be surprised if you find the Crown Valide more assured of her position. The soldiers of Percheron do not answer to her directly but she is now the titular head of our realm. Zar Boaz and Zaradine Ana have welcomed a son and heir, Zar Luc. The infant will take the throne when he is of an age. Until then, Herezah will be known simply as Crown. Please let it be known, although I'm sure she'll organize a ceremony soon enough to formalize the title." He saw the man's expression turn to one of dismay. "Trust me on this, Captain. Herezah's tremendously capable, and Percheron needs a steadying, strong mind at the top. And remember, Captain, Herezah is a grieving mother as much as she is our new Crown. Please tell the men to remember this."

"Yes, Spur."

Lazar nodded and left the man as he strode to find the woman who had brought his child. He found her admiring the Sapphire Pools. She swung around in fright as he entered the chamber.

"Spur Lazar," she said, "you scared me."

"My apologies. Also for keeping you waiting."

"Oh, don't be sorry. I never thought I'd ever see the inside of the palace. I could stay here forever and never want to leave."

"Don't be too sure of that. I'm sorry, I don't remember your name. I was expecting the other woman, the wet nurse."

"I am Harras, Spur. The woman who fed your baby was not feeling terribly well. She asked me to bring him to you."

"I'm very grateful for the hospice's swift help and I would like to make a donation. Will you tell the senior woman in charge that I will organize that soon?"

"Of course."

"I also wanted to thank you in person. Is there anything else that the palace can do for the hospice? You have, after all, just assisted the new Zar of Percheron."

She giggled coquettishly, and then suddenly appeared coy, as if embarrassed by his personal attention. He'd seen that expression and heard that girlish laughter many times and sighed softly to himself that he was unlikely to ever respond to a woman again. The two women he had loved had both died. There was no room in his shattered heart for a third love.

"No, Spur, the palace provides kindly for us, although if you'd bring your donation in person, I know your presence would brighten many of the grieving mothers."

"I'll do that once we have settled Percheron back into some sense of normality. The wet nurse—is she going to be all right? What does she do for a living? Perhaps I can find her a position."

"Again, that's most generous. I shall find out. She looked

very poor. The child she lost last night was her first son, so perhaps she would appreciate a chance to start afresh."

"Please make sure to let me know. I won't forget her name—Alzaria."

"Actually, Spur Lazar, I should tell you, for she made it rather clear to me to advise you—Alzaria is not her real name."

"Oh?"

"I think she was mindful of repercussions. The child was conceived outside of a marriage."

"I understand. What is her real name, so I can commit it to memory?"

"She asked me to tell you that her name is Garjan."

Lazar felt his blood turn to ice.

"Spur Lazar, are you all right, sir?"

He grabbed her by the shoulders, unable to stop himself. "Harras, tell me exactly what Alzaria said to you."

She looked at his fingers digging into her flesh, terrified, but repeated word for word, her eyes scared by the intense way he regarded her. "Is something wrong, Spur Lazar? The child is fine, isn't he?"

He let her go, smoothed the fabric of her robe. "Please forgive me. I'm so sorry for scaring you . . . again." He seemed very calm. "Did you leave him alone with her?"

"Only briefly, Spur. Barely moments."

"That's all it takes," he murmured, frowning.

"Pardon, sir?"

"Nothing, Harras. I'm sorry to have startled you. The name she used came as a shock."

"That's all right, Spur. Garjan? I don't know it. May not be from these parts."

"It isn't. It's Galinsean."

"Oh? Is that bad?"

"It's neither here not there," Lazar answered, distracted. "Is she still at the hospice?"

"That's where I left her, Spur Lazar. She said she needed to rest."

"All right. Thank you again, Harras," he said, his mind spinning toward his son's safety. "One of my men will escort you out." He showed her to the door, signaled to one of the guards, and mustered a distracted smile for her in farewell. He closed the door to think.

Maliz was already here in Percheron. How could that be?

He needed advice. *Beloch?*

Yes?

Maliz is here!

I've just learned that Ezram felt him.

What? I thought you were not connected to the demon?

We're not. But your magic that released us from his spell also made us sensitive to his presence . . . Ezram more so than me, it seems.

So, where is he?

We believe he has entered the city.

How can that happen? He was traveling across the desert. I thought I had time to prepare for him.

Lyana rose. When he is fully empowered, he has new magics at his fingertips.

He held my son.

There was a terrible silence across their link.

Beloch!

What happened? Lazar could hear the trepidation in the giant's voice.

He posed as a wet nurse.

And Luc?

Well, I'm going to check him again but he seems fine. He was delivered to the palace, gurgling happily enough, then sleeping, as babies do, through his finest hour.

Lazar, you know that cannot be right.

I do. I'm thankful he's safe, relieved beyond belief, but also utterly confused.

Me, too. Wait, let me bring Ezram into this. Ezram, tell Lazar what you sense about Maliz. I feel nothing.

I can't feel him anymore, Ezram answered. *It was an initial sense of nausea and it got worse for a while. I told Beloch after you'd arrived that it might mean Maliz had entered the city. I can't know for sure—I was assuming.*

No, you were right. He was here. He held my son.

Then your son—if he is concealing Lyana—should be dead, Beloch interjected.

I know. It doesn't make sense, does it? Why would he leave him untouched?

Ezram sighed. *Because your son is obviously not shielding the Goddess.*

Lazar paced, frustrated. *Where is she, then? Ana died for this! Who else is going to be hiding the Goddess if not Luc? Who?*

Be calm, Lazar, Ezram soothed. *I cannot feel Maliz any longer. It is as if he is no longer here. Perhaps the threat has passed?*

Lazar gave a sound of disgust.

But Beloch sided with his twin. *It's true. I can't feel him at all. My attention was diverted when we arrived, but even then, whatever I felt was weak enough not to impact me.*

What Ezram felt was obviously far more potent.

He was in full blazing power, I tell you. I felt unsteady from Lyana's rising, which provoked that power. Now there's nothing. And if he was still around, apart from the absolute fact that Luc would surely be dead, we would be fighting against his spell-making again.

You know, Iridor always told me that Maliz could not be killed by a mortal. Perhaps he was wrong. The woman Alzaria was definitely sickening. Maybe she is dead and he was lost with her? Lazar asked.

I can't believe that, but something strange has certainly occurred, Ezram said gravely.

Lyana is obviously up to something more cunning than Maliz ever imagined, Beloch said. *All we can do is wait. What do you wish us to do now, Spur? I think our presence is too unsettling for everyone.*

Where would you go if you could?

Back to the mountains, they said as one. He heard them chuckle softly.

Then go. Take the others as well. You have done more than we should ask of you, and Maliz is obviously biding his time, wherever he is, whoever he is.

We're never far. We can be with you in moments should you need to call upon us. When you're ready, we'll help you tear down the temples and rebuild them for Lyana.

Lazar nodded. *The priests will not make it easy for us, so it will happen slowly. The Galinseans may need some transport back to Romea, by the way,* he added, *and I may need swift passage somewhere, too.*

I'll get the Galinseans home, Ezram offered. *Beloch can take you wherever you need.*

Thank you, Lazar said. *No sign of those riders?*

No, Beloch confirmed. *But if they're smart, they'll wait for dark.*

Of course. And that's precisely what Arafanz will do. Nevertheless, alert me to anything suspicious.

37

She watched him pace, the quishtar she had ordered and elegantly poured with her own hand left untouched to lose its fragrance and to turn cold. It had been two days since Falza had nearly taken her head off. She still couldn't prevent herself from touching her throat from time to time in some sort of lingering reflex. She had insisted on supervising Bin's corpse all the way to the palace morgue and had personally commiserated with his parents at the loss of their brave son. She desperately missed his calming way and Lazar was not helping her nerves one bit as she tried to figure out this daunting, exciting new role of hers.

"You know this wet nurse?" he suddenly said, startling her.

"Yes, she's not from the hospice. She's a woman I've known from my days as odalisque, Lazar." She saw his expression change. "No, she's not feeding Luc, obviously. It's her daughter, who seems to never stop giving my friend grandchildren."

"And you were there when she fed him?"

"Yes, I've said it before. She didn't even know what I'd called her there for. I kept to your strange secret arrangements to the letter. And she's here now, in the next room, under guard, feeding him. No one but myself or Elza will care for his needs beyond the feeding. What are you frightened of?"

"I can't go into it, Herezah. But precautions must be taken. The woman I spoke of, Garjan?" She nodded. "She was a danger to him. How he survived I still don't know."

"You haven't explained anything, Lazar. But I know you're grieving like me and I can forgive you your curious behavior. Listen to me, Lazar. Please pay attention and cease your restless pacing."

He swung around, exasperated. "What is it?"

"I am going to make you a promise today. I want you to know that I make it with great honesty. I have no intention of breaking it."

"Go on."

"It's about us. No, wait—you must hear me out." She forced him to hold her gaze, standing up and insisting he let her take his hand.

"Herezah, I—"

"Hush. Now listen to me. Percheron has entered a new era. I am part of it. You have made me integral to it. And I will not let you down, or my poor dead son, or the faith my husband, Joreb, showed in me at the outset. As much as he might turn in his grave to know that a woman leads Percheron, I think he would approve that it is me."

"I do, too."

"I know. And that is why I make you this promise that what has passed is now the past for me. As much as I desire it, I now realize you and I can never be together in the way I would like and I would rather call you friend and feel the warmth of your smile than call you lover and feel the coldness of an insincere kiss. I took advantage of you, Lazar, but you must know it was driven by a genuine need, a genuine love, even if I allowed my own ambition to cloud my good sense. I make no claim upon you. I will never make you feel uncomfortable or awkward around me. I want us to be friends. And by that I mean that I look forward to your companionship for supper now and then, to your advice and constant counsel. I make no other demands of you physically or emotionally. I realize no one will take Ana's place."

"Thank you," he said, and she heard the deep relief in his voice.

"We're raising your son together. He needs us both. I know you will want to tell him about his mother, as much as I must tell him about his 'father.' Will you ever tell him the truth?"

"I don't know. I can't think that far ahead. I am worried that he simply gets through this night, let alone the coming years."

"Stop worrying. There are Elim guarding all our doors. Your giants are never far. It's time for you to let the fear go, Lazar. Luc is safe. Percheron is safe. And I am safe, which—"

"Whatever makes you say that, Valide?"

They both swung in startlement at the sound of Arafanz's voice as he stepped lightly from the balcony into the chamber.

"Zarab save me! He has Luc," Herezah hissed, hardly able to credit what she was seeing.

"Zarab will not save you, Valide. Lazar, don't think of drawing that weapon. If either of you call out to the guards I will slit the child's throat."

"What, when you committed your life to this child sitting the throne?" Lazar sneered. But Herezah heard the fear for his son underneath his bravado.

"No, Spur, I committed my life to destroying the royal structure of Percheron. I wanted the faith changed, which I gather has already been discussed; the harem disbanded, which I hear will occur soon; and Joreb's only remaining spawn dead, which you seem to have done very ably for me."

"What does he mean?" Herezah asked.

"Didn't Lazar tell you everything that unfolded in the desert?" He made a soft sound of admonishment toward the Spur.

"Arafanz—"

"You see, Valide," Arafanz continued, moving deeper into the room, Luc nestled comfortably in his arms, making room for his Razaqin to enter. One was unhooded, and Herezah recognized him, her disbelief deepening. "I'm not sure how Lazar explained away the death of your son but whatever he did say probably didn't give you the ghoulish detail that it was he who murdered the unarmed Zar, cleaving his head from crown to neck."

Herezah let go of Lazar as if burned. "What?" She felt as if all her breath had been sucked from her. "Lazar?"

"Tell her, Spur. Tell her the truth."

"It's true."

She stared at him, shock and fright mingling to make her feel weak-kneed and dizzy.

"Herezah, I will explain it but you need to know that Boaz had suffered some sort of change. He planned to kill Ana, to kill me, perhaps even Luc. He'd entered a madness from which there was no escape."

"You lie," she said, shaking her head slowly.

"Of course he lies," Arafanz taunted. "He wanted Ana all to himself."

"Herezah, I have no reason to lie to you."

"He wanted his child on the throne, Valide. Imagine it—Galinsean blood atop the Percherese throne. Falza must love it!"

"I'm sure he does," Lazar countered, and Herezah heard the ice in his voice. Recognized it. Lazar spoke like this when he was supremely confident. He didn't feel at all threatened by Arafanz's taunts. "But if I merely wanted to put a Galinsean on the Percherese throne, I could have helped my father's cause and taken it myself. This new Zar is half Percherese and he will be raised by and will learn to govern from a Percherese grandmother, chosen by royals, whether he's blood or not. Does this sound to you like someone who simply wants a Galinsean on the throne, or does this sound more like someone who is following Lyana's wishes?"

Herezah didn't understand why Lazar was talking about bringing the Goddess into the fray but he certainly seemed obsessed with her, what with changing over the faith and tearing down the temples of Zarab. She couldn't care less about it but she watched Arafanz struggle to answer Lazar's challenge, so presumably the rebel knew what the Spur was talking about.

"We're on the same side, Arafanz. I did your task," Lazar said, "because I didn't know if you'd live to fulfill it."

"I'm here to finish it," the rebel said.

"What do you want?" Herezah demanded.

"Your death, Valide."

"Why?"

"My task was to destroy the old guard of Joreb's structure."

"It's already torn to shreds. Let her be. She will herald your new era, trust me," Lazar assured.

"Trust you?" Arafanz sneered. "No. Now make a choice, you two. I don't need this child on the throne. You're right,

Lazar, the changes have already been rung in. His death makes no difference. I see giants roam the land again, which tells me Lyana has prevailed."

"What choice?" Lazar demanded.

"You, Valide, your death in exchange for the baby's life."

"This is madness," Lazar said. "Nothing will be achieved through her death. Nothing!"

"Satisfaction that I fulfilled my role. Now choose."

Herezah knew that Luc was too precious. His existence had made it possible to barter their peace with the Galinseans. His existence meant peace and empire for future generations. She was dispensable. Percheron was safe, Boaz was dead, Lazar would never be hers. She didn't allow herself another moment's thought, for fear of losing her nerve. She stepped fully away from Lazar. "Give the child to Lazar."

"And then I have no bargaining power, Valide."

"Herezah, wait!" Lazar cautioned.

"No. This is how it must be," she said. "Salazin can take my life as you hand the child to Lazar, Arafanz. Is that fair? Are you a man of your word?"

"Absolutely I am, Valide. I'm impressed by your heroics. I promise you both father and son will be left safe once you are dead."

She nodded. "How do I say 'do it cleanly' to the mute?"

Arafanz laughed. "He is not mute. You can tell him yourself."

It was just one more shock she couldn't be bothered to turn her mind to. Life had been enough of a blur these last few days. She stood still as Salazin approached, drawing a vicious-looking dagger from his belt.

"Arafanz! This—"

"Quiet, Lazar. Don't draw that sword. Here, catch your son."

Herezah held her breath in readiness but it all happened so fast. She watched Arafanz throw Luc at Lazar, who frantically grabbed for the child in the air. When she looked back at Salazin, he was empty-handed. She turned and stared at the rebel's surprised face, the dagger sticking from his throat. Arafanz just had time to switch his gaze from Lazar to Salazin.

"Why, son?" he gasped before he fell heavily to the ground, dead before he hit it.

"He had become dangerous," the young man said into the shocked silence. Then he said to Lazar, "I'm glad your son is safe," before he leaped off the edge of the balcony, escaping. Herezah felt her knees give and then her world blacked out.

She inhaled a deep breath of the balmy late-summer air and smelled the sweet jasmine in it.

"I walked through the harem today," she said. "It is a very lonely place. But then it was never a terribly happy place."

"You won't miss it."

"No, not one bit. And we shall find homes for all the girls. Some may return to their parents."

"How are you feeling?"

"Ridiculous with this huge bruise on my forehead that not even a wretched veil will cover. I'm sorry I fainted. I'm fine, Lazar, really."

"I plan to leave this evening."

"I wish you'd let it go."

"I can't. It must be done."

"I know. Well, I'm sure we're safe. Captain Ghassal takes no notice of me, anyway, so I presume you've left him with his orders?"

"I have. The city is calm."

"You're not going to explain any of it, are you? The desert, the fortress, Boaz, Arafanz, none of it."

"You said what has passed is the past. That is a fine creed. One day I will tell you what Arafanz put us through that terrible night and why killing Boaz was the kindest act I could show him. But right now it is too raw, Herezah. I have lost a lot of people that I cared about. I, too, must do some healing. Please believe me when I tell you that Boaz did not die in vain."

She nodded, far too pragmatic to continue her argument. Nothing would bring back Boaz. The Spur had no reason to lie to her, not now. She ruled Percheron. "Go, Lazar. Return safely to us."

"Only when I am satisfied that he is dead."

"You carry my hate with you all the way to him," she said as he bowed in farewell.

38.

*W*ho is this boy? Beloch asked as he carried Lazar east,
skimming the northern mountain range.

*His name is Teril. He was an inflictor's assistant. After I was
flogged and nearly died, he helped me. He also helped me when
I needed to return to the city to see Ana, and he got a message to
Iridor when I was hardly capable of supporting myself. He never
got over the death of a young inflictor, named Shaz, who the boy
maintains was murdered for his silence.*

*And he knows for sure this is the right direction? We are headed
well beyond the area I know.*

*Apparently our prey hails from a place to the east. Teril over-
heard the whispered arrangements, spied on them. We keep following this river and then we head south. The place is called Komassee.
All I know is that it has a cave network.*

Which suggests rocky foothills?

Yes, I imagine so.

Then I see them in the distance, Lazar. We shall be there soon.

He couldn't have made it that far in the time he's had.

Ah, wait. I see a smoke by the river. Three figures, horses, a cart?

Your eyesight is good! Sounds like my quarry. Set me down as close as you can. I'll stalk them on foot now.

And then what?

Wait for me. If I don't call to you within two days, I haven't survived. Go to your mountain home.

Survive, Lazar. Your son, Luc, needs you. Percheron needs you. Beloch knelt and set Lazar down as gently as he could.

I don't want them to see you, Lazar said.

It may be too late. But he's not expecting you now, is he?

Lazar grinned and began running.

The three men had seen nothing in the dim dusk. It was the evening of the second day since Beloch had spotted them. Lazar hid in the bushy undergrowth not far from where they had chosen to camp, and watched.

"How much longer?" one man said.

The one he addressed shrugged. "As long as it takes."

"We are far from home. Too far," the third man whined.

Salmeo scowled. "I am paying you enough."

"But we don't even know where we're going?" the first complained, trying to sound reasonable.

"I do," Salmeo replied, looking enormous in the falling dusk.

"Another two days, I imagine," Lazar heard Salmeo add, and then all three men were aware of his presence. The third man's head flew from his shoulders while his body remained stoically upright, spurting blood around the fire.

"What the—" was all the other companion had time to

scream before he found Lazar's blade poking through his middle and out past his spine. Lazar kicked the man off his sword, wiping it down on the now dead man's chest.

"Don't bother running," he said over his shoulder. "You're much too slow."

"Can I offer you some quishtar, Spur?" Salmeo had the audacity to ask in his feminine lisping way. Lazar had to hand it to the eunuch. He was as cold as the lizard he looked like when his tongue flicked out between that hideous gap in his teeth.

"No."

"But you must have traveled so far alone from Percheron. The least I can do before you start dragging me back is to pour you a cup of the hot brew."

"Perhaps with a drop of poison or two in it?"

"Ah."

"That woman you so callously murdered, Salmeo, was my mother."

The fat man shrugged. "Not intentionally, Spur. I'd really rather hoped to kill the Valide." He sighed. "So you want to begin the journey immediately, I take it?"

"Whatever makes you think we're going anywhere together?"

And for the first time since he'd laid eyes again on the huge eunuch, Lazar saw fear in the man's face. "Well, I presumed you would want to take me back for the usual humiliation—the chance to see justice done."

"No, Salmeo, I think I can mete out this justice," Lazar said, amazed at the calm in his voice. He had imagined hacking the eunuch, limb from limb, leaving him dismembered in a bloodied pile for the ants to finish off. But now, suddenly, the blood rage had dissipated. "You get to choose."

"What can I choose, Spur?" the eunuch asked in a delicate voice.

"Precisely how that justice is delivered."

"Not a pleasant choice, then."

"More than you ever offered any of the victims of your betrayals. Choose, Salmeo. By sword, or by poison. I'm sure you have brought some along."

"To be run through or to gasp, choking?" Salmeo mused.

Lazar was impressed by the man's composure. "What is it to be?"

"Swords are so messy. And these are my favorite traveling silks. Let's go with the poison."

"Where is it?"

Salmeo pointed. "In the sack. A small dark glass vial."

Lazar dug around, finally withdrawing a deep blue bottle, small and innocuous-looking. "May I?"

"By all means, Spur. It's an old friend for you."

Lazar pulled the cork and sniffed it. "Ah, drezden. I should have guessed."

"It's very potent when taken orally."

"I know. A single drop sustains me through the legacy of its poisoning when I get my fevers."

"Do you just want me to drink it all down?"

"I don't care how you do it, so long as you're dead by nightfall."

"Oh, I think I can guarantee you that. You don't mind if I take it with some quishtar?"

"By all means. Here, let me do it for you." Lazar busied himself preparing the death concoction, remembering how Zafira had traditionally poured the liquid from jug to jug, cooling it.

"You pour as if you've been doing that for years, Spur," Salmeo lisped.

"I had a good teacher," he admitted. "I'm told the best brew is made from the wild husk of the desert cherry."

"Oh, bravo, Spur Lazar. You have learned well. It is indeed and this is it."

"I recognize the fragrance."

"Such a pity to spoil it with the drezden, no?" Salmeo urged.

Lazar actually smiled at the huge man's dark humor. "All of it?" he asked, holding up the cup in one hand and the poison in the other.

"That's probably best. I'm not exactly small, am I?"

Lazar tipped the contents of the vial into the cup and carefully placed the porcelain down before the eunuch, stepping back swiftly.

"I didn't even think of throwing it over you, Spur," Salmeo assured him.

"I don't take unnecessary risks with my enemies." Lazar said, moving away to sit down.

"Oh, you and I, we're not so different, you know, Lazar," Salmeo said, reaching for the cup. It looked tiny in his huge, meaty hands, hands that nevertheless held the fragile porcelain with such care.

"And why is that?" Lazar replied conversationally.

Salmeo blew gently on the brew. "Well, you are the son of a king. You are the heir to a throne. And whether or not you choose to take that throne, you carry your pride, your obvious royalty, with great aplomb. It's why people accuse you of arrogance. You were born to rule, to lead, to be a man whom your people look up to."

"And you?"

Salmeo shrugged. "I am also the son of a king. I am an heir to a throne. But Percherese slavers slashed the throat of my mother, humiliated my father until he took his own life, dying in dirt on the roadside to Percheron. They made a whore of my sister, a princess. They cut away my manhood. In spite of all that, I remain a prince. I was born to rule, to lead, to be a man for my people to look up to. But I was denied my birthright, turning instead into what you see."

Lazar had stared at Salmeo, incredulous at the eunuch's dark tale. "I, too, was captured as a slave, Salmeo; it gives you no right to murder."

"Perhaps not. But you at least were permitted to fight your way to freedom, an opportunity that was not offered to a black slave boy from a village in the eastern provinces." He blew again on the quishtar. "I think this is ready. You are permitting me some small measure of dignity, Lazar, for which I am grateful, though I suppose I shouldn't be surprised. I have hated you but I could never accuse you of being a cruel or unfair man. So let me thank you for not dragging me back to Percheron. At least this way I die free amongst the plants I recognize and smells I love. This is my land. I was almost home." He raised his cup to the Spur. "Sherem," he said and gave a gap-toothed smile.

Lazar nodded. "Sherem!" he said softly, watching as the eunuch swallowed the contents of the cup.

"Farewell, Lazar," the eunuch said, grimacing at its bitterness.

"Farewell, Salmeo."

Later, after the thrashing death throes had ceased, as night choked off the last light of the day, Lazar severed the former Grand Master Eunuch's head from his body.

It's over, Beloch. Can you fetch me? Where you see the fire.

I see it, the giant replied, and Lazar heard the relief in his friend's voice. *Coming.*

Lazar picked up the heavy head and carefully wrapped it in some linen he found, placing it in a sack he'd brought along for the purpose. Herezah would no doubt enjoy seeing Salmeo's head on a spike, but until he delivered it to her, he would treat the chieftain with the respect due a king.

Eight years later . . .

Maliz seethed. He wished his smelly, lice-ridden body would die, forcing him to find a new host, but as long as it still breathed, he knew it was the best disguise for him. Frail and wizened, it required very little to keep alive, allowing him the opportunity to roam the city in his spirit form, watching helplessly as more of the dismaying changes were made.

The temples of Zarab—three of them—had been razed. Two had already been rebuilt in Lyana's honor. Crown Herezah ruled. As much as it galled him, she was doing a worthy job. The child had grown strong and sturdy. Although he was the image of his beautiful mother, Maliz was sure that, as the boy grew and turned into a man, the truth of who sired him would be apparent. But the youngster was already incredibly beloved by his people, and his so-called grandmother went to great pains to make him accessible so that his popularity was constantly fueled.

Galinseans had stayed. Bloods had mixed. Already there were children running through the streets who were a product of both realms. Trade moved freely between the nations and the whole region was enjoying great prosperity. The harbor had never been busier, and the new "Jewelled Road," as it was known, had caravans regularly crossing the desert between Percheron and Romea.

And Lazar, Zarab rot him, remained as Spur, filling his lonely life with teaching the young Zar—to ride, to fish, to hunt, and to fight with two swords.

Maliz had seen the fat eunuch's head rotting on the tall spike outside the palace. Old Salmeo had had many enemies, it seemed, and he had remained there for years. When the spike had finally been taken down, it had been quietly removed and, unbeknownst to the populace, was replanted in the gardens of the harem, watching over its now long-defunct and empty hallways and chambers, no doubt a final satisfaction for Herezah.

None of this mattered to Maliz, however. He was in the dormant stage of his cycle when he was, in the normal way of things, victorious and spent. But, although glad to be in this phase, he was confused this time. Had he won? He thought he had . . . and yet it had been years since he had felt that wonderful sense of power overwhelm and claim his body. And he had owned it only so momentarily . . . a matter of hours, in fact. Even that was of no consequence, however, when he considered the lack of confrontation. The only conclusion he could draw was that Lyana had been scared off; perhaps she had decided to abort this battle, but that seemed unlikely. She may be no match for him, but she certainly didn't lack courage and had faced him bravely on previous occasions.

He thought that she'd been at her most cunning this time

and was amused he'd been hoodwinked into believing she traveled in the guise of a newborn. A newborn who was heir to the throne of Percheron and Galinsea, no less.

Where was she? Oh, he could scream out to the heavens this evening! He'd been surviving in this pathetic excuse for a body for years now, waiting for a likely new host to come along but none had presented itself so far. All had been as vile and wasted a creature as the man who presently carried him. He should have been Zar. He should have been living an exalted lifestyle by now, biding his time in a beautiful, pampered body.

His fury spilled over this particular evening at the opening of the days of festivity in honor of Lyana. It was a new tradition that began with the first blow of the Samazen, almost always a midsummer night during the summer solstice. It was a superstitious time, anyway, for the region, and he had always hated it because people believed it was a brief period when the pathways between worlds were open, when spirits from other planes could enter this one. It was all old women's babbling! He relieved his pent-up fury into Lyana's waters at the rim where land meets sea.

"I piss on you, Lyana, and all who love you," he said, his toes wet as the water lapped around them, the music of the festival loud in his ears.

Despite his anger, he enjoyed the water's mildness, its invitation to take a few steps farther into its salty freshness. He felt guilty for even appreciating it, knowing the sea—like the other natural elements—was said to be owned by Lyana.

The notion irritated him that anyone would imagine anything so powerful as the sea answering to a fallen Goddess. He hawked a gob of spit as far as he could launch it. "And I spit on you, Lyana. If I could move my bowels, I would do that right now, too. All the wastes of my body I would give to you. I pay you homage with Zarab's excrement." And he gave a high laugh in his old-man's cackle at his jest.

"Ah, there you are."

Maliz looked around, startled to be confronted by a figure he realized he knew.

"Salazin?"

"My name is Razeen."

Maliz felt his already frail body weaken with fear. "What are you doing here? I . . . you were dead. We left you in the desert!"

"Or did I leave you?" the young disciple asked, smiling fiercely in the moonlight.

"What do you want?" Maliz screeched, hating his pathetic, thin voice.

"We have been looking for you, this night of all nights."

"'We'?" Maliz asked timorously, his tiny head swiveling in all directions but seeing no one. "Why this night?"

"Midsummer's Night. Surely you above all would grasp its import. A night when anything is possible. When magic abounds . . . especially at the most potent of all locations . . ." Razeen's voice trailed off as he looked down.

Maliz followed his gaze to where the mild waters fizzed and babbled around his feet.

"At the magical rim where land meets sea and worlds collide," Razeen finished. "I could kill you now, but we wanted to do this the right way."

"You keep saying 'we.' I see no one but you."

"Us," Razeen said, gesturing toward the waters.

Once again Maliz followed the man's gaze and was struck with horror to see a young girl floating in the waters. She was exquisite but wraithlike, her image one minute solid, the next faded. She glowed with golden light.

"We meet again," she said, her voice young, her figure so small.

"Lyana?" he croaked. "But—"

She drifted closer to him. He shrieked in his thin voice, shrinking back only to feel Razeen's chest behind him.

"There is no Iridor to trigger your rising now, Maliz. And Lyana doesn't exist in this plane to help fuel your powers either. You have only your faithless god to call upon and he doesn't hear you."

"How can this be? How can *she* be?" he begged.

"There were two," Razeen explained, pushing the man forward into the water so that it now lapped at his bony ankles. "Zaradine Ana gave birth to two children. The second was Lyana. I helped to birth her in the desert beneath the howl of the Samazen, and as her mother kissed her farewell and died, I gave the infant to her guardian, Ellyana. It was midsummer that night, too, Maliz. It is a time for great magics to occur. Worlds, planes, touch one another. The Goddess was immediately taken to another plane . . . perhaps you felt the dwindling of your powers from that moment on? She grew safe without your threat and you grew lazy without hers. Now she's strong. She's ready to have the fight you wanted. Except you are not strong and you are not ready. How ironic."

"No!" Maliz howled, now up to his calves in the Faranel.

"No one can hear you. Everyone is at Lyana's festival. But Lyana is here, Maliz. She has come to claim you."

"She has no substance. She cannot touch me."

"Oh, Maliz, how wrong you are. Once you are in her waters, she has all the substance she needs to drag you down into its depths. No fanfare, no audience, no theatrical battle for you, demon. Lyana wants you to simply slip beneath the surface, joining her beloved Zafira and Pez, who you gleefully destroyed, but both of whom beat you at your own game. You know Iridor survived long enough to keep Lyana, her brother, Ana, and Lazar safe, don't you? Oh, you didn't? How gut-wrenching it must be to learn this now, having spent so many years suffering in your weakened guise.

"First, her waters will suck away your life and cast your demon soul into its depths for ever. Then she will allow her fish to pick clean this stolen body of yours—cleansing it of your touch and laying its bones to rest serenely on her ocean floor, so that you are nothing more than a dulled memory."

"Help!" Maliz screeched, although no one could hear him, his voice as drowned by the laughter and happy celebrations, the fireworks and music of Lyana, as his body would be in the waters of the Faranel.

"Don't fight us, Maliz. This time Lyana wins. You have lost. Zarab has lost."

"Noooo!" Maliz screamed.

"Come, Maliz, come into my darkest depths," the girl called sweetly, dipping in the water and grabbing his hands.

No one heard the soft gulp as the man slipped beneath the surface and the Faranel Sea swallowed him. But the silent witness greeted Razeen as the warrior walked back up the sandy foreshore.

"Tell me we are rid of him."

"It is done, Spur Lazar. The long vigil is over. Your daughter, the Goddess Lyana, has prevailed."

Turn the page for an excerpt from the new series from

FIONA MCINTOSH

◆——————◆

ROYAL EXILE

BOOK ONE OF THE VALISAR TRILOGY

An extraordinary epic fantasy saga of
unassailable courage, relentless peril, and wild adventure

One

→→-◄◄←

"Could he do this?" he wondered, as yet another wail began. He knew he had no choice if the Valisars were to survive.

Two great oak doors, carved with the family coat of arms, separated King Brennus from his wife's groans and shrieks, but despite the sound being muffled, her agonized cries injured him nonetheless. He knew his beautiful and beloved Iselda would never have to forgive him because she would never know of his ruthlessness at what he planned for his own flesh and blood. He looked to his trusted legate and dropped his gaze, shaking his head. They were all servants to the crown—king included—and serve he must by presenting the infant corpse in order to protect the realm.

"It never gets any easier, De Vis," he lamented.

De Vis nodded knowingly; he had lost his own wife soon after childbirth. "I can remember Eril's screams as though they were yesterday." He hurried to add: "Of course, once the queen holds her child, majesty, her pain will disappear."

They were both talking around the real issues—the murder of a newborn and the threat that their kingdom was facing its demise.

Brennus's face drooped even further. "In this you are right, although I fear for all our children, De Vis. My wife brings into this world a new son who may never see his first anni."

"Which is why your plan is inspired, highness. We cannot risk Loethar having access to the power."

"If it is accessible at all in this generation. Leo shows no sign at this stage . . . and Piven . . ." The king trailed off as another agonized shriek cut through their murmurs.

De Vis held his tongue but when silence returned and stretched between them, he said softly: "We can't know for sure. Leo is still young—it may yet come to him—and the next prince may be bristling with it. We can't risk either child falling into the wrong hands. And as for Piven, your highness, he is not of your flesh. We know he hardly possesses his faculties, majesty, let alone any power."

The king's grave face told his legate that Brennus agreed, that his mind was made up. Nevertheless he confirmed it aloud as though needing to justify his terrifying plan. "It is my duty to protect the Valisar inheritance. It cannot be tarnished by those not of the blood. I hope history proves me to be anything but the murderer I will appear if the truth ever outs. Is everything in place?"

"Precisely to your specifications," De Vis answered.

Brennus could see the legate's jaw working. De Vis was feeling the despair of what they were about to do as deeply as he was. "Your boys . . ." the king muttered, his words petering out.

De Vis didn't flinch. "Are completely loyal and will do their duty. You know that."

"Of course I know it, De Vis—they might as well be my own I know them so well—but they are too young for such grim tasks. I ask myself: could you do it? Could I? Can they?"

De Vis's expression remained stoic. "They have to. You have said as much yourself. My sons will not let Penraven down."

Brennus scowled. "Have you said anything yet?"

De Vis shook his head. "Until the moment is upon us, the fewer who know the better. The brief will also be better coming directly from you, majesty."

Brennus winced as another scream came from behind the

door, followed by a low groan that penetrated to the sunlit corridor where he and De Vis talked. He turned from the stone balustrade against which he had been leaning, looking out into the atrium that serviced the private royal apartments. Breathing deeply, he drank in the fragrance of daphne that the queen had personally planted in boxes hanging from the archways and took a long, sorrowful look at the light-drenched gardens below she had tended and made so beautiful. Trying for an heir had taken them on a torrid journey of miscarriages and disappointments. And then Leo had come along and, miraculously, had survived and flourished. But both Brennus and Iselda knew that a single heir was not enough, however, and so they had endured another three heartbreaking deaths in the womb.

It was as though Regor De Vis could read Brennus's thoughts. "Do not fret over Piven, your highness. If the barbarian breaches our walls I doubt he will even glance at your adopted son."

Brennus hoped his legate was right. Brennus was aware that Piven had made it quietly into the world and had remained mostly silent since then. These days odd noises, heartbreaking smiles and endless affection told everyone that Piven heard sound, though he could not communicate in any traditional way.

And now there was a new child who'd managed to somehow cling on to life, his heartbeat strong and fierce like the winged lion his family's history sprang from. There had been so much excitement, so much to look forward to as little as six moons ago. And now everything had changed.

The ill-wind had blown in from the east, where one ambitious, creative warlord had united the rabble that made up the tribes who eked out an existence on the infertile plains. It had been almost laughable when Dregon sent news that it was under attack from the barbarians. It had sounded even more implausible when Vorgaven sent a similar missive.

De Vis could clearly read his mind. "How something we considered a skirmish could come to this is beyond me."

"I trusted everyone to hold their own against a mere tribal warlord!"

"Our trust was a mistake, majesty . . . and so was our confidence in the Set's strength. It should never have come to this. And, worse, we haven't prepared our people. It's only because word is coming through from relatives or traders from the other realms that they know Vorgaven has fallen, Dregon is crushed and cowardly Cremond simply handed over rule without so much as a squeak. I'm sure very few know how dire the situation is in Barronel."

Brennus grimaced. "Ormond might hold."

"Only if we'd gone to his aid days ago, majesty. He will fall and our people will then know the truth as we prepare to fight."

The king looked broken. "They've never believed, not for a second, that Penraven could fall. Food is plentiful, our army well trained and well equipped. Lo strike me, this is a tribal ruffian leading tribal rabble!" But as much as the king wanted to believe otherwise, he knew the situation was dire. He no longer had options. "Summon Gavriel and Corbel," he said sadly.

De Vis nodded, turned on his heel and left the king alone to his dark thoughts. Minutes after his departure, Brennus heard the telltale lusty squall of a newborn. His new son had arrived. Not long later the senior midwife eased quietly from behind the doors. She curtsied low, a whimpering bundle of soft linens in her arms. But when she looked at the king her expression was one of terror, rather than delight.

"I heard his battlecry," the king said, desperately trying to alleviate the tension but failing, frowning at her fear as she tiptoed, almost cringing, toward him with her precious cargo. "Is something wrong with my wife?" he added, a fresh fear coursing through him.

"No, not at all, your highness. The queen is fatigued, of course, but she will be well."

"Good. Let me see this new son of mine then," Brennus said, trying to sound gruff. His heart melted as he looked down at the baby's tiny features, eyelids tightly clamped. The infant yawned and he felt an instant swell of love engulf him. "Hardly strapping but handsome all the same," he said, grinning despite his bleak mood, "with the dark features of the Valisars." He couldn't disguise the pride in his voice.

The midwife's voice was barely above a whisper when she spoke. "Sire, it . . . it is not a boy. You have been blessed with a daughter."

Brennus looked at the woman as though she had suddenly begun speaking gibberish.

She hurried on in her anxious whisper. "She is beautiful but I must warn that she is frail due to her early arrival. A girl, majesty," she muttered with awe. "How long has it been?"

"Show me," Brennus demanded, his jaw grinding to keep his own fears in check. The midwife obliged and he was left with no doubt; he had sired a girl. Wrapping her in the linens again, he looked mournfully at the old, knowing midwife—old enough to have delivered him nearly five decades ago. She knew about the Valisar line and what this arrival meant. *How much worse could their situation get*, he wondered, his mind instantly chaotic.

"I fear she may not survive, majesty."

"I am taking her to the chapel," he said, ignoring the woman's concerns.

Their attention was momentarily diverted by Piven scampering up, his dark curly hair its usual messy mop and his matching dark eyes twinkling with delight at seeing his father. But Piven gave everyone a similar welcome; it was obvious he made no distinction between man or woman, king or courtier. Everyone was a friend, deserving of a beaming, vacant salutation. Brennus affectionately stroked his invalid son's hair.

The midwife tried to protest. "But the queen has hardly seen her. She said—"

"Never mind what the queen instructs." Brennus reached for the baby. "Give her to me. I would hold the first Valisar princess in centuries. She will go straight to the chapel for a blessing in case she passes on. My wife will understand. Tell her I shall be back shortly with our daughter."

Brennus didn't wait for the woman's reply. Cradling his daughter as though she were a flickering flame that could be winked out with the slightest draft, he shielded her beneath his cloak and strode—almost ran—to Penraven's royal chapel, trailed by his laughing, clapping five-year-old boy. Inside he locked the door. His breathing had become labored and shallow, and the fear that had begun as a tingle now throbbed through his body like fire.

The priest came and was promptly banished. Soon after a knock at the door revealed De Vis with his twin sons in tow, looking wide-eyed but resolute. Now tall enough to stand shoulder to shoulder alongside their father like sentries, strikingly similar and yet somehow clearly individual, they bowed deeply to their sovereign, while Piven mimicked the action. Although neither Gavriel nor Corbel knew what was afoot for them, they had obviously been told by their father that each had a special role to perform.

"Bolt it," Brennus ordered as soon as the De Vis family was inside the chapel.

A glance to one son by De Vis saw it done. "Are we alone?" he asked the king as Corbel drew the heavy bolt into place.

"Yes, we're secure."

De Vis saw the king fetch a gurgling bundle from behind one of the pews and then watched his boys' brows crinkle with gentle confusion although they said nothing. He held his breath in an attempt to banish his reluctance to go through with the plan. He could hardly believe this was really happening and that the king and he had agreed to involve the boys. And yet there was no other way, no one else to trust.

"This is my newborn child," Brennus said quietly, unable to hide the catch in his voice.

The legate forced a tight smile although the sentiment behind it was genuine. "Congratulations, majesty." The fact that the baby was among them told him the plan was already in motion. He felt the weight of his own fear at the responsibility that he and the king were about to hand over; it fell like a stone down his throat to settle uncomfortably, painfully, in the pit of his stomach. Could these young men—still youthful enough that their attempts to grow beards and moustaches were a source of amusement—pull off the extraordinary plan that the king and he had hatched over this last moon? From the time at which it had become obvious that the Set could not withstand the force of Loethar's marauding army.

They had to do this. He had to trust that his sons would gather their own courage and understand the import of what was being entrusted to them.

De Vis became aware of the awkward silence clinging to the foursome, broken only by the flapping of a sparrow that had become trapped in the chapel and now flew hopelessly around the ceiling, tapping against the timber and stone, testing for a way out. Piven, nearby, flapped his arms too, his expression vacant, unfocused.

De Vis imagined Brennus felt very much like the sparrow right now—trapped but hoping against hope for a way out of the baby's death. There was none. He rallied his courage, for he was sure Brennus's forlorn expression meant the king's mettle was foundering. "Gavriel, Corbel, King Brennus wishes to tell you something of such grave import that we cannot risk anyone outside of the four of us sharing this plan. No one . . . do you understand?"

Both boys stared at their father and nodded. Piven stepped up into the circle and eyed each, smiling beatifically.

"Have you chosen who takes which responsibility?" Brennus asked, after clearing his throat.

"Gavriel will take Leo, sire. Corbel will . . ." he hesitated, not sure whether his own voice would hold. He too cleared his throat. "He will—"

Brennus rescued him. "Hold her, Corbel. This is a new princess for Penraven and a more dangerous birth I cannot imagine. I loathe passing this terrible responsibility to you but your father believes you are up to it."

"Why is she dangerous, your majesty?" Corbel asked.

"She is the first female to be born into the Valisars for centuries, the only one who might well be strong enough to live. Those that have been born in the past have rarely survived their first hour." Brennus shrugged sorrowfully. "We cannot let her be found by the tyrant Loethar."

De Vis sympathized with his son. He could see that the king's opening gambit was having the right effect in chilling Corbel but he was also aware that Brennus was circling the truth.

In fact he realized the king was distancing himself from it, already addressing Gavriel.

". . . must look after Leo. I cannot leave Penraven without an heir. I fear as eldest and crown prince he must face whatever is ahead—I cannot soften the blow, even though he is still so young."

Gavriel nodded, and his father realized his son understood. "Your daughter does not need to face the tyrant—is this what you mean, your highness . . . that we can soften the blow for her, but not for the prince?"

De Vis felt something in his heart give. The boys would make him proud. He wished, for the thousandth time, that his wife had lived to see them. He pitied that she'd never known how Gavriel led and yet although this made Corbel seem weaker, he was far from it. If anything he was the one who was prepared to take the greatest risks, for all that he rarely shared what he was thinking. Gavriel did the talking for both of them and here again, he'd said aloud for everyone's benefit what the king was finding so hard to say and Corbel refused to ask.

"Yes," Brennus replied to the eldest twin. "We can soften the blow for the princess. She need not face Loethar. I have let the realm down by my willingness to believe in our invincibility. But no one is invincible, boys. Not even the barbarian. He is strong now, fueled by his success—success that I wrongly permitted—but he too will become inflated by his own importance one day, by his own sense of invincibility. I have to leave it to the next generation to know when to bring him down."

"Are we going to lose to Loethar, sire?" Gavriel asked.

"We may," was Brennus's noncommittal answer. "But we can do this much for the princess. Save her his wrath." His voice almost broke upon his last word and he reached to stroke her shock of dark hair, so unlike Leo's and Iselda's coloring.

"And Piven?" Gavriel inquired.

All four glanced at the youngster. "I am trying not to worry about this child," Brennus replied. "He is harmless; anyone can see that. He is also not of our blood," he added, looking down awkwardly. "If anything happens to him he will know little of it and if he survives, nothing will change in his strange internal world. It's as though he is not among us anyway. I am prepared to take the risk that the barbarian will hardly notice him."

The De Vis family nodded in unison, although whether they believed him was hard to tell.

"The queen, er . . ." Gavriel looked from the king to his father.

"Will be none the wiser," De Vis said firmly. "It is enough that most of us will likely die anyway. We can spare her this."

"Die?" Gavriel asked, aghast. "But we can get the king and queen away, taking Leo and the baby across the ocean to—"

"No, Gav. We can't," his father interrupted. "The king will not leave his people—nor should he—and I will not leave his side. We will fight to the last and if we are to fall, we fall together, the queen included. But we cannot risk the royal children."

Brennus took up the thread again, much to De Vis's relief. "Piven is not seen as an heir but he is also no threat. And while I sadly must risk that Leo is found, tortured, abused and ultimately exploited for the tyrant's purposes, I am giving him a fighting chance with you, Gavriel. That said, I won't risk the possibility of my daughter falling into Loethar's hands."

That sentence prompted a ghastly silence, broken finally by Corbel, who looked uncomfortably away from the dark eyes of the baby that stared at him from the crook of his arm. "Tell me what I must do," he asked.

The king sighed, hesitated. De Vis's encouraging hand on his arm helped him to finally say it. "Today, my daughter must die."

FIONA MCINTOSH'S

MASTERFUL EPIC FANTASY
THE PERCHERON SAGA

ODALISQUE 978-0-06-089911-0

In the exotic land of Percheron, the fifteen-year-old heir to the throne, Boaz, must assume the mantle of leadership, guided by his trusted warrior adviser, Lazar. In the midst of roiling covert intrigue, a headstrong young woman is brought to Boaz's harem, inflaming unexpectedly strong feelings in both Boaz and Lazar. And, unbeknownst to all, the gods themselves are rising in a cyclical battle.

EMISSARY 978-0-06-089912-7

Lazar offered up his life to protect Ana, a prisoner in the forbidden harem of the great Stone Palace of Percheron, accepting punishment intended for the bewitching odalisque. Now, with Lazar's guiding hand absent from the city, Percheron has become a darker, more treacherous place, as the young Zar Boaz has to battle the machinations of his mother Herezah.

GODDESS 978-0-06-089913-4

While enemy ships threaten Percheron's harbor, heroic Lazar lies afflicted with the drezden illness. And Zaradine Ana has been taken prisoner by the mysterious Arafanz and his warriors, and is believed to be with child—carrying the heir to the throne, the unborn son of Zar Boaz.

LEGENDS OF THE RIFTWAR

HONORED ENEMY ▶ 978-0-06-079284-8
by Raymond E. Feist & William R. Forstchen
In the frozen northlands of the embattled realm of Midkemia, Dennis Hartraft's Marauders must band together with their bitter enemy, the Tsurani, to battle *moredhel,* a migrating horde of deadly dark elves.

MURDER IN LAMUT ▶ 978-0-06-079291-6
by Raymond E. Feist & Joel Rosenberg
For twenty years the mercenaries Durine, Kethol, and Pirojil have fought other people's battles, defeating numerous deadly enemies. Now the Three Swords find themselves trapped by a winter's storm inside a castle teeming with ambitious, plotting lords and ladies, and it falls on the mercenaries to solve a series of cold-blooded murders.

JIMMY THE HAND ▶ 978-0-06-079299-2
by Raymond E. Feist & S.M. Stirling
Forced to flee the only home he's ever known, Jimmy the Hand, boy thief of Krondor finds himself among the rural villagers of Land's End. But Land's End is home to a dark, dangerous presence even the local smugglers don't recognize. And suddenly Jimmy's youthful bravado is leading him into the maw of chaos . . . and, quite possibly, his doom.